Praise for the Zoe Chambers M
D0194161

LOST LEGACY (#2)

"Intriguing, with as many twists and turns as the Pennsylvania countryside it's set in."

– CJ Lyons,
New York Times Bestselling Author

"A vivid country setting, characters so real you'd know them if they walked through your door, and a long-buried secret that bursts from its grave to wreak havoc in a small community—*Lost Legacy* has it all."

– Sandra Parshall,
Author of the Agatha Award-Winning Rachel Goddard Mysteries

"A big-time talent spins a wonderful small-town mystery! Annette Dashofy skillfully weaves secrets from the past into a surprising, engaging, and entertaining page turner."

– Hank Phillippi Ryan,
Mary Higgins Clark, Agatha and Anthony Award-Winning Author

"As well-crafted as the mystery is, and if you figure this one out before the end you should be a detective, it's the characters that make this series so unique and appealing."

– Bobbi Carducci,
Author of *Confessions of an Imperfect Caregiver*

CIRCLE OF INFLUENCE (#1)

"An easy, int read, partially because the townfolks' lives are so scandalously intertwined, but also because author Dashofy has taken pains to create a palette of unforgettable characters."

– *Mystery Scene Magazine*

"Dashofy takes small town politics and long simmering feuds, adds colorful characters, and brings it to a boil in a welcome new series."

– Hallie Ephron,
Author of *There Was an Old Woman*

"The texture of small town Pennsylvania comes alive in Annette Dashofy's debut mystery. Discerning mystery readers will appreciate Dashofy's expert details and gripping storytelling. Zoe Chambers is an authentic character who will entertain us for a long time."

— Nancy Martin,
Author of the Blackbird Sister Mysteries

"I've been awestruck by Annette Dashofy's storytelling for years. Look out world, you're going to love Zoe Chambers and Pete Adams, and *Circle of Influence* is just the beginning."

— Donnell Ann Bell,
Bestselling Author of *The Past Came Hunting* and *Deadly Recall*

"New York has McBain, Boston has Parker, now Vance Township, PA ("pop. 5000. Please Drive Carefully.") has Annette Dashofy, and her rural world is just as vivid and compelling as their city noir."

— John Lawton,
Author of the Inspector Troy Series

"An excellent debut, totally fun to read. Annette Dashofy has created a charmer of a protagonist in Zoe Chambers. She's smart, she's sexy, she's vulnerably romantic, and she's one hell of a paramedic on the job. It's great to look forward to books two and three."

— Kathleen George,
Edgar-Nominated Author of the Richard Christie Series

"This is a terrific first mystery, with just the right blend of action, emotion and edge. I couldn't put it down. The characters are well drawn and believable...It's all great news for readers. I can't wait to meet Zoe and Pete again in Vance Township, Monongahela County, PA."

— Mary Jane Maffini,
Author of *The Dead Don't Get Out Much*

"The author has struck gold by delivering a wonderful story...Betrayal, teenage angst, dysfunctional relationship and deep dark secrets will keep you turning the pages in this very enjoyable debut novel!"

— *Dru's Book Musings*

LOST
LEGACY

**Books in the Zoe Chambers Mystery Series
by Annette Dashofy**

CIRCLE OF INFLUENCE (#1)
LOST LEGACY (#2)
BRIDGES BURNED (#3)
(April 2015)

LOST LEGACY

A ZOE CHAMBERS MYSTERY

ANNETTE DASHOFY

HENERY PRESS

LOST LEGACY
A Zoe Chambers Mystery
Part of the Henery Press Mystery Collection

First Edition
Trade paperback edition | September 2014

Henery Press
www.henerypress.com

All rights reserved. No part of this book may be used or reproduced in any manner whatsoever, including Internet usage, without written permission from Henery Press, except in the case of brief quotations embodied in critical articles and reviews.

Copyright © 2014 by Annette Dashofy
Cover art by Fayette Terlouw

This is a work of fiction. Any references to historical events, real people, or real locales are used fictitiously. Other names, characters, places, and incidents are the product of the author's imagination, and any resemblance to actual events or locales or persons, living or dead, is entirely coincidental.

ISBN-13: 978-1-940976-24-2

Printed in the United States of America

In memory of my dad, John I. Riggle.
You are my sunshine.

ACKNOWLEDGMENTS

Alzheimer's is an ugly disease. I spent years watching and agonizing as my dad succumbed to it. To deal with his loss, I turned to my writing. Creating Pete's father, Harry, was a labor of love. He's not my dad, but he has some of Dad's characteristics (a passion for chocolate milkshakes) and uses some of his phrases ("Hello, Sunshine!") Spending time in this story allowed me to once again feel connected to the man I miss every day of my life.

As always, I need to thank the other sets of eyes who keep me on track: My online critique partners, Donnell Ann Bell, Mike Beifler, and L.C. Hayden; my face-to-face critique group, Jeff Boarts, Judy Schneider, and Tamara Girardi; and my beta readers, Diana Stavroulakis, Mary Sutton, Joyce Tremel, Paula Matter, and Martha Reed. It's fabulous having a team I trust with my words and my heart. Love you guys.

I also want to give a shout-out to Susan Meier who, during our annual Sisters in Crime chapter's retreat, helped me whip the opening chapters—and my writing as a whole—into shape.

Thanks to the gang at the Crime Scene Writers group for being there to answer all my procedural questions.

I owe a huge debt to Pennwriters and Sisters in Crime. I shudder to think where I'd be without them.

And to my husband, Ray (who suffered an avulsion fracture of his foot several years back and whose misery became fodder for Pete's dilemma), I love you, babe. Thanks for putting up with me and for going fishing so I could have quiet time to work.

Finally, I am grateful beyond words for my editor extraordinaire Kendel Flaum, editorial assistant Erin George, cover artist Fayette Terlouw, and the entire Hen House family at Henery Press. Thank you.

ONE

Zoe Chambers' teeth chattered in response to the rush of adrenaline, never mind the ninety degree heat of June in southwestern Pennsylvania. She flipped on the siren as the ambulance approached an intersection along the tarred and chipped country road.

"Jeez, I hate these kinds of calls," her partner Earl muttered. He cut the wheel hard, making the sharp left onto Ridge Road. The medic unit swayed and jounced over the ruts.

"Me, too." Zoe shifted in the passenger seat and studied the incident report in her lap. *Farm accident. Caller reports victim may be DOA.* In rural Vance Township, nearly every summer produced one of these. A year ago, a tractor rolled over, pinning the driver. Another time a farmer was run over by a hay wagon. Before that, someone lost an arm in a piece of machinery. The possibilities were endless. None of them were pretty. But even more than the type of call, the address on the report contributed to her unease.

Threatening gray clouds loomed in an otherwise pale blue sky. Not a hint of a breeze disturbed the tall grasses stretching across the field.

"It's gonna rain," she said.

Earl grunted a response.

They topped a hill, and a picturesque farm lay before them. "That's it." She clenched her jaw to quell the chattering. Once she got to work on the task at hand, the jitters would stop. At least, they usually did.

A two-story farmhouse with a sagging porch faced the road like a sentinel to an ancient barn. The doors, large enough to easily accommodate massive farm machinery, stood open in a wide yawn. Outside, two tractors hitched to wagons stacked high with fresh-cut baled hay waited.

Their patient was inside. Zoe had put up enough hay to know that was the only reason loaded hay wagons would be sitting idle with a storm approaching.

She picked up the mic. "Control, this is Medic Two. We are on scene."

"Ten-four, Medic Two," came the response, followed by the time. "Seventeen thirty-two."

Earl parked the ambulance behind one of the hay wagons. When Zoe swung open the door, a wave of hot air slammed into her. It was thick with humidity and perfumed with the scent of freshly cut fields. She offered up a silent prayer. *Please, don't let the patient be up in the hay loft.* If it was ninety degrees outside, it would be at least a hundred and twenty up there.

She tugged on a Monongahela County EMS ball cap and grabbed the jump kit from the patient compartment.

A pair of young men sat in the grass several yards away. Their sun-bronzed arms contrasted sharply with the pallor of their faces. A third, his back to them, stood doubled over, heaving. Another group of stoic, but ashen, helpers gathered in the shade of a silver maple, smoking cigarettes with unsteady hands.

An older man stepped down from his perch on one of the tractors, flicked away the butt of a cigarette, and approached the paramedics. "What the hell took you so long?" His voice sounded as rough as his weather-beaten face. Without waiting for a response, he added, "He's in here," and directed them toward the barn.

As they moved closer to the structure, the sweet smell of mown hay gave way to the stench of rotting flesh. At the gaping doorway, Zoe fought back a gag reflex. Her nose told her what was inside before her eyes grew accustomed to the dark interior.

The body hung in the center of the barn from a rope looped over a rusty pulley high in the rafters. The other end of the rope was tied to an upright support beam. Nearby, a wooden ladder leaned at an awkward angle, reaching toward the loft. The sickening buzz of ravenous flies filled the barn.

Earl pressed a handkerchief to his mouth and nose. "Nothing for us to do here." He shot a glance at Zoe. "Or at least nothing for me, Miss Deputy Coroner. I'm going to radio it in and request the cops."

Zoe gave a nod. At least pronouncing this one wouldn't require checking for vitals or unpacking the portable EKG. There was no question he was dead. That much was obvious. No, the questions were how long and—the big ones—cause and manner.

The sight of a body hanging in that barn did nothing to quash the apprehension she'd been experiencing since she'd first heard the address. She'd grown up hearing stories about this place. And about another hanging.

The farmer watched Earl retreat to the ambulance before turning to Zoe. "Where's he going? What did he mean about requesting the cops? The old man's dead. Cut him down and get him out of here so I can unload this hay."

She blinked. But clearing her eyes didn't change what she'd heard. Was he really that callous? "Who are you?"

"Name's Carl Loomis."

"You know the victim?"

"Yeah. It's Jim Engle." Carl motioned toward the house. "Jim owns this farm. I've been putting up the hay for him since he's been sick."

Jim Engle? *James* Engle?

Zoe looked down at the thick layer of dust on the rough-hewn floor. Several clear boot prints marred the surface. "Did anyone go inside the barn?"

Loomis blanched. "Hell, no. I opened the doors so we could pull the wagons in, and there he was. Half my boys tossed their cookies when the smell hit them."

Without stepping inside, Zoe leaned forward and squinted at the body. Engle's face was pale gray, and his tongue protruded between his lips. Milky opaque eyes stared, unseeing, at the hay stacked on the opposite side of the barn. Zoe doubted she'd have recognized him if she'd met him on the street. But that name? She knew the name.

She'd seen enough. The stench and the buzz of the flies drove her farther outside, gasping for air.

The farmer was eyeing the sky. The ominous dark clouds had all but obliterated the blue. A breeze kicked up, hissing through the maple trees surrounding the house. "So how about getting him down and out of here? I really need to get moving if I want to keep this here hay dry."

"I'm afraid we can't just cut him down."

Loomis leaned closer until the odor of tobacco smoke on his breath made her wince. "Why not? I know it stinks, but—"

"Not because of the smell. This is a crime scene. The police will need to investigate—"

"*Crime* scene?" He laughed. "This ain't no *crime* scene. Jim's been threatening to end it all for weeks. Hell, months. The man was dying of lung cancer. Said he wanted to go out on his own terms. Well, God bless him, he did. The only crime being committed here is you keeping me from getting my hay in this here barn before the rain ruins it."

Earl jogged up to them. "The cops are on their way. Franklin Marshall, too." He nudged Zoe with his elbow. "You lucked out. The boss himself will be here to process the body."

"Darn." Zoe made no effort to hide her sarcasm. When she'd taken on the deputy coroner role, she'd expected to investigate homicides and mysterious deaths, solve puzzles and make sense of the senseless. Television made it seem so exciting. But the reality was more like this...calling the time of death on a poor cancer-riddled old man who opted to take his own life rather than waste away any further.

"Franklin Marshall? The coroner?" The farmer clenched his fists as if he wanted to slug both of the paramedics. "Process the body? Are you people friggin' nuts? Jim farmed this land for almost fifty years. He'd be the first one to tell you we need to get this hay inside before it gets soaked."

"Then he should've picked a better place to kill himself," Earl said.

The farmer's eyes bulged, and Zoe feared he might take a swing at her partner. She placed a hand on Earl's arm and was about to suggest he cool it when she spotted an SUV with emergency lights flashing cresting the hill and roaring toward them. "The police are here," she said. To Carl Loomis, she added, "You might want to locate another barn. Or maybe tarp the wagons. But an unattended death like this will have to be investigated. Until the coroner gives a ruling of suicide, the police will treat it as a homicide."

The farmer gave no indication of hearing the last part. "Another barn? Look around, missy." Spittle flew from his lips. "There ain't another barn for more 'n two miles." He scowled. "Jim might have some tarps in there, though."

Loomis made a move for the door, but Zoe stepped in front of him. "You can't go inside."

"Then how do you expect me to tarp my goddamn wagons?" He continued with a stream of cursing that threatened to singe her ears.

The Vance Township Police vehicle rolled to a stop next to the ambulance. The chief of the department stepped out, tall and striking with his salt-and-pepper hair and piercing blue eyes. Zoe's pleasure at seeing Pete Adams extended far beyond mere relief—she trusted his commanding presence would calm the irate farmer. She resisted the urge to give Pete a wide smile, embarrassed by her own infatuation with the man. They'd been dancing around their mutual attraction since last winter, neither brave enough to take things further, considering their equally lousy romantic histories.

"What do we have?" he said as he approached.

Zoe caught the slightest hint of a grin cast her way, and her face warmed. She opened her mouth to give an official status report, but Loomis cut her off, offering his personal take on the situation, concluding with, "I need to get these two wagonloads of hay inside before it rains, so can you folks please cut him down and get him outta there? No disrespect intended."

Pete eyed Zoe, his eyebrow raised in a question. She shrugged. "I advised Mr. Loomis that we have to treat this as a crime scene, but—"

"I keep telling you, it ain't no crime scene." Loomis' face had blossomed into a shade of red that made Zoe fear he might explode. Or at least have a stroke.

A second Vance Township police vehicle rolled into the driveway.

Pete tipped his head toward the barn. "Well, Mr. Loomis, why don't you tell me exactly how you found Mr. Engle." He pointed a finger at Officer Seth Metzger, who was climbing out of the township cruiser. "Call dispatch and get Kevin and any of the part-time guys that are available out here. And request County and the crime unit. We're going to need the help. Then start getting statements from all these guys." Pete motioned to the farm workers, who still hadn't regained their color.

He turned a fuming Carl Loomis to the barn entrance. Zoe blew out a sigh, glad someone else was now the focus of the farmer's rants. Not that she didn't understand his concerns. She suspected more than one farmer in the area was frantically trying to get his hay in right about now. No trace of blue sky remained. The wind was kicking up dust devils in the driveway. And the air was so thick, if she could grab a chunk and squeeze, she was sure moisture would pour from it like a saturated sponge.

Alone for the moment with her partner, she caught his arm and drew him away. "Do you know anything about the Engle family?"

Earl shrugged. "Just that they've lived in the area and owned this farm forever."

"No." She studied the house. One of the shutters appeared ready to drop to the ground. A broken upstairs window had been replaced with a sheet of plywood. And no way would she trust the rickety steps to the front porch to hold a person's weight. "They haven't owned this farm forever. Don't you remember hearing the stories about this place?"

"Stories? What stories?"

She motioned to the barn where Carl Loomis flung his arms in animated outrage as Pete calmly jotted notes. "James Engle isn't the first person to hang in that barn."

In all Pete's years with the Pittsburgh Bureau of Police, he'd never faced anything like Carl Loomis. The man was livid, not because a friend was dead, but because two wagonloads of hay were on the verge of getting soaked. Of course, being a city cop transplanted to the role of Police Chief in rural Vance Township meant he didn't know shit about things like wet hay.

Thunder rumbled, sending Loomis closer to the edge of hysteria. "You don't understand," he said for the fourth or fifth time. "I can get better 'n five bucks a bale for this hay, but not if it gets wet. Do you know what that adds up to?"

Pete sympathized. But the coroner and the county crime unit hadn't arrived yet. He had to keep everyone away from the body. "What about covering it?"

"That's what that girl said. I don't exactly have a tarp in my hip pocket. And she wouldn't let me in the barn to look for one."

Pete spotted Zoe deep in conversation with her partner. So she'd already attempted to solve Loomis' problem? Naturally. She'd grown up in Vance Township and lived on a farm. She'd know better than he what this guy was going through. Pete looked for Metzger. The young officer was speaking with a group of Loomis' workers who milled around one of the wagons. "Seth!" he called.

"Yeah, Chief?"

"Pull the tarps out of the vehicles. You and those boys get busy covering the wagons."

"Yes, sir."

Lightning cut across the sky. In mere seconds, thunder rumbled.

Loomis' rage subsided. He glanced at the sky. "I need to go help my boys."

Pete waved the appeased farmer away and watched the road for the coroner and the team from County as the men made short work of covering the hay.

The first large raindrops plinked on the tin roof, forcing Pete to step inside the reeking barn. He stared up at what remained of Jim Engle. What would it take to drive someone to end his life in such a gruesome manner? Loomis said the man was dying of cancer. Surely he'd had access to drugs—morphine. A simple overdose had to be a more preferable form of suicide than hanging.

Unless it hadn't been a suicide.

"Pete?"

He swung around to find Zoe standing in the rain at the barn entrance. Wisps of her short blond curls fringed her EMS ball cap.

"Franklin just pulled in," she said. She held a pair of latex gloves, wringing them like an old washcloth.

"Thanks."

She didn't move, but caught her lower lip in her teeth.

"Is something wrong?"

"I don't know for sure." She paused, took a glance at the body, and wrinkled her nose. "Do you know the history of this barn?"

"No." From the look on Zoe's face, he suspected it must be relevant.

"I'm not sure of all the details, but I remember hearing stories when I was a kid. My mom's family once owned this farm. There was some hoopla about two of her uncles being found dead here. In this barn. One was hanged. I can't remember about the other. But I do remember my mom despised the Engle brothers, including James Engle." Zoe tipped her head toward the corpse.

Okay, so this particular history lesson sparked Pete's interest. "And why did she despise the Engles?"

Zoe glanced over her shoulder at Monongahela County Coroner Franklin Marshall who was lugging a large duffle bag toward them.

"Because," she said to Pete, lowering her voice, "Mom believed James Engle was responsible for the deaths."

TWO

"What have we got?" The clipboard Franklin held over his head served as a poor substitute for an umbrella against the windblown rain.

Pete wondered the same thing. He stepped back just far enough into the barn to allow Zoe and Franklin shelter without disturbing the footprints in the dirt and motioned to the body hanging from the rafters. "I'll get my camera and shoot some photos," Pete shouted over the roar of the downpour on the tin roof. "Then *you* can tell *me*."

"Do you guys need my help?" Zoe asked as four more police cruisers crested the hill and rolled toward the farm.

"I don't believe so," the coroner said. "Looks like we have plenty of manpower on the way. You and Earl can go back to saving the living."

Pete dashed through the deluge with her to their vehicles and motioned for her to get into the passenger seat of his SUV. He removed his cap and mopped his face with a handkerchief. "What else do you know about those other deaths?"

"Not much." Zoe panted from the run. "It was an old family lore sort of story. There's probably nothing to it, but I thought I'd mention it."

"Aren't your mom and stepdad coming to visit soon?"

She rolled her eyes. "Soon? Yeah. I have to pick them up at the airport tomorrow morning. First time they've been back from Florida in years. I can hardly wait."

Pete chuckled at her sarcastic tone. "I bet. Maybe you could ask her about those old homicides. Find out what happened."

"Do you think there's a connection?"

"How long ago did all this take place?"

"I don't know. Way before I was born."

He gazed through the fogged windshield at the barn. That would make the cold case more than thirty-five years old. If it even was a case. "I doubt Jim Engle's death has anything to do with your great uncles. But you know how I hate coincidences."

"Yeah. I'll ask Mom when I see her." Zoe reached for the door handle.

Pete caught her arm. "Are you coming to the poker game tomorrow night?"

She gave him a devious grin. "I'll be there. After spending the day with Mom and Tom, I'll need to get away." She dove from the SUV and rushed around it to the medic unit.

Pete watched her climb into the ambulance. The paramedic uniform with its lumpy cargo pants and gadget belt did a good job of camouflaging her figure, but his imagination stripped away the obstacles. He'd wanted to ask her out a half-dozen times since the mess with her ex-boyfriend last winter, but he always thought better of it. Reluctantly.

She kept stressing how much she valued their friendship. Friendship? What stirred in him at the moment sure didn't bear that particular label.

At least they still saw each other socially for the weekly card game whenever she wasn't on duty.

Someone pounded on his window, jarring Pete out of his fantasy regarding Zoe sans uniform. He made out the form of County Detective Wayne Baronick through the rain-streaked glass. Pete powered the window open, and a dripping Baronick rested his arms against the door. "Hey, Pete." The young hotshot presented his usual broad smile. "Think it'll rain?"

Pete grunted. Smartass.

"You getting the photographs?"

"Yep." Pete reached into the backseat of the SUV and retrieved his evidence collection kit, including his digital camera. He hit the button to close the window, forcing Baronick to jerk his arms out of the way. Stifling a smile, Pete climbed out.

Baronick fell into step beside him as they jogged to the barn. Lightning sizzled across the sky, followed immediately by a crack of thunder that shook the ground beneath their feet. "Holy shit," Baronick said, diving the last few feet into the barn.

Pete bit back a laugh and set his bag on the dusty floor.

"What do you think, Franklin?" Baronick asked. "Suicide?"

The coroner jotted notes on a pad. "You know I'm not going to make any declaration until after the autopsy."

"The farmer who found the body thinks so," Pete told Baronick. "Says the old man had lung cancer and has been threatening to kill himself for a while."

Baronick gazed out through the rain. "Is that the victim's house?"

"Yep."

"Anyone else live with him?"

"Not according to Carl Loomis. Engle's wife passed away five years ago. His brother lives about a mile north of here." Pete dug his camera from the bag and thumbed it on.

"Has the brother been notified?" Baronick asked.

"Not yet." Pete lifted the camera to his eye and snapped a wide-angled shot of the barn with the victim hanging in the center.

"Okay." Baronick cleared his throat. "You document the scene. I'm going to check out the house. Maybe we'll get lucky and this poor sap left us a clear and concise suicide note."

Pete silently rolled the slim odds of that happening around in his head.

"When you're done with the pictures," Baronick continued, "my guys can take over processing the barn and help Franklin with the body. Then you and I can pay a visit to the other Mr. Engle."

Pete placed a ruler on the floor next to one of the footprints to indicate scale and focused the camera. He knew Baronick hated to call on the next of kin as much as he did. But if Jim Engle's death turned out to be a homicide, family members would also be their prime suspects.

By the time Pete and Baronick stepped onto Wilford Engle's front porch, the storm had blown past, and the skies were clearing. Carl Loomis had informed Pete that the victim's brother was in his mid-seventies, but the man who opened the door appeared old beyond time. His flesh was so pale Pete guessed it hadn't felt the sun within the last decade. Ironic that the brother hanging in the barn looked to be the healthier of the two.

"Wilford Engle?" Pete said.

"Yeah." The old man squinted at Pete and his uniform.

Baronick held up his badge. "May we come in?"

"No."

Pete studied Engle. With the rain gone, both the heat and humidity were on the rise. In spite of it, Engle wore a long-sleeved cotton shirt from which bony wrists and hands protruded. Stained denim coveralls made for a much heavier man hung on his frail frame. But the man's dark eyes suggested steel forged by years of hard work and hard living. Wilford Engle took no bull from anyone. Ever.

"Sir." Pete softened his voice. "We're here about your brother."

Engle blinked. "My brother? Jim?"

"I'm sorry to have to tell you, Mr. Engle," Baronick said, "but your brother is dead."

Engle's shoulders shifted downward, as did his gaze. "Well, that's it then. I knew it was coming. Just thought we had a little more time is all. Thank you, officers, for letting me know." He stepped back, his hand on the door, ready to close it.

Pete blocked the door open with his foot. "I'm afraid Detective Baronick didn't make himself clear. Your brother didn't die of natural causes."

Engle stiffened. "He didn't?"

"No, sir. His body was found this afternoon hanging in his barn."

Engle's face might have lost its color if it'd had any. The old man's knees buckled, and he slammed sideways into the doorjamb. Pete grabbed for him, but the awkward angle threw Pete off balance. His foot caught on an uneven board, and his ankle rolled as Engle dragged both of them to the porch floor, Pete on the bottom. For a bag of bones, the old guy was damned heavy.

"Mr. Engle? Are you all right?" Baronick knelt beside them.

Engle moaned. "Yeah." He squirmed, grinding a sharp elbow into Pete's sternum. "Help me up, goddammit."

Baronick grabbed an arm, and Pete pushed from underneath. Groaning, the old man struggled to his feet. But not before stepping on the ankle Pete had twisted. He bit back a yelp of his own and hoisted himself up as Baronick helped Engle into the house.

The old man shuffled to a faded, battered sofa and flopped onto it.

"I'm sorry about that." He rubbed the shoulder that had impacted against the doorjamb. "I take these spells."

Pete's ankle screamed when he put weight on it, but he gritted his teeth against the pain. "We need to ask you a few questions."

"I guess I got a few of my own," Engle said. "You sure it was my brother?"

"Carl Loomis gave us a preliminary identification," Pete said.

"Pre-what?"

Baronick jumped in. "Preliminary. The coroner will confirm the ID with dental records or fingerprints. But Mr. Loomis was certain it was him."

"Well, Carl would know." Engle frowned at his hands in his lap. "Hanged, you say?"

"Yes, sir." Baronick pulled his notebook from his shirt pocket. "I searched your brother's house."

Engle's eyes darkened. "You had no right—"

"I found his suicide letter."

Engle choked. "You what?"

"Found a letter. It was handwritten. Lying on the kitchen table."

The old man shifted on the sofa. His mouth worked as though forming words, but no sound came until he said, "I don't believe it. Where is this letter? I want to see it."

"I'm sorry. It's evidence."

"Evidence?" Engle's voice went up an octave. "Can't you tell me what it said?"

"Yes, sir. I copied it word for word." Baronick looked down at his notes and read, "I've done things in my life I'm not proud of. Now the good Lord is punishing me with this disease. I deserve every excruciating minute of torture it brings. But I pray my death will offer some light to the darkness. Forgive me. This is the only way. Goodbye, brother."

Engle's hands trembled. "I can't believe he went and done it."

"Excuse me?" Baronick said.

Engle's eyes narrowed on the detective. "I want you to stay out of my brother's house."

"We can't do that." Pete straightened, ignoring the flames licking his ankle. "Until the coroner tells us otherwise, we consider his house a crime scene."

The old man glared at him and gave a grunt.

"When was the last time you saw your brother?" Pete asked.

"What's today? Friday? Must have been...oh, Tuesday. I drove him to a doctor's appointment in Brunswick."

"And what doctor was that?"

"Dr. Weinstein. In the old National Trust Bank Building on Main Street."

"Mind telling us what the doctor said?" Baronick asked.

"He said Jim was dying. What the blazes do you think he said?" Engle pulled a bandana from his hip pocket. "Moron," he muttered into the fabric before blowing his nose.

"Did your brother give you any hint he intended to commit suicide?"

The old man grew pensive and leaned back, sinking into the sofa. "Yes." Engle's gaze shifted to the window. "I didn't believe he'd really do it, though."

"Is it possible that someone killed your brother and made it look like suicide?"

The old man sputtered. "Are you out of your mind? Who would go to the trouble to kill a man who's only got a couple of weeks to live? No one, that's who. Moron."

Pete cleared his throat.

He'd have preferred to be armed with more information before questioning the old farmer, but he wanted to see the man's reaction. "There's something else I'd like to know about."

Engle gave an exasperated sigh.

"I've been told your brother wasn't the first person to die in that old barn."

Engle gave Pete a hard, cold stare. "Yeah? So? Farming's a dangerous way to make a living."

"But the case I'm speaking of wasn't a farming accident." At least he didn't think it was.

"I suppose you're talking about the Miller brothers."

Pete waited for Engle to continue.

"That was a long time ago. One brother killed the other, then killed himself. It was over a woman as I recall."

Baronick scribbled furiously in his notebook. "What woman?"

"I don't know. Ain't like I was their—whatcha call it—social secretary."

"I understand one of the men was found hanged," Pete said.

Engle's eye twitched. "Could be. It was a long time ago."

"Does it seem odd to you that a man hanged himself in your brother's barn all those years ago and now your own brother's done the same thing?"

The grizzled farmer stood up with a grunt, his joints cracking. "No, I don't think it's odd. It's just what it is. A coincidence. We're done here. I got things to do. Like plan a funeral."

"Coincidence," Pete said through clenched teeth as he and Baronick made their way toward his SUV in Wilford Engle's driveway. He'd have parked closer if he'd known he'd be walking on a busted-up ankle. But he refused to limp. "I hate coincidences."

"Me, too." The detective slapped his notebook against his palm. "Do you believe him?"

Pete looked back toward the house. Engle stood at the screen door watching their departure. "No. He's hiding something."

"Yeah. He sure didn't like that I was snooping around in his brother's house. Makes me believe I need to do a little more digging out there. And what was that about another hanging in that barn?"

"Just something I heard today." Pete slid behind the wheel, relieved to be off his feet at last. "I think I need to find out a little more about our local history."

And he knew just the person to ask.

THREE

Zoe was right about one thing. Carl Loomis hadn't been the only farmer racing to get his hay in ahead of the rain last night.

Two wagons overloaded with fresh green bales stood in the center of the indoor riding ring at the Kroll farm. She breathed in the fragrant aroma—perfume to a farm girl. Then again, she enjoyed the earthy tang of fresh horse manure, too.

Although the farm currently boasted fifteen boarders, Patsy Greene was one of the rare few willing to jump in and help with the barn chores, and the only one who offered to help with the hay. Patsy had almost ten years on her, but Zoe often commented that Patsy acted more like a twenty-something than a forty-something.

They stood shoulder-to-shoulder, gazing up at the mountain of work. "What time does your folks' flight get in?" Patsy asked.

"A little after ten." Zoe checked her watch. Seven a.m.

"Guess we'd better get busy." Patsy nudged her with an elbow, grabbed a manure fork, and headed toward one of the two dozen stalls that ran along both sides of the arena.

Zoe selected another fork from the feed room and entered the stall next to the one Patsy was mucking. "Thanks for the help. I'd never get done in time to leave for the airport on my own. And with the hay to unload this afternoon, I'll have enough to keep me busy."

"No problem. How's Mrs. Kroll doing?"

"Pretty good. She's still in remission."

In addition to her duties as a Monongahela County paramedic and one of Franklin Marshall's deputy coroners, Zoe also managed the Kroll farm. She'd needed a place to board her Quarter Horse gelding. When Mrs. Kroll was diagnosed with leukemia, she and her husband—

both well into their seventies—needed someone to keep the horse operation running while they dealt with her health issues. They'd been a perfect match. Zoe took over the riding and boarding facility in exchange for a stall for Windstar and half of the huge nineteenth century farmhouse for her and her cats. She picked up a little extra spending money by giving riding lessons on occasion.

"When was the last time you saw your mom?" Patsy called from the next stall.

"I drove down to Florida six years ago." And swore she'd never take on that task again. "They haven't been up here for probably ten years."

"To what do you owe the honor of their presence now?"

Zoe sifted sawdust bedding through the tines, keeping the brown lumps of manure on the fork. She had been pondering that question ever since her mother phoned a month ago to announce their visit.

"Well?" Patsy said.

Zoe tossed the manure into the wheelbarrow positioned by the stall door. "I really don't know." She wasn't entirely sure she wanted to, either. Life was never peaceful when Kimberly Chambers Jackson was around. Plus Zoe hated how she always reverted to the age of twelve in her mother's overpowering presence.

"How long are they gonna be here?"

"I don't know that either. Probably a week." A week that would feel like a month.

Patsy poked her head around the corner, a big grin on her face. "If they're still here on Friday, be sure and bring them to my birthday party. Barbecue and a keg at my house."

"My folks at your party?" Zoe snorted. "I thought you wanted your birthday to be fun."

Thirty minutes later, they'd cleaned almost half the stalls. Sweat trickled down Zoe's forehead, and she wiped it away with the back of her arm. "I thought it was supposed to be cooler today."

"It is." Patsy laughed. "Instead of ninety-two, it's only going to get to eighty-eight."

"Great." Zoe would have to grab a quick shower before heading to the airport. Meeting her mother and Tom in her old Chevy pickup was bad enough. If she stank like a farmhand on top of it, her mother would be appalled. Not a good way to start a visit.

Patsy deposited one more forkful of soggy bedding onto the mound in the wheelbarrow. "My turn," she said, propping the fork against the wall and wheeling the load toward the door and the manure pile. "Hey," she called over her shoulder. "Here comes Mr. Kroll."

The throaty rumble of the quad he used to travel between the house and the barn grew louder. Zoe heard him cut the engine and shout a greeting to Patsy before he appeared at the door. "Zoe!" he yelled across the barn. "You have company."

"What? Who?"

"Your folks. I hope you don't mind. I let them into your place."

"My folks?" Crap. "They weren't supposed to be here for..." She glanced at her watch again. Yes, it was only seven-thirty. "...two-and-a-half more hours."

"That may be so, but they're here. Now."

Patsy returned with the emptied wheelbarrow. "I'll finish up. You go."

"Are you sure?" Zoe looked down at her filthy hands and dusty jeans and shirt.

"I'm sure. Go."

"Want a ride?" Mr. Kroll pointed to his quad.

She'd ridden with Mr. Kroll before and nearly been bounced off into a ditch. "No, thanks. I'll walk."

Instead, she jogged. What in the world were her mother and Tom doing here so early? Had she misunderstood their arrival time? And now she was going to greet them, not only late, but looking like she'd been toiling in a barn. Which she had. Much to her mother's chagrin. Kimberly had never appreciated Zoe's passion for the outdoors or her love of animals.

Zoe arrived at the small stoop outside her kitchen door and kicked out of her grungy sneakers. She patted the dust from her Wranglers as best she could and slipped inside.

Her kitchen, long and narrow with appliances that would have been considered retro except for the fact they actually were that old, ran along the back side of the house.

In stocking feet, she padded across the floor to the swinging door leading into one of the two huge downstairs rooms she called home.

Summoning her courage, she plunged in.

Kimberly Chambers Jackson, wearing a cream suit with some kind of glitter on the lapels and honey blond hair done up in a curly cascade that even a hurricane wouldn't have budged, spun toward Zoe with a smile that froze into a look of horror.

"Hi, Mom." Even if Zoe'd had the urge to hug her mother, the thought of transferring sawdust and sweat onto that spotless suit—not to mention Kimberly's horrified reaction—stopped her cold. Then again, it might be amusing to see Kimberly bolt for the door after only a fifteen minute stay.

However, Tom Jackson, tall and still ruggedly handsome even though well into his sixties, strode across the room to her without hesitation. "Hiya, Sweet Pea," he said. A big grin beneath his graying mustache kicked up a ripple of creases that Zoe remembered as dimples.

"Hey, Tom." She surrendered to being caught up in a bear hug that lifted her off her feet. A rush of affection for the man who had been her late father's dearest friend, and who had stepped in to raise the distraught eight year old and comfort the grieving widow, swept through her.

He set her down and planted a kiss on her cheek. "It's good to see you, Zoe."

She brushed some transferred dirt from his blue polo shirt. "You, too. But what are you two doing here? I thought I was supposed to pick you up at ten."

Kimberly clasped her hands in front of her as if afraid to touch anything. Especially Zoe. "We caught an earlier flight and decided to rent a car. We didn't want you to have to drive us everywhere, after all."

Zoe kept her relief to herself.

"So this is where you live?" Kimberly did a slow pivot, taking in the room.

Zoe imagined her mother's thoughts as she inspected the furniture. The lumpy couch, the set of worn easy chairs—one of which was currently occupied by a pair of sleepy orange tabbies—and the wobbly end table had come with the house. The small dining table and chairs were products of a shopping trip to IKEA. Other odds and ends had been garage sale and flea market finds. Any other day, Zoe loved the lived-in atmosphere. Comfortable chic, she called it. But through her mother's eyes, she realized it could also be considered dilapidated and cheap. "Be it ever so humble—"

"It's charming," Tom said, giving his wife a look that said *be nice.*

"Where will we be sleeping?" Kimberly leaned a little to peer into the other downstairs room without moving her feet.

"Not there. That's my office. You can have my bedroom on the second floor." Zoe reached for a pair of the suitcases stacked at the foot of the stairs.

Tom intercepted her. "I'll get those. And we really don't want to put you out of your own bed."

Zoe caught the look her mother gave him. Clearly, displacing Zoe didn't bother Kimberly.

"It's okay." Zoe motioned to the lumpy couch. "That's a sleeper sofa. It's pretty comfortable, actually." If you liked having springs poking you in the back. "I don't mind. Really."

"See." Kimberly smiled at her husband. "She doesn't mind. And goodness knows there isn't a decent hotel within twenty miles of this place."

A hotel. Now there was a thought. Zoe made a mental note for their next visit.

Then again, if history were any indicator, that wouldn't happen for another ten years or so.

Tom tucked a bag under each arm, plus caught the handles of the other two, one in each hand. "Lead the way, Sweet Pea."

"Oh, Tom, you don't have to take them all in one trip," Kimberly said. "Let Zoe carry some."

"*You* could take one," Zoe said to her mother, knowing full well *that* wasn't going to happen.

Kimberly looked appalled at the suggestion.

"I can handle them," Tom said.

"I'll help." Zoe wrestled two of the bags from him and started up the stairs. When the house had been a single-family unit, Zoe's staircase had been the back one. It was enclosed, narrow, and steep. Tom followed and the clop of Kimberly's high heels indicated she was bringing up the rear.

"Oh, dear," Kimberly said. "Spider webs. And it's so dark. You should put more lights in here."

Zoe suppressed a string of sarcastic remarks. "Yes, Mom."

The *thump thump thump* of a miniature stampede mingled with a shriek, as Jade and Merlin, the two cats, raced up the stairs brushing past their ankles.

The top of the stairs opened into Zoe's bedroom. "I've cleared a couple of drawers for you. And there's space in the armoire." She'd moved a bunch of her things into the office downstairs.

The cats had taken possession of the double bed, daring the interlopers to make them move.

Tom dumped their bags on the floor. "I'm sorry we're putting you out." He crossed to the window and looked toward the view of the barn and rolling pastures. "Wow. No wonder you like it here."

Kimberly tested the mattress's firmness with her fingertips, while keeping an eye on the felines. "I didn't realize you had such a small bed. And these cats won't have the run of the place the whole time we're here, will they?"

Tom spun, a dark scowl on his face. "Kimberly, stop."

Zoe bit her lip to keep from smiling.

"But—"

"But nothing. This is a lovely old house and your daughter is bending over backward to give you a place to stay. So stop your bitching."

Pretending she didn't notice the storm clouds gathering in her mother's eyes, Zoe set the bags she'd been carrying in the middle of the floor and pointed at the door opposite the staircase. "That's the bathroom."

Kimberly cleared her throat. "You mean you'll have to come through here to use the facilities?"

"Kimberly..." Tom's voice was a low growl.

"I've arranged with the Kroll's to use their guest bath while you're here."

Kimberly's eyes lit up, the storm clouds gone. "Is it nicer than this one?"

Tom closed his eyes and shook his head.

"It's only half as big." Zoe nodded at the door. "Mine has a big claw-foot tub and a shower."

"Oh. Well. This'll be fine then."

Zoe headed for the stairs, but remembered the one thing she wanted to talk to her mother about. "Can I ask you something?"

"Of course. Anything." Kimberly's body language said otherwise.

"Do you remember the Engle farm?"

Kimberly turned her back to Zoe and popped the latch on one of the suitcases. "You mean the old Miller farm." It wasn't a question, but a correction.

"Yeah. I recall you telling me something about your uncles being killed there. What was that all about?"

Tom had been examining the armoire. "This is interesting. Where did you get it?"

"Yard sale," Zoe said without looking away from her mother's back. "Mom?"

"My uncles Vernon and Denver Miller owned that farm. They were a couple of bachelors. One morning, they were found dead out in the barn. One was shot, the other hanged."

"Kimberly, do you want to unpack now?" Tom interrupted. "Maybe you want to lie down and take a nap first."

Zoe scowled at her stepfather. What was up with him? To her mother, she said, "Wasn't there a connection to James Engle?"

Kimberly flung the dress she'd been unpacking down on the bed and faced Zoe. "The police said that Uncle Vernon and Uncle Denver fought over a woman and that it was a murder-suicide. But we all knew James Engle was responsible."

Tom crossed to Zoe and took her by the shoulders. "Your mother's tired. Can't this wait until later?"

Funny. Kimberly didn't look tired to Zoe. "It'll just take a minute. *Who* thought Engle was responsible? And why?"

"My mother for one. That was our family farm. It should have gone to her in their wills. But for some reason, the wills had been changed a few months before Vernon and Denver died, leaving everything to James Engle."

Whoa. There was a lot more to the story than Zoe had known. "When did all this happen?"

Kimberly looked to Tom. "How long was it? Forty? Forty-five years ago?"

He sat on the edge of the bed with a sigh. "Closer to forty-five."

"Why all the interest in family history?" Kimberly asked.

Zoe thought about the gruesome body hanging from the rafters the night before. "James Engle was found hanged in his barn yesterday."

Kimberly's eyes widened and she looked at her husband. "Oh my God. Tom? I'm so sorry."

Sorry? Zoe stared at her mother, then at Tom. "What's going on?"

Kimberly touched his shoulder and their eyes met. "There was a time when Tom looked up to James almost like a father."

FOUR

Pete hobbled across his kitchen to answer the pounding at the door. His damned ankle still hurt like hell. He'd promised Franklin he would be at the morgue by nine. The last thing he needed was company to delay him further.

He swung the door open to find a grandmotherly version of the Pillsbury Dough Boy wearing a pink t-shirt and khaki shorts. Sylvia Bassi, his former police secretary turned township supervisor, didn't wait for an invitation and bustled inside.

"I got your message," she said. "What did you want to talk to me about?"

He'd expected her to call him back. Not simply drop in. But he sure wasn't about to tell *her* that. He closed the door to block out the heat of the morning sun. "Did you hear about James Engle?"

"Yes, I did. Terrible thing. I can't imagine how much agony he must have been in to end it that way." She shivered.

Pete took one step on his bad leg, gritting his teeth against the pain, and eased into a chair. "What do you know about the Miller brothers?"

"The Miller brothers? Good heavens, you're going back a few years."

"That's why I called you."

"Pete Adams, are you insinuating I'm old?" Sylvia planted her plump fists against her ample hips.

"I would never insinuate such a thing. But you're the biggest local history buff I know."

"Bullshit. I *am* old. That's why I know my history. I lived it. Let me think. The Miller boys were bachelors. Quite the ladies' men. Handsome devils, the both of them."

Pete wondered about the faraway twinkle in her eyes as she took a seat at his dining room table.

"It was a tragedy. Rumor has it they got into a fight over a woman."

"What woman?"

Sylvia opened her mouth. Shut it again. Scowled. "There were rumors galore at the time, of course. But I don't think anyone ever narrowed it down. Anyhow, apparently Vernie shot Denver. Then, when he realized what he'd done, Vernie hanged himself." Her eyes widened. "It all happened in that barn. The one from yesterday."

"That's why I asked about it. Was there any connection between the Millers and the Engles?"

Sylvia tapped one finger against the table's surface. "Well, one of the Engle boys worked as a hand on the farm for several years before this all happened. When the wills were read, there was some sort of dust-up because Vernie and Denver left the farm to him instead of their sister and her family." Sylvia stopped tapping and shook the finger at Pete. "And their sister happens to be Zoe's grandma."

"Which Engle? James?"

"I believe so, yes."

"Makes you wonder who will get it now. I met Wilford. He doesn't look well either."

"I can't help you there. I do remember there was an investigation of sorts at the time, although nothing came of it. You should give Warren Froats a call."

"Froats?" Pete had replaced the old chief of police almost ten years ago. "Was he chief back then?"

"Warren was chief when the dinosaurs walked these hills. He'd probably still be chief if his cardiologist hadn't put his foot down and insisted he retire." Sylvia's face pinched into a scowl. "Good thing, too. Everyone loved Warren, but he wasn't much of a stickler for details, if you know what I mean. I'm not sure how many cases he solved. Mostly I think he just talked folks into forgetting about them."

"Yet you think I should speak with him about the investigation into the Miller homicides?"

She shrugged. "I can promise you one thing. If he did find any-thing, he'll still remember it. Nothing wrong with the man's memory."

"Okay." Pete added a stop at Froats' house to his itinerary for the day. After his trip to the morgue.

Sylvia pushed up from her seat with a grunt. "I'd better be going. I imagine you have an autopsy to attend to."

Pete stood, careful to keep his weight off the bad ankle without being obvious about it.

She paused in front of him. "You never said. Do you think there's a connection between Jim Engle and the Miller brothers' deaths?"

"Probably not. I'm just checking all the angles."

"All right then." She made a move toward the door and then hesi-tated. "And what happened to your leg?"

"My leg?" Pete straightened, striking the best invincible pose he could.

"Yes, your leg." She pointed at his right one. "The one you're try-ing hard to pretend doesn't hurt like the dickens."

He eyed her, but gave up the charade. "Injured in the line of duty. I'll be fine."

"Uh-huh. Get the doctor to look at it. And I don't mean the pathologist."

"Yes, Mother," Pete quipped and then leaned down to plant a kiss on her cheek.

She opened the door to leave. "Oh. You have more company com-ing."

Damn it. He glanced at the clock on the wall. Eight-fifteen. He needed to be on the road no later than eight-thirty to be in Brunswick by nine. Whoever was paying him a surprise visit this time had better make it quick.

He looked past Sylvia to see a black sedan parked at the end of his walk. A tall, slender woman wearing her brunette hair in a ponytail was helping an elderly man from the passenger seat.

Realization hit Pete with the force of a baseball bat.

No. Not now.

Sylvia nodded politely to the pair as she ambled down the side-walk toward her white Ford Escort, showing no signs of recognition. Why would she? She'd never met his sister and father.

"Hello, Pete," his sister said as the couple approached his door.

"Hey, Sis. Hi, Pop." Pete tried to keep the *what-the-hell-are-you-doing-here* tone from his voice.

"Son," Harry Adams said, beaming. He caught Pete in a hug that forced him to put full weight on his bad ankle. The old man mistook the groan as a result of his embrace and laughed, flexing his muscles. "I still work out in the gym, you know."

Nadine deposited a gargantuan purse on one of the kitchen chairs. "Come on, Dad." She guided him toward the living room. "I think your favorite TV show is on."

TV? Pete opened his mouth to protest. How long did they plan on staying? But his sister shot him a look that reminded him of his mother when he'd been in serious trouble as a kid. He closed his mouth.

Once the old man was settled on the sofa in front of the television, Nadine returned to the kitchen. "We have to talk."

No man alive wanted to hear those four words from any woman. "I wish you'd have called first. This isn't a good time for a visit."

"Which is precisely why I *didn't* call first. It's never a good time."

"But this really isn't. I have to be in Brunswick to attend an autopsy in a half hour."

"Tough."

"What?"

"You heard me." Nadine stripped the bright red elastic thing from her hair and made a production of slicking back the few stray wisps before rebinding them. "I've been taking care of Dad with virtually no help from you for almost five years now."

"You volunteered to take him into your house when they first diagnosed him."

"Yes. Because the Alzheimer's wasn't that bad yet and I didn't want to see him put in a home." She drew a deep breath and blew it out. "I still don't. But I need some help from you."

"I work. You don't."

"I do." She slammed a fist down on the table. "I work from home."

Pete winced. "You know what I mean."

"You said exactly what you meant. Your work is more important than mine because you go out into the world and arrest bad guys and all I do is transcribe doctors' notes."

Pete wanted to charge across the room and grab his sister by her shoulders. Shake her. But that would mean putting weight on his ankle. "What do you expect me to do? Quit my job?"

Nadine stuck her chin out. He remembered this same obstinate pose from when they were kids. One time he'd given in to temptation and belted her. He'd been six. She'd been four. But their dad had made it clear that hitting a girl—any girl, but especially his sister—would not be tolerated.

"I'm the one who's quitting," Nadine said.

"What?"

"Okay. Not quitting. I'm taking a vacation."

Oh. Were she and Dad headed somewhere and simply dropped in along the way? Was this entire argument over nothing? But somehow, that chin and the look in her eyes...

"I need a break. You never listen to me when I tell you I need you to take Dad for a weekend every now and then. If you'd even come stay with him for a few hours once a week so I could go shopping. But no. You have your precious job."

"Now hold on. I come out to visit every chance I get."

"Oh, sure. Once, maybe twice, a month. Never when it's convenient. Never with enough advanced warning I could plan to do something while you're there. Fine. I've had all I can take. If I don't get away for a few weeks, I'm going to...I don't know. I don't want to find out."

So she and Dad weren't going on vacation. "What are you getting at?" Pete knew the answer, but hoped—prayed—he was wrong.

"Dad will stay with you for the next two weeks. Maybe three. I'm going to the ocean to rest and regain my sanity."

Damn it. He wasn't wrong. "Nadine, I can't take him today—"

"I'm not asking you. You'd never say 'Okay, Sis. Sure I'll take him.' It's always 'Not today.'" Her impersonation of his voice wasn't particularly flattering. "I'm telling you. This is how it will be. He's all yours. I have a suitcase of his stuff in my car. You can bring it in. It's the black one. The other suitcases are mine."

He glared at her. She glared back. And he knew damned well, she was not going to back down.

Nadine hoisted her massive handbag from the chair and thumped it on the table. She flung it open and dug around inside, coming up with a large zippered plastic bag filled with pill bottles. "These are Dad's meds."

Holy shit. There had to be a whole pharmacy in there.

After more digging, she came up with a sheet of paper, which she shoved at Pete. "This tells you all you need to know. Which pills he gets when. Don't mix them up or forget."

Pete took the paper and unfolded it. "Are these all for his Alzheimer's?"

"No. The donepezil is for his dementia. The lisinopril and atenolol are for his heart and blood pressure." She waved a dismissive hand. "You don't need to know what they're all for. Just make certain he takes them on time. And I made sure there's enough so you won't have to bother with refills."

Pete read down the list of drugs, dosages, and times to a paragraph at the bottom. "What's this?"

"Dad needs to keep to a routine as much as possible. That's his favorite shows, meal times, bath time—"

"*Bath* times?"

"Relax. He can still bathe himself. You just have to remind him to do it."

"Great."

"And on occasion, he gets rambunctious in the evenings."

"Nadine, how am I supposed to conduct police business with Dad around? Take him with me?"

She shrugged. "Not my problem. For the next month, it's up to you to work it out."

Month? "You said two weeks."

"I said maybe three. Maybe even four. My plans are what you call open-ended." She added arms-crossed-in-front-of-her-chest to the jutted-chin pose.

Pete knew he didn't stand a chance. Reining in his anger, he dropped the bag of pharmaceuticals and the note regarding the care and feeding of his father on the table. He flung the door open, and attempted to storm across the porch. The best he could manage was a stomp and a hop. Damned ankle.

"Why are you limping?" Nadine called after him.

For a fleeting moment, he pondered playing the pity card. But he'd never used that one before in his life. He wasn't going to start now. "It's nothing. I'll be fine."

As he heaved his father's weathered black bag from Nadine's trunk, he struggled with the worst part of the situation.

His sister was absolutely right.

Pete had largely been avoiding his dad since he'd starting showing the early signs of dementia. Harry Adams had always been a tough old cuss. Take no prisoners. Take even less shit. Seeing the old man deteriorate in bits and pieces had been too hard. When Nadine volunteered to be caregiver, Pete had happily—and gratefully—allowed her to take on the role. He'd never intended to become an absentee son. But his work gave him every opportunity to do just that.

Now Nadine had thrown down her cards. Pete had no grounds to argue with her.

When he returned with the bag, Nadine was in the living room kneeling next to their father. She whispered something to him and kissed him on the cheek before rising and bustling past Pete, snatching her purse, and bustling out the door.

Pete gazed into the other room at the old man who was engrossed in whatever was on the TV. How the hell was he going to manage taking care of his dad while investigating a possible homicide?

"Hey, Pop," he called. "Feel like going for a ride?"

Pete entered the Monongahela County Morgue in the Brunswick Hospital basement exactly fifteen minutes after nine with Harry shuffling alongside him.

Coroner Franklin Marshall and Forensic Pathologist Lyle "Doc" Abercrombie, both in blue surgical scrubs, stood next to a stainless steel table on which lay James Engle's body. A short, stocky autopsy tech had already created the Y incision and was cutting through the ribs with a pair of loppers very much like the ones Pete used to prune his shrubs.

"You're late," Franklin said. "And who did you bring with you?"

Pete introduced his father to the coroner and the pathologist with a cursory mention of a surprise visit before directing Harry to a metal stool on one side of the room.

"You can sit here, Dad."

"Okay. Where are we?"

"The morgue. I'm observing an autopsy." Pete had answered the same question at least five times since he parked his car.

"As long as it isn't mine." Harry winked at him. At least the old man's sense of humor was still intact.

"Stay here. And don't touch anything." Pete wasn't much concerned about his father contaminating anything. But he knew the condition of some of the bodies in this place. God only knew what diseases some of those stiffs carried.

"He can watch if he wants," Franklin said.

"Thanks, but he's fine where he is." Pete didn't care to explain that he hadn't brought his father along because he was interested in his son's work, but because he hadn't had time to find someone to sit with the old man.

The tech set the loppers aside and lifted the sternum with portions of the ribs attached away from the chest, as though removing a lid from a box.

Franklin picked up a camera and snapped some shots of the chest cavity before the tech made a few snips and removed the heart. He set it in a scale, the way ladies at the market used to weigh their produce. Doc Abercrombie stepped in and moved the organ to a cutting board on an adjacent stainless steel counter where he used a scalpel to slice some tissue samples. As he worked, the pathologist mumbled notes into a recorder.

"I thought Detective Baronick would be here as well," Franklin said, his voice low.

"He's at the victim's house again this morning." Searching for whatever had the surviving Engle so spooked. "Did I miss anything here?" Pete asked.

"Nothing unexpected. Petechial hemorrhages indicate asphyxiation. The bruising on the neck is consistent with hanging by rope. The ligature marks slant upward from left to right."

"So no indication he had assistance?"

"None yet. It'll be at least a week or so before we get the tox screens back. Of course, with advanced lung cancer, I'd expect a high level of morphine in his blood."

"Time of death?"

"Considering the temperature in that barn and the rate of decay, I'd say our victim had been dead a couple of days before they found him."

The pathologist bent over the body, peering into the open chest cavity. "Gentlemen, I think we have a problem."

Pete and Franklin moved closer. With the victim's heart out of the way, they had a clear view of the lungs.

Abercrombie made a few cuts with his scalpel and lifted one of them out of the body.

Franklin squinted, removed his glasses to wipe his eyes, and put them on again. "Well, I'll be damned."

Whatever fascinated the two death experts eluded Pete. "What am I looking at?"

Franklin scratched his head. "Didn't you say this man was dying of lung cancer?"

"Yes. His brother said he only had days or weeks to live."

The pathologist gave a short laugh.

Franklin pointed to the mound in Abercrombie's hands. "Chief, this is one of the healthiest-looking lungs I've ever had the pleasure to autopsy." He motioned to Engle's chest cavity. "And from what I can tell, that one's a perfect match."

Pete looked at Franklin for some sign the coroner was joking, but found none.

Doc Abercrombie nodded his agreement. "I'm going to run further tests, of course. But from what I see here, this man did not have lung cancer."

Pete stepped back and winced when his ankle reminded him of its presence. With a swarm of questions buzzing in his brain like angry bees, he turned away from the body. No lung cancer? What was going on? Both Carl Loomis and Wilford Engle had told him of the diagnosis. Had they both lied? Had James Engle lied to them? Or had Wilford Engle lied to his brother's farm worker to cover up a murder?

Pete blinked away the litany of questions when a new one overpowered them. Across the room sat an empty stool.

Where the hell had his father gone?

FIVE

Zoe often threatened to hang a thermometer in the hay mow, but figured she didn't really want to know how hot it was. Sweat, mingled with chaff and dust, trickled down her back. She squirmed against the itchy stuff sticking to her skin under her shirt.

"Hold up down there," Patsy shouted over the racket of the hay elevator to Mr. Kroll and Tom, who were unloading the wagon parked in the indoor riding arena and tossing bales onto the contraption.

Patsy played catch at the top, handing the forty-pound bales to Zoe, who stacked them in the loft above the stalls that flanked the arena on the two long walls of the barn. In her effort to position the bales in the perfect pattern—fit the most hay in the cramped space without having the whole darned thing come crashing down like a house of cards—she'd fallen behind the pace. At the moment, Patsy had half a dozen bales at her feet waiting for Zoe.

"What are you girls doing up there?" Mr. Kroll shouted to them. "Quit your lollygagging. We're almost done."

The harassment was all in jest. During hay season, no one ever criticized the help. It was too sparse. Zoe had been shocked when Tom accepted her request that he assist. She had an ulterior motive, of course. She hoped he'd open up about his relationship with James Engle, but her questions would have to wait until the work was done.

Patsy lugged two bales back to the corner where Zoe perched five rows up, wrestled a bale into the space against the sloped roof. "You never mentioned your dad was so good looking."

"*Step*dad." Zoe emphasized the *step* part of it. "My real dad died when I was eight. And isn't Tom a little old for you? He's in his sixties."

"Age has nothing to do with it. He's hot."

Zoe glanced over her shoulder at her grinning friend. "You plan on stealing him away from my mom?"

"Maybe." Patsy winked at her.

"Good luck with that. For some reason, he's completely devoted to her." A fact that had always puzzled Zoe. Patsy was right about Tom. Zoe remembered thinking what a hunk he was back when she'd been a hormonal teenager. Her mother, on the other hand, had always been self-absorbed and needy. More so after the car crash that claimed Zoe's father's life.

Poor Tom. He could have had his pick of women. Instead he played caretaker to Kimberly and her daughter, marrying the young widow less than a year after the accident.

Patsy heaved another bale up to Zoe. "Your mom's a lucky woman."

"I guess."

"Don't you get along with your stepdad?"

"He's great. Mom, on the other hand, is a little too perfect for my taste. I'll bet she's on the phone right now calling in a cleaning service to sanitize the house. My half at least."

"As long as she pays for it. And at least you know your parents. I never did."

Stunned, Zoe shot a puzzled look at Patsy before snagging another bale. "What are you talking about? I've met your mom."

"I mean biological parents. I'm adopted." Patsy sneezed from the dust before Zoe could ask more. "Shall I ask the boys to crank up the production line again?"

Zoe crammed the last of the bales into place and jumped down from her perch. "Yeah. Let her rip."

They returned to the top of the hay elevator which continued to clatter, chains driving paddles up a stainless steel slope that reminded Zoe of a sliding board. Or the uphill part of a roller coaster.

"Okay, fellows," Patsy shouted over the noise of the electric motor. "Let's wrap this up."

Mr. Kroll stood on the wagon deck with the last few bales ready at his feet. "Amen to that." He tossed one of them to Tom, who dropped it onto the elevator.

With assembly line precision, they finished off the load within minutes. Tom yanked the elevator's cord from the electric socket, and glorious silence fell over the barn as the machine rattled to a stop. Patsy headed for the ladder, but Zoe climbed onto the elevator and slid down, easing over each of the paddles on the way to the barn floor.

"Tom was just telling me that you were over at Jim Engle's place yesterday," Mr. Kroll said once Zoe's feet hit the ground.

"Yeah." She glanced toward her stepdad, but he was busy helping Patsy move some sacks of feed. "Did you know him?"

"Yeah, I knew him." Her landlord eased down from the wagon, accepting Zoe's hand to steady him. "Didn't have much use for him, but I sure wouldn't wish something like this on anyone."

"Why didn't you like him?"

"Oh, now, Zoe, you know it ain't polite to speak ill of the dead."

"I understand." She wondered if Pete and Franklin had uncovered anything interesting. The autopsy would have been completed by now. "I don't suppose by any chance you knew the Miller brothers who used to own that farm?"

Mr. Kroll dusted off his coveralls. "The Miller brothers? They were a bit before your time, weren't they?"

"Yeah. But they were my mother's uncles, so I've heard stories."

Mr. Kroll moved toward the tractor hitched to the now empty wagon and climbed into the seat. "I didn't realize they were your relatives. I knew of them by name. Don't recall ever meeting them, though."

"Oh." Zoe made no effort to hide her disappointment.

Mr. Kroll fired up the Massey-Ferguson. With a sputter and a roar, the old tractor lurched out the big doors.

When the barn fell quiet again, Tom appeared at Zoe's side. He slung an arm around her shoulders, putting her in a playful neck lock. "Well, kiddo. What d'ya say we head back to the house and get cleaned up?"

"A cool shower sounds great right about now. I itch from head to toe." Zoe leaned against her stepdad, resting her head briefly against his chest.

She'd forgotten how much she missed him. No matter how rough things got with her mother or with her teenaged exploits, Tom had always been Zoe's champion.

"I'll take you and your mom out to lunch," he continued. "Is that hot dog shop still open in Dillard?"

"The Dog Den? Yeah. It's still there. I can't imagine Mom eating there, though."

He released her. "You don't give your mom enough credit. What about your friend?" He turned toward the tack room. "Hey, Patsy. Want to join us for lunch at the Dog Den?"

Patsy appeared at the door armed with a bucket full of brushes. "Thanks, but I'm going to take Jazzel out for a ride while I have the chance. By the way, did Zoe invite you and your wife to my picnic?"

Tom shot a curious glace at Zoe. "Picnic? No, she didn't."

"My birthday's next Friday. I'm having barbecue and beer at my place. If you're still here, I'd love for you to come."

He nodded. "Sounds like fun. Count us in."

"Terrific." Patsy grinned. "You all have a nice lunch."

Zoe gave her a sour look to match her sarcastic, "Thanks."

Patsy headed to the far end of the barn.

"I wanted to talk to you about something," Zoe said as she and Tom strolled outside.

"Okay. What about?"

"James Engle. I never knew you and he were friends."

The smile faded from Tom's face. "Your mother overstated the matter. We weren't really that close."

But Zoe wasn't ready to give up on the matter. "Then why were you trying so hard to change the subject this morning when I was talking to Mom about what happened with her uncles?"

Tom stopped. He removed his eyeglasses and studied the specks of chaff on the lenses. "I wasn't aware I was doing that."

Zoe didn't believe him. "You must know something about what was going on back then."

He tugged a handkerchief from his jeans pocket and wiped his glasses with it. "Sorry to disappoint you, but as far as I know, those stories you've heard about it being a murder/suicide are true."

"James Engle never told you anything?"

"Nope." Tom shoved the handkerchief back in his pocket and put on his glasses, which even Zoe could tell were still smudged. "Jim never said a word. And I never believed the stories your grandmother spouted either. But that didn't make me especially popular with her, so I learned to keep my opinions to myself. Your mom likes to carry on the family grudge, spreading rumors. I'd hate to see you picking up the banner and running with it. Jim's gone. Let the whole mess end here."

"But what if there's a connection between Engle's death yesterday and Vernon and Denver's all those years ago?"

"How could there be? Jim committed suicide. I don't think there's any doubt about that. Is there?"

Was there? Zoe wished she knew what was going on at the Monongahela County Morgue. "Probably not."

"Then drop it," he said, a note of finality in his soft voice.

Zoe deflated. Tom was right. Once again, he proved to be the voice of logic and reason. She'd hated that about him when she was growing up. She didn't much care for it now, either.

"Okay?" he asked.

She struggled to find a suitable argument against his rationale and came up blank. "Okay," she muttered.

"Good. Now let's go drag your mom out to lunch."

"To the Dog Den? Drag may be exactly what you have to do."

How the hell could an old man move so damned fast? Pete's injured ankle prevented him from charging down the hallway outside the morgue, only adding to his frustration.

Harry Adams was nowhere to be seen.

Elevators to the hospital's upper floors loomed at one end of the hall. Glass sliding doors to the underground parking lot flanked the other. Terrific. Was his father wandering aimlessly around the hospital's interior or had he slipped outside?

With a faint whoosh, the glass doors slid open. But it wasn't his father who strolled in.

"Hey, Pete," Wayne Baronick said. "Is the autopsy done already?"

"Not yet. Did you happen to see an older man out there? About seventy, six foot, gray hair, blue eyes?"

"No. But I saw about five guys fitting that description hanging out at the coffee shop down the street. What's up?"

"It's my father. He's..." Pete hated admitting his old man had Alzheimer's. The word dementia didn't sit well with him either. "He tends to wander off."

"I didn't think you had a father," the detective said. "I figured you'd just hatched from an egg. Like an alligator."

Pete resisted the urge to bite the young punk's head off. Like an alligator. "Go back outside and see if you can spot him. I've already called security, but I'm going to head upstairs and look for him myself."

"Yeah, okay." Baronick backed toward the glass doors. "But, Pete, there are like ten or eleven floors to this hospital."

"Don't you think I know that?"

The detective shrugged and jogged outside.

As Pete limped toward the elevators, the door to the men's room halfway down the hall swung open.

"Well, hello, son," Harry said. "What are you doing here?"

Relief poured from Pete in a sigh. "Pop. You scared the hell outta me. I told you to stay put."

"I didn't think I needed your permission to take a leak." The old man sniffed in disdain.

Pete rubbed his temple where the seed of a headache had taken root. "You're right. You don't. Just let me know where you're going next time."

"I don't need you keeping tabs on my whereabouts, you know. I'm not a child. Your sister treats me like a damned six-year-old. I won't have it from you, too."

Pete smiled in spite of himself. Yep, that was his old man, all right. "Okay, Pop. Let's go back inside."

"Inside where?"

"The morgue."

"Oh."

As they turned, Baronick charged through the glass doors. "There's no one out there matching that description—" He stopped midsentence and midstride.

"I found him," Pete said.

"Damn it. I wasn't lost," Harry said. "I was in the damned can."

Pete cleared his throat. "Wayne Baronick, meet Harry Adams. My father."

A slow smile spread across Baronick's face. "I can see the apple didn't fall far from the tree."

Pete bit back a remark about being neither an apple nor an alligator egg. "Did you find anything at Engle's house?"

"You first. Did the autopsy reveal anything?"

"Only that Jim Engle had a perfectly healthy set of lungs."

Baronick's smile faded. "Get out. I thought he had lung cancer."

Pete shrugged. "Apparently not."

The detective swore under his breath. He placed a hand on the morgue door and swung it open, holding it for Pete and Harry.

Inside, the tech had peeled the skin back from the top of the corpse's head. Franklin handed him a small power saw.

"Find anything else?" Pete asked.

"His liver shows signs of some excessive drinking, but not to the point of being life threatening," Doc Abercrombie said. "Otherwise, I see nothing here that would be cause for impending death."

"So if he committed suicide in order to cheat death..." Baronick's voice trailed off.

"Then he was the one who was cheated, I'm afraid," the pathologist said.

"Of course, we're not done yet," Franklin added. The tech fired up the saw and laid the blade against the skull.

Pete eased his father back onto the stool. He considered telling the old man to stay put, but that hadn't worked so well the first time he'd tried it. Instead, he pulled up a second stool and sat down next to Harry, relieved to be off his ankle. "Now," he said to Baronick. "What did you find at the house?"

"A lot of very neat files. Either James Engle was the definition of anal or he'd done one fine job of putting his affairs in order."

"That's it?"

"Not quite. One of the crime scene boys was crawling around, looking in and under everything. He found a crumpled piece of paper under the sofa. Turned out to be another interesting note."

"Another suicide note?"

"No. A letter dated two weeks ago. I sent it to the lab."

"What kind of letter?"

"I'm not sure." Baronick pulled a folded sheet of paper from his pants pocket. "I made a copy of it. Thought maybe you'd have some idea of what it's about."

Pete took the paper from him and read. At first, the name didn't register with him.

Dear Mrs. Jackson,

I suppose you're wondering why I would be writing to you now. My days are numbered and I hope to make things right as much as possible while I still can.

As part of that mission, I feel I need to let you know about your husband. Gary was just trying to do what's right. Mrs. Jackson, your husband did not die in that car crash.

I wish I could tell you more.

With Deepest Remorse,
James Engle

"What do you make of it?" Baronick asked. "Almost sounds like the old guy was playing private eye."

Pete stared at the words on the page. The weight of their implication crushed down on him. "Engle wasn't playing detective."

"What then? Who the hell is Gary Jackson?"

"Chambers," Pete corrected him. "Gary Chambers. He was killed—supposedly—by a drunk driver over twenty-five years ago."

Pete didn't remember the case firsthand. Back then, he'd still been in the police academy in Pittsburgh. But he knew the name.

Gary Chambers—Zoe's father.

SIX

Cause of death—asphyxiation due to strangulation. Manner of death—undetermined pending toxicology results.

Such were Coroner Franklin Marshall's rulings. Undetermined. At least that left the case open for Pete to investigate. Had the ruling been suicide, there would've been no case.

And Pete intended to investigate. Something about this thing stunk worse than James Engle's decomposing corpse.

Harry gazed out the passenger side window of the SUV. "Where are we going?" he asked for the third time since they'd left Brunswick.

"To Wilford Engle's house." Pete figured he could have told the old man Disneyland, and it wouldn't have stuck either.

It had been a process of elimination regarding who to talk to first. Pete had called Warren Froats, but the former Chief of Police was away on a fishing trip, according to his wife, and wouldn't be home until late. Dr. David Weinstein, James Engle's physician, was out of his office until Monday morning. That left the victim's brother. And Pete wasn't about to call ahead and give the old coot a chance to make travel plans.

Harry turned to Pete. "Engle? Isn't that the guy they were just cutting up back there?"

Pete took his eyes off the road for a moment to study his father, stunned that he remembered the autopsy, let alone the victim's name. "His brother. I need to ask him a few questions."

"He the next of kin?"

"Yeah."

"So he's the prime suspect, huh?" Harry beamed. "I watch those TV shows. I know how you cops think. The next of kin is always the prime suspect."

Pete chuckled. "Something like that, Pop."

But Pete doubted Wilford Engle had killed his brother. At least not without help. Wilford could barely support his own weight, as Pete's throbbing ankle still attested. No way could the old man hoist a body—live or dead—off the ground to make it look like a suicide by hanging. At the moment the biggest question in Pete's mind had to do with whether Wilford really believed James was dying of cancer. Or was Wilford the one fabricating the whole tale?

Ten minutes later, Pete pulled into the surviving Engle's driveway. He reached for the ignition, but hesitated. He couldn't very well shut off the engine—and the air conditioning—if he intended to leave Harry sitting there. Not with the temperature outside teasing the ninety-degree mark. But was it a good idea to leave Harry unattended?

Of course it wasn't. Pete cursed his sister under his breath. How was he supposed to do his job while babysitting his father?

"Well, what are you waiting on?" Harry asked. "Let's go. Do you want me to play good cop or bad cop?"

Pete bit back a grin in spite of himself. "How about you play silent cop and let me do all the talking. It is my job, after all."

Harry scowled at him. "Anybody ever tell you that you're no fun at all?"

"All the time."

Pete cut the ignition, and they climbed out of the vehicle.

"You again," Wilford Engle muttered when he opened the door. He eyed Harry. "Who's he?"

Pete made the introductions, and Harry extended a hand. Engle glowered at it for a moment then took it without much enthusiasm.

"Mind if we come in?" Pete asked.

"I do. But I don't expect that makes much difference to you." Engle stepped back, and Pete followed Harry inside.

As hot and miserable as it was outside, the interior of the house was worse. None of the windows were open. The blinds shuttered the room against the sun, but no fans circulated the stagnant air. The place reeked of old chewing tobacco and dust.

Engle didn't invite either of them to sit, but Harry sank into an easy chair.

Pete leaned against the same wall as yesterday, keeping his weight off his bad ankle, and pulled his notebook from his pocket. "I'd like to ask you a few questions."

"I didn't figure you were here to see how I was holding up." Engle gave a disdainful sniff. "What do you want to know that I haven't told you already?"

"When was the last time you were over at your brother's place?"

"Tuesday. I told you before. I took him to his doctor's appointment."

Pete made a small production of squinting thoughtfully at his notes. "And this doctor's appointment was with his oncologist?"

"Oncalla-who?"

"Oncologist. The specialist treating him for his cancer."

Engle stared at Pete as if he had sprouted a second head. "He wasn't seeing no specialist. I took him to Dr. Weinstein in Brunswick. I told you that yesterday. That's who I always took him to."

"Is there any particular reason why your brother wasn't being treated by a specialist?"

Engle's gaze shifted toward the sofa, and Pete suspected he would prefer to sit down. "I guess Dr. Weinstein didn't see no need for it." Engle's voice developed a quiver of doubt.

"So, if your brother was only seeing a general practitioner, why pick one that was fifteen miles away in Brunswick? Why not go to Dr. McCarrell in Philipsburg? That's who you see, isn't it?"

Pete braced for a tirade from the old farmer about poking into his business. In truth, Pete was only guessing about McCarrell. But while the man might come across as a folksy country doctor, without a court order, he'd flat out refused to comment on whether or not he ever treated either Engle, citing doctor-patient confidentiality laws. Pete hoped that Wilford was like virtually every other Vance Township resident over the age of sixty and chose the doctor who had been in the area for decades.

The tirade never came.

"Well, yeah. I do go to old Dr. McCarrell," Engle said, his voice soft. "So did Jim before the illness."

"Then why did he switch to Dr. Weinstein?"

"Because Weinstein's younger, I suppose. Knows more about treating lung cancer."

"Did you go in to see the doctor with your brother?"

"Why should I?" The vitriol was back in Wilford Engle's voice. "Jim was a grown man. He didn't need me holding his hand."

"Did you ever talk to the doctor? Maybe have a family meeting to determine a course of treatment?"

"I'm telling you, there wasn't no need for it. Jim might've been dying of lung cancer, but there wasn't nothing wrong with his mind. He took care of his own affairs."

Pete glanced at Harry, who was staring across the room, his face a blank mask.

"Why the blazes are you asking all these questions about Jim's doctor?" Engle said.

Pete forced his thoughts away from the cruel irony of James Engle's sound mind and body—save for the suicide—juxtaposed against Harry's Alzheimer's-riddled brain. It was time to get to the crux of the matter. "Mr. Engle, who told you Jim had lung cancer?"

"Jim, of course." The old man frowned in puzzlement. "What difference does that make?"

Pete tapped his pen against his lips. Either Wilford Engle was an Oscar-worthy actor, or he had no clue about the true state of his brother's health. Pete's instincts told him it was the latter. "Because the autopsy on your brother showed no signs of cancer. Lung or otherwise."

"What?" Spittle flew from the old man's lips as he sputtered. "What are you talking about? Didn't really have cancer? Of course he had cancer."

"Not according to the coroner. Your brother's lungs were healthy."

"You're a goddamn liar." Engle trembled. His face flushed a vivid crimson.

Harry snapped out of his daze and leapt to his feet. Damn, he was nimble for an old guy. "Pete's as honest as the day is long."

Engle ignored him. "What kind of con are you trying to pull on me, you goddamned cop?"

Harry clenched his fists and took a step toward Engle. "Who do you think you are, talking to my boy that way?"

Pete pushed away from the wall and caught his father's arm. "Cool it, Pop," he whispered.

A muscle twitched under the skin of Engle's jaw. "You think you'll rattle me, and I'll go to pieces? Confess to something I didn't do? I know how you stinking cops operate. Well, it won't work. 'Cause I didn't do nothing. My brother had cancer. He killed himself because he didn't want to become a burden."

Even in the dim light, Pete spotted tears welling in the old man's eyes. There was something else there, too. Engle shifted his gaze downward as his brows drew into a wrinkled peak. Then slowly, he appeared to cave in on himself.

Pete released Harry and jumped to catch Engle before he hit the floor for the second time in two days. This time, Pete managed to keep his balance and not go down with him, even though sharp pains shot up his leg when he put full weight on his ankle.

"Careful there," Pete said, easing Engle onto the sofa.

"Sorry," he muttered, brushing Pete away. Engle rubbed the day-old stubble on his chin and stared at the floor in front of him. His breath came hard and loud, but when he spoke, his voice was barely a whisper. "Jim didn't have cancer? But—why? I don't understand."

Pete gave Engle a moment to process the reality of the situation before asking, "Can you think of any reason your brother would lie about being sick?"

The tears were gone. Engle's eyes once again turned dark and cold, his jaw set. "No." He met Pete's gaze. "And I want you to leave. Now. I got nothing else to say to you."

"Okay." Pete knew the old man had given him all he intended to for the day. He'd have to get answers elsewhere. "If you think of anything that might help explain—"

"If I think of anything, you'll be the last person I call. Get out."

Pete turned to find Harry standing where he'd left him, a perplexed look on his face. "Come on, Pop. Let's go home."

Harry eyed Pete, glanced at Engle, and then around the room. "Yeah. Let's go. This place gives me the heebie-jeebies."

Zoe wondered if Saturday with Kimberly and Tom would ever end. Lunch at the Dog Den had been the disaster she'd predicted. Kimberly, flaunting an oversized necklace and earrings and attired in a bright pink tank top and shorts, told the waitress they should change their menu to include healthier, more nutritious fare. The woman gave Kimberly a look to suggest she should get back on her spaceship and return to her home planet. Sooner rather than later. So while Zoe and Tom dined on footlong hot dogs smothered in chili and onions with sides of greasy fried cauliflower, Kimberly sipped a can of diet ginger ale.

Lunch was followed by an afternoon of Kimberly's complaints regarding the lack of decent shopping or cultural amenities within the township even after all the years she'd been away. The abundance of cattle, horses, and bars held little appeal for her.

By late afternoon, Zoe was all too happy to give Tom a list of eateries in Brunswick that might suit Kimberly's delicate palate and pack them off in their rental car for a romantic dinner. Zoe climbed into her two-tone—three-tone if she counted the rust—Chevy pickup and headed for Dillard. She picked up a case of Pepsi at the beer distributor before circling through town to Pete's place. His Vance Township Police Department SUV sat alone in the driveway. Good. With any luck, she was the first to arrive at the poker game and could talk with him alone. What would he think about her discovery that James Engle had inherited that farm from the Miller brothers when it should have gone to her grandmother? Had the autopsy confirmed Engle's manner of death as suicide or something else?

"Hello?" she called through the screen door. A TV blared from the interior of the house.

Pete appeared and waved her in. "You're early."

"I know. Mom and Tom left for an evening in Brunswick, and I wanted to get out of the house before they changed their mind."

Pete gave a terse laugh and took the Pepsi from her arms, carrying it to the kitchen counter. His usual commanding stride seemed a little uneven.

"What happened? Are you limping?"

"No," he said, a growl in his voice.

Okay. Not a good subject for conversation.

With Pete's back to her, the hint of muscles beneath his t-shirt distracted Zoe from her curiosity about the case. Her gaze drifted downward as she indulged in the guilty pleasure of checking out the rather nice shape of his ass. Too bad he didn't wear his jeans a bit tighter, though. For one brief moment, she flashed back on the one and only kiss they'd shared last winter. She squeezed her eyes closed. *Stop it.* As sweet as that kiss had been, her chronic bad judgment where men were concerned had sworn her off all romantic involvement. Especially one with a close friend like Pete.

A peal of familiar laughter from the living room distracted her. "Sounds like Sylvia's here early, too." So much for a little alone time.

He turned to face her. Lines creased his forehead. His jaw was clenched and his lips pressed into a thin line. Zoe had seen him this tense before, but at work. Not on a Saturday poker night. There was something else wrong besides the limp. Before she had a chance to ask him what it was, he motioned for her to follow and led the way into the living room.

The ancient television in the corner was set to an old episode of *Seinfeld*. Zoe realized in the years she'd known Pete, she'd never seen him watch TV. Sylvia sat on the couch next to an older gentleman with eyes the same ice blue as Pete's.

"Zoe." Sylvia smiled up at her. "I didn't hear you come in. Have you met Pete's dad yet?"

Pete's *dad*? "Uh, no." Zoe shot a glance at Pete's pained expression.

The older man climbed to his feet, a bright smile on his face. Of course. Add twenty-five years or so to Pete and this would be the result.

Pete made the introductions in a strained voice. "Zoe, this is Harry Adams. Pop, this is Zoe Chambers."

She extended a hand, and Harry took it in both of his. "Zoe," he said. "What a lovely name. Very fitting for a lovely young lady."

Over Harry's shoulder, Zoe caught Sylvia's raised eyebrows and huge grin. It was shaping up to be an interesting night of poker at the Adams' house.

"Care to join us?" Harry motioned at the TV. "I love this show."

Pete caught Zoe's elbow. "I need her help in the kitchen, Pop."

"Sure you do, son." Harry gave a couple of obvious winks in Pete's direction before reclaiming his spot on the couch.

Pete let out a low groan as Zoe followed him into the other room. "I didn't know your father was staying with you," she said.

"My sister dropped him off this morning. Unexpectedly." Pete pressed his fingers into the space between his eyebrows.

"Headache?"

"You have no idea."

"Oh, I think I do. I'll trade my mom for your dad in a heartbeat."

Pete met her gaze head-on. There was something in his eyes Zoe had never seen before. She couldn't quite put a name to it. Regret? Maybe. Exhaustion? Definitely. But more than that.

"Pete? What is it?" she asked.

He opened his mouth, but before he could speak, someone else knocked at the door.

"Hey," Earl Kolter shouted through the screen. "You guys ready to lose your shirts? I'm feeling lucky tonight."

"It's open," Pete called out. Then he leaned closer to Zoe and whispered in her ear, "Can you stay after everyone else leaves? I need to talk to you."

The urgency in his voice, combined with that haunted look on his face, stirred myriad questions in her mind. Something was going on. But what? Was it the case? Or was it this surprise visit from his dad?

Before Zoe had a chance to respond, he'd already moved toward Earl who was coming through the door with a stack of pizzas. She jumped to grab the top four boxes.

"I've got them," Pete protested.

"Yeah, but no matter what you say, you're limping, and I don't want to be eating pizza off the floor."

"Limping?" Earl scowled at Pete. "What happened?"

"Nothing. I'm fine."

"You know you have the county's best team of paramedics here in your house right now." Earl winked at Zoe. "We could check you out."

"Doesn't anyone around here understand simple English? I'm fine." Without a hint of a limp, Pete crossed to the kitchen and thunked the pizzas down.

Earl raised a questioning eyebrow at Zoe. She gave him a shrug before carrying the rest of the boxes to the counter.

The door swung open again, and Vance Township Police Officer Seth Metzger stomped in, toting bulging plastic grocery bags. Fire Chief Bruce Yancy, who lugged a case of beer beneath each burly arm, followed. Sylvia and Harry joined the crowd in the kitchen, and the decibel level in the small house rose to a pitch akin to that of Heinz Field during a Steelers game.

"Looks like the gang's all here," Sylvia shouted above the din. "Let's eat."

Zoe grabbed a slice of pepperoni pizza, ducking out of the kitchen before the vultures swept in. Seth, Earl, and Yancy shouldered one another in an effort to pile their plates high. But when Sylvia cleared her throat, they sheepishly made room for her.

Zoe set her plate on the table and slid into a chair. Only then did she notice Harry standing alone near the arched doorway to the living room, a vexed look on his face. Pete had spotted him, too, and crossed to his dad's side. The limp was back.

Pete whispered something to Harry, who shook his head. Then Pete took him by the elbow and led him into the other room.

Something was definitely wrong. Zoe abandoned her pizza and followed them. Pete was easing his father onto the sofa.

"What's going on?"

Pete glanced up. "Nothing. Go make sure everyone can find what they need."

Unaccustomed to being the recipient of Pete's curt orders, she bristled. "The hungry hordes can take care of themselves. And don't tell me nothing's wrong."

Harry gazed up at her, the perplexed look still on his face. "Do I know you?"

Zoe opened her mouth to remind him of her name, but realization hit her before she could speak. She turned to Pete and finally put a name to what she saw in his eyes.

Anguish.

She smiled. "Hi, Mr. Adams. I'm Zoe."

Harry brightened. "Zoe. What a lovely name. Are you Pete's girl-friend?"

Heat singed her neck and crept to her cheeks. "Um, no—I—um—"

"She's just a friend, Pop," Pete said, putting a serious chill on her embarrassed blush.

Just a friend. Well, that *is* what she insisted she wanted. Wasn't it?

"That's too bad." Harry studied her with a raised eyebrow.

Zoe had always feared Pete could read her mind. Now she suspected his father of having similar abilities. She lowered her gaze to her shoes.

"Son, why aren't you dating this girl? Look at her. She's a knockout."

The heat around Zoe's neck burst into an inferno.

"I know she is." Pete cleared his throat. "Are you hungry? I'll fix you a plate."

"I could go for a bite."

"I'll be right back." Pete caught Zoe's arm and drew her toward the kitchen, but stopped short of the doorway. "Sorry about that," he whispered.

"About what?"

In reply, he shot a glance over his shoulder at Harry.

She wanted to tell Pete he had nothing to apologize for, with the possible exception of his too-quick denial of her role as his girlfriend. "Alzheimer's?"

"Yeah."

So that was why he wanted her to stay after everyone else left. He needed a friend to confide in. Maybe not a girlfriend, but the kind of friend who could provide comfort in trying times. She smiled. "Let's get him something to eat."

SEVEN

Pete stared at the pair of queens and pair of threes he held in his hand. Drawing one lousy card hadn't helped him a bit. The TV blaring from the living room helped even less.

Sylvia, Yancy, Earl, and Seth sat around the dining table. Zoe had offered to skip the game and keep Harry company.

"You playing or what?" Yancy asked him. "It'll cost you two bucks."

Pete studied the faces around him. Earl and Yancy had folded. Sylvia kept a steady eye on Pete. The woman had the best poker face of the bunch. Hard to tell what she was holding. Seth, on the other hand, broke out in a sweat every time he bluffed. Right now he was biting back a smile while fidgeting in his chair.

"I'm out." Pete tossed his cards down, leaned back in his chair, and allowed Sylvia and Seth to battle for the pot.

Meanwhile, Zoe was in the other room, babysitting Harry.

Damn it. Pete hated dumping his problems on his friends. Especially Zoe. He'd cringed at the look on her face when she'd recognized Harry's illness. Pity. She'd felt *pity*. For Harry, who would've detested anyone thinking of him as pathetic. And for Pete, for being stuck with a father who couldn't remember shit.

Plus, there was that embarrassing little exchange with Harry insisting that Pete ask Zoe out. Little did his dad know how much he longed to do just that. But she'd already turned him down, insisting she valued their friendship too much to risk it. She had a point. He'd made a lousy husband to his ex-wife. Now he realized what a lousy son and brother he was as well. *Friend* was about the best he could muster.

And how was Zoe going to react to the letter? Pete had made a copy of the crumpled note Baronick had found under James Engle's couch. He'd contemplated taking it directly to Zoe's mother. But the case was old. The note probably didn't mean a thing. He'd never met Kimberly Chambers Jackson. How would she respond to something like this? No, he'd show the copy to Zoe first and let her decide how to deal with her mother.

"Hey. You in?" Sylvia thumped him on the arm. "Ante up, bud."

Pete blinked. Seth was raking in his winnings, a victorious smile on his young face. Never mind that he was still down five bucks for the evening. The kid needed to work on containing himself.

Pete glanced over his shoulder at the clock on the wall. Eight-thirty. Poor Zoe had been sitting in there, watching TV with Harry for over an hour. "Deal me out of this hand." His ankle throbbed, but he fought to ignore the pain as he entered the living room.

The TV was tuned to some sort of dance competition. But Harry and Zoe weren't sitting back and watching it as Pete had expected. Harry perched on the edge of the sofa, his face etched with tension. Zoe had her back turned to Pete, but he noticed her hand on Harry's arm.

"What's going on in here?" Pete kept his voice light.

Harry sprung to his feet. Zoe rose slower and turned toward Pete. Her lips were pressed into a troubled frown, her eyes communicating volumes without saying a word.

"Where's Nadine?" Harry demanded. "I want to go home."

"Nadine's out of town. You're staying with me for a few weeks. Remember?" Pete winced at his own words. Hell, no, Harry didn't remember. That was the problem.

Harry squinted at Pete. Then his face softened. "Pete? Is that you? What are you doing here?"

Pete sighed. "I live here, Pop. How about I show you to your room and get you ready for bed."

Harry looked around, obviously confused. His eyes settled on Zoe. "Who are you?"

"I'm Zoe." Her voice sounded tired, but patient.

Pete wondered how many times she'd answered that question during the course of the evening. He took his father's elbow. "Come on, Pop."

"Okay."

As Pete turned his dad toward the hallway at the back of the house, he felt Zoe's fingers brush his arm. He met her gaze for a moment and wasn't sure which stung most. The vacant look in his dad's eyes. Or the look of sympathy in hers.

"You've done your time," Pete told her. "Go play some poker."

Pete finally settled Harry into the guest room after considerable arguing. Had the raised voices been heard all the way out in the dining room? Pete hoped not.

He left his father's room door ajar and the hall light on. As he hobbled through the living room, the absence of poker player chatter struck him as a bad sign. Sure enough, the dining room and kitchen were empty, except for Zoe, who looked up from a game of solitaire.

"Did Pop's bellowing scare everyone off?"

Zoe motioned toward the clock on the wall. "No."

Eleven o'clock. How did that happen? Pete sunk into the chair across from her with a groan. His ankle was killing him. "I guess I'm a lousy host."

One at a time, she flipped the cards face down. "No, you're not. Did you get your dad settled?"

Pete wiped a hand across his eyes. "Finally."

"It's called sundowning."

"What?"

"Sundowning. A lot of Alzheimer's patients get...unruly...later in the day."

Pete recalled Nadine's words. *And on occasion, he gets rambunctious in the evenings.*

"Plus he's in an unfamiliar setting," Zoe said.

"Unfamiliar," Pete echoed. And whose fault was that? He longed to blame this all on his sister. But as much as it pained him to admit it, Nadine had been right. "How do you know all this?"

Zoe scooped up the cards and tapped the edge of the deck against the table. "Patsy Greene—she boards her horse at the farm? Her mom had Alzheimer's. I used to help her out sometimes."

Terrific. Zoe was more help to a friend than he was to his own sister.

"It's a horrible disease," Zoe added. "You've never mentioned your dad had it. In fact, I don't remember you ever mentioning your dad at all."

"He lives with my sister in Pittsburgh. She's taking a vacation for a few weeks."

"Caregivers need a break every so often." Zoe reached across the table and rested a hand on his arm. "It's great that you're pitching in to help."

He eased away from her touch, leaning back in the chair. What would she think if she knew the truth?

"What do you need me to do?" Zoe asked.

"Do?"

"You asked me to stick around after everyone else left. I figured you wanted to ask me to help out with your dad."

Damn it. The letter. He'd almost forgotten. "Um, actually, no. That's not what I wanted to talk to you about."

"Oh?" She frowned, but then her eyes widened. "Oh. The autopsy. What did Franklin find out? Was it really a suicide?"

"We don't know yet. There's nothing to indicate anyone helped Engle along, but Franklin ruled the manner of death as undetermined."

"So you're still investigating?"

"Oh, yeah." Pete met her eyes. "There've been a couple of unexpected developments today."

"Really? Such as?"

"First, James Engle didn't have lung cancer."

Zoe choked. "But—wasn't that the reason he supposedly killed himself?"

"According to his brother."

"And Carl Loomis," she reminded him.

Pete had almost forgotten about the irate farmhand. He made a mental note to add Loomis to his list of interviewees.

She turned the deck over in her hand, cut it, and shuffled. "I talked to my mom about her uncles."

"And?" Pete slipped the letter from his pocket, but kept it palmed.

"The story goes that their deaths were a murder/suicide."

"That's what I heard."

She shuffled the deck again. "But their wills left the Miller family farm to James Engle instead of their sister...my grandmother. Apparently both wills had been changed a few months before they died."

"Interesting." Pete fingered the folded paper. "Still, I have a hard time finding a logical rationale to link a forty-five year-old case to Engle's hanging."

Zoe set the deck of cards down on the table. "James Engle and his hanging *are* the links."

Pete held up one hand with what he hoped was the same authority he used to stop oncoming traffic. "I didn't say I'm not going to look into it."

Her posture softened. "Oh." She pointed to his other hand. "What've you got there?"

"I said there were a *couple* of unexpected developments. The health of Engle's lungs was only one of them." He slid the folded paper across the table to her. "This is the other."

Zoe eyed the note on the table between them. It looked like a standard page of copy paper folded twice. A little rumpled around the edges, the whole thing was slightly rounded from having been in Pete's hip pocket. She reached for the page and found it warm to her touch. Pete's body heat. But that look in his eyes? This wasn't good news.

Bracing herself, she unfolded it and read.

Dear Mrs. Jackson,

I suppose you're wondering why I would be writing to you now. My days are numbered and I hope to make things right as much as possible while I still can.

As part of that mission, I feel I need to let you know about your husband. Gary was just trying to do what's right. Mrs. Jackson, your husband did not die in that car crash.

I wish I could tell you more.

With Deepest Remorse,
James Engle

What the hell?

A million questions crashed around inside her head, jamming in her throat. When one finally found its way out, her voice was little more than a squeak. "What is this?"

Pete leaned forward, his elbows on the table, his hands folded. "It's a photocopy of a letter the crime scene guys found crumpled under James Engle's couch."

"Crumpled? So he never sent it?"

Pete shrugged. "That's one possibility."

She reread the words. "Gary. My dad?"

"So it would seem."

Vague, distant memories flashed across her mind. Her dad had died when she was only eight. Mental pictures of him were limited to the old, faded photographs she kept in a shoebox in her closet. A tall, handsome fellow with sandy hair and wide smile holding a much younger version of herself. Her father helping her learn to ride a two-wheeler. Leading her on a spotted pony.

Try as she might, she couldn't conjure up any memories of her own beyond the sense of being deeply loved. And the intense loss of that unconditional devotion cut her like a stainless steel blade, even now, twenty-seven years later.

He'd been killed in a car crash. What did this mean? He *didn't* die in the car crash? Then how?

Her eyes blurred. She blinked. When her vision cleared, she realized her hands were shaking. She laid the paper on the table, smoothed it with her palms, and read further. "What was Dad trying to do right? Pete?"

He shushed her gently, and she realized her voice had risen. She pressed her trembling fingers against her upper lip.

"It may mean nothing at all." Pete took her other hand in his. "It's very possible that this is simply the ravings of a demented mind. He'd told everyone he was sick when he wasn't. Who knows what motivated him to write this? I was going to ask your mother about it, but I didn't want to upset her unnecessarily. So I thought I'd show it to you first."

Zoe looked up from the letter, gaping at Pete. She gave a short laugh that sounded frantic even to her. "You thought you'd upset me instead?"

His lips slanted into a lopsided grin. "I know you. I don't know your mother."

She wasn't sure if it was the warmth of his touch, his easy smile, or his attempt at humor, but the tightness in her chest and neck relaxed. With a clearer head, she read the letter a third time. And this time, only one question—and another potential meaning—shouted inside her mind.

Zoe met Pete's gaze, seeking answers she knew he didn't have. "It says he *didn't die* in that car crash." She swallowed hard. "Pete, is my dad still alive?"

The road leading into Warren Froats' place had been named for his family. Froats Lane. It crossed an ancient iron bridge and wound its way along the edge of Buffalo Creek. A canopy of cool, green leaves created a tunnel through which the Sunday morning sun trickled, splashing through Pete's windshield. He tugged his Vance Township PD ball cap a little lower over his eyes.

He'd only met Froats a handful of times. The former chief had turned into a bit of a recluse after retirement, preferring to stand thigh-high in a river somewhere, casting dry flies to spending time with those he used to serve and protect.

Froats had phoned Pete at six in the morning, stating he had plans for the day. If Pete wanted to talk, it would have to be before nine.

Harry had been restless during the night, but had finally fallen into a sound slumber, evidenced by his wall-shaking snores. Thankfully, Sylvia, also an early bird, agreed to come over to the house and be there when he awoke.

As Pete dodged the ruts in Froats Lane, he fought to keep his mind on the discussion he wanted to hold with his predecessor. But Zoe's distraught face kept crowding out his mental list of questions.

Was Gary Chambers still alive?

Pete had tried to reason with her. If her father were alive, where had he been all these years? Was he the kind of man who would walk away from his young daughter and never try to contact her?

That question gave Zoe pause. She admitted she didn't think so.

But she refused to focus on any of the other potential meanings to the letter. Or the likely possibility that Engle had either been trying to stir up trouble or had been certifiably nuts.

Damn it. Pete shouldn't have shown the blasted thing to her. If she insisted on believing her dad was still alive, she was setting herself up for heartbreak. She'd eventually have to face facts. It would be like losing him all over again.

Pete steered his SUV around yet another wide bend in the road. As the road straightened, the trees opened to full sun and a wide clearing. He jammed on the brakes. His tires spewed gravel from the road's tarred and chipped surface, as he almost skidded past Froats' driveway. Cutting hard to the right, Pete maneuvered the vehicle across an old wooden bridge, the planks clanking beneath him. Ahead, a single-wide house trailer, sporting a deck larger than the mobile home, nestled in a shady grove of skinny maples.

Pete pulled next to a red Ford pickup with mismatched white and brown side panels. In lieu of a tailgate, bungee cords stretched across the back of the truck bed. He killed the engine and stepped out.

"Well, if it isn't Pistol Pete Adams," came a gruff greeting. Warren Froats reclined in an Adirondack chair, an oversized mug clenched in his equally oversized paw. His yellowed Bass Pro T-shirt strained to contain a barrel chest and beer keg belly. "How the hell are ya?"

Pete's ankle stung enough to let him know it was still there, but hiding his limp was less of an effort as he climbed the two steps onto the deck. He extended his hand and Froats snatched it without rising. "Good to see you, Warren."

Froats tipped his head toward a second chair. "How about a cup of coffee?" Without waiting for Pete's reply, Froats bellowed, "Sally Jo! Bring Chief Adams a cup."

Pete lowered himself to the edge of the offered seat.

"What brings you out here to my little corner of heaven?"

"I imagine you've heard about James Engle."

Froats face pinched into a frown. "Engle? No. I've been on the river. Haven't heard any news. What about him?"

"He's dead. A farm worker found him hanging from his barn rafters Friday afternoon."

The screen door swung open, and a woman wearing a long gray

ponytail stepped through it carrying a mug emblazoned with a Pittsburgh Steelers logo. She handed the coffee to Pete who thanked her before she ducked back inside the trailer without a word.

Froats gazed across his front yard toward the creek, his eyes narrowed as if watching something Pete couldn't see.

"I understand you investigated another hanging in that barn," Pete said.

Froats made a rumbling noise in his throat. Then he hoisted himself out of the Adirondack chair. "Let's go for a walk." He didn't wait for Pete, but thumped down the steps.

Pete left the mug on the arm of the chair and followed, grateful Froats' stride was more of a shuffle.

"You think there's a connection between James Engle's death and the other case?" Froats asked once they were away from the trailer.

"I doubt it. Just covering all bases. There wasn't much detail in the reports from back then."

Froats grunted. "Never did care for paperwork. Let me think." He stopped, closed his eyes, and rubbed the stubble on his chin. "You're talking about Vernon Miller. Found hung in his barn. That same barn Engle owns now. Or *did* own, I should say. That was a suicide. Miller, I mean. How about Engle?"

"The coroner isn't sure yet."

"The Miller case was pretty cut and dried. Folks who knew 'em said the two brothers were both in love with the same woman. They fought over her. One of them got hold of a gun and killed the other. The remorse was too much for the poor sap and he hung himself."

"Who was the woman?"

"Ah, hell, I don't know. Those two boys were no better 'n a pair of tom cats. Both in their forties and never married. Good looking cusses. All the gals acted like they were movie stars or something. We're talking about back in the days of hippies and free love. Well, they took advantage of the *free* part."

"What about the gun?"

"Gun?"

"You said Vernon shot his brother. What happened to the gun?"

Froats' scowl deepened. He waddled away from Pete.

The spongy loam beneath them was punctuated with tree roots

and moss-covered rocks. Pete's ankle didn't appreciate the irregular terrain, and he picked his way along.

"Never recovered the gun," Froats mumbled.

Stunned, Pete looked up to catch the former chief's expression, but Froats had turned his back. Pete stumbled and came down on his bad leg. Hard. Searing pain shot all the way into his hip. He grabbed a tree to steady his balance and let loose a string of expletives.

Froats wheeled toward him. "You okay?"

"Just great," Pete said through gritted teeth. "What do you mean you never recovered the gun? How do you know Vernon was the one who pulled the trigger?"

Froats shrugged. "A witness."

"A witness? Someone saw the fight?"

"No. The bullet dug out of the body was a .38. It oughta still be around in evidence somewhere, by the way. Anyhow, a witness claimed Vernon owned a .38. Also claimed the boys had both been seeing the same woman and argued about her. What the devil's wrong with you, Pete? You look like you're about ready to pass out."

His ankle burned like someone was driving red-hot spikes into it. He clung to the tree trunk, sorting the pain from the anger and struggled to keep his breath even. "What witness?"

"You mean you don't know?" Froats said. "It was James Engle."

EIGHT

With her two tabbies observing from the back of the sleeper sofa, Zoe folded her bed into itself and wedged the cushions into place.

Overhead, muffled conversation mingled with footsteps and the occasional screech of furniture being moved. Zoe sighed. Her mother apparently didn't agree with the bedroom arrangement.

This was not the time to argue about it, though. Her mind was stuck on last night at Pete's. And that letter.

She retrieved her purse from behind the couch and removed the folded note from a side pocket. Heavy footfalls descending her staircase interrupted before she could open the letter. Not that it mattered. The words were burned into her brain. She'd read the thing at least twenty times since Pete had first shown it to her.

Mrs. Jackson, your husband did not die in that car crash.

What did that mean? Zoe slipped the paper into her hip pocket as the door at the foot of the staircase opened.

"Good morning, Sweet Pea."

The sight of her stepfather brought her up short.

Tom Jackson wore a black and gray pinstriped suit, a charcoal shirt, and a navy blue tie. With his six-foot-plus frame and his distinguished salt-and-pepper hair and mustache, he could have stepped from the pages of *GQ*.

"Wow," Zoe said. "You look great. Where are you going?"

He tipped his head and eyed her. "It's Sunday. Your mother and I were hoping you'd come to church with us."

Oh.

"Um. Well, I can't. I have stalls to clean and a riding lesson to teach at eleven."

"Kimberly's not going to be happy."

Zoe sighed. "Tom, in case you haven't noticed, Mother isn't happy with me most of the time."

"I know. That's why I hoped you'd agree to join us. It would be nice to have one day without a squabble."

Mrs. Jackson, your husband did not die in that car crash.

She touched her pocket containing the letter. Fat chance.

The *clip, clip, clip* of high heeled shoes echoed from the staircase, punctuated with a disgusted squeal. Kimberly appeared at the bottom, swiping madly at her bangs. "Good heavens, Zoe. Spiderwebs. Couldn't you dust this creepy staircase once in a while?"

"I could, but it would mess up my Halloween decorations. I've started early."

Kimberly primped her blonde hair and smoothed her charcoal jacket. Zoe wondered for a moment if they had intentionally color-coordinated their attire. But only for a moment. Of course they had. Or at least, her mother had.

"Why aren't you dressed?" she demanded.

Zoe glanced down at her own Sunday outfit. Blue jeans and a faded Monongahela County EMS t-shirt. "I am dressed."

"Not for church, you aren't."

She opened her mouth to give the same reply she'd given Tom, but changed her mind. Mother wouldn't care if the little Rankin girl missed her lesson on her favorite pony.

Zoe slipped the note from her pocket. "I want to talk to you about something."

Kimberly spun on her four-inch heels and swaggered toward the kitchen. "It'll have to wait until after church. I hope you have coffee made."

Zoe followed her. "There's a fresh pot ready." The necessity of coffee was one thing she and her mother agreed on. "And we can talk while you have a cup."

"No, we can't. Because you'll be getting dressed." Kimberly snatched a mug from the cabinet and the pot from the Mr. Coffee machine.

Zoe unfolded the paper. "Did you receive a letter from James Engle?"

Cradling the mug in her manicured hands, Kimberly inhaled the steam. "A letter from James? Heavens no." She took a sip. Her nose wrinkled. "What kind of coffee is this?"

"It's my own blend. I mix light roast with French vanilla."

"Ick." Kimberly dumped the brew down the sink. "Don't you have any Italian roast?"

So much for agreeing on coffee. "Sorry. Look, Mom, I need to ask you about this letter."

Kimberly opened another cabinet, scowling at the contents. "I don't know what letter you're talking about, dear." Not finding what she was seeking, she moved to another cabinet.

"This letter." Zoe thrust the paper in front of her mother's face.

"What's this?" Kimberly took the letter and squinted at it.

"Yes, what is that?" Tom asked from the doorway.

"It's a copy of a note the crime scene guys found at James Engle's house after he died."

Tom moved to his wife's side. "How did you get it?" he asked.

"Pete—Chief Adams gave it to me."

Kimberly stretched her arm in front of her, tipping her head back. "I can't read this. They made the font too damned small. What's it say?"

Tom took the paper from her. Kimberly returned to rummaging through Zoe's kitchen cabinets.

"It says that Dad might not be dead."

The bluntness of Zoe's words had the desired effect.

Tom choked. Kimberly whirled so fast she had to catch herself against the counter to keep from falling off her heels. "What?"

Tom clenched the paper in his fist. "That's not what this says."

Kimberly snatched the letter from her husband. "Give me your reading glasses." She snapped her fingers at him.

He removed them from his suit pocket and handed them over. On Kimberly, the dark rims looked comical. Not the least bit stylish. Nor did she appear to care. As she read, the color drained from her face. "Where did you say they found this?"

"In James Engle's house," Zoe said. "The original was crumpled up under a sofa or chair or something."

Tom rubbed his chin. "Obviously, Jim never mailed it."

Kimberly turned to her husband. "But why even write it?" She shook the paper. "This makes no sense."

"Could it be true?" Zoe asked. "Could Dad still be alive?"

"That's not what it says," Tom repeated.

"It says he didn't die in that crash."

Neither Tom nor Kimberly replied.

Zoe caught her mother's arm and squeezed. "The casket was closed. I never saw Dad's body. Did you?"

Kimberly stared at the letter. Just as Zoe had done last night. "No. I didn't. I couldn't bring myself to...to see Gary like that."

"Like how? Dead?"

Tom touched Zoe's shoulder. "Stop it."

She pulled away from him, releasing her mother's arm as well. Pressure boiled behind Zoe's eyes. "Stop what? I need to know. This is my dad we're talking about."

"He's dead." Tom's voice was soft.

"Is he?" Zoe snapped. "Everyone told me he was dead. But part of me never really believed it."

"Because you didn't want to believe it," Tom said. "Not because it wasn't true."

Zoe turned her back to him and was stunned to see tears in Kimberly's eyes. "Mom, if you didn't see his body either—"

"I couldn't. I wasn't strong enough." Kimberly met Zoe's gaze. "He'd been burnt in the crash."

Zoe's stomach did a slow roll. "Burnt?" This was news to her. She'd been told he was badly injured. But no mention of having been burnt.

"Beyond recognition, they said." Kimberly set the letter down and removed Tom's glasses. "I didn't want to see him like that. To remember him...*like that*. And I certainly wasn't going to let you see his body in that condition either. You had nightmares as it was."

"Who were 'they'?" Zoe demanded.

Kimberly blinked. "What?"

"Who told you he was burned beyond recognition?"

Kimberly squinted into space. "I don't remember. The people at the funeral home, I suppose."

Tom took the letter back from his wife, but didn't look at it. "It was a difficult time for your mother, Zoe."

"Did *you* see his body?"

"No." Tom placed a gentle hand on her shoulder. "I didn't have to. He died in that car crash. No letter is going to change facts no matter how much you want them to."

He was right about one thing. Zoe wanted the facts as she'd known them to be wrong. For almost three decades, she'd missed her dad. She'd suffered a void in her soul. There had been no closure for her. No sense of finality. Just a hole. And now she understood why. "But you didn't see a body. None of us did."

"Someone did," Kimberly said.

"Who?"

"The funeral director. The coroner. The police at the scene of the wreck." Kimberly took Zoe's hands in hers. "I know you loved your dad. He adored you, too. But you need to stop this silliness. I have no idea why James wrote that letter. Gary is dead."

Zoe pulled away. Her eyes blurred. Funeral director. Coroner. Police. Of course there had been witnesses to her father's death. Officials who could confirm it.

Crap.

She took the letter from Tom. Reread it.

Mrs. Jackson, your husband did not die in that car crash.

Zoe drew a deep breath, and her vision cleared. Or there were officials out there who could confirm her father had *not* died that night. Her mind raced with names, faces, questions. Who had been coroner twenty-seven years ago? Franklin could help with that. And Pete was talking with the old chief that very morning. She met her mother's teary eyes. "Who was the funeral director who worked on Dad?"

Kimberly sighed and shook her head. "Oh, Zoe."

Tom grabbed Zoe and spun her to face him. The usual jolly grin was gone, replaced by an unyielding glare. "I'm telling you to stop this. Your mother doesn't need to relive that night any more than you do. It's over. Wishing your dad alive won't do anything except break your heart all over again."

"I can't stop it. Not until I know for sure." She met his stern gaze with her own stubborn, determined one. "Who was the funeral director?"

Tom gave an exasperated growl, but turned to Kimberly with raised eyebrows.

Before she could answer, the phone rang.

"You'd better get that," Kimberly said.

"The machine will pick up."

It rang again.

"It was so long ago." Kimberly touched fingertips to her forehead as though willing the memory from some long forgotten corner of her mind.

"Okay," Zoe said. "What funeral home?"

The phone rang again.

"Oh, that's easy. There was only one in Philipsburg back then. What was the name of it, Tom?"

The answering machine cut off the fourth ring.

Tom shook his head. "I don't know."

"I do," Zoe said. She'd been there last winter when her friend, Ted Bassi, had been killed.

The incoming message blasted from the machine in the other room. "Damn it, Zoe, where are you?" Pete's voice demanded. "Call my cell phone as soon as you get this. I'm in the hospital."

Driving to Brunswick Hospital wasn't Zoe's preferred method of avoiding church attendance with Tom and her mother. Thankfully, Patsy had answered her phone and agreed to pinch hit at the riding lesson.

The emergency department's waiting room was relatively quiet when Zoe bustled through the electronic doors. The chair at the registration desk stood empty, and she drummed her fingers on the sign-in clipboard. Several minutes passed before a thin, dark-haired woman in scrubs appeared.

"Sign in and have a seat," she said without looking up. "I'll be right with you."

Zoe recognized the harried nurse. "Hey, Cindy."

The woman lifted her head and blinked. "Zoe." Her gaze took in Zoe's civilian garb. "I didn't recognize you. What d'ya need?"

"Pete Adams called me and asked—"

"Oh." Cindy rolled her eyes. "Say no more. He's back in eight.

Please get him out of here. Leon?" she called to the security guard. "Let her through."

Zoe thanked her with a grin. The guard punched a code into the keypad next to a door labeled, "Authorized Personnel Only," and Zoe slipped from the quiet anxiety of the waiting room into the frenetic hubbub of the ER.

Somewhere within the department, someone was wailing. Whether from grief or pain, Zoe couldn't tell. She hurried around a corner and passed a room where the curtain was drawn, but it didn't damper the argument going on behind it. Cutting another corner, she dodged a pair of orderlies scurrying from the nurses' station in the heart of the department. Room eight sat across from the station.

Odd. Not only was the privacy curtain drawn, the sliding glass door was shut.

Zoe opened it a couple of inches. "Pete?" she called softly.

"It's about time," came the familiar growl. "Get me out of here."

She stepped into the room and fingered the curtain. "Are you decent?"

"How the hell can anyone be decent in these goddamn hospital gowns with your ass hanging out?"

Zoe choked back a laugh and slipped through.

True to his word, Pete lay on the bed, wearing a dark scowl and a flimsy gown. Both his head and his legs were elevated, his arms crossed firmly in front of him. His right foot and lower leg were encased in a cast-like splint.

She pointed at it. "What happened?"

His jaw twitched. "I took a bad step. Avulsion fracture, they called it. Said I'll need to see an orthopedist." He muttered something else that Zoe couldn't make out and didn't think she wanted him to repeat.

"A bad step? Where? And how'd you get here?"

"Out at Warren Froats' place. He dumped me here and took off."

Zoe studied Pete. Police Chief Pete Adams. Always in control. Pete, who never took crap from anyone. Pete, who could calm the township's fears or shut up a pushy newshound with one look. And now here he sat. Helpless. With his ass hanging out of a hospital gown. Unfortunately for her, he was lying on his back.

"Well," Zoe said. "That was just plain rude of Froats, wasn't it?"

Pete glared at her. "Are you going to get me out of here or not?"

She bit her lip to keep from laughing. "Okay. Let me ask at the nurse's station about posting your bail."

"Ha. Ha."

She swept the curtain aside, saw the door, and turned back to him. "Why is your door shut?"

His eyes narrowed. "They got tired of me yelling, I guess."

No amount of lip biting could contain the laugh this time. She ducked out into the hallway before he had a chance to wing an emesis basin at the back of her head.

An hour later, Zoe helped Pete and his new pair of crutches struggle into her truck. She'd had to cut the seam on the right leg of his jeans to fit over the splint. For someone who'd just been sprung from captivity, Pete remained in a foul mood.

Maneuvering the side streets of Brunswick, she risked a glance at her passenger and decided a few questions weren't likely to irritate him any more than he already was.

"How did your meeting with Warren Froats go?"

He snorted and motioned toward his leg.

Okay, maybe that wasn't the right question. "Besides that. Was he able to tell you anything about my great uncles?" Or her dad. But one thing at a time.

"Damn sloppy police work," Pete muttered.

"What?"

"According to Froats, the gun used to shoot Denver Miller was never recovered."

"How can that be? If Vernon shot Denver and then hanged himself, why wasn't the gun found with the body?"

Pete grunted.

"So maybe Vernon wasn't the shooter," Zoe said, thinking out loud.

Pete shifted in the seat. "I probably shouldn't tell you the rest of it either."

She shot a glance at him. "What?"

"The so-called *witness* that claimed the gun belonged to Vernon..."

Zoe guessed before he could say it. "James Engle."

"Yeah."

She braked the truck to a stop at a red light while her mind raced on. "Did you get a chance to ask Froats about my father's car crash or that note?"

"No, I—" A burst of tinny music interrupted him, and he dug his cell phone from his hip pocket.

The light turned green. Zoe steered south onto Route 15 toward Vance Township. Even over the rumble of the Chevy's engine, she could make out the frantic voice on the other end of Pete's call.

"Calm down, Sylvia," he said. "Nate Williamson's on duty today. His number's in my Rolodex right there by the phone...Yeah.. Good. Call him and have him start a search. He couldn't have gone far...I'll be there as soon as I can."

"Your dad?" Zoe asked as Pete closed the phone.

He gave a loud sigh. "Yeah. Harry's missing."

NINE

Pete rooted his good foot into the floorboards and clutched the armrest as Zoe accelerated out of one of the bends on Route 15. She may have been a skilled ambulance driver, but passing slow-moving vehicles on a two-lane road without benefit of lights and sirens set his teeth on edge. He had told her they needed to get back to Vance Township *now*, but he preferred to arrive with only the one broken bone. "If you get a speeding ticket, don't expect me to fix it for you."

"You said to hurry."

"We're not going to be any good to Harry if we're dead."

Zoe snorted. "When did you become such a weenie?" But she did back off the gas.

Pete's cell phone rang again. Officer Nate Williamson's number flashed on the screen. "Nate, what've you got?"

"I'm at your house with Seth and Kevin. We're gonna start knocking on all the neighbors' doors. The fire department is calling in a crew to help with the search. Your father's on foot, so he couldn't have gone far."

Pete checked the clock on Zoe's dashboard. "We're still about ten minutes out. Call me if you find him."

"Will do, Chief."

Pete rammed the phone back in his pocket.

"I can make it in five," Zoe said.

"Ten'll do."

"He'll be okay, you know," she said. "They'll find him."

"Yeah." But in what condition? Nadine had been caring for their father for years, and the old man had been fine. Less than thirty-six hours and Pete had lost him *twice*.

They covered the next mile or so in silence except for the roar of the engine and the rush of the wind through the open windows. Then Zoe blurted, "I need a favor."

Pete turned to look at her. She stared straight ahead, focused on the road. But he could tell from the set of her jaw and the narrowing of her eyes, she wasn't asking him to fix a speeding citation. She was still obsessed with that damned letter.

"I need to talk to Warren Froats," she said.

"Why?"

"I never saw my dad's body."

"That doesn't mean—"

"Neither did my mother. Or Tom. No one saw his body. They were told he'd been burned beyond recognition."

"Then it makes sense. Even the best mortician couldn't do anything with someone in that condition."

Zoe waved a dismissive hand. "But what if it's just a ruse? That note said he's still alive. What if there was a big cover up back then to make it look like he'd died when he didn't?"

"A cover up? Zoe, don't you think you're stretching a bit? Why would your father fake his own death? He had a wife, a beautiful little girl. He had everything to live for."

"I don't know. But I need to find out. I figure there are three people who can tell me what I need to know. Three people who were there. Who saw—or didn't see—what went into that casket." She held up one finger. "The coroner." She held up a second finger. "The funeral director. And..." Three fingers. "...Chief Warren Froats."

Pete rubbed his temples. The pain killers they'd given him for his foot weren't doing a thing for his head.

"I'm going to call Franklin to find out who was coroner back then," Zoe went on. "But if you can arrange for me to talk to Chief Froats—"

"*Fine.*" If the old chief could answer Zoe's questions once and for all, it was a favor Pete would gladly grant. The longer she clung to this fantasy, the deeper her loss when reality struck.

"When?"

"Huh?"

"When can you arrange a meeting?"

"Do you mind if we find Harry first? He hasn't been missing quite as long as your dad, but..."

"Of course." She shook her head. "I'm sorry."

Pete winced. "No. I'm the one who should apologize." He reached across the back of the wide bench seat and rested a hand on her shoulder. For a moment he wondered if maybe she *would* find her father.

Just as Pete was losing his.

A Vance Township fire engine blocked Pete's street. The police department's cruiser idled in front of Mrs. Taggart's house. Pete spotted Seth on her front porch.

"I guess they haven't found your dad yet," Zoe said. She eased the pickup around the jammed traffic and pulled into Pete's driveway.

A red-eyed Sylvia met him at the passenger-side door before he could open it.

"I'm so sorry." Her voice caught. "I just went to use the restroom. When I came back to the kitchen, he was gone. If something has happened to that sweet man, I'll never forgive myself."

Pete reached through the open window to pat Sylvia's arm. "It's okay. I'm sure he's fine."

Pete hoped she bought his lie. He wasn't sure he did.

Zoe appeared next to Sylvia and yanked the door open, taking the crutches from him.

Sylvia gasped. "My heavens, Pete. What happened? I knew you were limping around last night, but—"

"I thought so, too," Zoe interrupted. "You said you broke your ankle at Warren Froats' place *today*."

These women were going to hound him to death. "It was my foot. And I did."

Sylvia was opening her mouth to demand details, but Nate jogged up, a walkie-talkie in one hand and a clipboard in the other.

For Nate's impeccable timing, Pete made a mental note to give the officer a promotion. "What have you got?

"We've checked every house within a three-block radius. Lots of folks aren't home from church yet, but we'll check back if we need to."

Meaning if Harry was still missing.

"The guys from the fire department are ready to search the cuts."

The un-reclaimed strip mines on the outskirts of town. Damn it. Pete hadn't considered that possibility. The "cuts" were rugged territory. Mounds of slag, an abandoned rail line...Not to mention a number of deep ponds scattered back there.

Harry, where the devil are you?

Pete's usually steady hands shook as he fumbled with his crutches. Zoe took them from him and jammed them into the ground. "One hand on the door, the other on the crutches," she directed.

"I've got it," he muttered. But when he slid down from the seat, the jarring impact sent daggers of pain shooting up his right leg. He caught Nate eyeing the cast. "I'm fine."

"I didn't say a word. Do you want to take over command?"

What Pete wanted was to get out there and look for his father. But thanks to his bum foot, that wasn't going to happen. "Yeah."

Nate held out the clipboard and walkie-talkie, but Pete's hands were occupied with the crutches.

"I'll take those." Zoe collected the stuff from Nate and motioned toward the house.

Once inside, she set the clipboard and radio on the kitchen table. Pete hopped to a chair and flung himself into it.

Sylvia had trailed in behind them and stood fretting by the door.

Pete studied the list of names and locations. Searchers and their assignments. Nate had done an excellent job planning out the search and tracking its progress.

Where the hell was Harry? Was he injured? Or simply wandering around somewhere in a daze?

The handheld radio crackled to life. "Metzger to base."

Pete snatched it up with a silent prayer for good news. "Base here."

"State Street is clear all the way to Lincoln."

Pete made a note next to Seth's name. "Copy that. Start checking residences on Lincoln from State to Dunbar."

"Roger."

He looked up to see two worried females standing over him. "Sylvia, where was Harry the last time you saw him?"

"Sitting right where you are now." Sylvia pointed at a cold, half-full cup of coffee near Pete's right hand. "He'd had his breakfast and was on his second cup. I got up to use the bathroom. I couldn't have been gone more than five minutes." Her voice broke. "When I came back, he was gone. I checked the bedrooms. I looked in the garage and outside around the yard. I called and called for him." Tears streaked down her face. "I'm so sorry, Pete."

"Don't be ridiculous." He held out a hand which she clutched. "It's not your fault. He sneaked out on me yesterday at the morgue, too."

"He did?"

"Yeah." Pete forced a grin. "Scared the hell outta me."

Sylvia tried to smile, but didn't quite make it.

Zoe put a hand on her shoulder. "I think the guys could probably use some coffee. Why don't you put on a fresh pot, and I'll tell Nate to spread the word."

Sylvia stood a little taller and puffed out her ample chest. A woman with a task. "Good idea." She shuffled toward the kitchen counter.

"Thank you," Pete mouthed to Zoe.

"What about you? Do you need anything?"

Harry back safe and sound would be good. Plus a handful of Vicodin. "No. I'm fine."

"Okay. I'm going to talk to Nate. And Yancy, too. He and I have discussed forming a mounted search-and-rescue team. If they don't find your dad in town, I can call in the gang from the barn and trailer the horses here to search the cuts."

Zoe headed for the door without waiting for a reply. Horses. Pete should call in the state canine unit, too.

The walkie-talkie crackled again. "Piacenza to base."

"Base here."

"No sign of him on Veterans Way. I'm moving up to Main Street."

"Copy that, Kevin." Pete slammed the radio on the table a little too hard and the battery cover popped off. Swearing, he fumbled with the piece of plastic. He wanted to be out there, finding his dad. Not stuck in his own kitchen.

Sylvia dumped a pot of water into the coffee maker and flipped the switch. "Did you get a chance to talk to Warren?"

Pete snapped the battery cover back in place. "I did."

"And?"

"The man wasn't much of an investigator."

"I never said he was. He was popular, but not because he solved a lot of cases." Sylvia pulled out the chair across from Pete and sank into it. "Thankfully, back then there wasn't a lot of crime in these parts. His job mostly involved writing speeding tickets and directing traffic if there was an accident."

"Well, he may have had a double murder to solve forty-some years ago, but he dismissed it as murder/suicide."

"You're talking about the Miller boys?"

"He never recovered the gun Vernon allegedly used to shoot Denver. Just the .38 caliber slug they dug out of the body. And the witness who claimed Vernon owned a .38 conveniently hanged himself two days ago."

The crackle of the radio interrupted him. "Pete? This is Yancy."

"Go ahead, Yancy."

"I've got a team of my boys getting ready to head out into the cuts. Zoe's making calls to line up some horses and riders to help."

Pete rested his head in his hands and closed his eyes. But he couldn't block the images of Harry lost out there. Hurt. Or worse. "Thanks, Yance."

When he looked up, tears glistened in Sylvia's eyes. "This is all my fault," she said, choking on her words.

He reached across the table to pat her arm. But before he could say anything, something clanked somewhere in the house.

"What was that?" Sylvia asked.

Pete held up a finger to silence her. He listened.

Nothing.

He climbed to his feet. Pain in his foot threatened to knock him back down, but he clenched his teeth and grabbed his crutches.

He took two slow, quiet steps. Stopped. Listened. *There.* A faint shuffle. Then a clunk.

"Harry?" Pete called.

"Hello?" came a faint reply.

"It's coming from the basement." Sylvia was on her feet.

She and Pete moved for the door at the top of the steps at the same time. Pete reached it first and flung it open. "Harry?"

"Yeah? I'm here." The voice was shaky. "Help."

"Oh, heavens." All color drained from Sylvia's face. "I never went downstairs. I called from here, but didn't get a reply. My knees have been bothering me and...Oh, dear, I should've gone down anyway."

Pete waved a hand at her. "We'll talk about this later." He fumbled with his crutches. How was a person supposed to maneuver with a pair of sticks in their hands?

"Hello?" Harry's voice filtered up from the basement.

Pete tossed the crutches. They clattered on the floor. "Get on the radio and tell them to call off the search," he said to Sylvia. "And get the paramedics in here." He grabbed the railing and pounded down the steps, ignoring the searing pain.

He spotted Harry standing next to Pete's workbench, fingering the reproduction flintlock rifle stock he'd been carving.

"Pop?"

Harry looked up with dazed eyes. Then his face broke into a smile. "Son. I'm so glad to see you. I—I can't seem to remember how to get out of here."

Pete sagged against the railing. "Are you all right?"

"Of course. I'm fine. I came down to see your workshop." He patted the gunstock. "You do this?"

"Yeah."

"Jaeger, right? Nice."

"Thanks."

"Anyhow, I sat down to rest." Harry pointed to the ancient recliner tucked behind the staircase. "Must've fallen asleep."

"Pete?" Sylvia called from the top of the steps.

"He's okay," Pete called back.

Footsteps thudded behind him, and he turned to see Zoe.

"Hey, Mr. Adams," she said when she reached the bottom.

"Well, hello." Harry beamed. "I didn't know we had company. Zoe, isn't it?"

She raised an eyebrow at Pete. "That's right. What are you doing down here?"

"Taking a nap," Pete whispered to her.

"Checking out my boy's handiwork," Harry said. "Now will you two kindly show me how to get out of here?"

Zoe crossed to Harry's side and took his arm, directing him toward the stairs. "Right this way, Mr. Adams."

"Oh, please. Call me Harry."

Pete hopped out of the way. From the top of the steps, voices drifted down. Sounded like the whole damned rescue team had crowded into his kitchen.

Pete watched as Zoe assisted Harry up the stairs. Then he looked down at the cast on his foot. He grasped the railing. Placed the bad foot on the first step. When he put his weight on it, the pain set off fireworks behind his eyes.

Nope. That wasn't going to work.

Footsteps descending the stairs drew his attention. Zoe, again. This time she had his crutches in her hands.

"Do I need to call in the rescue squad to carry you out of your own basement?" she asked with a wink.

"Don't be cute."

She doubled up the crutches and showed him how to use them in one hand while keeping the other on the railing. "Step up with the good foot first."

It worked. "Smartass," he grumbled.

In the kitchen, Harry sat with a fresh cup of coffee, while Sylvia fussed over him. Seth, Yancy, and a pair of firefighters milled about, eyeing Pete.

"What are you looking at?"

Seth snapped to attention. "Nothing, Chief. Just wanted to make sure everything was all right before we head home."

"Everything's fine. Get out of here and enjoy the rest of your weekend."

Seth grinned. "Okay then. See ya."

"Hey," Pete called as the team headed for the door. "Thanks."

"No problem." Yancy gave him a nod.

As Seth opened the door, Nate pressed in. Pete considered reaming him out for not checking the basement earlier. But the look on the officer's face stopped him.

"Chief, I just got a call from emergency dispatch." Nate's gaze shifted past Pete.

Pete glanced over his shoulder to Zoe.

"There's been a shooting." Nate took a breath. "At the Kroll farm."

TEN

A shooting at the Kroll farm. *Her* farm. Home.

Zoe mashed the gas pedal to the floor. The engine of her old pickup roared in response. Ahead of her, Nate's police cruiser screamed along Route 15. Medic Two filled her rearview mirror. Sirens in stereo blasted her eardrums. Pete and his crutches occupied the other side of her truck's bench seat, his cell phone pressed to his ear.

"Okay," he said to the county emergency dispatcher at the other end. "If you find out anything more, call me back." He snapped the phone shut. "The caller reported a male gunshot victim. No shooter at the scene. Nothing else." His voice was low, calm.

It did nothing to sooth Zoe's panic. Male gunshot victim? She started ticking off the possibilities, but couldn't bear the thought of any of the men at the farm being hurt. Or worse.

Over the roof of Nate's cruiser, she spotted a box truck rumbling along ahead of them, making no effort to pull over for the sirens. A semi barreled toward them in the other lane. She rammed the heel of her hand into the horn, expecting a whoop. Instead, the honk startled her. In the adrenaline rush, she'd forgotten she wasn't behind the wheel of the EMS unit. Her pickup had been tucked in between police cruiser and ambulance as a courtesy.

"Take it easy," Pete said. "Or I'll drive."

With that bum ankle? But instead of pointing out the obvious, she asked, "They can't give you any idea who the victim is?"

Once the semi roared past, Nate swung his vehicle around the lumbering box truck. Zoe floored the accelerator and kept with him. Medic Two clung to her back bumper. As they flashed past the truck, she glanced over to see the driver talking on his cell phone.

"Hang it up," Pete bellowed at the window while pumping his fist up and down in a sign language version of his order.

Whether or not the driver understood or obeyed, Zoe didn't know. Or care. Her eyes burned into Nate's car. Her mind, a mile ahead—at the farm.

"Apparently the caller was on the verge of hysteria." Pete answered the question she'd almost forgot she'd asked. "The dispatcher was lucky to get as much information as she did. She's been trying the call back number, but there's no answer."

Hysteria? That sounded like Kimberly.

Zoe's fingers itched to grab her own cell phone, but she knew better. Especially at this speed. Still, she wanted—no, *needed*—to know who had been shot. A *male* gunshot victim. She prayed it wasn't Tom. But that meant wishing the fate on someone else. Of the fifteen boarders at the farm, only a few were men. But the younger girls' fathers often drove them there. And the older girls sometimes brought a boyfriend to the barn.

The emergency procession approached a car and a van. Brake lights glowed as both vehicles dove toward the right shoulder. Or as far as they could without dropping over a ten-foot embankment into a pasture. Nate swept around them. Zoe followed.

Route 15 swung in a wide arc to the right followed by one last lazy bend back to the left before straightening out again and splitting the Kroll farm in half.

With home in sight, Zoe risked a glance out her window at the barn. Cars, trucks, and horse trailers crowded around the building. In all the excitement, she hadn't had a chance to call off the search and rescue mission.

Nate's brake lights reminded her to slow down, although he barely did. The cruiser bounced and kicked when it hit the gravel farm lane. Zoe followed close on his bumper, glad for the seatbelt digging into her lap and preventing a mashed head against the truck roof. Pete's cast thumped against the floorboards, and he let fly a string of profanity.

"Sorry," she said.

Churning up gravel, she tailed the cruiser. Threatened to push him up the lane next to the farmhouse. The graveled road then looped behind it and toward the barn. A slender figure in a bright red shirt and capris stood in the backyard, waving the vehicles on. Kimberly. If she'd been the hysterical caller, as Zoe assumed, this explained why she wasn't responding to the dispatcher's callback attempts.

They topped the rise above the house and rolled down the other side to the barn. Two long aluminum horse trailers blocked the road. Nate steered around them, spewing dirt and grass under his wheels. Zoe stayed with him. When the brake lights came on again, she had to jam her own brake pedal to keep from acquiring a police car as a hood ornament.

One of the boarders, a short bulldog of a man in a Western hat, appeared in the barn doorway and signaled frantically.

Nate leapt from the cruiser before Zoe could shift the truck out of gear. Her first instinct was to race after him, but Pete's fingers closed around her arm.

"Let Nate make sure the scene is secure," he ordered.

Seth Metzger dashed past the passenger window. He must have followed the emergency units in his own vehicle.

"But EOC said the shooter was gone," Zoe said. Besides, she wanted to point out, there were at least a dozen folks milling around just inside the door. Probably ready to load up their horses and help with the search for Harry. If there was a nut case with a gun still hanging around, the bystanders would have scattered. Or, knowing this gang, taken the shooter down themselves.

Pete's grip tightened. "Let Nate confirm it."

She met Pete's ice blue eyes and saw—what exactly?—concern? He was worried for her. And with his foot in a cast, he was helpless to protect her. The thought of Pete Adams wanting to keep her safe would have given her heart palpitations on any other day. Right now, all she wanted was to dive into the fray and find out what was going on in her barn.

The handheld police radio on the seat between them crackled to life. "It's clear," came Nate's voice. "Get the paramedics in here."

Pete released Zoe's arm, and she bolted from the truck.

Inside the building, onlookers clad in jeans and boots gathered in a semicircle around something. Someone. Zoe elbowed through them. And froze at the sight laid out before her.

The farm tractor with a manure spreader hitched to it sat in the middle of the riding arena. The faint smell of diesel hung on the air.

Nate and Patsy knelt next to the tractor's massive left rear tire, her face deathly pale. In front of them, Tom Jackson bent over the still form of a man, both of Tom's hands pressed into the form, obviously applying pressure to a wound. Seth attempted to herd the bystanders toward one corner, away from the crime scene.

Zoe sprinted forward.

"Zoe." Patsy's voice was little more than a squeak. "Thank God."

Tom looked up. Blood smudged his stoic face. His bare arms glistened, wet with the stuff.

Zoe's gaze dropped from Tom to the motionless man between them.

Mr. Kroll. Zoe's landlord. The man who had offered her half his home as her own. The sweet, gentle soul who cared for his sickly wife and whose throaty laughter drifted through the walls of the old farmhouse.

Who could possibly want to harm Mr. Kroll?

Tom's hands pressed into the older man's upper chest, left of his sternum, below his clavicle. Blood drenched Mr. Kroll's shirt and the ground around him. Zoe launched into paramedic mode and dropped to her knees. Her fingers settled against her landlord's neck, searching for a carotid pulse. Please God, let there be a pulse. The sounds around her—Patsy sobbing, the soft whimpers and murmurs from the dozen or so horsemen who'd been corralled near the feed room, Seth's calm, authoritative voice, sirens shrieking somewhere down the valley—all grew muffled and distant inside her head. She shifted her fingers, listened with them. And detected a faint rhythm.

She closed her eyes. Mr. Kroll was alive.

When she opened them again, Pete was leaning on his crutches, studying her with his jaw set. She forced something close to a smile and gave him a nod. His jaw relaxed.

Zoe shifted her focus to her watch, counting beats as the sweep second hand marked off time. Without looking up, she asked, "What happened?"

"I don't know," Patsy wailed. "I came out to the barn to get Jazzel ready...you know...to come help with the search. And there he was. Right there." Her voice cracked. "There's so much blood..."

Barry Dickson and Curtis Knox, paramedics from the ambulance service's B crew, jogged up, wheeling a Stryker gurney loaded with equipment. Nate rose and helped Patsy to her feet. "Let's give them room to work," the officer said. "I need to ask you some questions anyway."

Barry Dickson, as big as a Steelers linebacker, knelt beside Zoe. "What've we got?"

"His pulse is 116 and thready," Zoe reported.

"Do we have a name on him?"

"Mr. Kroll. Marvin. Marvin Kroll."

Knox, tall and reedy in contrast to his muscle-bound partner, wiggled his fingers into a pair of latex gloves and tossed a second pair to Zoe. He leaned over the patient. "Marvin? Can you hear me?"

"He's been unconscious since I got here," Tom said through clenched teeth.

Ignoring him, Knox dug his knuckles into Mr. Kroll's sternum. "No response to pain stimulus. We need to check for an exit wound, guys."

Zoe snatched the cervical collar from the jump kit and eased it around the farmer's neck.

Barry eyed Tom. "Sir, are you okay there?"

He gave a quick nod.

"All right then. You're doing a great job. Try to keep that pressure on while we move him."

Zoe held traction on Mr. Kroll's neck while Barry and Knox log-rolled him just enough to take a look underneath.

"No exit wound," Knox announced.

Zoe nabbed the stethoscope draped around Barry's neck and listened to Mr. Kroll's lungs while Knox proceeded to pack sterile dressings against the wound. No longer needed, Tom backed away.

"Breath sounds are good," Zoe reported. At least the bullet hadn't pierced a lung.

"Damn it," Knox muttered as blood soaked through the bandages as fast as he applied them.

Barry positioned the long backboard next to Mr. Kroll. Zoe helped them maneuver him onto it. All the while, she fought the impulse to look at her landlord's clammy, pasty face, the slightly parted lips—

fought against the questions raging inside her head. Who would do this? And why?

She swiped her arm across her face to catch the accumulating beads of sweat before they had a chance to burn her eyes—and to brush aside her thoughts before they could singe her brain.

"Let's move," Knox said, a tinge of urgency in his otherwise steady voice.

Zoe shot a glance at Tom, standing alone. His skin, streaked with blood, had paled beneath his Florida tan.

The three paramedics grabbed the gurney and hustled their patient out of the barn to the awaiting Medic Two.

Outside, the sun momentarily blinded Zoe, but she kept moving, past the trucks and the trailers, past the township police cruiser and her own pickup. An unmarked black sedan had joined the party. The car may have been unadorned, but it might as well have shouted Monongahela County Detectives.

At the back of the medic unit, they stopped. Barry flung the patient doors open, and without a word, they hoisted the gurney and Mr. Kroll inside and climbed in beside him.

Blood soaked through the dressings. Knox muttered something then said, "We need to get an IV started before this guy bleeds out."

The cramped space left little room to maneuver. Barry snatched the IV equipment from the cubby in front of him. Knox readied the O2. And Zoe automatically flung open the LifePak.

Knox caught Zoe's wrist. "We need you to drive."

She blinked. Drive? The ambulance? Lights and sirens the entire fifteen miles to Brunswick Hospital? Fifteen miles to think about who was in the patient compartment? And if he took a bad turn...She swallowed hard and opened her mouth to say okay.

"No."

Zoe snapped around to find Pete standing at the rear of the ambulance.

"She's too close to the patient," he went on.

Zoe wanted to argue. If she excused herself every time she responded to a call involving an acquaintance, she'd spend her entire professional life on the lumpy couch back at the garage. But Pete locked her in his hard gaze, and she kept quiet.

"Kevin just arrived," he said. "He'll drive."

She spotted the young officer loping toward them from the barn.

Next thing she knew, Pete was offering his hand as she stepped down from the ambulance's patient compartment. Kevin slammed the back doors and headed around to the front.

The ambulance lurched away from them, swinging into the grass to get around the two trailers still blocking the lane. Then it topped the rise and dropped over the other side.

Other than a voice or two that carried from the barn and the trill of cicadas in the woods on the hill, silence settled over them. Zoe drew a breath. Felt her legs go weak. And in that moment, she was in Pete's arms, her face pressed against the soft cotton of his t-shirt. She clung to him, his crutches biting her elbows, and fought against the sobs that threatened to wrack her body.

ELEVEN

Pete drew Zoe close. At first, she held her body rigid as tremors rolled over her like small earthquakes. She'd gone pale at the sight of the old man bleeding in the barn. No way was he going to permit her to drive the frigging ambulance in her condition.

If she argued, which he fully expected her to, he had an ulterior motive for keeping her where she was.

Eventually, she softened against him. But just for a moment. Then she drew a ragged breath and pressed away from him. "Sorry."

"What for?"

She dug a tissue from her jeans pocket and pressed it to her nose. "For...you know...going to pieces like that."

He resisted the urge to pull her back into his arms. Instead, he touched her cheek. "You're entitled."

"It's unprofessional."

Pete fought back a smile. "You and I don't always have to be professional with each other."

She gazed at him over the tissue. Something—some emotion—passed over her eyes like a cloud, but he couldn't decipher it. Then she looked away. Stuffed the tissue back in her pocket. Grew a little taller. Gave her head a shake. "I could've driven the ambulance. I'm sure you have plenty of work for Kevin here."

This time, he didn't fight the grin. Zoe could be painfully predictable. "It's under control. The county detectives are helping Nate and Seth question your boarders. Besides, I need a favor."

She raised an eyebrow at him. "A favor?"

Pete sobered. "I need to question your stepdad. While I'm doing that, I'd like you to let the victim's wife know what's going on."

Zoe looked toward the house. "Poor Mrs. Kroll. I should drive her to the hospital."

Damn it. Zoe was bound and determined to go to Brunswick this afternoon. "No. Maybe your mother and stepdad can do that once I'm done questioning him."

"But—"

Pete held up a hand to silence her. "Have you forgotten that you're *my* ride today?"

"I'm sure Nate or Seth would give you a lift home."

"I'm not going home. Nate has to finish up here, and Seth is supposed to be off duty. I don't think the board of supervisors would appreciate paying him overtime to be my chauffeur. Besides, I think I can make it worth your while."

She narrowed her eyes. "How?"

"First, you drive me over to Carl Loomis' place."

"Carl Loomis? Why?"

"I have a few questions for him regarding his employer's health."

"You mean James Engle's lung cancer?"

"Or lack thereof. By then Nate should be finished here. I'd appreciate you driving both of us over to Warren Froats' place so we could pick up my car. I left it there this morning. And you mentioned wanting to talk to him."

"Oh." She dragged the word out into about three syllables. "I suppose I could convince Mom and Tom to take Mrs. Kroll to the hospital."

Atta girl.

Zoe jogged toward the house. Pete's gaze lingered on the curve of her very nice ass in those tight jeans. He blinked and turned away before his imagination carried him off to one of his favorite fantasies. The one that did not include the jeans.

Clearing his throat—and his mind—Pete crutched his way back to the barn. At the doorway, he nearly collided with a man and a woman wearing Mon Valley Riding Club t-shirts and ball caps.

"Chief," the man said. "I hear they found your father. How is he?"

"We were going to help search for him when this happened," the woman added.

"He's fine." If only it were true. "Thanks. I appreciate that you were willing to give up your Sunday."

"Any excuse to get on a horse." The woman blushed. "Of course, now we don't feel much like riding."

"Your officer talked to us and said it was okay for us to leave." The man took off his cap and used a red bandana to wipe sweat from his bald head before replacing the hat.

Pete thanked them again and tried to ignore the pitying look they gave him as he hobbled into the barn.

Seth stood next to a young woman seated on a hay bale, his notepad open. Nate was questioning the short, muscle-bound cowboy who had flagged them down when they'd first arrived on the scene. Across the barn, Wayne Baronick and another county detective were similarly occupied. Two girls stood near the feed room with their heads together. Pete spotted four more moving in and out of stalls, tending to their horses.

But Zoe's stepfather was nowhere to be seen.

Pete made his way across the riding arena to Seth, who was tucking his notepad into his shirt pocket.

"Thanks for your help," he told the woman. "If you think of anything else..."

She rose and gave him a shy smile. "I'll be sure and call you." She glanced at Pete before walking away.

"Did you get her number?" Pete asked.

Seth grinned. "Yep." His face grew serious. "So far we have nothing. Patsy Greene was the first on the scene. She didn't touch or move the victim, but called 9-1-1 and the main house from the phone over there." He hoisted a thumb at an ancient black telephone on the wall next to the doors. "Says Tom Jackson responded and tried to stop the bleeding. Then everyone else showed up."

"Where's Patsy now?"

"Inside the feed room sitting down. She's pretty upset."

"And where's Tom Jackson?"

Seth glanced around. "He's probably out back washing up. I bagged his clothing and took swabs from him, so I told him it was okay."

"Good." Pete gazed toward the door at the back of the barn and calculated how many steps it would take for him to make it there.

Seth must have guessed what he was thinking. "I'll go tell him you wanna see him."

"Thank you."

As the young officer loped away, Pete surveyed the crime scene. The tractor and manure spreader. The ground next to the machinery, marred from the rescue effort, was dark with the victim's blood.

"If the last few days are any indication, it isn't safe to be a farmer in Vance Township."

Pete turned to find Baronick wearing his usual smug grin. "You think?"

The young detective shrugged. "The first one looks more and more like a suicide. But this guy didn't very well shoot himself off his tractor."

"You think he was on the tractor when he was shot?"

"We'll process the scene more thoroughly once we finish taking statements. But there appears to be blood and hair on the corner of that..." Baronick wrinkled his nose and nodded toward the machinery. "...that trailer thing that's full of shit."

Pete snorted. "You haven't been around a farm much, have you?"

"As little as possible."

"It's called a manure spreader."

"Oh. Right."

Seth approached from the far end of the barn escorting a ramrod-straight man wearing one of the department's disposable white jumpsuits. His dark hair and a mustache bore just a hint of gray. Only the deep lines and creases on his tanned face gave evidence of his age.

So this was Zoe's stepdad. He carried a towel and was buffing his arms.

"Chief, this is Tom Jackson," Seth said.

Pete offered his hand and then introduced Baronick while Seth excused himself to find another witness to question.

Pete eyed Jackson and knew the man was inspecting him right back. Tall—even a bit taller than Pete—and fit, Jackson was obviously no stranger to a gym. He might've had a couple of decades on Pete, but this was not a man he'd want to tangle with.

How much did Jackson know about him and Zoe? Then again, there wasn't much to know. *Just friends.* Pete removed his notepad from his hip pocket. "Mr. Jackson, when did you arrive on the scene?"

"Must have been close to three-thirty. Patsy Greene—my daughter's friend—called the house to say something had happened in the barn. Marvin—Mr. Kroll—had been hurt and needed help. I noticed the clock on the mantel read twenty-five after." Jackson slung the towel around his neck. "I got out here as fast as I could."

"Who else was here?"

"Just Marvin and Patsy."

"Did you say you were in the house when Patsy Greene called you?"

"That's right."

"Did you notice anyone pulling in or out of the farm lane before she called?"

Jackson rubbed his forehead and winced. "To tell you the truth, I wasn't paying attention. I only arrived yesterday, but already I've noticed boarders come and go around here all the time."

"Did you hear anything? A gunshot? Maybe you thought it was a truck backfiring? Or fireworks?"

"No. Nothing."

Pete scribbled *heard zilch* in his notebook. "How well do you know the victim?"

"Only met him yesterday. I helped him and Zoe—my daughter—unload a wagon full of hay."

That answered Pete's earlier question. Apparently, Jackson didn't realize Pete knew who Zoe was. Just as well. "Did he mention anyone he might have had an argument with?"

"No."

"Did he say anything to you while you were helping him?"

"He was unconscious when I got here, and he stayed that way the whole time. I wasn't even sure he was alive until Zoe checked his pulse. Look, I really don't know anything that could help you fellows. If you don't mind, I'd like to get back to the house and get a proper shower."

"Of course. Thank you for your time." Pete handed him a business card. "If you think of anything else, give me a call."

Jackson palmed the card and nodded.

Just then, another matter occurred to Pete. "You didn't happen to know James Engle, did you?"

Jackson's unwavering gaze locked onto Pete. "No, I didn't."

"All right. Thanks."

After Tom Jackson walked away, Baronick turned to Pete. "Jackson. Any connection to that letter?"

"Yep. Husband of the recipient."

"So either Engle never mailed the letter or the wife kept it a secret."

"Or Tom Jackson is lying."

Baronick gazed after the man with narrowed eyes. "Or that."

"I do know one thing. Jackson's hiding something."

The detective's focus snapped back to Pete. "He answered all our questions without hesitation. There was no sign of evasion or nervousness. Why do you think he's hiding anything?"

Pete shrugged.

"Oh. Your gut."

That was as good a way to describe it as any. Something Jackson had said—or hadn't said—gnawed at Pete. But he didn't know what. Not yet.

Mrs. Kroll might have weighed ninety-five pounds if she were wearing a parka and snow boots. In her thin cotton house dress, the elderly woman felt like nothing more than bones in Zoe's arms. However, she acted anything but frail as she pulled free of Zoe's embrace.

"There's no time for this." Mrs. Kroll dabbed at her rheumy eyes with a tissue. "I have to call our son, Alexander. He'll want to be here for his dad. And I need to get some of Marvin's things to take to the hospital. His shaving kit. Pajamas. He hates those flimsy things they call gowns the hospital gives you."

Zoe smiled, remembering Pete's same complaint just hours ago.

Was it only hours?

While Mrs. Kroll bustled around the house, mumbling to herself and gathering her husband's things, Kimberly stood in the middle of what the Kroll's called the "parlor" and pressed her fingers to her lips. "Why isn't Tom back yet?"

"Pete—Chief Adams needed to get his statement first."

Kimberly dropped her hand to her side. "Statement? Certainly he doesn't believe Tom had anything to do with this?"

"Everyone who was in the barn will give a witness statement. You never know who might have seen something. Maybe without even realizing it."

"Oh." The lack of furrows in Kimberly's brow led Zoe to wonder if her mother may have an intimate knowledge of Botox.

"Mom, when Tom does get back, could the two of you drive Mrs. Kroll to the hospital and stay with her until her son arrives?"

Kimberly's eyes held the scowl her forehead couldn't produce. Definitely Botox. "The hospital? I don't know…"

Somewhere in the house, a door slammed. "Hello?" Tom's voice filtered through the walls. "Kimberly?"

Zoe brushed past her mother, through the parlor door. She crossed the old farmhouse's wide center hall and opened the door into her office. "Tom?"

He stood in the middle of her living room, attired in one of those disposable jumpsuits the police handed out when clothing was collected as evidence. "Where's your mother?"

"Here." Kimberly breezed into the room and rushed to her husband. "What happened to your clothes? And what's that on your face?"

He brushed a hand across his cheek, but still missed the smudge. "I got some of Marvin's blood on me." He kept his voice low.

"Blood?" Kimberly shrieked. "Are you hurt?"

Both Zoe and Tom shushed her.

"I'm fine," Tom said in the same soft tone. "It's Marvin's blood. Not mine."

"Marvin's blood?" came Mrs. Kroll's frail voice.

Zoe spun to find her landlady standing right behind her. If it were possible, she appeared even paler than before.

"How bad is he?"

Tom glanced at Zoe, and she caught the dilemma in his eyes. The truth wouldn't do the old woman any good right now.

Zoe took Mrs. Kroll's arm. "He was holding his own when I put him in the ambulance. Barry Dickson and Curtis Knox are two of the best paramedics I know. And Mr. Kroll's a fighter, right, Mrs. Kroll?"

"You're right about that," Zoe's landlady said. "He *is* a fighter."

"Why don't I help you get his stuff together?"

"No, dear. I'll do it." Mrs. Kroll patted Zoe's hand and headed for the staircase in the center hallway.

Tom gave an audible sigh.

Zoe turned to him. "Can you and Mom drive her to the hospital?"

"Now?" He looked down at his temporary clothing.

Kimberly shook her head. "I don't think we should. We don't really know these people. Zoe, you should be the one to do it."

For once, Zoe agreed with her mother. But Pete's request loomed over her. "Chief Adams has a broken foot and asked me to drive him somewhere. I'd really appreciate it if you could do this for me."

Tom shot her a puzzled look. "You know Chief Adams?"

"We're friends." The sensation of being in his arms earlier quickly faded into a more distant memory of a kiss. Savoring the sweetness of those memories, that word—*friends*—left a bitter taste on her tongue.

Tom appeared to process this tidbit. "Yeah. Let me grab a quick shower and put on some clean clothes."

"But, Tom." Kimberly's voice sounded like a whiny teenager's.

He patted her arm. "Zoe's asked us to help her out. She wouldn't do that unless she really needed us." He kissed his wife's cheek and headed for the back staircase.

Kimberly huffed. Then she turned to Zoe with a frown that even Botox couldn't counter. "Sitting in a waiting room with a bunch of strangers is not what I had planned for my vacation."

"None of us planned for this to happen," Zoe snapped.

Kimberly acted as if she hadn't heard. "I told Tom this would be a disaster. But he insisted we come here for a visit. These are your friends. *You* should be the one taking care of them."

"*Tom* was the one who insisted you make the trip?" Then again, why should this surprise Zoe?

"You're not hearing me. I don't care to waste my time sitting in a hospital waiting room with people I don't know."

Zoe wanted to ask why her mother bothered spending time with *her*, since she clearly didn't know her daughter either. Before Zoe could form the words, Kimberly wheeled and stomped after her husband.

Zoe shook her head. She didn't have time to deal with Mommy Dearest today. Someone she cared for had been shot. In the same barn where she spent countless hours. The exact barn where she should have been giving riding lessons if Pete and Harry hadn't taken her away from her routine.

It could have been her.

There wasn't time to think about that either. She strode across the living room and slammed through the back door on her way to the barn. And Pete.

TWELVE

Pain screamed up Pete's leg with each rut in Carl Loomis' red dog gravel lane. Heavy rains had carved tire tracks into trenches. Zoe drove half on, half off the side of the driveway, straddling the ditches. The ride was anything but smooth. Pete wondered how a car with low ground clearance would manage the half-mile long driveway without ripping out its undercarriage.

Freshly mown fields bordered the lane. Closer to the house, a woven-wire fence that had seen better days surrounded a cluster of squat, gnarly trees laden with small, green apples.

Zoe parked her truck behind a tractor and cut the engine. She leaned forward to look up at the blue sky marbled with billowing white and gray clouds. "He's probably out cutting hay, you know."

Pete gathered his crutches and opened the door. "Only one way to find out."

The house was sided in red asbestos shingles, and the roof sagged in the middle. The grass surrounding it reached halfway to his knees.

"I wonder if he plans to bale his yard," Pete mused out loud.

The wood-framed screen door banged as Carl Loomis stepped out onto the porch. He looked from Zoe to Pete. "Can I help you folks?"

Pete hobbled toward the house on a path worn in the deep grass. "Mr. Loomis, I'm Police Chief Pete Adams. We met Friday over at the Engle farm."

"Oh. Yes, of course." Loomis moved forward with an extended hand, which Pete accepted. "I didn't recognize you without your uniform. Or with crutches. What happened?"

Pete grunted. "Injured in the line of duty. Mind if we sit down? I'd like to ask you a few questions."

Loomis dug a pack of cigarettes from his shirt pocket and tapped one out. "Is this gonna take long? I just finished up supper and was heading back to the field."

"I'll try to keep it brief."

The farmer lit the cigarette and took a long drag. "Well, okay then." He motioned toward a set of pitted medal chairs on the uneven porch.

Pete studied the one lone step. And no railing. A vision of tumbling backward, thrown by the damned crutches and nothing to grab onto, flashed through his mind.

Zoe was either observant or clairvoyant. "Let's move a couple of chairs down here," she said.

A minute later, Pete and Loomis sat facing each other, and Zoe perched on the step.

Pete opened his notebook and clicked his pen. "You were pretty convinced that James Engle committed suicide."

Loomis fingered his cigarette. "Still am."

"Why is that?"

"I told you before. He's been threatening to pull his own plug for a while now."

"Did he give you a reason?"

"Weren't you listening the other day? The man was dying of cancer. He said he wanted to end it on *his* terms."

Pete watched Loomis take another long drag and blow out a stream of smoke. "Lung cancer, wasn't it?"

If the farmer caught the irony in Pete's voice, he didn't show it. "That's right."

"Who told you about his illness?"

Loomis paused. Frowned. "What d'ya mean?"

"I think it's a pretty clear question, Mr. Loomis. Who told you James Engle had lung cancer?"

"Well...Jim did. Why?"

"When was that?"

Loomis knocked the ash from his cigarette. "I don't know."

"Was it a week ago? A month? Maybe six months or a year?"

"I think it was late winter. Maybe early spring." Loomis took one more drag, then dropped the cigarette and ground it out with his boot.

"What difference does it make when he told me?"

Pete leaned back in his chair and studied the farmer's face. "Because the autopsy showed no signs of cancer."

Loomis' eyes widened, and his jaw went slack. "No cancer? Are you shittin' me?"

Pete held the man's gaze, but didn't reply.

After a few moments, Loomis looked away. "Huh. Well ain't that a kick in the head."

"Any idea why Engle might lie about being sick?"

Loomis' gaze snapped back to Pete's. "Lie? You think Jim was lying about having cancer?"

"You don't?"

"Hell, no. Look, Chief. The man was devastated. Absolutely devastated. If what you say is true, then he had a quack for a doctor."

"You think he was misdiagnosed?"

"Damn right. That's the only thing it could be. Old Wilford ought to sue that good for nothin' sonofabitch for malpractice. Can you arrest him for murder? Because Jim wouldn't be dead if he knew he wasn't really sick."

Pete closed his notebook and pushed up from the chair. Loomis could be right. He wouldn't know until he had a chance to talk to Dr. Weinstein in the morning. "Thanks for your time, Mr. Loomis. We'll let you get back to work now."

The farmer stood and tapped another cigarette from the crumpled pack. "If there's anything else you need, you just come on by."

Pete thanked Loomis and left him standing there twiddling his unlit smoke.

Zoe caught up to Pete as he headed back to her truck. "So do you think he's right?"

"About the doctor misdiagnosing Engle? I think Loomis thinks he's right. And it's as good a possibility as any. Makes more sense than faking an illness and then committing suicide over it."

She opened the passenger side door for him. "Yeah." But she didn't sound convinced.

And while a misdiagnosis did offer a tidy answer to the question of why James Engle had claimed to have a terminal illness, Pete wasn't convinced either.

*   *   *

Most days, the cab of Zoe's pickup felt cavernous, but with Officer Nate Williamson—whom they'd picked up at the police station—sandwiched between her and Pete, this wasn't one of them. She'd heard rumors that Nate had once played pro football. She believed it.

By the time they pulled into Warren Froats' driveway, the sun had dropped behind the surrounding hills, throwing the valley into shadows.

Zoe's head had been swirling with the day's events, from the call to pick Pete up at the hospital to Harry's disappearance to Mr. Kroll's shooting and finally, Carl Loomis' suggestion that all the questions surrounding James Engle's death could be answered so simply and so tragically as a medical misdiagnosis.

But now, as she parked next to the Police Department SUV Pete had abandoned when Froats drove him to the hospital, her attention focused with the intensity of a laser on one thing. Her father's death—if indeed he had died.

Froats' house trailer showed no signs of life. The windows were dark. The front deck stood vacant. "Maybe he's not home yet," Zoe said.

"Doesn't matter," Nate replied. He turned to Pete. "You have your car keys, right, Chief?"

"Uh-huh." Pete opened the passenger-side door, fumbled with his crutches, and slid down from the cab. Nate slid across the bench seat and stepped out beside him.

Zoe didn't move. Disappointment settled over her like the dusk settling over the valley.

Pete tossed his keys to Nate. "Go ahead and take it back to my place. I'll catch a ride home with Zoe."

"You sure?"

Pete caught Zoe's eye. "Yeah. I want to introduce her to Warren Froats."

"You're going to wait until he comes home?"

"Yep."

"Whatever you say." Nate gave her a nod. "Goodnight, Zoe."

"'Night."

Pete stood next to the open truck door as his officer drove his SUV away. Then he motioned to Zoe. "You coming?"

"But no one's home."

"He's home." Pete slammed the door.

She looked around, wondering what Pete knew or saw that she didn't. But she jumped out of the cab and rushed to catch up with him as he swept along on his crutches toward the house. Damn, he was getting good with those things.

"How do you know?" she demanded.

Pete tipped his head toward a patchwork-colored Ford pickup. "His truck's here." Pete stopped at the base of the porch steps and bellowed. "*Froats.*"

"Down here!" The throaty reply carried on the sultry evening air from somewhere in the shadowy woods.

Zoe glanced at Pete's cast. "Do you want me to go find him?"

Without responding to her, Pete shouted, "*Froats.* Get your ass up here."

The only answer was the rush of the nearby stream. But in a few moments, a twig snapped and leaves rustled. Zoe caught sight of movement in the woods.

A tall, rotund figure in waders strode toward them, a fishing pole in one hand, a minnow bucket in the other.

"Pistol Pete Adams? What are you doing back out here?" Froats pulled up short. "And who's this you brought with you?"

Zoe remembered the previous police chief as an imposing uniformed figure with close-cut hair. The scraggy mountain man with longish hair and a beard bore little resemblance to the picture in her mind.

"Warren Froats, this is Zoe Chambers," Pete said.

Froats moved closer, eyeing her. "Don't I know you?"

She extended her hand. "Yes, sir. I work on the ambulance. I was pretty new when you were still chief, but we responded to a few calls together."

He grunted. Switched the fishing pole to his left hand and wiped his right one on his shirt before taking hers. "I'll have to take your word for that. But it's your name that's ringing a bell for me. Chambers. Zoe Chambers." He held onto her hand while he squinted at her and frowned. Finally his eyes widened. "Traffic accident. Must've been...what...twenty-five years ago? Fellow's name was...Gary. Gary Chambers."

Zoe's pulse raced. "Twenty-seven years. He was my—"

"Father," Froats finished for her. "You were the little girl with the big eyes. Never shed a tear, though."

She hadn't? She remembered such devastating sadness that she'd thought she'd have cried for weeks. Months. "You remember the accident?"

He snorted and released her hand. "It was a bad one. You don't forget those. Never seen a body as badly burned as that."

Zoe felt the air leave her like a deflating balloon. "You saw the body?"

"I was at the accident scene. Of course I saw the body." He shook his head. "Damned shame. About as ugly a thing as I hope to ever lay eyes on. All charred."

She swallowed hard against a wave of nausea and thought of the closed casket.

Pete cleared his throat. "Zoe, why don't you give Warren and me a few minutes alone?"

He thought she couldn't handle hearing the truth. Well, he was wrong. "No. I'm fine." She fixed her gaze on the former chief. "How was the ID made?"

"Excuse me?"

"If the body was so badly burned, I gather identification must have been a challenge."

Froats rubbed his jaw. "Well, it's true a visual ID was out of the question. And the body was too burnt to lift fingerprints from him. As I recall, identification was made from personal effects. He was wearing his wedding band and a watch your mother had given him as a gift."

"That's it? What about dental records?"

"Probably."

"Probably?"

"It was twenty-five—twenty-*seven*—years ago. I don't remember every detail."

Exasperated, Zoe looked to Pete, who gave her a nod. "We'll check the records back at the station."

"Why all the questions about your father's accident?" Froats asked.

She opened her mouth to tell him about the note, but Pete cut her off. "Her mother's in town for a visit, and it's stirred up some conversation."

Froats grunted. "I see."

That made one of them. "Is there anything else you can tell me about the crash?" Zoe asked.

"Nothing you probably don't already know."

"That's just it. I don't know much of anything. My mother would never talk about it."

He made a growling sound in his throat and tipped his head toward his porch. "All right. Let's sit down."

Zoe followed Froats up the steps then turned back to Pete, who leaned on the railing at the bottom. "Do you need a hand?"

"I'm fine here."

Poor Pete. His foot had to be throbbing, and here she was, dragging him around on her own private investigation.

Froats set his fishing gear on a battered table. "Can I get you something to drink? A beer maybe? Or a can of pop?"

"No, thanks." She lowered to perch on the edge of a battered lawn chair. "What can you tell me about the wreck?"

The former chief dropped into a second chair. "Let me think. Well, it happened out in the game lands about a mile or so from Parson's Roadhouse. You know that windy road?"

She did. Intimately. "That much I do know." The exact bend in the road was burned into her memory, giving her chills every time she drove past it.

"Your dad's car was run off the road by a drunk driver. The drunk slammed into a tree and wasn't hurt too bad. But your father veered to miss him and went over a hill. Must've ruptured the gas tank. The whole car was incinerated."

Zoe cringed at the mental picture. The thought of her dad trapped in a car, plunging over a hillside, bursting into flame. She clutched the arm of the lawn chair, bracing against a fog of vertigo. "What was the COD?"

"Hmm?"

"Did he die of injuries sustained in the collision? Or..." Or was he burned alive?

"I'm afraid I don't know." Froats' voice was soft, as if he understood what she couldn't bring herself to ask. "You'd have to check with the coroner's office about that."

She swallowed a hard, dry lump in her throat. "I will. Thanks."

"I'm not sure what else I can tell you."

Zoe didn't know what else to ask either. "Thanks for your time." She stood and moved toward the steps.

Pete held up one finger. "Warren, the other driver...the drunk?"

"Yeah?"

"Do you remember his name?"

"Sure do. He was the town lush back in those days. Picked him up for drunk-and-disorderly at least three or four times a month. It's a damned shame it took something like that crash to sober him up, but to the best of my knowledge he hasn't had a drop since."

"His name?" Pete said.

"Loomis. Carl Loomis."

THIRTEEN

According to Zoe's watch, it wasn't yet seven-thirty in the morning when she approached Pete's door, but sweat already tickled down her back. With the humidity, she half expected to sprout gills at any moment.

As she stepped onto the concrete slab porch, the door swung open, and Sylvia stepped out. "I'm sorry, Pete," she was saying. "But there's just no way I can watch him today. Good morning, Zoe."

"Morning, Sylvia."

Pete stood in the doorway, wearing jeans and a t-shirt and braced on his crutches. Lines creased his forehead. "Thanks anyway."

Sylvia paused next to Zoe. "What are you going to do?"

"Take him with us, I suppose. Nothing else I can do."

"Harry?" Zoe whispered to Sylvia.

"Yeah," she replied, her voice low. "It was a rough night."

"It's been *two* rough nights," Pete corrected.

Sylvia shook her head. "Nothing wrong with his hearing," she said to Zoe.

"I can read lips," he muttered.

"I had my back to you," Sylvia snapped over her shoulder. Then she leaned close to Zoe's ear and spoke softly enough that Pete couldn't possibly hear. "I hope you're up to this. No woman should have to put up with two Adams men at the same time."

Zoe covered her mouth, feigning a yawn to hide her smile.

Sylvia fluttered a hand over her head as she ambled away. "Good luck."

Pete held open the door for Zoe as she stepped inside.

Harry sat at the kitchen table with a heaping bowl of Cheerios in front of him. "Good morning, Sunshine," he called to her with a grin.

"Eat your breakfast, Pop," Pete said. "We have to get going."

"Going? Where to?"

Pete sighed, and Zoe wondered how many times he'd already answered the question. "You're going with me to work today."

"Good. I like playing cops and robbers."

Zoe met Pete's gaze. Dark circles shadowed his tired eyes. "Are you all right?"

He snorted. "Yeah, I'm terrific. Any word on your landlord?"

"Nothing this morning yet. Mom and Tom didn't get home until around midnight. According to them, Mr. Kroll has a closed head injury in addition to the gunshot wound. Doctors are gonna do surgery on him today to remove the bullet." She pointed to Pete's foot. "And what about you?"

"I told you I'm fine."

"Uh-huh. That cast is only supposed to be temporary, right? Shouldn't you make an appointment with an orthopedist?"

"Have you been comparing notes with Sylvia?" He maneuvered a clumsy turn away from her and crutched into the living room. "Damned coddling females."

Behind her, Harry burst into gruff laughter. "Now you know how I feel with your sister always fussing over me."

Zoe grinned and followed Pete, but he stopped before heading into the hallway at the far end of the room and raised one finger. "Stay there and keep an eye on him while I get dressed."

"Okay." Yesterday's frantic search for Harry flashed through her mind. Obviously, it stuck in Pete's, too. "I'm a little surprised you want me to drive you around again today. I figured you'd have Seth or Kevin be your chauffeur."

"Seth's already getting overtime pay to be on patrol while I'm laid up." Pete hobbled out of sight, but called over his shoulder, "You work cheap."

She laughed. "You mean you're not placing me on the police payroll?"

"No," he said from the other room.

"Well, crap. So what's our itinerary?"

"First stop is the doctor who treated James Engle."

"He's in Brunswick, right?"

"Yep."

Zoe mulled over the possibilities. She should have no problem convincing Pete to swing by the hospital and check on Mr. Kroll's status. And if they were already at the hospital, she might be able to catch Franklin at the morgue or in his office across the street. Another thought occurred to her. "You didn't say much last night after we left Warren Froats. What did you think about Carl Loomis?"

A loud thud reverberated through the house followed by some choice swear words from Pete.

Zoe started toward the hall. "Are you okay?"

"I'm fine. Dropped my damned crutches."

"Oh." She backed up until she could see Harry through the arched doorway. He was still happily munching his cereal. "Does it seem odd to you that Carl Loomis turns out to be the man who supposedly ran my dad off the road?"

Silence greeted her question. "Pete?"

"Give me a minute to get dressed, will ya?"

She sighed. Fine. She returned to the kitchen and sank into a chair next to Harry. "How're you this morning?"

"I'm great." He tilted his bowl to corral the last of his Cheerios into his spoon. "Want some cereal?"

Zoe smiled. "No, thanks."

Having no luck with the utensil, he set it down and picked up the bowl. Bringing it to his lips, he slurped the last of his breakfast, finishing with a contented sigh. "Are you joining us today?" he asked as pushed the bowl to the center of the table.

"I'm going to drive. Pete hurt his foot."

"I know. Guess what else I know." Harry winked at her. "You're Zoe."

"Yes, I am. I'm glad you remembered."

"Me, too. I'm lousy with names. Always have been, but it's getting worse. Old age sucks."

Zoe snorted.

"I know something else, too." He shook a finger at her. "My boy's kind of sweet on you."

Her cheeks warmed.

"And I have a pretty good idea the feeling's mutual."

She stared at her hands on the table. Chewed her lip.

"Well?" Harry nudged her. "Am I right?"

Zoe considered admitting her feelings to him. After all, he'd probably forget all about the conversation within the next few minutes. Then again, he seemed to be quite lucid at the moment.

"Well?" he asked again.

"Well what?" Pete swung around the corner into the kitchen.

"Nothing," Zoe said.

Harry gave her an ornery grin. "I'm right. I knew it."

Pete looked at his dad. Then at her. He raised an eyebrow.

She jumped to her feet. "Are you ready to get going?"

Harry slammed both palms down on the table. "I sure am. Let's go. This is gonna be fun."

Fun. According to Harry, spending the day together investigating a suicide that may or may not be a homicide ranked right up there with a day at Kennywood Park. But all Pete could think about was the half-dozen calls he'd placed last night and this morning to Nadine, all of which went to voicemail.

Zoe drove Pete's township SUV with Harry riding shotgun. Pete had claimed the backseat so he could put his throbbing foot up. But he hadn't counted on the hard plastic being so uncomfortable. It wasn't often he'd been delegated to the rear seat, usually reserved for prisoners. In fact, this was a first. And, he decided, his last.

"You never said what you thought about Carl Loomis," Zoe said. "Should we question him again?"

We? "I don't imagine it would do any good. Warren said Loomis had no memory of the accident. He'd blacked out."

"But maybe he's remembered something since then. I bet no one's asked him about it in years."

"I thought you'd let go of this thing about your dad after Warren told you he saw the body with his own eyes." At least, Pete had hoped she would.

"He saw a body burnt beyond recognition. What if it wasn't really my dad?"

"Zoe..." Pete let his exasperation creep into his voice.

"What's this all about?" Harry asked.

"Nothing," Pete replied.

"My dad supposedly died in a car crash twenty-seven years ago," Zoe said. She proceeded to fill Harry in on all the details, from the closed casket, to the cryptic note found in James Engle's house, to suspecting her father was still alive.

Pete listened as he watched houses, barns, trees, and underbrush whiz past his window. In his heart, he understood Zoe's longing to have her dad back. Hell, he wanted his own dad back, and Harry was sitting in the same vehicle with them. In Pete's head, the whole scenario reeked of conspiracy-theory craziness.

In his gut, something felt off about the whole thing, but he wished Zoe would leave it alone. Let him quietly ask some questions. Do some digging. Then he could report to her what he found, *if* he found anything. And if he didn't...Well, she wouldn't have to experience that loss all over again.

"We definitely need to ask this Carl Loomis fellow some questions," Harry declared when Zoe finished her tale.

There was that *we* thing again. "But not today," Pete said. "Today *I* am investigating James Engle's death and Marvin Kroll's shooting."

Harry turned in his seat to scowl at Pete. "You're not being very helpful to this young lady."

They hit a pothole, and Pete's foot bounced on the unforgiving hard plastic seat. He gritted his teeth against the pain. "We—I—have a job to do and two active cases to solve."

"But my dad's supposed death may be tied to them," Zoe said. "After all, that note was written by one of the victims. Not to mention it was found in his house."

"Yeah." Harry sounded like a belligerent child.

Great. Now he had the two of them hounding him about a very cold case that probably wasn't a case at all.

Zoe slowed the vehicle as they approached the traffic light on the edge of Brunswick. "Maybe we could swing by Loomis' place on our way back to Dillard."

Harry nodded in agreement. "That's a great idea."

Pete dropped his head against the glass of the backseat door. "I doubt we'll have time. Once I finish interviewing Dr. Weinstein, we should stop at the hospital and check on your landlord."

"Okay."

Zoe agreed way too fast. Pete caught her watching him in the rearview mirror. A smile tugged at her lips. Damn. She'd played him. "That's what you wanted all along, isn't it?"

"Maybe." The light changed, and she hit the gas to make the left turn ahead of the tractor trailer coming the other way.

She probably figured on squeezing in a side trip to visit Franklin Marshall while she was there.

Sneaky.

Pete squinted into the morning sun to camouflage his smile.

Zoe's and Harry's protests echoed in Pete's ears as he waited for the elevator in the National Trust Building. He'd insisted they drop him off at the front door of the historical relic turned office building on Brunswick's Main Street and ordered them to find a parking space until he called on his cell phone to come pick him up again. The only reason Zoe had relented in her demands to go inside with him was the lack of on-street parking and his inability to walk two blocks, which was the location of the nearest spot. Convenient. He'd pondered how he was going to lose his entourage long enough to question Engle's doctor.

The doors opened, and he hobbled into an elevator small enough to remind him of a vertical coffin. The grinding and whirring sounds of the cables did little to instill confidence. He wondered how claustrophobic types dealt with the quaint early twentieth century amenities.

They probably used another doctor in a more modern building, he decided when the doors finally opened following a painfully slow ascent.

Dr. David Weinstein's small waiting room held about a dozen chairs, three tables stacked with golf and movie star magazines, and one potted palm tree that desperately needed water. But other than the condition of the plant, the space appeared tidy. An elderly couple occupied two of the chairs. A woman and a sullen teenage boy thumbing a cell phone claimed two others. Only the mother met his eyes, and she quickly looked away.

Pete crossed to the small sliding window with the "Please Register" sign taped to it. He stood there and waited as a blonde in blue scrubs ignored him from her desk on the other side of the window. After a minute or two, he cleared his throat.

"Please sign in, and we'll be with you shortly," the blonde said without looking up.

Pete wondered about the definition of *shortly*. "I'm not a patient."

She lifted a weary gaze and eyed his uniform shirt without any indication of being impressed.

He held up his wallet with his ID. "Pete Adams. Vance Township Police Department. Dr. Weinstein agreed to talk with me this morning about a case."

From the corner of his eye, he noticed the four patients in the waiting room giving him a long hard look. No doubt they were mentally calculating how much longer they'd be stuck there thanks to him.

The blonde ordered him to wait and disappeared. Minutes passed with no movement behind the registration desk. Then a nearby door swung open, held by a short, sinewy man with wire-rimmed glasses and a white lab coat. Pete sensed the doctor taking in the crutches, the cast—and the uniform and badge.

"Come this way, please." The man escorted Pete into a small office. Framed diplomas and degrees filled the walls. "I'm Dr. David Weinstein. How can I help you, Officer?"

"It's Chief, actually. And I'm looking into the death of a patient of yours."

"James Engle. Yes. I've been notified of his passing. It's quite sad."

"How long had you been treating Mr. Engle?"

"I believe he started coming to me six or seven months ago."

"What were you treating him for?"

The doctor's eyes narrowed. "I'm not sure I can discuss this with you. Doctor-patient privilege, you know."

"True, but your patient is dead."

"By suicide, as I understand it. I didn't think the police investigated suicides."

"There are some...irregularities regarding the circumstances. I'm just making sure we haven't missed anything."

Dr. Weinstein didn't look convinced, but he motioned toward a chair. "Have a seat."

As Pete gratefully obliged, the doctor picked up his phone and told someone on the other end to bring James Engle's chart.

"It'll just take a moment." Weinstein removed an expensive-looking pen from a marble desk set in front of him.

Pete wondered if the doctor's interpretation of *a moment* was the same as *the doctor will be with you shortly*. Which generally meant sometime between now and when you die.

Weinstein pointed the pen at Pete's cast, perking up as if he'd smelled fresh blood. "What happened?"

"Injured in the line of duty."

"If you need a referral for an orthopedist…"

If the doctor was truly guilty of misdiagnosing James Engle's cancer, there was no way he was getting his hands on Pete's bones. "It's been handled. Thanks anyway."

Weinstein smiled. "Good to hear."

The door opened and the same blonde who had manned the reception desk entered. She handed a folder to the doctor and left without acknowledging Pete.

Weinstein thumbed through the papers and reports, frowning and humming to himself. "Ah, yes." He tapped his upper lip with the pen. "You need to understand something about the way these things are treated. Finding the right balance of medication is tricky. Often the drugs make the situation worse. Hence all the disclaimers on the television advertisements."

"Disclaimers?"

"Yes. Thoughts of suicide. Deepening depression. I've been working with Mr. Engle to find the proper dosage. To make my job more difficult, he tended to take himself off his meds. Refused to refill the scripts I gave him because he didn't like the way the drugs made him feel. I can't be held responsible for a patient's death when he doesn't follow the recommended course of treatment."

"Exactly what were you treating him for?"

"Depression, of course."

"Depression? That's all?"

"Recently, yes."

"What about *not* so recently?"

"I don't understand what you're asking, Chief Adams. Why don't you tell me what you really want to know? It might make this conversation easier."

Pete considered his next move and decided the doctor might be right. "Was there ever a concern about Mr. Engle having lung cancer?"

"We ruled that out."

"But you did test him for it?"

"We did chest x-rays as part of his routine physical, but they came back clean."

Just like the autopsy.

The doctor skimmed his pen down the page. "The patient had complained of chest pains, but we ruled out any cardiac issues. Determined his symptoms were caused by stress combined with clinical depression. I referred him to a therapist. My receptionist set up the appointment for him, but he cancelled and never rescheduled."

"Doctor, do you have any explanation for James Engle leading his family and friends to believe he was dying from lung cancer?"

The pen slipped from Weinstein's fingers and clattered to his desk. "What? No. As I said, his chest films were clear."

"And Engle was aware of that fact?"

"Absolutely."

Pete started to close his notebook, but the letter to Zoe's mother flashed across his mind. "Besides the depression, did Engle suffer from any other mental or emotional impairment? Dementia, perhaps?"

The doctor reclaimed his fancy pen and replaced it in the holder. "No. In my professional opinion, he was in complete command of his faculties."

Pete slipped his own disposable pen in his shirt pocket. "Thanks for your time," he said, leveraging himself to his feet with the crutches.

The doctor muttered an unintelligible reply.

Pete made his way back to the waiting room where the four patients had been joined by a slump-shouldered woman and a white-haired man in a wheelchair. The receptionist called for one of them to come on back, but Pete didn't take the time to notice which patient. He was too busy solving at least part of the puzzle behind James Engle's death.

FOURTEEN

"You should ask Pete to help you," Harry said with a case-closed nod of his head.

Parked in a lot two blocks from the National Trust Building, Zoe had just finished pouring out her suspicions and doubts regarding her father's death and was a bit startled by Harry's response. One thing she'd discovered while helping Patsy with her mother was dementia patients were terrific sounding boards. They would listen intently and then promptly forget the entire conversation. So Zoe had considered her monologue nothing more than thinking out loud. "Pete thinks I'm making too much of it. So does my stepdad."

Harry shifted in the SUV's passenger seat to face her. "What does your heart tell you?"

She drew a deep breath and held it as she contemplated the question. "My *head* tells me they're probably right."

"That's not what I asked."

She met his steel-blue gaze. "My heart says I need to know for sure."

"Well, there you are then. You have to pursue it. Otherwise you'll always wonder. Always wish you'd done something about it when you had the chance. You'll never be at peace with your dad's memory." Harry tapped the side of his head. "Memories are damned important. Most folks don't give them enough credence. But when you start losing those memories, you really start appreciating them."

A flash of heat rose behind Zoe's eyes, and she blinked to prevent the rush of tears. She leaned across the gearshift and gave him a hug. With a gruff chuckle, he hugged her back.

From her jeans pocket, her phone erupted into a rendition of *I Fought the Law.*

"What's that?" Harry asked as she drew away from him.

"That's Pete." She dug for the phone and flipped it open.

"Come pick me up," he ordered.

"On our way."

Brunswick's Main Street had the quaint appearance of a nineteenth century village courtesy of a recent attempt to revitalize the dying downtown shopping area. Cobblestone sidewalks sported reproduction gaslights. Flowers cascaded from planters. The genuine historic buildings had been sandblasted and buffed to their original glory. While the county courthouse and a few office buildings created a certain amount of commerce—and kept the parking spots filled—traffic was light, so Zoe had no difficulty making the left turn out of the lot.

Pete leaned on his crutches on the curb in front of the old office building. Zoe pulled the Explorer next to him. For a moment, she considered popping on the flashing lights, but figured Pete wouldn't find it amusing. He might even insist on taking over the wheel, cast or no cast.

"Do you need a hand?" she asked as he fumbled into the backseat.

"No." He flopped down with a groan and slammed the door.

She eased away from the curb and just happened to head toward the hospital. "Did you find out anything from the doctor?"

"Not much. He denies ever diagnosing Engle with cancer. Says he was treating him for depression, but Engle wasn't exactly diligent about taking his meds."

"Depression?"

"Uh-huh. Supports Marshall's finding of suicide." Pete gazed out the window. "I gather we're on our way to check on your landlord."

"Do you mind? I'm worried about him, but I'm more worried about how *Mrs.* Kroll is holding up." She failed to mention her secondary reason for a trip to the hospital.

"Nope. I'd like to find out when Mr. Kroll will be up for some questions."

"Like who shot him?"

"That would be at the top of my list, yes."

The renovated portion of Brunswick gave way to decay within blocks. Zoe braked to a stop at a red light. On one corner, a brand new four-story brick building housed a bank. Part of the attempted renewal project. On the opposite corner, a dingy, sprawling Victorian with an overgrown weed lot for a lawn and plywood covering the windows appeared to house only rodents—or possibly a stray drug addict or two.

When the light changed, Zoe turned right, driving through a section of town devoted to rundown housing projects and beer distributors. A few blocks and a left turn brought them into an older residential area with plain, but well-kept homes lining one side of the street and Brunswick Hospital taking up two solid blocks on the other.

She bypassed the entrance to the underground parking lot, which connected to the morgue, with a glance at the Marshall Funeral Home right across the street. Instead, she pulled into the main entrance with its above-ground lot. Pete directed her to park in a tow-away zone near the front doors. "Official police business," he muttered.

Zoe wasn't exactly sure how official the trio looked. Harry, so sharp and clear during their conversation earlier, once again appeared dazed. Pete in his regulation uniform and not-so-regulation crutches lacked his usual air of authority. And Zoe, donning jeans and a Monongahela County EMS t-shirt, but driving a Vance Township police vehicle, felt a bit like an imposter.

A white-haired woman at the courtesy desk squinted at her computer screen. "Marvin Kroll is still in surgery." At Pete's request, she directed them to the surgical waiting room on the third floor. "Use the E elevators down that way." She pointed to the far end of the waiting room.

Pete thanked her. A few minutes later, he led their odd procession through a set of automatic doors into an obnoxiously cheery room filled with vinyl-upholstered chairs, a pair of couches and two institutional recliners. A pair of TVs in opposite corners were set to two different stations, the volume so low that neither produced more than some muffled background noise. An empty coffee pot sat on a table near the doors.

Zoe spotted Mrs. Kroll hunched in one of the chairs near an end table. On one side of her sat a man who appeared to be in his fifties. His face was a younger version of Mr. Kroll's, but his body had the soft look of someone who worked in an office rather than on a farm.

On the other side of her, Detective Wayne Baronick stood when they approached. "Chief Adams. I didn't expect to see you here."

"I could say the same about you." Pete motioned to the detective, and they moved toward the empty coffee pot.

Zoe claimed Baronick's vacated chair. "Has there been any word?"

"He's in surgery. It's taking so long."

The man next to her fingered a tattered magazine. "Not really, Ma. It just feels that way."

Mrs. Kroll put a hand on his arm. "This is my son, Alexander."

The younger Kroll gave her a weak smile and shook her hand.

Zoe noticed Harry gazing around the room with that lost expression. "Harry?"

He blinked. The curtain across his eyes parted, and he smiled. "Zoe. Where's Pete?"

"He's over there talking to a friend." She introduced Harry to the Krolls and then helped him take a seat next to Alexander. "So, have they given you any inkling about his prognosis?"

"The brain scan wasn't as bad as they feared, so they've told us there's room for cautious optimism." Alexander shot a worried glance at his mother. "But it's going to be a long recovery at best. Could be months of rehab."

Zoe took Mrs. Kroll's frail hand. "I'll be there to help any way you need me to."

"I appreciate that, sweetheart." The older woman forced a smile that couldn't hide the fear in her eyes. "But you have your own life."

Zoe met Alexander's gaze. "Please call me if they need anything."

He nodded. "It's good to know you're right there in the house with them. Thanks."

They fell quiet. Zoe looked over at Pete and Baronick, who were huddled in hushed conversation. If she wanted to slip away in search of Franklin, this might be her chance. She checked her watch—not quite ten o'clock—then eyed Harry.

Excusing herself from the Krolls, she motioned for Harry to come with her. Pete and Baronick's discussion halted when she approached. "Pete, do you have time for me to take Harry down to the snack bar? We're both hungry."

Harry raised a puzzled eyebrow, but kept quiet.

"Yeah. Fine." As she led Harry to the door, Pete called after her, "Just don't lose him."

In the hallway, Zoe slipped her hand into the crook of Harry's elbow and he tucked his arm into the pose of a perfect gentleman escorting a lady. "I don't remember mentioning I was hungry."

"You didn't. But I needed an excuse to get out of there for a little bit."

"Oh. Good. Because I do forget stuff sometimes."

"So do I. I hope you don't mind that I used you like that."

"Not at all. Where are we going?"

"I want to talk to Franklin Marshall. The coroner. About my dad's car crash."

"And we're being sneaky because Pete isn't being very helpful."

"Exactly."

Harry patted her hand. "Well, then I'm happy to be your partner in crime. And I won't tell Pete. There is one thing, though."

"What's that?"

"I really am hungry."

Zoe laughed. "We'll stop at the snack bar on our way back. We should have some food in hand to support our cover story anyway."

"Excellent."

They took the elevator down to the lowest level and exited into an empty hallway. Zoe guided Harry toward the morgue, but no light shone through the frosted windows in the door. "He's not here. Are you okay to take a little walk?"

"Lead on, my dear lady."

They headed farther down the hall and out into the cool darkness of the parking garage. Their footsteps echoed back to her as they crossed to the street entrance. Outside, the bright sunlight momentarily blinded her, and the stifling heat slammed her full in the face.

Traffic was light. They crossed the street and made their way up the sidewalk to the Marshall Funeral Home.

"Did somebody die?" Harry asked.

It took a moment for Zoe to process his question. "Franklin Marshall, who owns the funeral home, also happens to be the county coroner."

"And we need to talk to him to find out about your dad's accident."

Harry was staying on track today. Zoe smiled. "Right."

As soon as they stepped into the front foyer, the old familiar dizziness struck. The ever-present fragrance of lilies and carnations mixed with a few roses choked her. A plaque near a doorway on their left indicated a name she didn't know. She swallowed against the hard lump rising in her throat. God, she hated funeral homes.

Franklin's assistant, a woman with a face like the full moon, approached them from the rear of the building. "Zoe. It's so good to see you."

"Hi, Paulette. Is Franklin available?"

"He's in his office." The woman smiled at Harry. "Is this business? We have a wonderful preplanning program."

Zoe choked, sneaking a glance at Harry. "Not that kind of business. This is Harry Adams. Chief Adams' dad."

Paulette took his hand. "Lovely to meet you. I could give you a brochure about our services if you're interested."

Harry scowled at her. "No, thanks."

Zoe bustled him down the hall before Franklin's secretary could launch further into her sales pitch.

"Do I look like I'm ready to kick the bucket?" Harry whispered.

"Not at all. Business must be slow."

"I can't imagine why. People are dyin' to get into places like this." Zoe snorted.

She found Franklin in his office, bent over an Early American desk. He straightened as they entered. "Zoe. I didn't expect to see you here today."

"I know. I was hoping you could answer a few questions for me if you aren't too busy."

"Certainly." He pointed to the chairs across from him.

She nudged Harry, who was eyeing the three display caskets sitting in a darkened corner. "Huh? Oh." He moved toward the chairs, letting Zoe sit first.

She introduced the two men. Before Franklin had a chance to launch into the same sales pitch as his secretary had, she asked, "Who was the county coroner before you took office?"

Franklin scowled. "Before me? Richard Perryman. Why?"

"Was he the coroner twenty-seven years ago?"

"Heavens, no. Twenty-seven years? What's this all about?"

She looked down at her hands.

Harry cleared his throat. "We're investigating her father's death."

"You're— Excuse me, who are you again? Wait." Franklin looked at Zoe. "Adams. As in Pete Adams?"

Zoe opened her mouth, but Harry beat her to it. "He's my son."

She touched his arm. "Harry's helping me out today."

"Oh." Franklin's gaze shifted to Harry and back to Zoe. "What about your father's death?"

"I was hoping to talk to someone who worked the case. Maybe see a copy of the coroner's report."

"Is there a problem?"

A problem? "Not really. Well, maybe." She took another breath before telling him about the letter James Engle had written to her mother.

As she spoke, Franklin leaned back in his chair and steepled his fingers in front of his chest. Once she finished her story, he sat in silence, chewing his lip.

"Interesting," he said at last. "Unfortunately, you're not going to be able to talk to the coroner from back then."

"Why?" she demanded.

"Because Martin Dempsey, who was coroner at the time, died fifteen years ago."

Zoe deflated. "Oh. But, what about his records? Can I get a copy of his report on the accident?"

Franklin gave a short laugh. "Anything older than ten years is in storage."

"Where?"

"The basement of the courthouse. And if you recall, many of those old records were destroyed when the basement flooded during Hurricane Ivan."

Zoe slumped back into her chair. Even Mother Nature was in on the conspiracy to keep her from finding the truth about her dad. She ran Franklin's words through her brain again and grasped at the one word that had slipped by her the first time. "Many. You said 'many' of the records were destroyed. But not all."

"Well, no. Not all. The rest are in musty old boxes covered in cobwebs."

"How do I get to them?"

"Please tell me you're kidding. Have you any idea what the courthouse basement is like?"

She'd been in the basement of the farmhouse plenty of times and figured the courthouse couldn't be much different. "Yeah, I do. How do I get in?"

Franklin removed his wire-rimmed glasses and rubbed his eyes. "Look. If you're so determined, I'll have someone over there try to find the files." He replaced his glasses and picked up a pen. "Give me the date and year."

"How long will this take?"

"You know how it goes. A week. Maybe two."

"No. I'll do it myself."

"They aren't going to let you into the records room."

"Why not? I'm a deputy coroner. Doesn't that give me some official detective status?"

Franklin shot her a look. "You're a paramedic who is also a part-time deputy coroner with minimal training in the investigative end of it. You can call time of death and you can collect evidence at a crime scene. That's it."

She glared back at him. "I know that. Work with me here, Franklin."

"Why should I? You won't even come in to assist me with an autopsy every now and then."

True. She'd attended one, and the smell stuck in her nostrils for weeks.

"You know I plan to retire some day and I'd love to see you take my place."

This was news to her. "What?"

"If I were training you to take over for me, then you might possibly have the right to access all those old records."

Zoe studied Franklin's face. Was he saying what she thought he was saying? "How soon are you planning to retire?"

"Oh, not soon. But you never know. I'd rather know someone I trusted was ready to fill in for me at a moment's notice."

"Uh-huh. And when would this training begin?"

Franklin shrugged. "We could say it's already begun. If anyone asked. Like the folks at the courthouse."

He *was* saying what she thought he was saying. But her cell phone sang out *I Fought the Law* before she could respond. "Uh-oh, Harry. Pete's looking for us."

Harry had been dozing but snapped awake. "Tell him I had to use the men's room."

Zoe snickered. "Hey, Pete," she said into the phone.

"Where the hell are you?"

"On our way. Um, your dad had to use the restroom."

"Oh, God. You didn't lose him, did you?"

"No. He's right here with me. Are you still in the surgical waiting room?"

"I'm on my way down to the snack bar. Just wait for me there."

"Oh." *Crap.* "Okay." She pressed end and said to Franklin, "We have to go."

She rose and offered a hand to Harry, but he waved her off and stood up without any help.

As they headed for the door, Zoe paused and turned back. "Thanks, Franklin."

"No problem."

But he called out to her as she stepped into the hallway. "Oh, and Zoe?"

"Yes?"

"The next time I call you to assist on an autopsy, I damn well expect you to be here. On time."

FIFTEEN

Pete sat at one of the tables in the hospital snack bar, nursing a Styrofoam cup of coffee and fuming. Where the hell were Zoe and Pop? As if he didn't know.

She'd dragged his father with her to talk to Franklin Marshall. Pete wished he'd never shown her that damned letter. But how was he to know she'd fixate on her interpretation of one line? One stupid sentence. *Mrs. Jackson, your husband did not die in that car crash.*

He sipped the steaming brew and shifted his focus back to the real case he had on his hands. Someone had shot one of the township residents he'd sworn to protect. And not just any resident. A nice old man who took care of his cancer-stricken wife. Some asshole had walked into the man's own barn and shot him.

The same barn where Zoe spent most of her off duty time.

The same nice old man who shared a roof with Zoe.

She could easily have been there. Hell, if she hadn't been helping him look for Harry, she probably *would* have been there.

The idea of Zoe facing a crazed idiot with a gun made the coffee in Pete's stomach burn like battery acid. Granted it wouldn't have been the first time. She'd stood toe to toe with a gunman just last winter in that very same barn. That time, she'd managed to take the shooter down on her own with Pete arriving in time to do nothing more than call for an ambulance and take the wounded killer into custody.

Pete didn't want things to go that far ever again. He wanted whoever had shot Mr. Kroll in jail, and he wanted him there now.

Baronick had given Pete a rundown of what the county crime scene guys had found—damned little. No shell casings, so the guy had either policed his brass or used a revolver. They were running tests on the tissue and hair discovered on the manure spreader, but were fairly certain it belonged to Kroll. He'd apparently been shot while on his tractor, fell and struck his head on the way down.

Baronick had interviewed the wife upstairs in the surgical unit's waiting room. She hadn't given him anything useful. Her husband had no enemies, didn't fight with anyone. Mrs. Kroll didn't know of any new boarders and there hadn't been anyone hanging around who shouldn't have been. In fact, Mrs. Kroll had told the detectives, the only new faces she'd seen lately were Tom and Kimberly Jackson.

Pete's brain segued from Zoe's mother to Zoe's ancestors. The Kroll shooting may be his only real case, but the old Miller homicide/suicide gnawed at him, too. Why hadn't the gun been found? A man who was that overcome with remorse for shooting his brother wouldn't bother to hide the weapon before hanging himself. Unless someone else had hidden it. Someone like another shooter.

Pete had asked Baronick to do some digging in the county evidence lock-up if he had any spare time. The young detective might be a pain in the ass, but he loved a good mystery. Pete knew from the spark in Baronick's eyes that he'd make the time.

Pete shifted in the chair to reposition his throbbing foot, and his mind shifted to the other case with ties to Zoe and her mom. Gary Chambers. If James Engle hadn't been suffering from dementia when he wrote that note, what exactly had he meant by those cryptic words?

Sipping his coffee, Pete opened his cell phone and scrolled through his address book before pressing send.

"Wayne," he said when the detective answered. "While you're on the trail of information on that Miller case, do me a favor. See if you can find anything about the vehicular homicide of Gary Chambers." Pete gave Baronick the year.

"Twenty-seven years ago?"

"Nice to know you can do the math."

"Gary Chambers. Isn't that the name mentioned in the letter we found under James Engle's couch?"

"Right again. I'm not sure what I'm looking for, so anything you find would be appreciated."

"Got it. I'll be in touch."

Pete tucked the phone into his pocket as Zoe and his father appeared in the doorway. She gave him a guilty grin.

Pete held up a hand. "I don't want to know."

"But—"

"You didn't lose Pop. That's the main thing." In fact, his old man looked almost—perky.

Harry nudged Zoe. "Do I still get something to eat? I'm starved."

"Sure. What'll you have?"

"A milkshake. Chocolate."

Pete snorted. "That's not exactly a healthy lunch."

Zoe planted her fists on her hips and narrowed her eyes at him. "It's still too early for lunch. This is...brunch."

Harry nodded in fervent agreement. "Yeah."

"Chocolate milkshakes for brunch?"

Zoe dropped her stance and leaned down to Pete's ear. "At his age, if he wants a milkshake, I'm buying him a frigging milkshake."

With that she headed for the counter, leaving Harry rocking back on his heels and wearing a smug smile.

"I like her, Pete."

"I know, Pop."

"You should marry her."

Pete choked on his coffee.

Harry slid into the bench across from him. "I'm serious. She's a real sweetheart. And pretty."

Pete already knew that.

"And she treats me like a grownup instead of like a damned kid the way you and your sister do."

A grownup who orders a chocolate milkshake for brunch. "So where were you two just now?" Pete asked, not expecting a coherent answer.

"Talking to a guy at some funeral home. About Zoe's dad."

Pete sat back in the seat. Son of a bitch. His old man remembered all that? And Zoe's name. "What about her dad?"

But Harry's eyes clouded over, the old confusion returning. "I—I don't remember exactly. She's trying to find him, I think." He frowned. "You should help her. She's a nice girl."

"I know, Pop."

The next few minutes passed in silence before Zoe returned with two large Styrofoam cups and two straws. She handed one of each to Harry, who eyed the container. "What's this?"

"Your chocolate milkshake. I got myself one, too."

"Oh, I love milkshakes. And chocolate's my favorite. How did you know?"

She met Pete's gaze. "Lucky guess."

So much for the momentary return of Harry's faculties. Zoe slid into the empty seat across from Pete and tore the paper wrapping from her straw.

"I have a few questions I need to ask you," he said.

She pierced the flimsy plastic lid with the straw. "This sounds official."

"It is."

She blinked at him. "Oh. Okay."

"Do you have any idea who might have wanted your landlord dead?"

"Not at all." She took a long slow draw on the straw. Her cheeks sucked in from the force. "I wish I did."

"You spend a fair amount of time with him in the barn, don't you?"

She ran her tongue over her lips. "Sure. He can't do much manual labor anymore. I do most of that. But he loves to drive his tractor. And his quad. He's on one or the other all the time. Won't let anyone else behind the wheel of either of them."

"Has he had any arguments or disagreements with any of the boarders lately?"

"Nope. He gets along with everyone. He's our adopted grandfather."

"Do you have any new boarders?"

"How new? The last time we had stall space was back in March. A single mom and her preteen daughter brought in a small Appaloosa. They adore Mr. Kroll."

"Okay. How about strangers? Has there been anyone hanging around that shouldn't be? Or have any of your boarders brought friends around?"

"Nobody new. No strangers. Even the guy who delivers the feed is the same one we've had for years."

Pete braced to tread on tenuous ground. "How about your mother and stepdad?"

Zoe paused mid sip. "You don't think they had anything to do with this, do you?"

"Just covering all the bases. Do your stepdad and Mr. Kroll get along?"

"Yeah. Tom helped us with a load of hay, so Mr. Kroll loves him. And Tom did help save Mr. Kroll's life yesterday." She used the straw to stir her shake and gave a short laugh. "Poor Tom is having a lousy vacation. First he finds out his old friend has hung himself. Then we put him to work in the barn. And to top it off, there's this shooting, and he has to play first responder."

Pete struggled to maintain a calm façade. Keeping his voice level, he asked, "So your stepdad and James Engle were friends?"

"Um hum," she said around the straw. She swallowed and smacked her lips.

Pete held her gaze, willing her to elaborate. She didn't. Should he press it? Mention that Tom had apparently flat out lied to him about not knowing Engle?

No. Not yet. "What about your mother?"

Zoe snorted. "My mother doesn't get along with anyone. And she doesn't go anywhere near the barn. Ever. Trust me. If she were going to shoot anyone, they'd have to come to her because she couldn't be bothered to go to them."

Having dropped Pete and Harry off at the Vance Township Police Station and been freed of her escort duties, Zoe headed back to Brunswick behind the wheel of her own vehicle. Pete's questions replayed in her mind. Specifically, one question.

"So your stepdad and James Engle were friends?"

Her big mouth had done it again. She had to go and blather on about Tom's crappy vacation. And now she'd put him solidly on Pete's radar.

She hadn't mentioned Tom's friendship with Engle earlier for one very big reason. She feared her stepfather knew a lot more about the murder/suicide of Vernie and Denver Miller than he was letting on.

Why had Tom been so evasive when she'd questioned her mom about the whole thing? Tom, who was always open and above board. Tom, who defended her against her mother's nonsense.

What could he possibly be hiding from Zoe? Did he know what really happened between her great uncles all those years ago?

Could he have been involved in some small way?

Zoe struck the steering wheel with the flat of her hand. No. Tom would never have a part in anything so dark. But he was hiding something. That much she knew.

And now so did Pete. He hadn't been fooling her one bit. Maybe it was all those poker games, but as much as he'd tried to cover it, she'd seen the flash of excitement in his eyes when she'd mentioned Tom and Engle's friendship. He was no doubt wondering why she hadn't mentioned it before.

Now she and Pete were both keeping secrets from one another.

After two loops around the blocks nearest the courthouse turned up nothing in the way of empty spots spacious enough to accommodate a three-quarter ton pickup, Zoe headed to the lot she'd left a couple of hours ago. She fed the meter and hiked three blocks to the ancient stone courthouse.

She climbed the wide stone steps and entered through massive burnished oak doors. A uniformed guard watched as she deposited her wallet, phone, and keys in a plastic bin and stepped through the metal detector. The guard gave her a satisfied nod, and she reclaimed her stuff.

Inside the grand concourse, a pair of sweeping marble staircases mirrored each other. As it did every time she stood in this spot, her gaze followed the stairs up to the second level where the courtrooms were housed.

But she wasn't headed up today. Trudging down into the dungeon-like labyrinth of offices, archives, and storage areas, she anticipated her upcoming confrontation with the gatekeeper to the old records room. She pictured a skeletal old woman with white hair and whiter skin. Probably wore dark-framed reading glasses hanging from her bony neck on a tarnished chain.

Zoe made her way down a musty hallway to a tiny gray metal desk next to a door labeled "Archives and Records." Instead of her imagined gray-haired lady, the man who sat behind the desk struck her as looking more like former Pittsburgh Steeler Hines Ward. Without the smile.

"Hi." She extended a hand. "I'm Zoe Chambers with the coroner's office. I need to look at some records from an old case."

The Hines Ward-lookalike's security badge stated that he was actually Devon Wilkins. He gave her hand a brief, crushing squeeze, but showed no sign of being impressed by her title. "I need ID."

She handed over her driver's license.

His eyes flickered down to it then back to her face. "Your *department* ID."

Apparently the Department of Transportation wasn't good enough for him. "Department?"

He gave a weary sigh. "I either need your credentials from the Coroner's Office or something from the police department giving you access to the evidence."

Zoe plastered her best smile on her face. "Look, Mr. Wilkins, Franklin Marshall just approved me today. I don't have my credentials yet." She suspected she wouldn't see anything like that until after she'd satisfied Franklin's demands about autopsy attendance.

Wilkins shook his head. "Sorry."

"Couldn't you call Franklin? He'll verify I'm legit."

The clerk fixed her with a wordless stare.

"Fine." Zoe pulled out her cell phone. If Wilkins wouldn't place the call, she would.

At the same time she noticed the total lack of bars, the clerk gave a self-satisfied grunt. "There's no signal down here."

Wonderful. She stuffed the phone back in her purse and eyed the door. The information she wanted—needed—was so close. Only a couple of inches of solid wood and happy-go-lucky Mr. Wilkins stood in her way.

She retraced her steps to the airy courthouse concourse where her cell phone revealed five lovely bars, and she punched in Franklin Marshall's phone number.

Ten minutes later, she stood inside the archived evidence room, having bartered her way into a full half-dozen autopsies. Maybe she'd find a way to get used to the smell.

While the man standing guard had been nothing like what she'd expected, the room itself was closer to what she'd pictured. Enormous. Old. Dark. But there must have been a dehumidifier or air purifier running somewhere, because there was none of the mustiness she imagined.

Gray steel shelving units reached to the high ceiling, stacked with boxes—case numbers, names, and dates scrawled on the ends facing out. Zoe wandered through the cavernous space, scanning the years for a date that was engraved forever on her heart.

After exploring up one row and down the next, she finally found the year she'd been searching for. When she spotted the box labeled with CHAMBERS and the date her dad had died—allegedly—a chill embraced her.

The thing was too high to reach. Zoe jogged down the row to retrieve a step ladder leaning against the shelves. Her sneakers made only a faint squeak against the concrete floor, but the ladder clattered and scraped as she dragged it back to the box. She clanked it down and climbed to the fourth rung in order to reach her prize. Balancing precariously on her tiptoes, she stretched and maneuvered two other boxes stacked on top of the one she wanted. For a moment, she imagined dropping the whole stack, evidence scattering everywhere, and that unsmiling Hines Ward-lookalike tossing her ass out into the maze of underground hallways.

Forcing her breath to slow, she eased the box marked CHAMBERS out from under the others, letting them slide gently down into the vacated space. Then she hugged the container against her side as she backed down the ladder.

Zoe dropped to the concrete floor, her legs crossed yoga style, and set the box in front of her. Biting her lip, she eased the lid up.

A voice behind her nearly jerked her heart out through her chest. "And just what do you think you're doing?"

SIXTEEN

Pete leaned back in his chair and propped his foot on the desk. Why the hell hadn't he filled the prescription for pain killers the ER doctor had sent home with him? His entire leg throbbed, from his knee to his toes. He raked through the top drawer and found a bottle of Motrin. Dumped four of them into his palm and swallowed them dry. A quick check of the label revealed that they were almost a year past expiration.

He tossed the bottle back in the drawer and turned his focus back to his notes.

Tom Jackson. Pete hated the doubts he was having about the man who had raised Zoe. But how many coincidences was he supposed to ignore?

Tom Jackson had been one of the first on scene when Kroll had been shot. Pete double checked his notes. Patsy Greene had stated she found the victim and phoned the house. She reported that Tom Jackson arrived a few minutes later and tried to stop the bleeding, never leaving Kroll's side until after the ambulance arrived.

Jackson had lied about knowing James Engle. Not only was Jackson friends with the late James Engle, he was also friends with the late Gary Chambers. Zoe's dad.

But Jackson had Zoe as an alibi for Engle's homicide. She'd picked him and her mother up at the airport the morning *after* Engle's body had been discovered.

Even so, if Pete could connect Jackson to the Miller murder/suicide, he'd make a clean sweep of tying the man to every case, current or cold, that Pete was investigating.

An annoying chime from the front of the station signaled that someone had entered. Some chatter and the cackle of boisterous laughter drifted back to him. A moment later, Sylvia appeared in his door-way.

"As a member of the township board of supervisors, I must voice my disapproval of your choice of how to spend our taxpayers' dollars." She ambled into his office and eased into a chair across from him.

Pete shrugged. "So what else is new?"

Sylvia ignored the comment and continued to chastise him. "You're using our police secretary to babysit Harry—"

"Harry would loathe that you think he needs to be babysat. Nancy is *entertaining* him."

"On township time, may I point out. Plus here you sit when you're supposed to be on sick leave. We're already paying Seth overtime to take your shifts while you're gimped up."

Pete picked up a pen and flung it at her. It missed—as was his in-tention—and smacked the wall behind her. "I'm here on my own time."

"And throwing things at a poor defenseless old woman." Sylvia clutched at her ample chest and put on a better pouty face than any two-year-old.

"Poor defenseless old woman, my ass. What do you know about Tom Jackson?"

Sylvia blinked. "Zoe's stepdad?"

"That's the one."

Sylvia leaned back and fingered her upper lip. "What exactly do you want to know? He grew up around here. Handsome son-of-gun. All the girls chased him when he was a kid. I think he let a few of them catch him, too. At least until he married Zoe's mom."

"What kind of fellow was he? Did he get into trouble?"

"No more than any of the other local boys."

"He was a friend of Gary Chambers?"

"Oh, yeah. Those two were tight ever since they were kids. As I remember, Tommy was almost as torn up as Kimberly when Gary was killed. It was their mutual grief that drew them together. Plus Tommy felt a sense of responsibility."

"Responsibility? Why?"

"He made Gary some kind of pledge to look after his widow and daughter. Or so I heard."

"Before Gary died?"

"I don't know. You'd have to ask Tommy."

Pete jotted a note. "I might just do that. What about James Engle?"

"What about him?"

"Were he and Jackson friends?"

Sylvia squinted, as if trying to see something in the distance. "Now that you mention it, yes. I think I do remember the two of them hanging around together. Engle was a bit older. I think Tommy looked up to him. Admired him. But after that incident with the Miller boys, Jim and Tommy had some kind of falling out."

Pete's head threatened to explode. Strike four.

Zoe's heart pounded like a kettle drum against the inside of her sternum. One hand pressed against her chest to keep everything in there contained. The other clenched in a fist that she longed to connect to her interloper's nose.

Detective Wayne Baronick grinned down at her. "Did I scare you?"

"No," she snapped. Although she and Baronick crossed paths at the occasional crime scene or traffic collision, her only real contact with the man had been last winter when he'd given her a hard time over a case that hit too close to home. He'd just been doing his job, or so Pete had said. Baronick had in fact severely bent the rules to aid them in their investigation. But she still wasn't sure about the county detective in spite of his devilish smile.

"So what are you doing here?" Baronick asked. "And how'd you manage to get past Devon? He's not easily swayed from his duties."

No kidding. "Franklin Marshall promoted me to chief deputy coroner this morning."

"Really?" Baronick didn't sound convinced.

"Yes, really. Call him if you don't believe me."

"No, no. I believe you. If Devon let you back here, you must be telling the truth." Baronick hunkered down next to her and tipped his head to read the end of the box. "You're looking into your dad's crash." He narrowed his gaze at her. "You sure Marshall promoted you?"

"Yes, I'm sure. Of course, he might *de*mote me tomorrow. But for now, he's given me access to the forensic evidence from old cases."

Baronick gave a slow nod. "I see. As it happens, I was asked to look into this case, too."

Stunned, Zoe leaned back against the boxes behind her. "Who asked you?"

"Guess."

Her mind swept through the possibilities, and it didn't take long. "Pete?"

"Uh-huh. He's got me looking at two old cases—your dad's crash and those two brothers who died in the same barn where James Engle hung himself. They were related to you, too, weren't they?"

"They were my mom's uncles." So Pete was giving some credence to her suspicions after all. "Did you find anything?"

"Not yet. I just got here when I heard someone dragging a ladder around. Decided to see who else was spending a lovely summer day locked in this dungeon." Baronick motioned to the box in front of her. "Let's see what we've got."

Zoe drew a breath, blew it out, and lifted the lid. She and Baronick leaned forward to peer inside.

A folder lay at the bottom. Nothing else.

She reached in and removed it. "That's it?"

"So it seems." Baronick took the folder from her and flipped it open.

Zoe scooted around so she could read over his shoulder. "What's it say?"

He frowned. Thumbed through several pages. Then flipped them back again. "Not very damned much. We've got an accident report." He let his finger trail down the page as he read. "Ran off the road by a drunk driver. The car caught fire. Vance Township Volunteer Fire Department responded." He paused. "Whoa. Here's something interesting."

"What?"

"The driver of the other car was Carl Loomis. The guy who was raising a fuss at the James Engle farm on Friday."

"I know."

Baronick turned to look at her. "How?"

"Warren Froats told Pete. Pete told me."

"Froats." The detective blew a quick raspberry. "That old bag of wind."

Zoe snorted. "Don't hold back, Detective. Tell me what you *really* think of him."

Baronick shook the accident report at her. "See this? It's typical Warren Froats. Granted, I never worked with the man. He retired before my time. But whenever I have to look up information on an old case that he handled, it's like this. Nothing. The man hated details. I don't know how the DA ever won a case on the reports he wrote."

"What else is there?"

Baronick flipped to another page. "Here's your coroner's report."

Zoe snatched it from him. As she scanned the page, her hopes for answers melted into her shoes.

"It says cause of death was smoke inhalation. Method of death is listed as accidental." She flipped the page over, but the back was blank. She pointed at the folder in the detective's hands. "Where are the autopsy results?"

He thumbed through the remaining pages. "There's nothing here. Oh, wait. Look." He pointed at a faded notation on a sheet of lined notepaper. "It says no autopsy was performed at the request of the family."

Zoe choked. "That's crazy. It wouldn't matter if the family didn't want an autopsy. On a case like this, it would be done anyway."

He shrugged. "Sure. *Now.* Things were different back then, I guess. Maybe the old coroner was as incompetent as Froats."

"But how did they come up with a determination of smoke inhalation if there wasn't an autopsy? I don't suppose there're any lab results in that folder, are there?"

He scanned the few pages and shook his head.

"Toxicology reports?"

"Nope."

Zoe's mind spun. Instead of answers, the box only contained more questions. "Is this incompetence? Or a cover-up?"

Baronick frowned. "You lost me. Cover-up?"

She studied the detective's face. Would he think she was crazy, too? Biting her lip, she decided to chance it. "You saw the letter Engle wrote to my mother, right?"

"The one the crime scene guys found crumpled under his couch? Yeah."

"It said my father didn't die in that crash."

Baronick didn't reply, so she continued. "I think my father's still alive. I think he faked his death."

Instead of laughing, Baronick rubbed his jaw. Frowned at the folder, the sparse reports, then at her. "Why would he do that?"

"I don't know. But the only person I've found who actually says he saw my dad's body was Warren Froats."

"And you know what I think of him."

"What if Dad isn't dead? What if he and Froats made up the story about him being burnt in the crash so the casket would stay closed? Dad would know my mom wouldn't want to see that. They could have set the car on fire to fit their story."

Baronick wasn't looking at her like she was nuts. He wasn't looking at her like she was poor, delusional Zoe, either.

"But when I tell all this to Pete, he brings up one question I can't answer."

"Which is?"

"Why would Dad do that to Mom and me? How could he just disappear and let us think he was dead all these years?"

Baronick closed the folder and set it back inside the box. "I think I may know the answer to that one."

"I can't believe I let you coerce me into being your chauffeur," Sylvia muttered.

Pete fumbled for the lever to slide back the passenger seat in her white Ford Escort. "Don't bullshit me. You love any chance to pick up some new local gossip."

"But you won't let me share any of it. Police business." She huffed. "What good is gossip if a body has to keep it to herself?"

"Welcome to the wonderful world of law enforcement." He managed to release the seat a couple of clicks, making room for his legs and sighed in relief. Whoever had last sat in this seat must have been a midget. He half turned toward Harry in the backseat. "You doin' okay, Pop?"

Harry grunted. "Where are we going?"

"Zoe's house."

"Who?"

Pete closed his eyes. Here we go again.

"You remember Zoe, don't you, Harry?" Sylvia called back over her shoulder. "Pete's girlfriend."

Pete shot Sylvia his best I'm-going-to-kill-you look.

"Oh, sure," Harry replied. "She's a sweetheart."

"Indeed she is." Sylvia glanced at Pete. "And she's going to wring your neck when you show up to question her stepdad about three murders and a shooting."

"That's two alleged suicides, a shooting, a traffic fatality, and only *one* murder."

"Well, that makes a huge difference. She's still gonna wring your neck."

"Good thing she's not my girlfriend then."

Sylvia muttered something, but the only word Pete comprehended was "idiot."

"What did you say?" he demanded.

"Nothing. Not a thing." Sylvia clicked on her turn signal as they approached the farm lane. "Just don't come crawling to me when you're old and lonely."

At the moment his concerns had little to do with getting old. How was Zoe going to take his suspicions? Sylvia might be right about her wringing his neck.

A few minutes later, Pete crutched his way down the hill to the farmhouse's enclosed back porch. Sylvia and Harry, arm-in-arm and looking very much like a respectable older couple, trailed behind. Pete struggled with the big step onto the porch and hobbled to the door to Zoe's half of the house. He rapped lightly on the glass window in the door and expected the lace curtain to be brushed aside revealing Zoe's inquiring face.

Instead, the door swung open to a woman he'd never met before, but the striking blue eyes, blond hair, and incredible body were oddly familiar. This woman might have been a couple of decades older than Zoe, dressed in pristine matching pastels rather than a uniform or jeans, and must have used enough hairspray to keep her "do" in place even in a Florida hurricane, but otherwise the resemblance was striking.

"Kimberly Jackson?" Pete said.

The woman raised a critical eyebrow. "Yes?"

Pete held up his ID and introduced himself. "Is Zoe home?"

Kimberly crossed her arms in front of her and made no move to open the door any further. "No. And I don't have a clue as to when she'll be back."

A weight lifted from Pete's shoulders. If Zoe was going to strangle him, at least his demise had been given a reprieve. However, he couldn't help wondering where she'd gone. "How about Mr. Jackson? Is he in?"

"Yes." Kimberly's gaze shifted past Pete to his entourage. A flash of recognition crossed her face. "Sylvia," she said coolly.

"Hello, Kim." Sylvia's smile appeared forced. "How long has it been?"

Kimberly ignored the question and still made no move to invite them in.

Pete made a mental note to ask Sylvia about her past relationship with Zoe's mother. "Mrs. Jackson, I need to ask your husband a few questions."

Kimberly's eyes came back to his. He'd been mistaken. They weren't anything like Zoe's. The only sparkle in these baby blues was the hard glint of steel. She gave a disgusted sigh and stepped back, opening the door wider. "Tom's on the front porch."

Pete hobbled inside with a glance back to make sure Kimberly didn't slam the door on Sylvia or his father. The look on Sylvia's face told Pete he needn't worry.

He started across the space that served as both a living and dining room toward Zoe's office.

"Wait," Kimberly called. "I'll get Tom. You can talk here."

Pete paused and pivoted on his crutches. He shot a glance at Sylvia. "It's no problem. I'd rather meet with him out there."

Sylvia caught Kimberly's arm. "Why don't we fix some lemonade for the men?"

Pete bit back a smile. Good old Sylvia had picked up on his silent request. He needed some alone time with Zoe's stepdad.

Kimberly's voice shot up an octave. "Lemonade?"

As Sylvia led Kimberly to the kitchen, Pete continued through Zoe's office. Behind him he heard Sylvia introducing his father to Zoe's mother. He almost wished he could spy on the conversation going on behind that kitchen door. But he had more important matters to deal with on the front porch.

SEVENTEEN

"Damn it," Pete said through clenched teeth as he battled his way through the screen door to the front porch. He tried to block it open with one crutch while hopping on his good foot, but the second crutch snagged on the threshold, nearly toppling him onto his face.

Tom Jackson jumped to his rescue, catching the obstinate door and holding it open.

"Thanks," Pete muttered. He was supposed to be the one tending to his township's helpless victims, not the one needing assistance. Especially not from Jackson.

Pete thunked across the wood deck and cast a glance at the pair of Adirondacks flanking a table bearing a potted geranium and an open can of Coke. Weighing the aggravation of climbing back out of the low-slung chair versus standing, he opted to lean against the wide wooden porch railing.

"Chief Adams." Jackson reclaimed his seat. "If you're here to see my daughter, I'm afraid you've missed her."

"I'm not here for Zoe." Pete propped his crutches against a support pillar and took what he hoped looked like a casual stance. From the set of Jackson's jaw, Pete knew going head-to-head with this man would offer the same result as running into a brick wall. Better to keep things casual, if that were possible. "I hoped we could talk."

Jackson studied him. "About what? Because if this is about Mr. Kroll's shooting yesterday, I've already told you everything I know."

Pete reached into his pocket and eased out his notebook, but didn't open it. "All right then. What about James Engle?"

Jackson's right eye narrowed ever so slightly. Otherwise, the man showed no reaction to the name. Pete waited for a response. None came.

Pete hated losing in the game of chicken. But Jackson showed no hint of backing down. So much for staying casual. "You lied to me, Mr. Jackson."

The man's eyes never wavered. "Oh?"

Pete flipped open his notebook. "Yesterday I asked if you knew James Engle. You said you didn't."

The shift in Jackson's countenance was subtle. A slight downturn to his lip—a momentary narrowing of his eyes. "I didn't think my relationship with James Engle had anything to do with Mr. Kroll being shot."

Pete softened his own expression. "It was a simple question. I never said it was related to the shooting case."

Jackson picked up his Coke and sipped. Rolling the can between his palms, he said, "Yeah. I *knew* Jim. Past tense. I haven't seen him in years. Decades."

"How many decades?"

Jackson stopped toying with the can. "Exactly?"

Pete watched him without answering.

Jackson appeared to be looking back through his past. "Kimberly and I have lived in Florida for close to twenty years. I haven't seen Jim since before then."

"How well did you know him?"

Jackson again locked onto Pete's gaze, and Pete had the distinct feeling the man was trying to read him. "We were close. Once. A long time ago."

"How long ago?"

Jackson broke the staring match and chuckled. "About a hundred years."

Pete didn't share the laugh. "You look good for your age."

Jackson shifted in the chair, relaxing. "I was a kid. In my twenties. Jim Engle was—more than a friend. He was kind of a father figure to me. But people grow apart. Life gets in the way." He smiled beneath his mustache. "We haven't been close for a very long time."

"Life gets in the way," Pete echoed back to him. "By *life*, don't you really mean death? As in the deaths of Denver and Vernon Miller?"

Pete had hoped for a reaction. Instead, Jackson held the faint smile. "Now you're really stretching, Chief. Is business so slow around these parts that you have to go back forty-some years to find a case to work on?"

Pete crossed his arms and struck a laid-back pose. Or as laid-back as he could with his foot and ankle throbbing. He should have risked the Adirondack chair.

"I don't like coincidences, Mr. Jackson. James Engle's body was found hanging in the same barn the Miller brothers died in. Your own wife suspects Engle had something to do with her uncles' deaths. And rumor has it your falling-out with Engle happened about the same time. That's too many coincidences to suit me."

Jackson's smile had vanished. He seemed ready to go on the offensive, but appeared to swallow whatever argument he'd intended to use. "All right. Yeah. After Denver and Vernon's deaths, Jim changed. He started drinking. A lot. He shut me out."

"What do you know about the Millers?"

"Not much."

Pete wanted to stomp across the porch and grab the man, but knew he'd fall flat on his face. Instead he slammed his hand down on the railing. "Come off it, Jackson. Your so-called *father figure* inherited the farm that should have gone to your wife's family. Don't tell me you don't have some knowledge or insight into what happened."

"I hate to disappoint you, but I really don't know more than anyone else who was around back then. The Millers were both involved with the same woman and it got ugly. As for Jim inheriting? He worked damned hard for the brothers. They showed their appreciation by leaving him the farm. That's *it*."

For a moment, the only sound was a pair of robins squawking from the pines in the front yard. Pete studied Jackson as he asked his next question. "Who was the woman?"

Jackson remained nearly unreadable. Nearly. "I don't know."

Pete kept his own face expressionless in spite of his triumph. Tom Jackson was lying through his teeth. "Okay. As for James. Had you spoken with him?"

Jackson frowned. "I told you. No."

"You said you hadn't *seen* him," Pete corrected. "Did you have any contact at all? Phone call? Email? Letters?"

"Nothing."

Pete nodded as if he believed that one, too. "What about Gary Chambers?"

Jackson's eyes darkened. "I haven't talked to him recently either."

Now Pete allowed himself to smile. "I would guess not. I didn't take you for psychic. But you knew him?"

"Of course."

"How well?"

Jackson no longer made any effort to appear relaxed. He clenched the can so tight the aluminum crinkled. "We were best friends."

Pete pretended to read his notes. "You made a pledge to take care of Chambers' wife and daughter if anything happened to him. Isn't that right?"

"Who told you that?"

Pete leaned a shoulder against the pillar, confident he would win this game of chicken.

Jackson let out a slow breath. "Yeah. I said I'd watch out for them."

"When?" What Pete really wanted to ask was if he'd made that pledge before Chambers' death? Or after he'd allegedly *faked* his death? But asking that would have given credence to Zoe's wild suspicions.

"I don't know. It was just one of those things. We'd been drinking. Celebrating after Zoe was born, I think. He got emotional and made me promise I'd look after Kimberly and Zoe if anything ever were to happen to him."

Jackson sighed. "It was one of those drunken buddy moments. I told him I would. But I never in a million years expected..."

Pete reached into his shirt pocket and pulled out the copy of the letter from James Engle's house. The one about Zoe's dad's accident. Pete pressed away from the porch railing to hand the folded paper to Jackson. "What do you make of this?"

Jackson set the Coke can next to the flower pot and took the letter. He unfolded it and squinted at the words on the page for a moment, and handed it back.

Pete didn't take it. Instead, he folded his arms and resumed leaning on the railing.

A flash of annoyance crossed Jackson's face. He let his hand and the paper drop to his lap. "This is the damned letter that has Zoe in knots."

"So you've seen it before?"

"Yesterday morning. Zoe confronted her mother with it."

"And you hadn't seen the letter before then?"

"No."

"How about your wife?"

"What about her?"

"Had she seen it before?"

The screen door swung open, and Kimberly breezed onto the porch carrying a glass pitcher Pete recognized from Saturday night poker games here at Zoe's place. A smiling Harry followed with a bowl brimming with potato chips.

"Had who seen what before?" Kimberly asked. She set the pitcher on the table, carefully moving her husband's Coke aside.

Sylvia, carrying glasses, trailed behind and gave Pete an apologetic grin in reply to his glare. He'd hoped for a little more time alone with Zoe's stepfather. But Sylvia had a chance to redeem herself. Pete raised an eyebrow at her and shot a glance at Jackson's Coke can. Sylvia's minute nod let Pete know she understood.

Jackson waved the letter at his wife. Kimberly pinched it between her thumb and index finger and held it at arm's length, straining to see. "Oh." She crinkled her nose as if the page carried a stench.

"Well?" Pete asked.

"What?" Kimberly gave him a vapid look.

He waited. From the periphery of his vision, he noted Sylvia pour the rest of Jackson's Coke into one of the glasses. Slicker than a sleight-of-hand artist, she swept the can out of view.

"Oh," Kimberly said again. "Had I seen the letter before? No. Not until Zoe shoved it at me yesterday before church. I swear that girl does stuff like that just for the shock value."

Shock value? *Zoe?* Did Kimberly even know her own daughter?

Harry, still holding the chips, offered the bowl to Kimberly with one hand and held out the other one, palm up in an invitation to swap snacks for the letter. Kimberly eagerly complied.

"Any idea why Engle wrote it?" Pete asked.

Kimberly shrugged, uninterested. "How should I know?"

"He addressed it to you, Mrs. Jackson."

"But he clearly decided not to mail it," Zoe's stepfather said.

Harry frowned at the letter while Sylvia leaned closer and read it over his arm.

Pete glared at his pair of would-be assistants, but neither one noticed. He turned back to the Jacksons. "Do either of you have any idea what Engle meant when he wrote about Chambers not dying in the accident?"

Jackson took the bowl from his wife and examined the contents. "I can tell you what he *didn't* mean. He did *not* mean that Gary's still alive, no matter what Zoe says." Jackson popped a chip in his mouth.

Kimberly planted her hands on her hips. "Obviously it's the ramblings of an unstable man. Jim was dying, after all. He clearly wasn't in his right mind."

"Except he wasn't dying," Pete said.

Jackson choked on the chip. "What?"

Finally. An unmasked reaction. Pete made a mental note. Tom Jackson did not know about James Engle's feigned cancer.

"Hey. You two about done in here?" Devon, the clerk gatekeeper of the courthouse crypt, stood at the end of the aisle, scowling at Zoe and Baronick. "It's quitting time. I want to lock up and get home."

Zoe glanced at the thin folder lying in the bottom of the box in front of her. Done? She'd been done before she started.

Baronick shot one of his killer smiles at the clerk. "I need about fifteen more minutes, pal. Do you mind?"

Devon muttered something and disappeared.

Baronick stood and offered a hand to Zoe. She ignored it and climbed to her feet.

"Fifteen minutes?" She picked up the box. "What for? There's nothing here worth copying or signing out."

The detective took the box from her and slipped it back where they'd found it. "True. But this isn't the only case I was asked to look into. You can go, though."

"No way. Not until you tell me what you meant about knowing why my dad would disappear without a word to his family."

Baronick crooked a finger at her, beckoning her to follow as he strode off to another section of the storage room. "You say you think he may have faked his death. That no one saw his body?"

Zoe jogged along behind him. "No one I believe."

Baronick paused to orient himself. He looked around, grunted, and started off again. "Had your dad been involved in anything...shady?"

"No," she snapped. "What are you getting at?"

"Have you ever considered that he went into witness protection?"

Zoe stopped. "What?"

Baronick located the row he'd been searching for and veered down a new aisle, squinting at the faded labels on the boxes. "If he'd seen something he shouldn't have or testified against someone in a big case, someone who might have wanted payback, he may have gone into witness protection. The feds would have helped him fake his death. And he'd have just disappeared."

"That's nuts. He never testified against any mobsters." At least Zoe didn't think he had. "You've been watching too many old movies."

The detective chuckled. "Very likely." He stopped. "Ah. Here we are. Vernon and Denver Miller." He reached up and pulled out another box, this one in worse shape than the first.

Baronick set the box on the floor and hunkered down next to it just as Zoe's mind skittered back in time. Her memories of being eight years old were vague at best. Just about everything else had been obliterated by the agony of losing her dad. But what had gone on before that? Had he been involved in something? Seen something? Was there any merit to Baronick's bizarre theory?

A soft whistle from Baronick brought Zoe back to the present. She leaned over his shoulder. "Did you find anything?"

He held a pair of folders, not much thicker than the one for Gary Chambers. "Pretty sparse police report. No surprise there."

"Warren Froats was police chief way back then, too?"

"How'd you guess?" Baronick smirked. "And the coroner was the same, too. No autopsies."

"Did these guys do *anything* to earn their pay?"

Baronick scowled into the box. He reached in and picked something up. His eyes widened. "Someone did."

"Oh?"

He held up a lumpy small brownish envelope with smudged scrawls on the side.

Zoe leaned down for a closer look. "What is that?"

Baronick hastily tugged a glove onto one hand. With his thumb, Baronick popped open the flap. Then he carefully tipped the contents out into his gloved palm.

They both stared at the lump of lead.

"That, my dear," Baronick said with a grin, "is the bullet that killed Denver Miller."

EIGHTEEN

Pete surrendered the front seat on the way home so he could stretch out across the back of Sylvia's car and put his throbbing foot up. He really needed to solve these cases and get to the orthopedist.

"You know I absolutely adore Zoe," Sylvia said, "but that mother of hers is a real piece of work."

Pete grunted.

Harry continued to clutch the duplicate letter the way a kid might hang onto a stuffed animal. "Who?" he asked Sylvia.

"Zoe's mother," Sylvia replied, her tone softer. "Kimberly. She's the one we were just talking to."

Pete watched the back of his father's head and imagined his puzzled expression.

"She's the one who poured the potato chips into the bowl while I made lemonade," Sylvia went on.

Harry nodded. "Right. I remember now. Lovely woman."

Pete sighed. "How well did you know Kimberly before Chambers' accident?"

Sylvia adjusted her rearview mirror so she could see Pete. He watched her eyes reflected in it. "Not well. She's six or seven years younger than I am, so we didn't run in the same circle. Plus she grew up on a little farm a mile or so south of the Kroll place. I don't remember her hanging out around Dillard."

"What about Chambers?"

"Gary was always a really nice guy. He and Tommy Jackson were only a couple of years behind me in high school. Both were jocks. Both went off to college on football scholarships. There was a lot of talk that Gary might have gone pro, except he blew out his knee."

"That's when he married Kimberly?"

Sylvia's eyes narrowed in concentration. "Seems to me she was going to college when she met him. Maybe community college? I can't remember. Anyway, once she and Gary got married, they moved into an apartment in Philipsburg. Couple years later they built that house on the hill behind the Vance Plaza."

"You mean the Robertson's place?" Pete thought of the stone and cedar house that looked more like a ski lodge than a private residence perched on a hillside overlooking the valley between Philipsburg and Dillard.

"Back then it was the Chambers' place," Sylvia said as Pete spotted a twinkle in her eye.

"That house had to cost a pretty penny to build. Even back then."

"As I recall, Gary did okay for himself." She emphasized the *okay*, as if what she really meant was *only* okay. "Owned a little appliance store in Philipsburg. But Kimberly had a reputation for being a social climber."

"No," Pete said sarcastically.

Sylvia chuckled. "Hard to believe, huh? Gary was gaga over his beautiful wife and gave her everything he could. She set her heart on a showplace house. He built it for her."

"With what?"

Sylvia shrugged. "I have no idea."

Pete made a mental note to look quietly into Gary Chambers' life insurance. "By the way, where'd you put it?"

In the mirror, her eyes twinkled mischievously. "In my handbag."

Sylvia's purse sat on the backseat next to Pete. It had gained some notoriety in the past as a lethal weapon, so he hesitated touching it.

She must have spotted his trepidation. "Go ahead. It should be right on top."

He gingerly opened the bag. As Sylvia had said, a Ziploc containing Jackson's Coke can sat on top of the other contents. "Where'd you get the plastic bag?"

"I always carry them with me. You never know."

Pete chuckled and removed the evidence. "If you ever want to come back to work for me as an officer, just give me the word."

"I learned a thing or two after all those years as your secretary."

"I'd say so."

"What does this mean?" Harry asked, thrusting the letter he'd been studying into Sylvia's face.

Pete lurched forward to grab his old man's arm before Sylvia drove them into a ditch. But she beat Pete to it and calmly moved Harry's hand out of her line of vision.

Pete flopped back in his seat. "What is it, Pop?"

Harry jerked around. "Pete. I didn't know you were back there."

Pete closed his eyes in exasperation, sighed, and opened them again. "The letter, Pop. What does *what* mean?"

Harry looked at the letter in his hand as if he'd never seen it before. Then he gave his head a quick shake. "Oh." He held the paper up to show Pete, pointing at one sentence.

"*Gary was just trying to do what's right,*" Harry read. "What does that mean?"

Pete took the letter from his father and read it again. Zoe had been so focused on the next line, Pete had overlooked the rest of the note. "That," he said to his dad, "is a very good question."

Zoe slammed through her back door, sending both cats scurrying. She wanted to talk to her mom and Tom. Now. But their rental car was gone. She spotted a terse note on her table. *Gone out to dinner*. Great. When had they left? How long before they'd return?

She remembered next to nothing about her drive home from Brunswick, her mind stuck on what Baronick had said. Witness protection? Could her dad be out there somewhere, using a different name? With a new family? Would he simply abandon her and her mother to save his own skin?

No. Of course not. But to save theirs? Yes. That much Zoe could believe. He could and would sacrifice his life with them if it kept them safe.

But safe from what?

A knock at her door jarred her. She swung the door open to find Patsy Greene standing on the porch.

"I was out at the barn and saw you come home," Patsy said as Zoe waved her in. "Any word on Mr. Kroll?"

Mr. Kroll. Zoe had been so wrapped up in her own problems, she'd let him slip from her mind.

"I stopped at the hospital this morning. But he was still in surgery." She glanced at her answering machine. No blinking light. No message. "I don't know if Mrs. Kroll's home yet."

"She's not. I knocked on her door first." Patsy offered a tight smile as if apologizing for making Zoe her second choice.

"I could call Pete and ask if he's heard anything." Zoe reached for her phone.

Patsy shook her head. "Don't bother him." She jammed both hands in her jeans pockets. "To be honest, I'm not sure I want to know. I keep thinking how awful he looked yesterday. And all that blood."

The image wasn't one Zoe was likely to forget anytime soon either.

"I went ahead and fed everyone and turned them out. I hope that's okay."

In the winter, the horses usually stayed in their stalls all night and were turned out during the day. In the summer, the schedule was reversed. "That's great. Thanks. I owe you."

Patsy shrugged. "It's the least I can do. I feel just awful about what happened."

"Me, too."

"There is one thing I didn't do, though."

"What's that?"

Patsy kept her hands buried in her pockets and shifted her weight from one foot to the other. "The manure spreader is pretty full and—well, that's what Mr. Kroll had been getting ready to do yesterday. Empty it. But the tractor…"

Zoe understood. "It's Mr. Kroll's tractor." To be more precise, it was Mr. Kroll's baby. And no one else ever touched it. "I don't suppose he'll mind if I drive it." To be honest, she would love to have him home and well enough to chew her out for daring to fire up the old Massey-Ferguson. "I'll take care of it tomorrow."

Patsy nodded. "Thanks." She turned to go. "Call me if you hear anything about him."

"I will."

As Zoe watched Patsy climb the path to where she'd parked her pickup, Tom's rental car crept up the farm lane. Zoe folded her arms and waited.

"Oh, you're home," Kimberly said by way of a greeting. "We were going to order take out for you, but I wasn't sure you'd be here. Or what you'd like."

Zoe shot a look at Tom. It didn't surprise her that Kimberly hadn't thought to bring something home for her only child—and Zoe didn't for one minute buy the two offered excuses—but Tom? He not only knew precisely what Zoe liked to eat, he also usually remembered she existed. Usually. But from the dark expression on his face, she sensed the lack of a doggy bag wasn't entirely accidental. "That's all right. I'm not hungry anyway."

Kimberly brushed past Zoe. Tom followed. And he continued to follow as his wife headed straight to the stairs.

"Wait," Zoe called after them. "I wanted to ask you both something."

Kimberly let out an audible sigh, but Tom wheeled to face Zoe. The look on his face was one she'd rarely seen before. It made her step back.

"I think I've answered enough questions for one day," he growled. "In fact, I think I've answered enough questions for my entire lifetime."

Zoe frowned. She looked at her mother. Had Kimberly been grilling him about something? But Tom's anger wasn't directed at his wife. "I don't understand," Zoe said.

Kimberly stood with one foot on the bottom step and planted a hand on her hip. "Your friend, the police chief, was here."

"Pete?"

"You have more than one police chief friend?" Tom snapped.

Zoe stuttered. "Uh, no. What was he doing here?"

Tom placed his hands on Kimberly's shoulders and gently edged her back from the stairs. "You talk to her," he told his wife. "I've had all I can take for one day."

Zoe watched in stunned silence as her stepdad, the man who ordinarily championed her when her mother was too self-absorbed to bother, disappeared up the staircase.

Kimberly appeared only slightly less uncomfortable with the turn of events. "So," she said, dragging the word out. "Does your police chief always travel with an escort of senior citizens or only when he has a broken leg?"

Senior citizens? "Oh. His father's staying with him."

"Yes, I know. Harry. Charming gentleman. Can't say the same for the son." Kimberly breezed across the room, waving a hand over her shoulder like a flag, beckoning Zoe to follow. "Do you have anything to drink? Wine? Brandy?"

Zoe scrambled after her. "No. I might have a couple beers in the back of the fridge." From the last time she'd hosted the poker game.

"Beer?" Kimberly wrinkled her nose. "Oh, well. In a pinch, I guess it'll do." She pushed through the swinging door to the kitchen.

The rebound of the heavy oak door almost slammed it into Zoe's nose, but she caught it in time.

Kimberly raked through the refrigerator, emerging with two bottles. She held one out to Zoe, who waved it away. Kimberly replaced one and unscrewed the cap from the other.

When was the last time Zoe had seen her mother drink a beer? Never. "Mom? Are you all right?"

Kimberly reached into a cupboard for a glass and poured the amber brew into it. "No. I don't think I am."

Zoe sat on the stool she kept next to the antique Hoosier cabinet. "What's wrong?"

Kimberly gave a short laugh and took a sip. She made a face as she swallowed. "You have to ask? This hasn't exactly been a dream vacation, you know. I didn't want to come. It was Tom who insisted."

Zoe already knew that much, but hearing again that her mother had not wanted to come see her still hurt. "I'm sorry it's such a chore to spend time with your daughter," she said making no effort to hide her sarcasm.

Kimberly set the glass down hard on the counter. "That's not it, and you know it."

Zoe knew no such thing and hiked an eyebrow at her mother.

"Oh, Zoe." Kimberly blew out a disgusted breath. "It's not you I don't want to see. It's this place."

"My house?" Zoe knew that wasn't what her mother meant, but her inner obstinate teen had momentarily reared its ugly head.

"No, not your house." Kimberly swung an arm in an all-encompassing circle. "Vance Township. Monongahela County. Pennsylvania. There are just too many memories here."

"I'm sorry you hated your life here with me and Dad," Zoe said through clenched teeth.

Kimberly glared at her. "Stop being petulant." She sighed and picked up her glass again. "I loved my life here. I loved Gary. I loved you." Kimberly took a sip, shooting a look at Zoe over the rim of the glass. "I still do."

Zoe's eyes burned, and she blinked hard, swallowing against the lump that suddenly rose in her throat.

"Everything was just about perfect back then." Kimberly gazed at the liquid in her glass as if she could see her past in it. "I was married to the love of my life. I had a beautiful daughter. Wonderful friends. A lovely home. And then in the blink of an eye, everything fell apart."

"The accident," Zoe said softly.

Kimberly nodded.

Zoe's mouth had gone dry, and she wished she hadn't turned down the beer. "Mom, about the accident—"

"Don't start on that again, Zoe."

Zoe opened her mouth to argue, but reconsidered. Her mother was reminiscing about her dad and their lives together. Maybe…"Mom, before the accident, you said everything was perfect?"

Kimberly took a sip. Held it in her mouth and appeared to think back. Then she swallowed and licked her lips. "About as close to perfect as you can get, I imagine."

Zoe chewed her lip. "Did Dad act…differently at any point?"

"What do you mean?"

"Did he act strange? Scared? Did you get the feeling he was keeping secrets?"

"Scared? Secrets? No." Kimberly set the glass down again, gentler this time. "Why are you asking?"

Zoe slid off the stool and took a step closer to her mother. "Did he…did he testify in any court proceedings shortly before the accident?"

"No. Zoe, what are you getting at?"

She put a hand on her mother's arm. "Just listen to me for a moment, okay? Don't argue, just hear me out. You never saw his body—"

"Oh, for crying out loud."

Zoe held up a hand. "Just listen."

Kimberly frowned but closed her mouth.

"Could something have happened before the accident that might have put Dad's life or *our* lives in danger? Could he have seen something he shouldn't have?" Zoe locked her gaze hard on her mother's eyes. "Could he possibly have faked his death and gone into the witness protection program?"

The swinging door slammed open. Zoe spun around to find Tom standing there. He no longer looked angry. He looked exhausted.

"Witness protection?" He sounded even more tired than he looked. "You have to be kidding."

"Zoe," Kimberly said, her voice gentle. "This has gone on too long. You're taking it too far. Gary...your dad...is dead. He wasn't involved in anything that would put him or us in any kind of danger. There was no trial. He didn't see something he shouldn't. There was nothing."

Tom stepped up behind Zoe and rested both hands on her shoulders, giving them a gentle squeeze. "Your mother's right, Sweet Pea. You need to let this go."

Zoe turned to face him and looked up into a face that seemed to have aged twenty years in the last two days. "I can't. I *need* to know."

"There's nothing to know." He pressed his mouth into a tight thin line and shook his head. "Your mother was right about something else, too. We shouldn't have come. It's only stirred up a lot of ideas in your head." His gaze shifted over Zoe's head to Kimberly and a look passed between them. The kind of unspoken communication that comes with being married for so long.

Kimberly touched Zoe's hand with an awkwardness that embodied her lack of practice. "Tom and I were talking over dinner. We're going to take an earlier flight home."

Zoe looked back and forth between them.

"Tomorrow if we can," Tom said.

Zoe stared at him, stunned.

Kimberly dumped what remained of her beer into the sink. Without another word, she and Tom left Zoe alone in her kitchen.

Tomorrow. How was she going to get the answers she needed by tomorrow?

NINETEEN

Pete had planned on going into his office early the next morning in spite of being on medical leave. But Harry refused to be rushed, and Pete's foot slowed him down more than he'd anticipated. Damned crutches. By the time he called Kevin to drive them up the hill to the station, the clock read noon and the thermometer on his porch had inched past ninety.

Nancy, Pete's police secretary, gave him a forced smile when he mentioned letting Harry hang out with her. Again. Rather than wear out his father's welcome and risk losing yet another secretary, Pete decided to set up shop in the conference room and asked Kevin to find something for Harry to watch on the television they kept in one corner.

With Harry occupied, Pete instructed Kevin to drag out the white board. This whole damned mess was getting more and more complicated, and Pete needed to see everything laid out in front of him. He sank into one of the chairs and propped his foot up on the conference table. From there, he directed Kevin to write out the names of the cases, new and old, across the top. James Engle (COD: Undetermined). Marvin Kroll (Shooting Victim). Gary Chambers (Accidental Death, Named in Letter). Miller Brothers (Murder/Suicide).

Pete leaned back and studied the board. Gary Chambers didn't really belong up there, but Pete didn't like all the questions being raised by that letter. Chambers stayed. "Now," Pete said, "under James Engle, write Tom Jackson, Kimberly Jackson—"

Kevin shot a questioning look at his boss. "*Mrs.* Jackson?"

Pete shrugged. "Engle wrote her a letter shortly before he died. For some reason, Kimberly Jackson was on the man's mind."

Kevin nodded and added the name.

"Wilford Engle," Pete went on.

"Next of kin," Kevin said.

"Right. And Carl Loomis."

"Found the body."

"Under Marvin Kroll, write Tom Jackson and Patsy Greene." Pete scowled at that short list. He was painfully lacking suspects or witnesses in the Kroll shooting.

Pete had Kevin jot Tom Jackson, Carl Loomis, and James Engle under Gary Chambers' name. He finished by adding Tom Jackson, James Engle, and Unknown Female in the Miller Brothers' column. Who was this mystery woman the two siblings had fought over?

A knock at the open conference room door interrupted Pete's study of the names. He looked up to find Zoe standing there.

Kevin shot Pete a covert glance and nudged the white board with one foot, angling it away from Zoe's line of sight. "Hey, Zoe," the young officer said with a too-big grin.

The kid would never survive in one of their poker games.

Kevin cleared his throat. "Chief, I'm gonna go work on my reports."

Pete held a stern face. "You do that." After Kevin had left and closed the door, Pete turned his attention to Zoe. Attired in her work uniform, she appeared strictly professional. But for a fleeting moment, his thoughts of her drifted into the strictly unprofessional category. He shook them off. "You're not on duty yet, are you?"

"No." She was scowling in the direction of the white board. "My shift starts at four, but I need to make a few stops before I get there."

Harry turned from his television show. "Well, hello, Sunshine."

Zoe smiled. "Hi, Harry. What are you watching?"

"Darned if I know." He made a sour face. "Some young pretty boy talking about movie actors like they were real stars. None of them come close to the likes of John Wayne. Or Marilyn Monroe."

Pete sighed. "You can change the channel, Pop."

"No, it's fine." Harry went back to viewing the show, even without the Duke on the screen.

Zoe shifted from one foot to the other.

Pete motioned to a chair. "Have a seat."

She shook her head. "I'm not gonna be here that long."

He crossed his arms. "Then why don't you just tell me what's wrong." He knew, but he wanted to hear it from her.

"You came to the house yesterday to talk to my folks."

Yep. That's what Pete thought. "I did."

She fixed him with a look and raised a questioning eyebrow.

"Tom's name kept coming up. I wanted to ask him about a few things."

"Like what?"

Pete detected a sense of urgency in Zoe's voice and in her eyes. "The usual stuff. Zoe, what's wrong? Did he say something to you?"

She pressed her lips together into a thin line and flopped into the chair she'd refused a moment ago. "They're leaving."

"Leaving?"

She gave quick nod. "If the flights out today weren't all booked, they'd already be gone. Mom got them on stand-by for tomorrow. They're going back to Florida."

Pete mulled that one over.

"What did you say to them to make them leave?" Zoe demanded.

He wondered the same thing. Had one of his questions hit too close to home? He glanced at the white board.

Zoe followed his gaze. She narrowed her eyes at him and rose, crossing to where she could see the board. "What on earth? Pete, why do you have Tom's name listed under every case?"

Damn. "I told you. His name keeps coming up."

"And my mom?" Zoe swung around to look at Pete as if he'd somehow betrayed her. "Pete, Mom and Tom weren't even here when James Engle died."

"Engle addressed that letter to your mom. And he and Tom Jackson were friends who'd had a falling out at some point. Just because they're listed up there doesn't make them suspects." Something occurred to Pete, and he pulled out his notebook, flipping back through the pages. "By the way, what time did you pick your mom and stepdad up at the airport Saturday morning?"

Zoe seemed lost in thought, trying to make sense of Tom Jackson's name linked to all four cases. She gave her head a quick shake. "Um, Saturday morning? I didn't. They surprised me by taking an earlier flight and rented a car at the airport. They got to the farm around seven-thirty. I was still in the barn cleaning stalls."

Pete scowled. "Why did I think you'd picked them up?"

"Probably because I was supposed to. At ten."

Something whispered in the back of Pete's brain, but he couldn't quite grasp it.

"But, Pete," Zoe said, "it was still *after* Engle died."

"I know. I told you. Just because they're on the board doesn't make them suspects."

She continued to stare at the list of names, an odd, intense glint in her eyes.

"Zoe? What's going on?"

She blinked, as if coming out from under another spell, and she brushed a hand across her eyes. "I wanted to ask for your help with something."

He knew that wasn't what had been weighing on her mind as she studied the white board, but he decided against pressing it. For now. "What can I do for you?"

She took a deep breath. Let it out. "I was talking to Wayne Baronick yesterday about my dad. Wayne mentioned something I hadn't thought about." She met Pete's gaze. "What if my dad saw something or was involved in something." Her gaze became even more intense. "What if he faked his death and went into the witness protection program?"

Her words had come tumbling out of her mouth so fast, Pete had to take a moment to process what she'd said. "*Wayne?*" When had she run into him? And when had they gotten to be on a first name basis? "Witness protection? Zoe—"

"Just hear me out." She planted her hands on the table and leaned toward him. "I kept wondering why Dad wouldn't have let Mom or me know where he was all these years, but if he thought we'd be in danger? Yeah, he'd do it. He'd keep his identity and location a secret to keep us safe."

"*Did* he see something back then?" Pete asked, pondering this new theory.

"I don't know. I don't remember anything, but I was just a kid. I asked my mom, but she thinks I'm grasping at straws."

Pete didn't reply.

"You think so, too."

He hiked an eyebrow at her.

She straightened and folded her arms. "*Wayne* doesn't think I'm crazy."

Wayne again. Pete sighed. "And what do you think I can do about it?"

Zoe came forward again. "How can I find out? Who do I ask? Where do I start looking?"

Pete gazed into her eyes. The eager eyes of a child on Christmas morning. And Pete was the Grinch. "Zoe, witness protection—WitSec— is run by the U.S. Marshalls, and they do their job. I hate to tell you, but if your dad was in the program, there's no way the feds would give you any information on his whereabouts."

The excitement melted out of her. "But couldn't you do some digging?"

Pete shook his head. "They wouldn't give me any more than they'd give you. There's a reason WitSec exists. If the feds started giving out information on subjects, the entire program would be compromised."

Zoe slumped into one of the chairs.

Pete lowered his foot to the floor, ignoring the sharp pain that shot up his leg. Gritting his teeth, he stood, hopped to the chair next to Zoe, and flopped into it. He reached over and closed his hand over hers. "I know you don't want to hear this, but I don't believe your dad is still alive. If I did—" He squeezed her hand and lowered his voice. "If I did, I'd move heaven and earth to find him for you."

She met his gaze, her eyes gleaming with unshed tears. Swallowing hard, she rose. "I have to keep looking." Her voice sounded moist, strangled. "But thanks."

Pete watched her go. Damn Baronick. Why couldn't he keep his bright ideas to himself?

Across the room, a chair creaked. Pete glanced over his shoulder. Harry had turned away from the TV and was giving Pete the same look he used to give him when Pete had tormented Nadine as a child. "That girl just asked for your help," Harry growled. "And you sent her packing. What kind of numbskull move was that?"

* * *

Zoe had left home hours early for work with the intention of finding answers. The Vance Township Police Station had been her first stop, and Pete had been no help at all. Why had she been surprised? He hadn't been the least bit supportive of her quest to find her dad. Pete kept insisting the letter meant something else. Or nothing at all.

Yet, he'd asked Wayne to look into her dad's car crash. What was up with that?

She climbed into her pickup and headed for her next stop, the Volunteer Fire Department. The only person manning the station was a lanky young rookie who told her Bruce Yancy wouldn't be in for forty-five minutes. Rather than sit around and wait, Zoe moved to what she'd intended to put off until last.

Roth Funeral Home stood at the end of an old residential area in Phillipsburg. Zoe parked in the empty lot across the street from the well-kept red brick Colonial. Her throat tightened. The last time she'd been inside that building was last winter following the death of Ted Bassi, Sylvia's son and Zoe's best friend's husband. His murder and the aftermath had nearly destroyed the entire family. Right now, Zoe would give about anything to have Rose to talk to. But she'd taken the kids off the grid somewhere out west for the summer—to heal.

Zoe shut off the ignition and sat in the truck cab until the sweltering heat encroached on her, forcing her to finally step outside. She fought to swallow the lump rising in her throat as she passed through the front door into an atrium, sickly sweet with the scent of floral arrangements.

A stout young woman with mousy hair and wire-rim glasses appeared from a back office. She extended her hand. "Good afternoon. I'm Judy Roth. How may I help you today?"

Zoe accepted the hand and introduced herself. "I'm looking for information about a burial you folks handled twenty-seven years ago. Is there anyone around who might have worked here then?"

Judy's eyes widened. "Twenty-seven years ago? Oh. Our computer records only go back twelve years or so. It would take me some time to go through the old paper files."

"Thanks, but what I was really hoping for was to talk to whoever actually prepared the body in question."

"Twenty-seven years ago?" Judy repeated, her voice weighted with a heavy load of doubt. "That would either have been my father or Mr. Kurtz." She motioned for Zoe to follow her back into the office where Judy settled behind a polished cherry desk. Zoe took a seat across from her. "You may recall that Roth Funeral Home used to be Roth and Kurtz Funeral Home."

"I remember." Zoe might have avoided the building as much as possible, but Mr. Roth and Mr. Kurtz had been long-time residents of Philipsburg and she'd encountered them at various functions and businesses around town over the years.

"Mr. Kurtz retired six years ago and moved to Arizona."

"What about your father? Would he be willing to talk to me?"

"I'm sure he would." Judy smiled sadly. "If he were able to. I'm afraid he's in a nursing home over in Steubenville. He's had a number of small strokes and can't communicate anymore."

A sharp rap brought Pete's attention to Detective Wayne Baronick grinning at him from the conference room doorway. "Speak of the devil," Pete grumbled.

Baronick didn't wait for any further invitation and ambled in. "Now is that any way to talk to the man who's been doing your legwork while you just sit around?" He set a cup of Starbucks coffee and an evidence envelope in front of Pete.

Harry swung away from the television to inspect the newcomer. "Who are you?"

"Pop, you remember Detective Baronick? You met at the morgue."

"Hey, Mr. Adams." Baronick gave him a quick salute.

Harry had that all-too-familiar vacant look on his face. "Morgue? I ain't dead yet."

Baronick chuckled and stepped across the room to extend a hand and an introduction to Harry, as if they had never met before. Pete rubbed the pain in his forehead. How was it that everyone else could be so at ease with his dad's mental decline and not him? Pete knew the answer. It wasn't *their* dad going through it.

Harry went back to his TV show, and Baronick dropped into a

chair across the table from Pete. The detective pointed at the envelope. "Aren't you going to open it?"

Pete took a sip of the coffee first. Then he read the notations on the envelope. He glanced at Baronick who laced his fingers behind his head and gave Pete a self-satisfied smile.

Pete set the coffee down and carefully dumped the lead slug into his palm. "Froats said this was floating around somewhere."

"*Somewhere* being the courthouse basement. I ran into your girlfriend while I was there."

"Zoe?" That answered one thing that had been nagging Pete.

"You have another girlfriend I don't know about?"

He ignored the question. "What was she doing there?"

"Looking into her dad's accident. Same as you'd asked me to do."

"Did you find anything?"

"Not much. Accident report states Chambers was run off the road by a drunk driver and the car caught fire. And I understand you've already heard that Carl Loomis was the driver of the other car."

Pete dropped the bullet back into the envelope. "Yeah. Anything else?"

"Coroner reported COD as smoke inhalation. But—get this—there was no autopsy done at the request of the family."

"Kimberly Chambers Jackson made the request?" Pete's gaze shot to the white board.

"That would be my guess."

Pete looked back at Baronick. "I need you to do me two favors."

The detective shrugged. "Sure. If I can."

Pete pointed to the white board. "Write Kimberly Jackson in Gary Chambers' column."

"Easy enough. What else?"

"Drive me over to Carl Loomis' place."

TWENTY

With a promise from Judy Roth to dig up the funeral home's file on Gary Chambers, Zoe backtracked to the Vance Township V.F.D. to meet with Bruce Yancy. After striking out twice, her level of optimism had plummeted.

The same gangly young firefighter Zoe had talked to earlier buffed an already spotless red and white engine and waved her toward the fire chief's cramped office just off the truck bay. Boisterous laughter punctuated with some colorful language drifted out to her as she approached the door.

Yancy looked up with a smile when she knocked. "I heard you wanted to talk to me. Don't tell me you can't make it Saturday night."

Poker night. And this was Yancy's week to host the game. Zoe gave him a sheepish grin. "Sorry, Yance. I'm on duty."

Yancy's visitor, who had his back to her, turned with a grunt. "You remember my old pal, our former police chief, don't you?" Yancy said.

Warren Froats.

Zoe tensed. "Of course." She still hadn't decided if the man was part of the cover-up to help her father fake his death or was merely incompetent.

"So, Ms. Chambers, you're one of the suckers in the infamous poker circle?" Froats said with a gruff chortle.

Yancy choked out a short laugh. "I don't know who's the sucker here. She won twenty bucks from me over the last two weeks, and I intend to get it back." He shook a finger at Zoe. "Bring a pager. You can be on call from my house."

"We'll see." Zoe eyed Froats. She'd have preferred speaking with

Yancy alone, but Froats seemed quite comfortable and didn't appear to have any plans to leave. So be it. No way was she going to put this off again. She turned to Yancy. "I was hoping you could answer a question for me."

"Promise you'll come to the game Saturday night, and I'll tell you anything you want to know."

She forced a grin. "Promise none of our good citizens will get sick or injured and you've got a deal."

He gave one quick nod of his bulldog head. "You got it. What d'ya need?"

"You probably don't remember, but my dad was supposedly killed in a drunk driving accident—"

"I remember," Yancy said. "What's it been? Twenty? Twenty-five years ago?"

Zoe opened her mouth to answer, but he held up a hand to stop her.

"No. It was twenty-seven years ago. I know because I just celebrated twenty-seven years with the department, and that was the first really bad call I'd been on." Yancy shook his head. "Sorry, Zoe. You just don't forget the ones like that."

"Can you tell me about it?"

He gave her a long hard stare. "Why on God's green earth would you want to hear about that after all these years? Or ever for that matter?"

Her throat had gone dry and threatened to constrict. "I don't want to. I need to. No one's ever told me what really happened."

Froats' chair squeaked in protest as he shifted in it. "As I recall, I told you what really happened only a few days ago."

Zoe cringed under the old chief's scrutiny. Now she understood why he'd been so effective. That evil-eye of his would scare straight all but the most hardened criminal. "I know you did. But I still have questions."

"Then ask them," Froats barked.

She stood a little taller. "Fine. Is there any chance...Did my dad fake his own death?"

The tiny office fell silent. Both men exchanged stunned looks before turning back to her.

"Fake his own death?" Froats sounded aghast. "Why would you wonder that?"

Zoe considered telling him about the letter but remembered how Pete had cut her off the last time. "I have my reasons."

Froats crossed his arms in front of his barrel chest. "I'd like to hear them."

Zoe shot a glance at Yancy, who seemed to be struggling with a memory. She should have waited to speak to him alone. Too late now. And since he wanted to know, this might be the perfect time to tell him. "I did what you said. I dug up the coroner's report on the accident."

"And?"

"There was no autopsy."

"So?"

"From everything I've learned, the body in that car—"

"Your dad's body," Froats said.

"The body in that car," Zoe repeated with emphasis, "was burnt so badly no one could identify it except by personal effects, which could easily have been planted."

Froats face turned crimson. "Planted?"

"The cause of death in the coroner's report stated smoke inhalation, but with no autopsy, that was nothing more than a guess. Everything about the investigation was shoddy." Zoe debated whether to go on, but decided to hell with it. "Either everyone involved in the case bungled it, or they were covering up something."

Her implication wasn't lost on the retired chief. Froats climbed to his feet and took one menacing step, closing the gap between them. "You realize you're calling me incompetent."

Zoe held her ground. "You *and* the coroner at the time. Martin Dempsey, I believe."

Yancy jumped from his chair and put an arm in front of Froats, blocking him. "Zoe, you need to think this through. I saw the car and your dad's body, too."

"*A* body," she reminded Yancy. "Not necessarily my dad's." She glared up at Froats. "If you're not incompetent, that means you took part in a cover up. Was my dad involved in something back then? Did he testify against someone?"

Froats' eyes shifted slightly. His expression softened.

Yancy lowered his arm from in front of Froats and took Zoe by the shoulders. "What are you saying?"

"Witness protection."

Froats shook his head. "No."

The quiet tone of the former chief's voice startled Zoe. She'd expected denial. Of course he wouldn't come out and admit anything. What she hadn't expected was the troubled creases on his forehead.

"Your father didn't testify against anyone or do anything else like that." Froats lowered into his chair with a grunt. "But I do remember something, now that you mention it."

Zoe shrugged free of Yancy's grasp, locking her gaze on Froats. "What?"

Froats stroked his shaggy beard. "I'd forgotten all about it. Gary Chambers had been asking a lot of questions in those last few weeks before the accident."

Zoe's pulse quickened. "Asking who? About what?"

"I got the impression he'd been asking anyone who might know anything." Froats lifted his gaze to meet Zoe's. "About that other old case. The Miller brothers."

Zoe braced a hand on Yancy's desk. "What about the Miller brothers?"

"I'm not really sure. He'd called me the afternoon before the accident. Your dad had some questions he wanted to ask me. I assume that's what it was about, but he wouldn't say over the phone."

"You assume?" Zoe wanted to grab the man by his shirt collar and shake him. How could she get through to him how important this was to her?

The creases between Froats' brows deepened. "We never got the chance to talk. I'd told him to meet me for coffee at Parson's."

Zoe's eyes fogged as the weight of his words pressed down on her. "You mean..."

Froats let out a loud breath. "He never made it. Your father was killed on his way to see me."

"What do you hope to accomplish at Loomis' place?" Baronick wheeled his unmarked county sedan onto a narrow secondary road. The tires crunched on the surface, kicking up a cloud of dust. The open windows did little to cool the interior, baked by the afternoon heat.

Pete glanced over his shoulder at Harry in the backseat. His old man seemed mesmerized by the scenery flashing by his window, undaunted by the hot breeze mussing his white hair. "Loomis is another one with connections to more than one of these cases." Pete powered the window up to cut back on the wind in Harry's face. "Not only did Loomis discover James Engle's body, he also drove the car that ran Gary Chambers off the road."

"Let me guess," Baronick said. "Loomis was drinking buddies with one or both of the Miller brothers, too."

"I don't know. You can ask him when we get there." Pete removed his ball cap and pressed one shirt sleeve to his forehead, blotting the sweat. "Don't you believe in using air conditioning?"

"It's broken."

Figures. "By the way, don't you use your head for anything besides holding up your hat?"

Baronick jerked around shooting a puzzled glance at Pete. "What do you mean?"

Pete tugged his cap back on. "What did you think you were doing, feeding the idea of witness protection to Zoe?"

"Oh." Baronick shrugged. "She couldn't think of a reason a father would fake his own death and not tell his family. That's what came to my mind."

"Not 'a' father. *Her* father. And there's no evidence Gary Chambers was involved in anything that qualified for witness protection."

"So tell her that."

"I've tried, damn it. You don't know her like I do. She's worse than a dog with a bone where her father's concerned. If she gets an idea in her head, she'll never let it go."

Baronick slowed as they approached a crossroad. "Which way?"

"Left."

The detective cranked the steering wheel one-handed, the other arm hanging out the window. "From what I can tell, Zoe's no fool. If she thinks something's not quite right about her father's death, I'm inclined to give some credence to it." Baronick grinned. "But as you said, I don't *know* her like you do."

Pete bit back a retort to the innuendo. "She's no fool, but she's not thinking like an intelligent adult right now. She's back to being a desperate, lonely eight-year-old who just lost her dad."

"Son?" Harry's quivering voice was barely audible over the rush of the wind through the window and the crunch of gravel. "Are we home yet? I'm hungry."

"Sorry, Pop. We have a stop to make first."

"Okay." Harry's voice sounded much like that lonely eight-year-old Pete had been describing.

"Mind dropping us off back at my house when we wrap this up?" Pete asked Baronick.

"No problem."

They topped a hill, and Pete gazed out at one of the township's stunning vistas. Rolling farmland dropped away from them, dotted with trees and Hereford cattle. A nineteenth century farmhouse overlooked a cluster of sheds, while a massive barn stood sentry over a pond.

In contrast to the landscape that probably hadn't changed in more than a hundred years, a pretentious, modern mansion sat on the far hillside, probably benefiting from all the contemporary amenities while enjoying a view of the past.

A nagging voice had been whispering in Pete's brain and now began to shout. That letter. And the question Harry had latched onto. What had Gary been trying to make right? And that house he'd built for Kimberly while doing only "okay" with his appliance store.

Pete pulled his phone from his pocket while pointing to a mailbox ahead. "That's Loomis' drive. Turn here." Pete pulled up one of his contacts and hit *send*.

Baronick cast him a questioning glance.

Kevin picked up on the second ring.

"Look into Gary Chambers' life insurance coverage," Pete said.

There was a moment of dead air on the phone. "Gary Chambers? Hasn't he been dead for like twenty-five years?"

Pete didn't reply. Kevin knew full well how long Chambers had been dead.

"Um," the young cop finally said. "Chief? How am I supposed to do that?"

Baronick's sedan bucked and bounced over the ruts in Loomis' driveway, jarring Pete's foot and shooting searing pains all the way up to the top of his head. "You're a cop," he snapped. "Figure it out."

Pete and Baronick found Carl Loomis kneeling between his tractor and an unhitched baler. Dirt and grease streaked the farmer's sweat-soaked shirt and jeans. A cigarette dangled from his lips. He looked up with a scowl as Pete crutched toward him, Baronick on one side, Harry bringing up the rear.

"Now what d'ya want?" The cigarette bobbed around the farmer's words.

Pete didn't bother to make introductions. "I have a few more questions."

Loomis nodded at the external driveshaft spindle on the rear of the tractor. "I'm busy right now. Goddamn power take-off's busted, and if I don't get it fixed, I can't get nothing done."

Loomis was always busy, always full of excuses, and always eager to get rid of the police. Pete sighed. "I'll try to be brief."

Loomis muttered something incomprehensible, but he stood up, wiping his hands on a rag that looked even filthier. "Fire away."

"What do you know about the night Gary Chambers was killed?"

Loomis' face paled beneath its tan. He took the cigarette from his lips, letting it hang between his fingers. "I reckon you already know as much about it as I do."

"You were driving the car that hit Chambers' vehicle?"

"Yes, sir."

"And you were drunk at the time?"

After a beat, Loomis nodded. "Yes, sir. I admit all of it. I had a tendency to hit the bottle pretty hard back then."

"What can you tell me about the accident?"

"Not a goddamn thing." Loomis dropped the cigarette and ground it out with his boot. "I blacked out before it ever happened. I only know what they told me."

"What *who* told you?"

"You guys. The cops." Loomis' eyes glistened. "And Jim."

"Jim? Engle?"

"Yes, sir. I never been as sorry about nothing as I was about killing that man. I never had a drop since then. Not one drop." He slipped a pack of cigarettes from his shirt pocket and tapped one out. Pete noticed the farmer's hands shook as he lit up. "But I gotta tell you, seeing Jim's body in the barn like that the other night, about near drove me back to the bottle. Old Jim's been good to me. Hired me right after that accident. I been working for him ever since."

"But there's nothing you can tell us about the accident with Chambers? Something you might have remembered over the years?"

Loomis took a trembling drag from the cigarette. "Not a thing."

Yet another wasted trip. Pete thanked the farmer and started to maneuver a one-eighty on his crutches when Loomis called out to him.

"I did remember something else, though."

Pete turned back. "Oh?"

"You boys asked me if I seen anything suspicious around Jim's farm before he died."

Pete reached for his notebook, but Baronick snatched out his own. Good. Pete could keep both hands on his crutches. "And you remember seeing something?"

Loomis nodded. "I don't know if you'd call it suspicious, but I recall that Jim had company a couple days before he hung himself. On Wednesday."

Loomis might have found Engle's body on Friday, but the coroner had determined the time of death to be two days prior to that. *Wednesday.* "Do you have any idea who this 'company' might have been?"

"Actually, he had two different visitors. I was out cutting hay on that hill above Jim's house. Didn't think nothing of it at first, which is why I didn't say anything before. But then I heard about the shooting out at the Kroll farm. Made me remember. I saw a car parked over there in his driveway."

"What kind of car?"

"Beige. All cars look the same now."

Pete exchanged a glance with Baronick who rolled his eyes.

"It wasn't there all that long," Loomis said. "Then it was gone. I made a couple more passes when I noticed a white SUV parked in about the same spot. Ford, I think."

Great. How many white Ford SUVs were registered in Monongahela County? "Don't suppose you were able to get a license number on either of the vehicles?"

"Hell, no. I was too far away."

Pete and Baronick exchanged another look.

"Didn't need to see it for the SUV, though." Loomis took another drag on his cigarette. "I recognized the fellow that got out. It was Marvin Kroll."

Zoe closed her eyes and leaned back against the plate glass window in front of the ambulance garage. The shade cast by the building did little to lessen the early evening heat. The other members of the A Crew perched on folding chairs inside the open bay door. A pair of teenage boys skateboarded down the hill across Main Street, and the paramedics bet on their own response time to the inevitable mishap. Zoe blocked them all out, her mind crowded with questions from the conversation she'd had with Bruce Yancy and Warren Froats two hours earlier. Why had her father been digging into the deaths of her great uncles? Was it merely coincidence that he'd been involved in that so-called accident while on his way to talk to the chief of police?

A pain as sharp as a dagger pierced her heart as she realized for the first time since Pete had shown her that letter, she was toying with an alternate meaning to the words *Mrs. Jackson, your husband did not die in that car crash.* Maybe her father really was dead. Maybe someone had killed him to stop him from asking questions.

Something else gnawed at her. If Froats was right and her dad had been asking questions all over town, why hadn't Tom mentioned it to her?

From inside the ambulance bay, the tones sounded, indicating the county 9-1-1 center was calling them into service. The skateboarders' audience leaped up, dragging their chairs from in front of Medic Two. Zoe shook off her mental fog. She and Earl were up to take the call.

Tracy Nicholls, the newbie on A Crew, stuck her head out of the office door. "We've got another farm accident. Anonymous caller reports an ambulance is needed at 1482 Covered Bridge Road, one mile north of Ridge Road."

Zoe's heart kicked into high gear. "I think I know that farm. Did the caller give a name?"

"No. I told you the caller was anonymous."

"I mean the patient's name."

Tracy looked down at the call sheet in her hands. "Carl Loomis."

TWENTY-ONE

"I hope this call isn't as bad as the one last Friday," Earl said as they approached the lane to the Loomis farm.

The image of James Engle's bloated corpse hanging from the barn rafters flashed through Zoe's mind. "I don't think that's possible."

Earl swung the ambulance into the farm lane. As the rig rocked and jounced over the ruts carved by the heavy spring and early summer rains, Zoe's seatbelt was all that kept her from being tossed around the cab.

Ahead, a John Deere was parked in front of one of the farm's outbuildings. Wisps of smoke rose from what appeared to be a blackened pile of rags draped over the PTO port on the rear of the tractor.

"Better call for fire backup," Earl said. "Something's been burning. We don't want a flare up."

Zoe snatched the mic. "Control, this is Medic Two."

She didn't hear Control's response. Earl hit the brakes, throwing her forward against the shoulder harness as the ambulance skidded to a stop on the gravel.

"Shit." He slammed the shifter into park and dove from the ambulance's cab, running toward the tractor.

Zoe battled to draw a breath. A charred hand reached out from what she'd thought was a mound of burning rags.

"Medic Two? This is Control. Please respond." The voice on the radio made its way into Zoe's consciousness.

She keyed the mic. "We need police and fire response to this location. Repeat. Police and fire." She choked. "We may have a homicide."

Without waiting for Control to confirm her transmission, she grabbed the jump kit and defibrillator and pounded after Earl.

He knelt next to the still smoking body, pressing a bandana to his nose and mouth with one hand, gingerly searching for a pulse on the exposed wrist.

Cringing, Zoe glanced at the victim's face, charred beyond recognition. The stench of seared flesh and hair mingled with something chemical sent her reeling. She dropped to her knees, gagging, cramming her nose into the crook of her elbow. She nodded toward the blackened wrist Earl was palpating. "Anything?"

Wide-eyed and pale, he shook his head. "Did you call for police?" Earl's voice was muffled through his bandana.

"Yeah." Zoe tried not to breathe and failed. Turning away from Earl and the body, she retched.

Earl stood and reached down help Zoe to her feet.

"I'm all right," she insisted.

"I know you are."

"It's the smell." She'd held a man's brains in her hands one time and never so much as squirmed. But certain scents did her in. Burnt human flesh apparently was one of them.

She took a few unstable steps away from the body and surveyed the scene. The victim—she could only assume he was Carl Loomis—was mangled and contorted like a boneless ragdoll. She'd been to similar horrific accident scenes before. The spinning power take-off shaft—normally used to run mowers or bailers or other farm equipment attached to the tractor—would grab a loose piece of clothing and suck the hapless farmer in, slamming him against the equipment, often ripping off a limb. A scorched gas can lay a couple of feet away from the body along with a barely recognizable cigarette butt.

The combination told a tragic story. But something about it niggled the back of Zoe's mind.

Darkness had fallen before Pete arranged for Sylvia to sit with Harry and for Seth to drive him out to the Loomis farm. Damn foot.

Monongahela County's Crime Scene Unit was on the job. Generator-powered halogen lights had been set up in front of the barn.

In addition to the CSU's vehicle, a pair of fire trucks, an ambu-

lance, the coroner's wagon, and seven police vehicles—township, county, and state—plus his own, created a morbid circus atmosphere. Pete
started toward what was clearly the center ring.

"Do you need help, Chief?" Seth asked.

Pete waved him clear. "Go."

The young officer jogged ahead of the chief, like an eager teenager
planning to meet up with his buddies and see what the excitement was
all about. Pete, however, dreaded what awaited him. Only hours earlier, he and Baronick had stood there talking to Carl Loomis as he
worked on his tractor. Now Baronick stood in nearly the same spot,
watching the county forensic guys do their stuff.

Four of the local fire fighters climbed aboard one of the idling die-
sels as Bruce Yancy shouted orders over the rumble. The fire chief,
however, didn't join the men who were heading back to the station.

Pete finally located Zoe standing away from the action near the
tractor. She and her partner were engaged in deep conversation with
Franklin Marshall.

Zoe glanced Pete's way and blinked as though she didn't recognize
him. She looked spent, her eyes glassy, her skin ashen.

Marshall had followed her gaze. "Hey, Pete. Glad you could make
it." But there was no joy in the coroner's voice.

Pete moved to Zoe's side. She looked like she could use a hug, and
he longed to give her one. But this was neither the time nor the place.
"What have we got?"

Marshall motioned toward the tractor. "The victim was DOA.
Looks like he got an arm caught in the power take-off. Nasty business
all by itself, but then you add the burning cigarette and the gas can."
The coroner shook his head.

"Carl Loomis?" Pete asked.

"Presumably. Once I get him back to the morgue, I'll check dental
records for a positive I.D."

Zoe didn't say a word, but pressed her fingers against her mouth.

Bruce Yancy ambled up. "We're gonna head back to base."

"Did you have to put out the fire?" Pete asked.

"Nope. It'd burnt itself out by the time we got here."

"It was still smoldering when we arrived," Earl added. "So we
called for fire backup."

"No problem." Bruce patted Zoe's shoulder. "Funny thing, ain't it, Zoe? You and me talking about your dad earlier. This kind of puts me in mind of that call."

"Yeah, it's a laugh riot," Zoe said, her voice husky around her fingers.

Pete glared at the fire chief. Tact had never been the man's strong suit.

Bruce gave a quick salute and shuffled off to the remaining fire engine.

Earl put a protective arm around Zoe's shoulders. "Are you all right?"

"Yeah. I told you. It's just the smell."

"I'm gonna radio Control and put us back in service." With a nod to Pete, Earl hurried away.

Marshall heaved a deep sigh. "And I better check on the forensics guys."

Pete reached out to stop him. "Do you believe this was an accident?"

"I don't believe anything yet. Talk to me tomorrow, after the autopsy." Marshall paused and turned back to Zoe. "Which reminds me. You *will* be there tomorrow. Eight o'clock sharp."

Zoe dropped her hand from her mouth. "I'm on duty until eight."

"All right. Eight thirty. No later." Marshall trudged off toward the tractor and the body.

Finally, Pete was alone with Zoe. Or as alone as possible in the middle of a potential homicide investigation. "What was that all about?"

Zoe shook her head. "I made a deal with the devil, and the devil's name is Franklin Marshall."

Pete decided against asking her to elaborate. He had a more sensitive question in mind. "You talked to Yancy about your father?"

"Yeah. After I talked to you, I stopped at the funeral home and spoke with Judy Roth, but she wasn't able to tell me anything. So I went to see Yancy." Zoe fell silent for a moment. "Warren Froats was there."

"Oh?"

"I wanted to find out if Yancy remembered anything about my

dad's accident. You know. Anything more than what Froats had told us."

"And did he?" The fact that Zoe had referred to it as her dad's *accident* wasn't lost on Pete.

"Yancy said it wasn't the kind of thing he'd forget." Zoe's gaze drifted toward the tractor. "I guess it wouldn't be. The body burnt like that." Her voice cracked.

Pete took both crutches in one hand and pulled Zoe against him with his free arm. For a brief moment, she clung to him. Buried her face against his chest. Took a few deep, ragged breaths.

But then she steeled herself and stepped back. "I'm all right."

He wasn't buying it. "You should get out of here."

"There's something else." She brushed a hand over her face and looked up at him. "Froats told me that my dad was on his way to see him when he died."

"Your dad was on his way to see Froats? Why?"

"Apparently Dad had been asking questions all over town about the deaths of my great uncles. Froats told me he'd called and said he wanted to talk to him about something, but wouldn't elaborate over the phone. Froats assumed it was about Denver and Vernon Miller."

Over by the barn, Earl was helping Marshall drag the cot from the coroner's van. "Seems like asking and answering questions can be hazardous to your health," Pete mused.

Zoe gave him a perplexed look. "What?"

"Wayne and I were here earlier today talking to Loomis."

She stared at him a long moment, her face still, but Pete sensed a whirlwind of activity behind her eyes. "Why?" she asked.

Pete hesitated. "I wanted to find out if he remembered anything about the accident."

"My dad's accident?"

"That's the one."

"And did he?"

"He maintained he didn't remember a thing about it."

"That's not unusual. Especially if he suffered any kind of head trauma during the crash."

"Or if he was drunk."

"Which everyone agrees he was." Zoe narrowed her eyes at Pete.

"I'd given up hope finding out anything from him. I'm surprised you wasted your time questioning him again."

"I didn't say it was a waste of time."

"He told you something?"

"Not about the accident. But he remembered seeing a couple of cars over at James Engle's place last Wednesday."

Zoe's eyes shifted. "Wednesday?"

"The day Marshall thinks Engle died. Loomis didn't recognize the one car. But the other belonged to your landlord."

Pete watched Zoe try to process the information.

"But I remember Mr. Kroll telling me he never had much use for James Engle," she said. "Why would he go to visit him?"

"You talked to him about Engle?"

She nodded. "When we were unloading hay with Tom and Patsy. But he wouldn't tell me why he didn't like him. Didn't want to say anything bad about the dead."

Pete watched as Earl and Marshall lifted the body bag containing Carl Loomis' charred remains onto the cot. "Has Mr. Kroll regained consciousness?"

"Not last I heard, no."

Damn. "Do you think *Mrs.* Kroll would be up to answering some questions?"

Zoe met Pete's gaze with a scowl. "I can ask her."

He shook his head. "That's all right. I'll call her tomorrow. There's something else I want you to think about."

She raised a questioning eyebrow at him.

"I know you want to believe that your father's still alive out there somewhere—"

She reached out and touched his arm. "No." Her voice was little more than a coarse whisper. "I did want to believe that. But now that I've talked to Froats and Yancy." She shook her head. "Dad was asking questions. If he was really on his way to see the chief of police that night..."

"Someone might have wanted to shut him up," Pete finished the sentence Zoe struggled with.

"You think so, too?" she said.

"I think it's a possibility. And there's something I'd like to do—

with your permission—that might just tell us for sure."

"Anything." She studied him. "What?"

"I'd like to exhume your father's body."

The background chatter of emergency responders, the throbbing grumble of the generators running the halogen lights, the static and squawk of radio transmissions, all fell away into muffled silence as Zoe struggled to grasp Pete's words.

Exhume her father's body?

She hadn't considered that option. Or had she? Maybe she'd thought of it briefly and dismissed it as—what? Too extreme? Too gruesome? Too...absolute? She'd never seen her dad's body after the accident. Did she truly want to see it now? If his body was there, it would prove that he was really dead. And she'd have to come to grips with the loss once and for all. But that's what she'd wanted, right?

"Zoe?" Pete's voice cut through the veil of introspection.

She met his concerned gaze. "You think my dad was murdered?" Her voice stumbled over that last word. Considering the possibility was one thing. Pete giving credence to it was another matter altogether.

"I think there are too many unanswered questions dating back to the Miller brothers."

"You want to exhume their bodies, too?"

The corner of Pete's mouth twitched as if he were tempted to smile had the circumstances been different. "Let's start with your father and go from there."

Zoe thought about her mother. Kimberly, who couldn't face seeing the body twenty-seven years ago, would undoubtedly raise holy hell over the proposition of reopening old wounds. "Mom will have a fit. But she and Tom are leaving for Florida tomorrow anyway."

Pete frowned. "What time is their flight?"

What had Kimberly told her? "I think around 10:30 a.m. I know they were planning to leave for the airport right after breakfast."

The frown deepened, and Pete turned away from her, apparently watching Franklin and Earl load Carl Loomis' body into the coroner's van.

Suddenly she remembered the white board back at the police station and realized why he'd asked. "You think Tom had something to do with my dad's accident."

Pete didn't reply.

Which was all the answer she needed. She braced to chastise him for thinking such a thing. And yet, hadn't she had the same fears? Tom had been acting strangely ever since they'd arrived. He'd avoided her questions. He'd been downright surly with her on more than one occasion. And he'd completely neglected to mention that her dad had been asking questions about her great uncles' deaths shortly before his own.

The heavy night air sent a shiver through her. "How soon can we get Dad's body exhumed?"

TWENTY-TWO

The only way Zoe could make it to the morgue in Brunswick by eight-thirty in the morning would be to leave the ambulance garage in Philipsburg promptly at eight, hit zero traffic, and break a few speed limits along the way. Franklin knew the county well enough that he had to realize he'd made an impossible request. So when Zoe managed to get off duty a few minutes early, she figured she could make a brief stop at home, be a little late for Carl Loomis' autopsy, and still not get into too much trouble.

Although the sky had been clear at dawn two hours earlier, by the time Zoe parked behind the farmhouse, clouds had rolled in and transformed from a dull, leaden gray, to roiling black with flickers of lightning to the west—the leading edge of a cold front the weather station had been forecasting. Wind threatened to snatch Zoe's ball cap from her head as she stepped out of her truck, but the air was still thick with humidity.

Tom's rental car remained parked where it had been last night. Part of her wished he and Kimberly had left for the airport already, but Zoe wanted to talk to her stepfather—needed to talk to him. She intended to get answers. No matter what.

She stepped into the enclosed back porch and noticed Mr. Kroll's Muck Boots and a pair of Mrs. Kroll's garden Crocs sitting side-by-side on a faded rug next to their door. The old couple had been inseparable in all the time Zoe had known them. A heavy sadness settled over her at the thought one of them might never wear those boots again.

Bracing to deal with something she *did* have control over, she stepped into her half of the house.

Tom and Kimberly's luggage was lined up inside the door. Jade had made a nest on one of the bags and lifted her head to acknowledge Zoe's entrance. The cat yawned and tucked her nose under a paw, returning to her nap. Merlin was nowhere to be seen, leading Zoe to hope he hadn't packed himself *inside* one of the bags.

Zoe's round dining table was set for two. Not three. The aroma of coffee wafted from the kitchen along with the murmur of conversation barely louder than a whisper. Zoe side-stepped the suitcases and carry-ons, intent on storming into the other room. But the door between them swung open and Kimberly breezed through, coffee pot in hand.

"Oh." She stopped short, forcing Tom, who followed carrying a pair of steaming plates heaped with eggs and sausage, to dance an awkward jig or risk rear-ending her. "We didn't expect you."

Zoe glanced at the dual place-settings. "Of course not." She made no effort to disguise the annoyance in her voice. "Why would you? It's not like I live here or anything."

Kimberly huffed and reached for one of the cups. "You're too old to act like a spoiled brat. I made plenty of coffee. And there are more eggs and sausage if you want some."

Being called a brat by her mother did nothing to ease Zoe's mood. She eyed the plates Tom set on the table. Prompted by the aroma, her stomach let out a rumble. She pressed a hand against her belly to shush it. "I don't have time. I have to attend an autopsy this morning."

Tom shot a curious glance her way, but didn't say a word.

Kimberly's face had soured. "Zoe," she said sharply, "I do not want such talk at the meal table." She slid into one of the chairs and picked up her fork.

Ignoring her mother, Zoe kept an eye on Tom who settled his tall frame into the chair across from his wife. "Carl Loomis died last night."

The fork clattered from Kimberly's fingers to the plate. "Carl Loomis?"

Tom's expression remained as still as a mask.

Zoe considered taking a seat, but decided she held a slight advantage if she remained standing. "It's been a bad week around here. First James Engle. Then Mr. Kroll. Now Carl Loomis."

Tom sipped his coffee. Swallowed. Picked up a napkin and wiped his lip. "How did Loomis die?" He kept his gaze on his plate.

The tightness in Zoe's gut turned from hunger to dread as she realized she was thinking of her stepfather as a suspect. How much to tell him? God. Could Pete be right? "His arm got caught in his tractor's power take-off."

Tom buttered a slice of toast. "Farming's dangerous work."

Especially when someone is helping matters along. "It's a good thing you didn't get into town until Saturday morning." Zoe hoped it sounded like she was joking even though she was not. "Otherwise the cops might try linking these incidents to you two."

Kimberly slammed a well-manicured hand down on the table, rattling plates and silverware. "Enough. I told you, I want none of this kind of talk while I'm eating. It's not good for the digestion."

Zoe folded her arms in front of her, never taking her eyes from Tom. "I'm glad I caught you before you left for the airport. There's something I need to know."

He turned slowly to meet her gaze, but his face remained unreadable. "And what's that?"

Heat crept up Zoe's neck. "Why didn't you ever tell me Dad was asking questions about Denver and Vernon's deaths before he died?"

An exasperated and unladylike noise came from Kimberly's direction, but Zoe didn't look away from her stepfather.

Tom lifted his chin ever so slightly. "Was he? I don't recall."

The heat spread to Zoe's eyes. "You don't recall? From what I've been told, he was asking everyone in town. Including Chief Froats."

Kimberly choked. "Froats? You've been talking to that horse's ass?"

Her mother swearing caught Zoe off guard. She turned from Tom. "I need answers, and you two haven't been giving me any."

Kimberly's face reddened. "You do not need answers, my darling daughter. You need drama. You like to stir the pot just to upset me."

"I do not." Zoe hated the way her voice sounded like a whining teen. She swiped a hand across her eyes to stem the threatened flow of angry tears. She would *not* cry. Not now. "I do intend to find out what happened to my father—"

"You already know," Tom interrupted.

She swung back on him. "Do I? Do any of us? There was no autopsy. The police investigation was laughable. Now we find out he was digging around in an old case that raised a lot of unanswered questions. And people involved in one or the other or both of these old cases are turning up dead."

Tom didn't as much as blink at her tirade. Instead, he quietly said, "We?"

Zoe paused, her mouth open. "Huh?"

"You said *we* found out Gary was digging. Who's *we*?"

She swallowed. "Pete Adams. And me."

"The police chief." Tom said it as if the words tasted foul in his mouth.

The heat behind Zoe's eyes threatened to boil over into tears again. She tried to swallow them. No way should she ever play poker against this man.

She lowered her voice. "He's meeting with the DA right now to get a court order to have Dad's body exhumed."

"No!" Kimberly's cry sounded like something that might come from a wild animal. "No. I will not have Gary disrespected like that. For God's sake, Zoe, let him be at peace."

Zoe spun to face her mother. "How can Dad be at peace if he was murdered and his killer's still out there?"

Behind her, Tom's chair squawked against the wooden floor. "Zoe—"

A soft rap at the door cut short whatever he was about to say. Jade bolted from her perch on the stacked luggage.

Zoe glanced at the door, then back at her parents.

Kimberly appeared on the verge of a stroke, her face crimson, her eyes wide. "Tom, we have to stop this. I won't have Gary's grave desecrated." She tossed her napkin over her uneaten breakfast, stormed across the room and up the stairs.

Tom had climbed to his feet and towered over Zoe, his blue eyes dark as the storm clouds gathering outside the window. "I'm going to call our attorney. He'll have this blocked. And then we're leaving for the airport. I'd like to say it's been nice spending time with you, but..."

Whoever was at the door knocked again, louder this time. Zoe glared at her stepdad, feeling very much like the rebellious teen she had once been. But at least she hadn't let him see her cry.

She turned her back to him and crossed the room to answer the door.

Patsy Greene stood wide-eyed on the porch, and Zoe wondered how loud their discussion had been.

Zoe stepped back, motioning Patsy in.

"Mr. Jackson." Patsy offered a shy smile.

"Patsy." Tom's expression softened. "I'm afraid Kimberly and I are going to miss your birthday party on Friday. Now, if you'll excuse me, I have a flight to catch." He shot a dark glance at Zoe and strode to the stairs.

As his heavy footsteps faded, Patsy made a pained face at Zoe. "Sorry. I interrupted something, didn't I?"

"Yes." Zoe closed the door. "And you have no idea how much I appreciate it."

"Oh." Patsy's laugh was as uncomfortable as her expression. "I hate to bother you..."

"You're not bothering me. What is it?"

"Well. I was going to clean stalls for you this morning."

Zoe thought of the autopsy and looked at her mantle clock. Crap. She was going to be late for sure, and if she had to clean stalls, too? "Something's come up and you can't do it," Zoe finished Patsy's sentence for her.

"No, that's not it. It's...well...the manure spreader..."

Zoe slapped a palm to her forehead. "I was supposed to take it out and empty it."

Patsy nodded apologetically. "It's overflowing as is. I'd do it, but I don't know how to drive Mr. Kroll's tractor. I'm afraid I'd blow it up or something."

Zoe heaved a sigh. "My fault. I completely forgot about it. Let's go." She glanced at the stairs. When her mother and stepfather had arrived less than a week ago, she'd have claimed her relationship with them was as bad as it could get.

She'd been painfully wrong.

Pete swore under his breath as he juggled his crutches and the heavy wood door between the DA's outer office and the hallway. When he did manage to heave the oak slab open, he was met with a thud and a round of cursing.

Wayne Baronick caught the door and held it with one hand while pressing the other to his nose. "Chief Adams." The detective's voice carried a definite nasally twang. "It figures. Does breaking my nose on the DA's door count as being injured in the line of duty?"

Pete snatched Baronick's hand away from his face and studied the nose in question. No blood or other signs of injury. "Crybaby. It looks fine." Pete nudged the detective out of the way and hobbled past him.

The detective made a show of looking behind Pete. "Where's the rest of your posse?"

Posse? Oh. "Pop's at home. Sylvia came over to watch him."

"How'd you get here then?" Baronick glanced around a little too eagerly. "Zoe?"

"No." The detective's sudden interest in Zoe and her recent tendency to refer to him as *Wayne* irritated Pete. A lot. "Not that it's any of your business, but I had one of my officers drive me."

Baronick hoisted a thumb back toward the DA's office and fell into step beside Pete, who headed for the elevator in the courthouse annex. "Is Fratini on board with the exhumation?"

The sterile building lacked both the history and the charm of the old courthouse and neglected to make up for it with working modern amenities. The down button failed to light even after Pete's repeated jabbings. "Not at first. He didn't think we had strong enough evidence linking Gary Chambers' death to either the James Engle's case or the Carl Loomis investigation."

"But the letter from Engle named Chambers. And Loomis was driving the car that killed him—"

Pete leaned heavily on his crutches and silenced Baronick with a raised hand. "I explained all that. But the kicker was the botched case." Pete smiled, remembering the gleam in the DA's eyes. "No autopsy. Shoddy investigation all the way around. Do you know who the district attorney was twenty-seven years ago?"

Baronick scowled. "Is this a quiz?"

"A man by the name of Randall Taucher."

The detective's frown deepened as he clearly struggled to make sense of the name.

"You might be familiar with R.J. Taucher."

The light of recognition clicked on in Baronick's eyes. "Young hotshot attorney over in the public defender's office?"

"That's the one. Randall Junior. And, according to our illustrious District Attorney, the boy is eager to take a run at his late, great father's office." The elevator door pinged open, and Pete hobbled in.

Baronick blocked the door from closing. "So Fratini figures showing the old man screwed up an old case might shine a bad light on the kid?"

Pete shrugged. "Politics. But if it gets me what I want, so be it." He punched the button for the ground floor. It didn't light either.

"Anyway, I'm glad I ran into you." Baronick leaned against the elevator opening, keeping the doors from whishing shut.

"Oh?" This better be good. Pete wanted to get back to Zoe's and talk to the landlady, hopefully before Tom and Kimberly Jackson left for the airport.

"The lab just called me with some results you might find interesting."

Pete straightened, taking his weight off the crutches.

"The bullet they removed from Marvin Kroll?" A smug smile crept across Baronick's face. "Was fired from the same gun as the bullet that killed Denver Miller."

"That," Pete said, "is *very* interesting."

"There's more. They managed to lift a pretty good print off that letter the crime unit guys found in James Engle's house."

The letter to Kimberly. "Did they get a match?"

"Not through AFIS." Baronick was trying so hard to bite back a smile, Pete expected him to explode.

"But?" There was always a but.

"*But* they matched it to the prints found on that Coke can you picked up."

The can Sylvia had pocketed on Monday. At Zoe's house. Tom Jackson. Pete took a slow breath. He should be way more excited about matching two pieces of evidence and possibly nailing a killer. Instead, he ached, knowing he was about to destroy Zoe's world.

TWENTY-THREE

Thunder growled as Zoe clicked on the lights in the massive pole barn. Outside, it was darker than dusk. She could only hope the storm would swing to their south so she could empty the manure spreader without getting drowned.

She eyed the Massey-Ferguson still parked in the middle of the indoor arena, the lone silent witness to Mr. Kroll's shooting. The beast was his pride and joy. Old but sturdy and reliable, he would boast. A lot like the man himself. At least until three days ago.

"Seems almost sacrilege, doesn't it?" Patsy used a manure fork to scoop a smattering of dirty bedding that had tumbled off the spreader and tossed the stuff back where it belonged.

"You mean touching Mr. Kroll's toy?" Zoe managed a sad grin.

"Yeah."

"We can't leave it here like this. And a loaded manure spreader isn't exactly the kind of monument to a person's life anyone would want."

Patsy winced. "Monument? You make it sound like he's dead."

"Sorry. I didn't mean to." Zoe put one foot on the tractor's hitch and reached up to the seat.

"Wait." Patsy raised a hand.

"What?"

"You're not gonna start it yet, are you?"

She wasn't? "Uh. Yeah. Why?"

Patsy crossed her arms on top of the manure fork handle, resting her chin on her wrists. "I've watched Mr. Kroll start this baby at least a hundred times, and never once without checking the oil first."

As much as Zoe did not want to attend Carl Loomis' autopsy, she wanted to face Franklin Marshall's wrath even less. Besides, it was going to pour any second. "I think he'd forgive me if I overlooked it this one time."

"He always says the reason his farm machinery runs so good is because he always, *always* takes good care of his equipment. And checking the oil is one of the things he harps on the most."

"You're right." Mr. Kroll was meticulous about the care and feeding of his beloved gadgets, big and small. With a resigned sigh, Zoe glanced around for a rag. "Do me a favor. Grab a roll of paper towels from the tack room."

Patsy propped the manure fork against the spreader. "Sure thing." She scuffed off across the arena.

The windows and doorway lit up with a flash of lightning. Zoe flinched at the boom that followed. Blinking, she noticed the metal toolbox bolted to the back of the tractor, below the seat. Of course. Mr. Kroll kept something in there for wiping down a dipstick.

Zoe clanked open the lid revealing a wadded oily gray rag. "Never mind," she called after Patsy.

Grabbing the rag, Zoe tugged. But it was caught on the tools beneath. She gave another yank, freeing the cloth—along with a folded piece of paper that went scurrying across the arena floor, caught on a gust of wind from the open barn doors.

"Crap." Zoe tossed the filthy rag onto the tractor's fender before jogging after the elusive paper. She snatched it before the next breeze could send the thing to the opposite end of the building.

The paper turned out to be a dirt-smudged envelope. Maybe something important. A bill Mr. Kroll had intended to take into the house after he'd finished his work that day? Only he hadn't counted on being hauled away in an ambulance.

Patsy shuffled to Zoe's side for a closer look. "What's that?"

"I don't know." Zoe turned the envelope over, checking for a return address.

It took a moment to make sense of the awkward, nearly illegible scrawl. Another moment for the name scribbled in the upper left corner to register. *James Engle*

"It might be personal." Patsy shook her head emphatically. "You better put it back."

Ignoring Patsy's complaints, Zoe thumbed open the flap and snatched out the letter. The handwritten words in that now-familiar scrawl swam together before her eyes, but without reading a thing, she knew she was looking at the motive for Mr. Kroll's shooting.

Officer Nate Williamson was certainly big enough to qualify him as a linebacker. Yet for a personal vehicle, he drove a two-door Saturn Ion. Pete shoved the passenger seat as far back as it went and still couldn't get comfortable with his bum foot. Maybe he really should consider making that appointment with the orthopedic guy.

A gust swayed the small car, and Nate clicked on the wipers as the first few fat rain drops splatted on the windshield. "How soon before they dig up the body?"

"Fratini will go before the judge today to get the court order. Could happen later this afternoon." Pete glanced at the deepening black sky out the window. A jagged bolt of lightning transected the clouds. "Or tomorrow."

"I wonder how Zoe's gonna handle it."

Pete had told Nate about the fingerprint and wasn't sure if he meant that or the exhumation. Either way, the next couple of days were going to be rough for Zoe.

Pete pulled his cell phone from his pocket and rolled it over in his hand a few times. Should he call her and warn her about the prints? No. She was assisting with the Loomis autopsy this morning. He started to put the phone away, but thought better of it and punched in Kevin's number.

He answered on the second ring. "Yeah, Chief?"

"Did you find out anything about Gary Chambers' life insurance?"

"I did. I had to promise to let the gal at the agency go over my current policy with her, but she managed to dig up some old records."

Pete grinned to himself. "Was she cute?"

There was a self-conscious pause. "Uh, well, I only talked to her on the phone, but, yeah. She *sounded* cute."

"What'd you find out?"

"If you hoped to learn he had a million-dollar policy, I have to disappoint you. In fact, he had a pretty skimpy death benefit, even for the time. Two thousand dollars. His wife sure didn't get rich when he died."

"Damn." A million-dollar payout was exactly what he'd been hoping for. On the other hand, bumping Zoe's mom down a notch on the suspect list motive-wise wasn't such a bad outcome. "Thanks, Kevin."

Nate slowed the Saturn as they approached the bend before Zoe's place. Even though the car's clock read a little after eight-thirty on a summer morning, the storm-darkened sky made it look like closer to nine at night. Lightning momentarily brightened the landscape followed by a ground-shaking rumble of thunder. The raindrops were still fat and sparse, but Vance Township was only minutes, maybe seconds away from a gully-washer. Pete hoped he and his cast could make it inside before that happened.

With no vehicles coming the other way, Nate swung the small car wide to the left and made the near U-turn to the right, bouncing up the hill before the drive snaked toward the house.

Zoe's two-tone brown Chevy pickup sat in its usual spot. What was it doing there? She was supposed to be in Brunswick at Loomis' autopsy. Next to Zoe's truck, Patsy Greene's black Dodge Ram. The Krolls' white Ford would be in the antiquated garage across the farm lane, but Tom and Kimberly Jackson's rental car was noticeably absent. Damn.

In that moment, something he should have caught before leapt to his mind. He yanked his notebook from his pocket. It was already open to his last interview with Carl Loomis in preparation for asking Mrs. Kroll about her husband's visit there. Pete didn't even have to flip a page to find what he was looking for.

Loomis had reported seeing two cars at James Engle's house a week ago. Kroll's pickup was the second. The first had been a nondescript beige sedan.

The Jackson's rental car had been a nondescript beige sedan.

"Damn." Pete said it out loud this time.

Nate parked next to Zoe's Chevy. "What?"

Pete opened the door and hoisted himself out of the Saturn with a grunt. "Call Kevin. Tell him to check the rental car places at the airport. Find out if Tom Jackson rented a beige sedan. Ford. Loomis never said the sedan was a Ford, only the SUV." Pete could kick himself for not making the connection earlier. "Check for rentals last Tuesday or Wednesday." Rain pelted his back. He started to close the car door then jerked it back open. "If he doesn't find a rental in Tom Jackson's name, check under Kimberly Jackson. Or Chambers. And tell Kevin to check the airlines to find out exactly *when* they flew into Pittsburgh."

Nate already had his phone out. "On it, Chief."

Lightning sizzled overhead accompanied by a deafening roar that shook the ground. "And I want to hear the second he knows anything."

Pete slammed the door and swung down the sloping path to the back porch. The rain chose that moment, with him midway between car and house, to let loose in all its soaking glory. The grass beneath his crutches and one good foot was slick and made the going even tougher. By the time he reached the porch, water dripped from the bill of his department-issued ball cap. He fumbled with the door and the one step onto the porch, nearly falling on his face. But he made it into the enclosure, wet and winded.

He looked at each of the three doors across the back of the house—thought about the TV game show where contestants are asked to pick the one they believe holds the best prize. Pete based his selection on curiosity. He thumped to Zoe's door and knocked. No answer. She must have caught a ride to the coroner's office.

He made his way to the far side of the porch and rapped on Mrs. Kroll's door. Muffled thuds came from inside, and the door swung open to reveal the Krolls' son, his face haggard.

Pete braced his crutches under his armpits and extended a hand. "Alexander, isn't it? I'm Chief Pete Adams. We met Monday at the hospital."

"Yes, of course." They shook. "Please. Come in."

Pete removed his soggy ball cap and maneuvered into a small, tidy kitchen. "Is your mother up?"

Before the young man could reply, Mrs. Kroll's frail voice called out from the next room. "Chief? Is that you?"

Alexander directed him toward the dining room. "Coffee?"

"Please."

On a good day Mrs. Kroll was slight. She may have once been a hearty farm wife, but a long battle with leukemia had ravaged her body, leaving her pale and fragile. This morning, as she huddled over a steaming cup at the oversized antique table, her skin looked like worn tissue paper, stained dark under her eyes. Pete feared if he looked close enough, he could make out every bone in her face.

Pete eased into a chair across the mammoth farm table from the old woman. "How's your husband doing, Mrs. Kroll?"

"Holding his own, according to his doctors." She smiled wistfully. "I just wish he'd open his eyes. I miss seeing his eyes."

The old woman's words were a sucker punch to Pete's gut. She was clearly agonizing over her husband's condition and here was this cop about to demand answers about what might have brought the tragedy to their lives.

Alexander joined them carrying two mugs of coffee. He set one in front of Pete and sat down next to his mother while sipping from the other. "I didn't ask. How do you take it, Chief?"

"Black is fine." Though a shot of bourbon might help. "I hate to bother you both at a time like this, but I need to ask some questions."

"You said that much on the phone last night," Mrs. Kroll said. "I can't imagine what I could possibly tell you. I don't know who would have any reason to hurt my husband."

Her son placed a hand on her shoulder.

Pete cleared his throat. "Have you heard about Carl Loomis?"

"Yes. Terrible, terrible accident." She shook her head. "But then, we've had a spate of those lately, haven't we?"

"Yesterday, before his...accident...I spoke with Mr. Loomis. He mentioned seeing your husband over at James Engle's house last Wednesday. I was hoping you might be able to tell me why he was there."

The cup in Mrs. Kroll's hands began to shake. She slowly lowered it to the table before spilling the contents. "Marv was over at Jim's place?" Her voice trembled as much as the cup had. "That can't be right. Surely you heard wrong. Or Carl was mistaken."

"Why do you say that?"

"Marv never had much use for Jim Engle is all. His brother Wilford neither. Oh, they were all civil when they ran into each other at the Farm Bureau meetings or the fair and such. But I can't imagine Marv simply dropping by to visit, you know what I mean?"

Pete's cell phone buzzed in his pocket. Thinking it was Kevin, he yanked it out. "Yes, ma'am. I know what you mean. Excuse me a minute, please." The number on the screen wasn't Kevin's. He pressed the green button. "Zoe?"

Her voice was frantic or excited. Pete couldn't tell which. Her words tumbled over each other—something about toolbox and a letter. A house-rattling boom of thunder further distorted the connection.

"What?" he shouted into the phone.

The other end went quiet for a long moment, and Pete thought they'd been disconnected. But then Zoe's voice came through clear and strong. "Mrs. Kroll is the woman Denver and Vernon Miller died fighting over."

TWENTY-FOUR

Pete glanced over his reading glasses at Zoe, who leaned in the doorway between the Krolls' kitchen and dining room, still breathing hard from running through the rain from the barn to the house. Her hair hung in wet curls framing her face, and she hugged an oversized beach towel over her rain-soaked ambulance uniform.

Across the table, Mrs. Kroll and her son waited in silence while Pete tried to decide how to tackle the subject at hand. Namely another cryptic letter from the late James Engle. Judging by the perplexed looks on their faces, Pete felt certain that neither the old woman nor her son had ever seen the document before. And if Mr. Kroll had been keeping it from his wife, he might have feared she couldn't handle the contents.

Mrs. Kroll must have sensed Pete's indecision. "Read it to me, please."

He shot a questioning look at the son. Alexander nodded. "Go ahead."

Pete studied the crumpled sheet of paper before him and skimmed through it silently one more time before reading it out loud.

"Dear Marvin,

As my remaining days on this earth dwindle, I am making every effort to set things right with those who have been harmed by lies and deception. I am aware your wife is not well and has not been well for some time. I fear the burden of guilt she carries may have something to do with her illness and for that I am truly sorry. I wish I'd had the courage to face the evil in my life sooner.

For many years, your wife has believed the deaths of Denver and Vernon Miller were her fault. She, and others, believed the brothers fought over her resulting in murder and suicide. I am ashamed that I let this lie go on. Please do your best to assure her that Vernon really did love her, but she played no part whatsoever in what transpired that dreadful night.

With deepest remorse,
James Engle."

Pete lifted his gaze from the page to Mrs. Kroll's face. The room had fallen silent. She didn't move, except for her eyes, which shifted slightly downward.

After several long moments, Pete set the letter down and leaned forward, resting his forearms on the table. "Mrs. Kroll?"

Her eyelids fluttered, the trance broken. "I'm fine." She took a long breath, as if it were the first she'd drawn in a very long time, and Pete thought he noticed a trace of a wistful smile on her lips.

"Are you up to answering some questions?"

She blew out a forceful sigh. "Yes."

Alexander draped a protective arm across the back of his mother's chair.

Pete looked over at Zoe and tipped his head toward the empty chair next to him. She took the hint, pushed away from the jamb, and slid into the seat.

"Mrs. Kroll, did you know about this letter?"

"Good heavens, no." She fingered the now empty coffee cup in front of her. "I would have wanted to talk to Jim if I had. Find out what exactly happened."

Pete would have liked that opportunity, too.

Before he could form his next question, Zoe piped in, "You were the mystery woman?"

"Yes, I suppose I was. Although I didn't realize it was a mystery." Mrs. Kroll may have been gazing toward the window, but Pete suspected she was seeing something else entirely, from a different time. "I was just a girl when I fell in love with Vernie. He was so dashing. So handsome. Like a movie star. He made me feel like a princess. I'd have given my life for that man. And I wanted nothing more than to marry him and grow old with him. But he wasn't the type to settle down, I guess. When he wouldn't propose, I decided to make him jealous by dating his brother. It was stupid, I know. But I was young and foolish. And in love." She paused, as if gathering strength to continue. "Denver and I were just friends. He knew what I was up to. But instead of getting jealous, Vernie started seeing other girls. And then he got one of them pregnant." Her voice broke. "I was devastated. I turned to Denver for comfort and things...well, things went further than either of us had intended."

Pete noticed Alexander's face had turned a deep shade of crimson. No son, even one in his fifties, wanted to hear about his mother's love life. Especially with someone other than his father.

Mrs. Kroll's voice dropped so low Pete had to strain to hear. "It was a few days later when I got the news about the fight. Vernie and Denver. Both dead. Murder/suicide, they said, although I never could quite believe Vernie would kill his brother. But I was told they'd fought over me. I carried the guilt and the shame with me all these years."

"Who told you they'd fought over you?" Zoe asked.

Mrs. Kroll blinked, snapping out of the past, and looked at Zoe. "Why, Jim Engle I believe. But everyone around knew about it."

Everyone. Except for anyone Pete had asked.

A soft tapping drew his attention to the window that looked out onto the back porch. Nate stood there waving, and from the look on his face, he'd heard from Kevin. Damn. Pete hadn't had a chance to tell Zoe the latest revelations regarding her stepfather. Besides, Pete had one more question for Mrs. Kroll. He held up a finger to his officer. Nate nodded and struck an at-ease pose.

Pete patted the table to bring the old woman's eyes back to him. "Mrs. Kroll, I know this is painful for you, but you mentioned Vernon had gotten another girl pregnant."

Mrs. Kroll looked down. "Yes."

"Do you happen to know who that was?"

"Yes, of course. It was Mae Engle."

"Mae *Engle*?" both Pete and Zoe said at once.

Mrs. Kroll looked back and forth between them and nodded. "Jim and Wilford's younger sister."

"Sister?" Why was this the first Pete had heard of another Engle sibling? "Where is this sister now?"

A hard frown creased Mrs. Kroll's forehead. "I'm not really sure. You know, things were different back then. An unmarried girl getting pregnant was a shameful thing. So I assumed she'd gone away to have the baby. But she never came back. I wonder what happened to her. And to Vernie's baby."

Pete turned to Zoe, who looked as shell-shocked as he knew he must. She shrugged and gave her head a quick shake. "Yeah," he said. "I do, too."

Pete had excused himself to talk with Nate. Zoe had wanted to join him, but he told her to stay with Mrs. Kroll. Rankled, Zoe kept glancing at the kitchen door, which Pete had closed behind him. What on earth was he keeping from her?

Mrs. Kroll dabbed her nose with a tissue. "I'm sorry for getting so emotional."

Alexander put an arm around his mother, but the look on his face told Zoe he had no idea how to comfort her.

Zoe rose and moved around the table to sit next to her landlady. "It's perfectly understandable given the circumstances." She patted Mrs. Kroll's arm.

Muffled voices filtered through the door, but Zoe couldn't make out what the men were saying.

"Tell me something." Zoe pondered how to pose a delicate question that nagged her. "Did Mr. Kroll know about your past?"

"Oh, yes. Marv and I were friends all through school." Mrs. Kroll smiled at the memory. "Truth be told, he was a little sweet on me even then. And he was so kind after everything that happened with Vernie and Denver. You might say he picked up the pieces of my broken heart."

"So he knew them?"

"Of course."

Not the answer Zoe had hoped for. Especially when she distinctly remembered Mr. Kroll telling her he'd never met them.

A noise from the direction of the kitchen drew her attention. Nate passed the window on his way out.

At the same time, the door opened. Pete locked eyes with her and crooked a finger. First he'd ordered her to stay. Now he was beckoning her to come. If she wasn't so darned curious, she'd have snapped at him for treating her like a dog. Instead, she excused herself from the Krolls and joined Pete in the kitchen. Once again, he shut the door behind them.

"What's going on with all the cloak and dagger crap?"

He motioned for her to keep her voice low. She gave him her best angry glare.

"When did you say Tom and your mother arrived in town?"

The question took her by surprise. "Saturday morning. Why?"

"Are you sure?"

Zoe stared into the icy depths of Pete's eyes and didn't much like what she saw. Bad news lurked under the surface. Real bad. "That's when they showed up here."

"In a rental car."

It wasn't a question. "Yeah."

"A beige Ford sedan."

"Yeah. Pete, what's going on?"

He heaved a sigh. Looked away for a moment. Came back to hold her gaze. "I had Kevin check the airlines. Tom Jackson arrived in Pittsburgh on Wednesday morning and rented a beige Ford. He stayed Wednesday, Thursday, and Friday nights at Tonidale."

"Tonidale?" A landmark motel near the airport. "But why would they—"

"*They* didn't. Your mom arrived Saturday morning. Alone."

Zoe sagged into the antique ladder-back chair next to the door. Tom and Kimberly had lied to her. Maybe not outright, but by omission. Letting her believe they'd both flown in Saturday morning on an earlier flight and rented a car so she didn't have to pick them up as they'd originally planned.

"There's more."

"More?" Her voice squeaked in her ears.

Pete snagged a second chair and balanced on his crutches as he dragged it, legs screeching on the old linoleum, to face her. With a grunt, he sat. The crutches clattered to the floor beside him. Knees to knees, he took her hands in his. "Saturday, I came by to talk to your stepdad."

For a moment the heat and strength of his hands—and the thought of how well hers fit in his grip—distracted her from the situation. But then his words sunk in. "I know. Tom told me." She didn't mention how unhappy he'd been about the visit.

Pete squeezed, and she lifted her gaze to the steel-blue of his eyes. "I had Sylvia pick up a Coke can he'd been drinking from."

"You—what?" She did *not* like where this was going. At all.

Pete told her about the prints on the can matching those on the letter to Kimberly. The one that had been found in James Engle's house. Crumpled. Under the couch.

The room fell still except for the faint grinding of the ancient refrigerator, matching the churning thoughts inside Zoe's head. Tom had seen the letter. Had been in Engle's house. Before Engle had died. How soon before?

"Are you—" Her voice caught. She took a breath and tried again. "Are you going to have the police in Florida arrest him when their plane lands?"

"I don't have to. Their flight was delayed because of the storms. Airport Security picked him up at the departure gate."

She closed her eyes and pictured Tom, dragged out of the airport in handcuffs. Her mother going into a total meltdown, probably getting arrested for assaulting an officer. How long before Kimberly phoned Zoe, screaming to come bail both of them out of jail? Then again, the way they'd left things, Zoe might well be the last person her mother would call.

Pete squeezed again, bringing her back from the dark hole she'd descended into. From the crease in his forehead, she gathered he had more, and it wasn't good news to counterbalance the bad.

"I don't suppose you've seen a .38 caliber handgun around anywhere, have you?"

Zoe opened her mouth to ask why he wanted to know *that*. But she flashed to the afternoon in the courthouse basement with Baronick. "No." She dragged the word out and left it hanging out there with a question mark on the end of it.

"The gun that killed your Great Uncle Denver is the same gun used to shoot Marvin Kroll."

Maybe the news should have surprised her. But it didn't.

"Tom couldn't have carried a gun on the plane, so he must have had it stashed here somewhere. And he may have hidden it again before he left."

Maybe this *shouldn't* have surprised her, but it did. "Here?" She looked toward her side of the house as if she could see through the wall. "But I wasn't living here the last time they came for a visit—"

Pete released one hand and cupped her cheek, keeping her from looking away. "Zoe. He arrived in town on Wednesday. He could have had the gun hidden somewhere else and picked it up before he came to the farm."

Pressure built behind her eyes. "But this time he might have left it...hidden it...here."

Zoe stood in the doorway to the barn, listening to the steady drizzle plinking into puddles where the gutters leaked. Inside, Pete and Nate, who'd had no luck finding the missing gun in her half of the farmhouse, searched the feed room. Next they planned to check each stall. After that, the hayloft, although no doubt Nate would be doing that on his own while Pete barked orders from the ground.

And then? Zoe eyed the still overflowing manure spreader. Certainly Tom wouldn't have shoved it in there. Would he?

A sudden rush of anger toward the man who had raised her drove her out into the rain. She needed to walk—to cool down and clear her head—to have a good cry where Pete and Nate couldn't see her.

How could Tom have done all this? The same man who'd carried her on his shoulders, who'd defended her against Kimberly's self-serving demands, who'd called Zoe Sweet Pea.

She doubled over and choked. Had Tom killed her father, too? In all the hubbub over the letter in the toolbox and Mrs. Kroll's revelations, Zoe had completely forgotten to ask Pete about his meeting with the DA. She sniffed hard, straightened, and lifted her face to the sky. Let the rain wash away the salty streaks. Or give her something besides her childish weeping to blame them on.

As she turned to head back to the barn, her phone vibrated in her pocket. She dug it out and checked the screen. Franklin Marshall. Crap. Carl Loomis' autopsy.

"Where the heck have you been?" the coroner demanded.

"I'm so sorry, Franklin. But I found a piece of evidence and—"

"Never mind that. I've been trying to reach Pete Adams, but he must have his cell phone turned off. He wouldn't happen to be there, would he?"

She jogged the last steps to the shelter of the barn. "Ah, yeah. He's right here."

"Put him on the line."

Zoe crossed the indoor arena to the feed room where Pete and Nate were sifting through the contents of two barrels of grain. "Wouldn't he have hidden the gun where it wouldn't eventually be found?" she asked as she shoved the phone at Pete.

"Probably. Who is it?"

"Franklin. I missed the autopsy."

"So he wants me to arrest you?" Pete took the phone.

"He didn't say."

Pete turned his back to her to take the call. Zoe studied the spilled grain, raising an annoyed eyebrow at Nate.

He shrugged. "You know what they say. Leave no oat unturned."

Zoe bit back a smile in spite of herself. The crack of Pete's crutch against a metal shelf jolted her back to reality.

He made an ungraceful pivot and handed her phone back to her. "Marshall says you missed an interesting autopsy."

"Oh?"

"Carl Loomis didn't die because of the fire or smoke inhalation. COD was blood loss."

"From getting sucked into the power take-off?" Even as she asked the question, she suspected the answer would be *no*.

She was right. Pete shook his head. "Gunshot wound."

TWENTY-FIVE

After calling in a couple of Baronick's county guys to assist Nate in the search for the gun, Pete commandeered Zoe to drive him back to the station. He'd never be able to keep her away anyhow. Not after she heard about Tom and Kimberly Jackson being transported there for questioning.

The storms had cleared out for the moment, and patches of blue peered through tatters in the blanket of dark clouds. Almost a dozen vehicles jammed the Vance Township Police Department's parking lot. When Zoe wheeled her hulk of a truck off Dillard's Main Street, she jammed on the brakes to keep from rear ending a news van. Pete reached for the dashboard as the seatbelt grabbed his shoulder.

"Sorry," she said.

Pete scanned the lot. Baronick's unmarked sedan filled Pete's usual space. He also recognized Sylvia's Escort. A pair of nondescript cars he hadn't seen before were nosed against the front walk.

Three vans bearing local television station logos took up more than their fair share of the remaining parking spots. A handful of well-dressed reporters loitered by the station's front door accompanied by a trio of jeans-clad videographers, their TV cameras hanging at their sides.

"Do you want me to drive you to the back entrance?" Zoe asked.

"No." Pete pointed to the other side of the building—the half that housed all the other township offices. "Park over there."

She eyed his foot. "You sure?"

He was getting damned sick of being the local invalid. He glared at her without answering.

Zoe shrugged and eased her Chevy into the lot at the opposite end of the building. She jumped out and was at the passenger door before Pete untangled his crutches. From the crease between her brow and the tightness of her lips, Pete knew she was teetering on the edge.

He stepped down and caught her wrist as she reached to slam the door. "Maybe you should go back home."

She blinked. "My mom and Tom are in there." She tipped a thumb toward the police station. "I'm not going anywhere."

Pete leaned closer to her. He shifted his grip, intertwining his fingers with hers. He wanted to tell her he was sorry. That he would try to take it easy on her stepdad. That everything would be okay. But he wasn't at all sure that everything would be all right for Zoe. He didn't have the luxury of taking it easy on a suspect in a string of murders that went back forty-five years. Saying he was sorry seemed insufficient.

She must have sensed it, though. For a moment, she rested her forehead against his shoulder.

He let the crutches clatter against the truck, cupped the back of her head with his free hand, and closed his eyes, breathing in her scent.

Zoe drew away, clearing her throat. "I need to get in there before Mom tears the place apart."

Pete released Zoe and gathered his crutches. "Let me go first."

A murmur ran through the news crew as someone apparently recognized the police chief even out of uniform and on crutches. The videographers swung their cameras to their shoulders, and the reporters snapped to attention, microphones at the ready.

Maybe Pete should have had Zoe drive them to the back entrance if only to shield her from fifteen minutes of unwanted fame. "Stay close," he told her. "I'll use a crutch as a battering ram if I need to."

The reporters loomed toward them, tossing out questions so fast he couldn't distinguish who'd asked what. Not that it mattered.

"Give me a half hour, and I'll have a statement for you," he said.

"Chief, is it true that you've arrested someone for the string of murders in the township?"

"Can you give us a name of the person you're holding?"

"Do you think this is a serial killer targeting farmers?"

With Zoe clutching a handful of the back of Pete's shirt, he ignored the news crews and hobbled to the door, parting the group of reporters who obviously sensed those crutches could *accidentally* come down on someone's foot. Or whack a shin.

Inside the station, Nancy sat ashen-faced and wide-eyed behind the counter, pinching the phone receiver between her ear and shoulder, talking on one line while a second one started to ring. Officer Seth Metzger strode toward them from the back of the hallway. "I'm sorry, Chief. I didn't know you were here or I'd have—"

"It's all right. Where are Tom and Kimberly Jackson?"

Seth's gaze jumped between Pete and Zoe. He swallowed hard. "Tom Jackson is in the interrogation room with Kevin standing guard."

From behind Pete, Zoe let out a strangled breath.

"Mrs. Jackson," Seth said, "is in the conference room with Detective Baronick." The officer leaned closer to Pete and whispered, "I covered up the white board."

Pete imagined Kimberly seeing her husband's name in every column of that board and pitching the whole thing out the window—except there were no windows in the conference room. "Good move."

"Sylvia and Mr. Adams are in your office." Seth squirmed. "Sylvia mentioned having a dentist appointment—uh—soon."

Pete leaned on one crutch and rubbed a spot on the side of his head where a pain was blooming. "Thanks, Seth."

Zoe stepped between them and faced Pete. "I want to talk to my mother."

He shook his head. "Not going to happen. You know that. At least not until I've talked to her first."

"She's more likely to talk to me."

He huffed a laugh. "Really?"

"Well, she'll yell. But she'll talk. We have a long history of communicating that way." Zoe folded her arms in front of her. "And she despises you."

"Thanks." He thought of Sylvia waiting in his office. "I have that effect on women. Look, I can't have you doing anything to jeopardize this case—"

"Jeopardize? Pete, my mother may be self-centered, self-righteous, and stubborn with a capital S, but she's not a killer. Trust me on this. She wouldn't dirty her hands like that."

Pete studied Zoe. Maybe Kimberly wouldn't get her hands dirty, but perhaps she had someone else willing to do the scutwork for her. Tom, for example. "Let me do my job. Besides I need you to do something else for me."

Zoe narrowed her eyes at him. "What?"

He tipped his head toward his office. "Relieve Sylvia from Harry duty. Please."

Zoe held Pete's gaze. There was something going on behind her baby blues. "All right," she said after a moment. "But I want to talk to my mother as soon as you've finished questioning her."

He held out a hand. "Deal."

When she took it, the expression on her face was the same one she wore at their Saturday night poker games when she knew she had him beat.

Zoe kept her hand on the doorknob to Pete's office. He disappeared into the interrogation room farther down the hall. Seth had vanished into the front office to help Nancy man the phones. Zoe took a breath, hoping to settle her thoughts. Tom was being questioned as a murder suspect. Her mom was in the conference room only a few feet away. The police were searching Zoe's farm for a missing gun. The sweet old couple whose house she shared might somehow be mixed up in this whole mess. And yet rising to the surface of all the chaos in her life, was the memory of being in Pete's arms even if only for a moment.

She shook her head. Stop it. Now was not the time for romantic fantasies. She blew out the breath and pushed into Pete's office.

Sylvia looked up from her seat behind Pete's desk, her face strained.

Harry must have been pacing and stopped. "Nadine? It's about time. Can we go home now?"

Zoe glanced at Sylvia, who climbed to her feet. "He's not having a good day."

"Oh." Zoe shifted back to Harry. "It's me. Zoe. I'll take you home in a little bit, okay?"

"Zoe?" His expression was reminiscent of a child lost in department store. He shook his head. "Nadine's expecting me for dinner." He turned and resumed pacing the small room.

Sylvia sidled around the desk. "I hope you're here to take over for me. I have a dentist appointment in..." She checked her watch. "Good lord. In ten minutes. I'll never make it."

"Go." Zoe shooed her toward the door. "I've got things covered here."

Sylvia snagged her purse from edge of the desk. "Thanks." She shot a glance at Harry then whispered to Zoe, "Good luck." On her way out the door, she paused and added, "By the way, I'm so sorry about all this with your mom and Tommy."

Zoe managed a weak smile.

Alone with Harry, she watched him prowl back and forth like an old lion trapped in a cage. He turned toward her and pulled up short. "Nadine? Get me out of here. I want to go home."

Zoe longed to talk to her mother. Without Tom, without Pete, and without Wayne Baronick. Maybe then Kimberly would give her some straight answers. But right now Zoe faced a sad, lost old man. "Okay, Harry. I'll take you back to Pete's."

"Pete? My boy Pete?" Harry looked around expectantly. "Is he here? I haven't seen him in ages."

The ache in her chest deepened. In spite of the flashes of clarity, this was what the future Harry—funny, charming, insightful Harry—faced. "He's right down the hall. I need to get his house keys." She caught her lip between her teeth. Did she dare leave Harry alone while she went in search of Pete? The senior Adams had proven he had a penchant for wandering off.

Harry placed a hand on his belly. "Maybe he has some food at his place. I'm starved."

"I'm sure he does." She pulled out her phone and glanced at the time. One o'clock. No wonder he was hungry. When she stopped agonizing over the madness of the morning, she realized she could use a bite to eat, too. And surely she and Harry weren't alone. She thumbed through the numbers in her phone's address book. "Harry, what would you say to a big slice of pizza?"

A smile cleared the fog that had covered his eyes. "I'd say hell-o, darlin'."

She choked on a laugh and pressed the button for the new pizza joint down the street.

While the number rang through, Harry pointed a finger at her. "I know you. You're not Nadine."

"I'm not? Then who am I?"

Creases deepened in his cheeks. Creases that had probably been killer dimples at one time. "You're Pete's girlfriend."

A stoic Tom Jackson kept his arms crossed and both feet planted firmly on the floor as he stared at the far wall. Pete had excused Kevin, so it was just the two of them. And for all the interaction Jackson offered, Pete might as well have been alone.

He leaned back in his chair and swung his aching foot onto the table that separated the two men. "Do you want to hear what I think?"

Jackson's dark gaze settled on Pete for a moment. "No. I'm not talking to anyone but my lawyer."

"You don't have to talk. Just listen." Pete didn't mention that he'd also be watching Jackson's every move.

Zoe's stepdad didn't respond other than to turn his gaze back to the space over Pete's shoulder.

Pete made a production of pulling his notebook and pen from his pocket. He retrieved a pair of reading glasses from another pocket and set them on his nose before deliberately thumbing back through the pages. "Let's start at the beginning. The Miller brothers. I understand that you and James Engle were pretty tight up until that incident. You must have been about twenty at that time, right? And the alleged fight between the brothers was over a girl. Everyone thought it was Bernice Kroll. But it wasn't her at all. The fight was over Mae Engle. Vernon Miller had gotten her pregnant."

Jackson shot a startled glance at Pete, but recovered and went back to staring at the wall.

"Except," Pete said, "it wasn't Vernon who got James' sister in trouble. It was James' best friend. You."

With Harry in tow, Zoe met the pizza delivery guy at the station's front door and paid for the two large pies. The cost would be well worth it if extra cheese enticed some answers from her mother.

Zoe stopped at the front office, dealt a pair of paper plates to Nancy and Seth, and held open the lid of the top box so they could help themselves.

Harry ran his tongue over his lips as he watched. "That smells wonderful."

Zoe smiled at him. "Come on. Let's find a place to sit down." She knew exactly where she intended to sit.

Juggling the boxes and the extra plates with one hand, she fumbled with the doorknob to the conference room, bumping the door open with her hip.

Inside, Kimberly sulked, her arms crossed, shoulders hunched, and wearing a look that would freeze molten lava.

Across the table from her, Wayne Baronick jumped to his feet. "Zoe? What are you—?"

She breezed into the room and thumped the boxes onto the table. "I knew you must be hungry. I brought lunch. Harry, have a seat."

"Wait. I don't think you're supposed—" Baronick's stuttering ceased when he sniffed the aroma wafting from the boxes. "What kind do you have?"

"One with extra pepperoni." She cast a furtive glance at her mother. "And one with mushrooms and extra cheese."

Either Kimberly wasn't hungry, was angrier than even Zoe expected, or had changed her preference in pizza in the last ten years. Her fierce countenance never wavered.

Zoe set up Harry with two slices and left him happily devouring the first one while she collected two plates and waited for Baronick to stretch a long thread of mozzarella.

"So have you finished questioning my mother?"

"Finished?" He snorted. "I haven't gotten word one out of the broad." He glanced at Zoe and winced. "Sorry."

"So is there any legal reason I can't sit with my mom and have a chat over lunch?"

He eyed her. "Legal? No. But I don't think it's a good idea."

"Oh, I *know* it's not a good idea." Zoe slapped a slice of pepperoni pizza on one plate for her and a slice of mushroom on the other for Kimberly. Licking her fingers, she gave the detective a grin. "Enjoy your lunch."

He grunted around a mouthful of cheese.

Zoe ambled around the long conference table, set a plate in front of her mother, and slid into the chair next to her.

Kimberly eyed the pizza, gave a delicate sniff, but made no move to reach for it.

Zoe wondered if she should have bummed a plastic fork and knife from the delivery guy to go with the plates. She'd forgotten her mother wasn't a finger-food kind of person. "Eat up, Mom. It's really good." Zoe punctuated her statement by cramming a major portion of her own slice into her mouth.

The action stirred the result she'd hoped for.

"Oh, for heaven's sake, Zoe. Just because you live on a farm doesn't mean you have to eat like a pig."

At least she had her mother's attention. "And just because you're on the verge of going to jail doesn't mean you have to live on bread and water. Eat."

Kimberly huffed but leaned forward and inspected the contents of the plate in front of her. She picked up the slice, handling it as if her nail polish was still wet.

Zoe waited until her mother had taken a couple of bites and visibly relaxed before breaking the silence. "Why didn't you say anything about Tom flying in three days ahead of you?"

Kimberly chewed slowly. Swallowed. "You never asked."

Zoe glared at her. "Don't be a smartass, Mother."

"Watch your mouth." Kimberly turned her attention back to her pizza. "I had commitments at the end of the week and couldn't take time away until Saturday. Tom was eager to see you, so he left early."

"But Tom didn't come see me. I never saw him until you both showed up. Together."

Kimberly sighed dramatically. "True. When he picked me up at the airport, he told me he'd run into some old friends and ended up spending time with them instead of you. He felt so bad. We decided not to say anything because we knew your feelings would be hurt."

Zoe choked out a short laugh. "That's a switch. You never worried about my feelings before."

Kimberly flung the slice of pizza down onto the plate. "This is why we never should have come here. You take such pleasure in playing the poor wounded little girl. Well, grow up, Zoe. Believe it or not, Tom and I really do worry about you."

Zoe let her slice drop as well, her appetite gone. "All right. What about after you learned of James Engle's death. Didn't you wonder about Tom then?"

"No. Heavens, no. You can't possibly believe Tom had anything to do with that, do you?"

Zoe leaned back in the chair crossing her arms. "Think about it, Mom."

"I don't have to. Tom did not kill Jim Engle."

From inside Zoe's pocket, her phone buzzed. She ignored it. "Okay. What friends did he run into and spend time with when he got here?"

Kimberly shifted in her chair and took another look at her plate, pushing what was left of the pizza around in a small circle. "I don't know."

"Did you ask?"

"No. I don't care who he spends time with."

Zoe considered reaching over and giving her mother a shake. Was she really so naive? "You don't care? Really? What if the friend was a woman?"

Kimberly turned to Zoe with a raised hand. For a fleeting moment Zoe believed her mother was going to slap her. But Kimberly must have reconsidered. She sat taller in her chair. "Tom loves me. I trust him implicitly. He wouldn't cheat on me. And he sure as hell wouldn't kill anyone. Ever. I'm ashamed of you for even suggesting such a thing." She shoved the plate and the half-eaten pizza at Zoe. "Take your damned peace offering or bribe or whatever it is and get away from me."

Even with their ragged past, the venom in Kimberly's voice stunned Zoe. With trembling hands, she gathered the plates and walked back to Harry and Wayne Baronick, who had done a fair job of emptying both pizza boxes.

The detective gave her an exaggerated sheepish grin. "I hope you didn't want seconds."

"No, thanks."

The smile faded. "I couldn't help overhearing. Are you okay?"

"Just terrific," she lied.

"Well, if it's any consolation, you got way more out of her than I did." Baronick lowered his voice. "And I have to be honest, Zoe. Your mother scares me."

Zoe huffed a laugh.

Baronick's phone rang, reminding Zoe that she'd missed a call. While the detective answered his cell, she dug hers from her pocket and pulled up her voicemail.

The wild accusation failed to produce the angry response Pete had hoped for. Jackson's eyes never wavered, but his mouth drew to one side in a fleeting hint of a smirk.

Pete flipped a page in his notebook. "Let's jump ahead a few years. Your good pal Gary Chambers was married to a beautiful young woman. They had an adorable little girl. You decided you were in love with Kimberly, but Gary was in the way, so you arranged for him to have a fatal accident. You drove him off the road and set up Carl Loomis, the town drunk, to take the fall."

Jackson's face relaxed a bit, but his eyes never shifted.

"Then your old friend James decided after all these years to clear his conscience. He wrote a letter to your wife—the wife you rescued from widowhood—and threatened to tell her how Gary really died. But you intercepted the letter and came back to Pennsylvania for a visit to shut him up."

Jackson's face darkened again.

"Which brings us to Marvin Kroll." Pete tapped the notebook. "While James was busy setting everyone straight, he decided to tell Kroll who really got Mae pregnant and stirred up the fight between the Miller brothers. Kroll confronted you about it so you had to get rid of him, too." Pete set the pen down. "But Patsy Greene walked in and caught you, so you started CPR to make it look like you were a big hero instead of cold-blooded killer."

Jackson leaped from his chair and swept an arm across the table. Pete's notebook and pen went sailing. "You son of a bitch. You have no idea what you're talking about. All you're doing is alienating my daughter from me."

Pete gripped the edges of the table, fighting an urge to lunge at the man. "You mean Gary Chambers' daughter."

"*My* daughter. *I* raised her. *I* helped her with her homework. *I* held her while she cried over the stupid boys in school who broke her heart. Me. As for that story of yours? If that's the kind of police work you do, Chief Adams, you might want to consider a new career. Because this one is going to get you sued for slander. And that's just for starters."

For a moment, Pete thought Jackson might throw a punch at him, but a knock at the door saved him from finding out. Before Pete had a chance to call out, the door swung open and a large man in a charcoal suit stormed in.

"Not another word, Mr. Jackson. Chief Adams, you weren't interviewing my client without me being present, were you?"

Pete lowered his foot to the floor and rose, extending his hand. "Mr. Imperatore. Of course not. I was simply entertaining your client with a story."

"I figured it must be something like that." Anthony Imperatore, Esquire, grasped Pete's hand. "Nevertheless, you'll excuse us now."

Pete gathered his crutches and hopped over to where his pen and notebook had landed on the floor. He scooped them up, nodded to a seething Tom Jackson, and maneuvered to the door with as much dignity as he could muster with a bum foot. As he stepped out into the hall, his phone rang. He glanced at the screen before answering. "What have you got, Marshall?"

"A body," the coroner said. "At least I'll have it in another couple of hours. Your court order came through. Gary Chambers is being exhumed as we speak."

TWENTY-SIX

Pete expected to find Zoe and Harry waiting in his office. When he discovered it empty, he knew exactly where she'd gone with his father.

The conference room door swung open as Pete reached for the knob, and Baronick charged out, nearly bowling Pete over. "I'm glad you're here," the detective said. "I just got a call from the county lab."

Pete peered over Baronick's shoulder. Kimberly Jackson huddled at one end of the table, Harry at the other with Zoe standing over him talking on her phone. Everyone present and accounted for. Good. No discernible bloodshed. Even better. "And?"

"The bullet the ME dug out of Carl Loomis matches the others."

Pete breathed a sigh. He needed to call Nate to check on the search at the Kroll farm. But Pete knew damned well if they had found the gun, he'd have heard about it already. Find the gun, solve this entire string of homicides. "Did you get anything out of Mrs. Jackson?"

"Not a thing. Zoe talked to her, though."

"What?" If he didn't have the crutches, he'd have grabbed Baronick by the throat. "You let Zoe talk to her mother? Alone?"

"Not alone. I was in the room. And the conversation was too loud to be considered private."

Pete relaxed. A little. "Learn anything?"

Baronick glanced back into the room, apparently making sure Zoe wasn't in earshot. He lowered his voice. "I learned I'm sure glad Kimberly Jackson isn't *my* mother. Beyond that, the woman is staunchly convinced her husband is the most honest, trustworthy man on the face of the earth."

Pete grunted.

"Did you get anything out of him?" Baronick motioned toward the interrogation room.

"I talked. He listened. Mostly." Pete pictured Tom Jackson coming over the table at him. "The man has a temper. And I believe he's absolutely capable of violence."

An eager smile spread across Baronick's face. "So you think we've got our man?"

That very question had been nagging at Pete since he'd left Jackson with his lawyer. "No. Truth be told, I don't."

Before Baronick could respond, Zoe pushed between him and the doorjamb. "You don't what?"

"Nothing." Pete shot a look at Baronick and then turned on Zoe. "I told you to wait until after I talked to your mother."

Zoe dismissed the subject with a quick shake of her head. "I just got a phone call."

"A lot of that going around," Pete said.

"Oh? Well, mine was from Mrs. Kroll. Mr. Kroll is awake."

"Really? That's great. Can he talk?"

"I don't know. She sounded ecstatic so he must be doing well. I was gonna head to the hospital to see him. If you still need me to keep an eye on Harry, I can take him with me."

Pete's mind raced, sorting out the latest developments. "You can take both of us. I need to question Marvin Kroll. Hopefully he saw his shooter. And I had a phone call, too." He lowered his head, fixing his gaze on Zoe. "Your father's body has been exhumed. It's being transported to the morgue right now. Marshall intends to do the autopsy this evening."

A gasping cry caused all three of them to turn toward the conference room. "What?" Kimberly stood a few feet inside the door, her trembling fingers pressed to her lips. "You dug up Gary's body? Without my consent?"

"We didn't need your consent, Mrs. Jackson," Pete said. "Your late husband's part of an open, ongoing case. A judge issued a court order this morning."

Kimberly took two staggering steps toward them. Pete thought for a moment she might collapse. But her eyes grew damp and fierce, and she pointed a shaking manicured finger at Zoe. "You. This is all your doing. You've insisted on seeing his body. You couldn't just let him rest in peace. That man loved you. And Tom loves you. But it's not enough.

Nothing is ever enough for you. How dare you desecrate your father's grave…his memory?" Kimberly's voice broke. "How *dare* you." With a movement as smooth and as fast as a cat, Kimberly swung, slapping Zoe full across her face.

The crack echoed down the hall. Zoe gasped. Staggered. Pete grabbed for her, dropping a crutch that clattered to the floor. Baronick made a move to block Kimberly, but too late. Harry snatched the woman from behind by her shoulders, and pulled her away from her daughter.

"That wasn't very nice," Harry said.

Kimberly appeared as stunned as the rest of them. She brought both hands to her face, and her eyes widened in shock. Whimpering, she sagged back against Harry. Baronick jumped to catch her before she could slump to the floor taking Pete's father with her.

In Pete's peripheral vision, he noticed Harry and Baronick ease Kimberly into a chair at the conference table, but his full attention was on Zoe, rigid against his chest. Her breath came in short, choking huffs, refusing to surrender to tears.

"Detective," Pete called over Zoe's head, "take care of charging Mrs. Jackson with assault. Pop? Help me get Zoe out of here."

A smile spread across his father's face. "You got it, son." He stepped away from Kimberly, but stopped and turned back. He shook his head at her. "That wasn't very nice at all."

Zoe's face finally quit stinging by the time she parked her truck at the Brunswick Hospital, but the slap had penetrated much deeper. Her mother may have done a lot of insensitive things to Zoe over the years, but Kimberly had never once struck her. Until now.

The drive to the city was silent, and the silence continued during the ride in the elevator. Flanked by Pete and Harry, Zoe hugged herself against the memory of her mother's fury. Her driver's license might state she was thirty-five, but at that moment she felt as lonely and raw as when she lost her dad twenty-seven years ago.

As if reading her thoughts, Harry put a fatherly arm around her shoulders.

A flush of heat boiled up behind her eyes. She blinked hard and sniffed back the threatening tears. She would not cry. Bad enough to ache as if she'd lost another parent—because she had—but she wouldn't let Harry and Pete see her bawling like a child.

Leaning against Harry, she forced her thoughts to the murders. Could Tom really be a cold-blooded killer? Now that Mr. Kroll had regained consciousness, they would find out for certain. Tom would either be charged and tried. Or cleared.

The doors swished open, and the three of them stepped out. Arrows directed them to the ICU where they were greeted by a pair of automatic doors labeled with signs restricting patients to no more than two visitors at any time. Another placard indicated that to be admitted, use the green phone. Pete reached for the receiver.

"Zoe?" a frail and familiar voice said.

She turned to find Mrs. Kroll and Alexander coming up behind them.

"Zoe dear. I'm so glad you came." The older woman drew her into a feeble embrace. "Isn't it wonderful? Marvin's going to be all right."

Ashamed of being so wrapped up in her own self-centered woes, Zoe smiled at the love and relief in Mrs. Kroll's voice. "It's definitely wonderful, Mrs. Kroll."

Pete shook hands with Alexander. "I hoped to be able to speak with your father. He might be able to clear up a few things."

"Yes, of course." Alexander glanced at his mother. "We haven't spoken to Dad about what happened. I didn't want to upset him. But he's doing remarkably well. All things considered."

Mrs. Kroll picked up the phone that Pete had reached for and pushed a button.

Zoe frowned at the sign limiting visitors to two per bedside. She wanted to be there when Pete questioned Mr. Kroll. She wanted to know who had been killing area farmers for over four decades—who may have been responsible for her father's death as well.

Pete must have figured out what she was thinking. He took her hand. "I need you to stay with Harry."

"But, Pete—" She winced, hating the whine in her voice. Took a breath and tried again. "But, Pete, I need to find out—"

He gave her hand a squeeze, gentle but firm. "I'll find out for you. We can't both go in there and leave Harry out here."

She looked at Pete's dad and was once again struck by the resemblance. Except Pete maintained his air of authority, while Harry appeared lost, gazing down the hallway toward the elevators, a bewildered look on his face.

Zoe heaved a resigned sigh. "I know. Go ahead. I'll take care of him."

Pete gave her hand another squeeze. But instead of releasing it, he drew her closer, leaned forward, and pressed a kiss to her forehead. "Thanks," he whispered into her hair.

Mrs. Kroll hung up the phone, and the automatic doors crept open. "Chief Adams? We can go back now."

Pete held Zoe's gaze for a moment before turning and hobbling through the doors with Mrs. Kroll at his side.

As the doors drifted shut, Zoe became aware of the silence and noticed Alexander grinning at her, obviously aware of the moment that had just passed between her and Pete. Her cheeks warmed. She cleared her throat and looked to Harry, who had missed the whole thing. He continued to look toward the elevators with that befuddled look on his face.

She moved to his side. "Harry? Are you all right?"

Startled he looked at her wide-eyed. Then smiled. "When did you get here?"

Zoe opened her mouth to remind him she'd driven him here, but thought better of it. "Just now. How are you?"

"Fine and dandy." But he scowled when he lifted his gaze to the elevators again.

"Harry? Is something wrong?"

He gave his head a shake and reached up to rub his forehead. "It's hell to get old. I could swear I just saw someone I know, but I can't recall his name. If he comes back, I'm gonna feel like an idiot. He'll know me, but I won't know him."

Zoe looked down the empty hallway. She hadn't seen anyone come or go since they'd arrived. "Don't worry about it." She patted Harry's arm. "Whoever it was probably left and won't be back."

The possibility didn't seem to placate him. "I can't place him, but I know I've seen him before." Harry's eyes narrowed. "And I don't think I liked him much."

* * *

Pete hesitated in the doorway to Marvin Kroll's cubicle. The old gentleman had always seemed so robust. An unstoppable source of energy who loved to drive his tractor and his quad and take care of his farm. Lying there, his head swathed in bandages—tubes, lines, and catheters streaming from his body—he reminded Pete of a deflated balloon.

Mrs. Kroll struggled into a paper gown she'd removed from a shelf outside the room. "You'll need to put one of these on, too, Chief."

"Yes, ma'am." Pete helped her get her second arm through, then he selected a gown of his own and suited up.

The small room smelled of antiseptic. A monitor above the bed tracked Kroll's heart rhythm. Two machines produced intermittent beeps of different tones.

Mrs. Kroll shuffled to her husband's bedside, rested a small hand on his arm, and bent over to kiss him on the cheek. He stirred. With a smile, she whispered something to him, and he smiled back.

A cavern opened inside Pete's chest. He ached for what these two old folks had. A bond so close that it had survived decades of for better or worse, in sickness and in health. He'd had it once. He thought. But nowhere in his marriage vows was there any mention of sticking out the long hours and fears involved in being wed to a cop.

Mrs. Kroll fingered a strand of her husband's white hair sticking out from the bandage. "Marv, honey? Chief Adams is here to see you. Do you think you can talk to him?'

Kroll moved his head slightly, as if trying to get a good look at Pete. Taking the hint, Pete crutched closer to the bed. "Hello, Mr. Kroll. How are you feeling?"

He managed a weak shrug. "Like I've been run over by a hay wagon."

"I'll try to be brief. Can you tell me who did this to you?"

Kroll's forehead creased. "I wish I could. But I don't remember anything about it."

"Nothing? Maybe you remember having company? Did anyone come to see you? Talk to you?"

"I wouldn't know I'd been shot in the barn if Bernice hadn't told me." With what looked like Herculean effort, Kroll tried to shift in his bed. He let out a groan as he settled back where he'd started. "I don't even recall going to the barn. To be honest, I'm not sure I remember getting up that morning. Doctors say I have retro— retro—"

Mrs. Kroll patted his arm. "Retrograde amnesia, dear."

He nodded. "They tell me I may never remember the stuff I did right before the accident."

Except it wasn't an accident. Damn it. Pete had hoped Kroll could solve this string of crimes by giving him one lousy name. But Pete knew about head traumas and had been afraid this might be the case. So he tried another route. "Mr. Kroll, do you remember going to see James Engle last Wednesday?"

The old man became even more still. Only that zigzagging line of mountain peaks and valleys on the monitor gave evidence of life. After several long moments, Kroll blew out an audible breath. "Yes."

"Why did you go see him?"

"I had some questions for him."

"Questions? About what?"

Kroll continued to stare unblinking at Pete. "I...I'd rather not say."

"Did these questions have anything to do with the letter you'd hidden in your tractor's tool box?"

The old man's eyes widened, and he shot a glance at his wife.

"It's okay, honey," she said, her voice soft. "I've seen the letter. I know all about it."

Kroll grimaced. "I didn't want you to find out about it until..."

"Until what?" Pete asked.

The question appeared to pain him more than his injuries. "I wanted more information than what that no account rattlesnake provided in that damnable letter of his. It was a tease is all it was. He didn't really say a blamed thing."

Mrs. Kroll laid a hand on her husband's chest. "He said I wasn't at fault for Vernie or Denver's deaths. That's something."

He met her gaze, tears rimming his eyes. Pete noticed the old man's heart rate had rocketed.

"It wasn't enough. I wanted to know why the blazes he let this go on for all these years. Why he let you suffer. That son of a—" Kroll pressed his lips closed in a hard frown. "I figured James had done it. Killed those men. And I wanted him to admit it to me." Kroll looked at

Pete. "And to you, too, of course. I wanted him to come clean. As punishment. Not only for the crimes, but for what he's put my girl through all these years. Letting her believe she was responsible for the deaths of those men. The guilt she carried—" The old man's voice cracked and a tear traced alongside his cheek, to his pillow. "And for him to suggest that burden may have contributed to her illness and never do anything about it."

Mrs. Kroll swept a hand across his face, brushing the tear away, then bent down and kissed his forehead.

Pete gave them a minute. Once Kroll seemed composed, Pete said, "And did you get him to admit anything?"

"In a manner of speaking. He said he was protecting his sister."

"His sister?" Pete checked his notes. "Mae? Vernon Miller had gotten her pregnant."

Kroll raised an eyebrow. "You knew?"

"I told him," Mrs. Kroll said.

"So did James say his sister killed the Miller brothers?"

Kroll appeared to consider the question. "No. He didn't say anything concrete. Just that Mae had been sweet and they were protecting her."

"They?"

"I assume he meant him and his brother. But when I asked him about it, he clammed up. Told me he'd said as much as he was free to."

Pete jotted a reminder to press Wilford Engle on the matter. "Mr. Kroll, how did James seem when you left?"

"Seem?" The old man pondered the question. "I guess I'd have to say he seemed glum. Despondent. But to be perfectly honest, the few times I've seen him over the last few years, he's been that way. A real sad sack."

Which meshed with Dr. Weinstein's diagnosis of depression. "Did you see anyone else around James' place while you were there?"

"No, sir."

"Any other cars? Maybe you might have thought they were just passing by, but could have stopped after you pulled out?"

Kroll started to shake his head, but winced. "No. I didn't see a living soul."

"Just one last thing. Why didn't you say anything about this sooner? Especially after you heard the man had died."

Kroll shifted his moist gaze to his wife. "Because I didn't know what to say to Bernice. I thought I might go back and talk to him again, but then he went and killed himself two days later."

"Actually, Mr. Kroll, James Engle died that same day you talked to him."

Kroll choked. "What?"

"His body wasn't found until Friday night, but the coroner believes he died sometime Wednesday."

"Son of a..." Kroll fell silent for a moment. "I didn't think one thing had anything to do with the other. Could my questions have driven James to...to kill himself?"

"I don't believe so."

A nurse breezed into the room and snatched a pair of Latex gloves from a box on the wall. "I'm sorry. I'll have to ask you folks to step out for just a couple minutes."

Pete folded his notebook into his pocket and repositioned his crutches. "I have all I need for right now, anyway." He thanked both of the Krolls for their time and made his way out of the room.

In the hallway, Pete stripped out of the paper gown and slamdunked it into the trash bin. Had Marvin Kroll's questions driven James Engle to kill himself? Ironic that for years Bernice Kroll carried the guilt of having pushed two brothers to murder and suicide, and now her husband felt the same kind of culpability.

Could James Engle's death truly have been at his own hand? From what Pete could determine, Kroll had been the last person to see him alive, but Pete wasn't buying Kroll as a killer. Besides, the old man had been unconscious in his hospital bed when Carl Loomis had been murdered. And while James may very well have killed the Millers all those years ago, he certainly hadn't shot Kroll. Or Loomis.

Which meant there was still someone out there.

Or back in Pete's jail.

TWENTY-SEVEN

Zoe glanced at the waiting room door as she thumbed through a tattered six-month-old Hollywood gossip magazine. Harry fidgeted in the chair next to her like an impatient eight-year-old. "When can we go home?" he asked for the fourth time.

"As soon as Pete comes out from visiting Mr. Kroll." Also for the fourth time. She didn't mention her father's autopsy, which was scheduled to start within the hour.

She heard the electronic doors out in the hallway hiss open and expected to see a doctor or nurse cruise past the waiting room, just like the other dozen times. But this time several long seconds passed before someone appeared, and that someone was Pete.

Zoe jumped up. "How is he?"

Alexander Kroll rose from his seat as well and moved next to her.

"Considering what he's been through, he looks good," Pete said. To Alexander he added, "You can go back now if you want."

Alexander thanked him and hurried off.

"Well?" Zoe prodded. "Who did he say shot him?"

"He didn't." Pete checked his watch. "We better get down to the morgue. Come on, Pop."

Harry sprung from his chair. "Are we going home now?"

"Not yet." Pete did an awkward pivot and hobbled away.

"What do you mean, 'he didn't'?" Zoe caught Harry's arm and guided him after Pete.

"Kroll doesn't remember. In fact, he doesn't remember much of anything that happened earlier that day."

"Crap."

"Watch your mouth, young lady." Harry's voice sounded reprimanding, but his eyes twinkled.

Zoe feigned being dutifully rebuked. "Yes, sir. Sorry."

Harry grinned and tucked her hand into the crook of his elbow. A gentleman escorting a lady.

To the morgue.

Zoe drew Harry alongside Pete. "Did you learn anything from Mr. Kroll?"

Pete pressed the down button at the elevator. "Yeah. I don't believe he killed James Engle."

She shot a look of annoyance at Pete. He ignored her which irritated her even more.

The doors pinged open, and they rode down to the sub-basement level.

They found Franklin Marshall in the office, already wearing his scrubs and ready to step through the doors into autopsy. He glanced at each of them before his gaze settled on Pete. "We have quite an audience today, don't we?"

Zoe noticed a look pass between the two of them. "What?"

Pete started to answer, but Franklin held up a hand. "Zoe, I know I've hounded you about participating in autopsies, but I'm afraid this isn't one you should attend."

She slipped free of Harry's arm. "That's my father in there."

"Which is precisely why you shouldn't be."

"No. Oh, no." She shook her head. "Not again." A gentle hand touched her shoulder. She wheeled on Pete, nearly knocking him off balance. "No one let me see my dad when I was little. You're not going to keep me from seeing him now."

"Franklin, keep an eye on Pop for me." Pete held Zoe's gaze and tipped his head toward the hallway. "Walk with me for a minute."

"It's not gonna make a difference."

"Just hear me out." Pete shifted both crutches to one hand and slung the other arm over her shoulders, leaning on her. "Come on."

They left Harry and Franklin behind and stepped into the empty hallway.

Under different circumstances, the physical closeness to Pete, the warmth of him, the scent of him, would have made her dizzy. Instead, she braced against what she knew was coming. Another "for your own good" speech.

"I need to see my father." She held her voice steady and low when what she wanted was to scream.

"I know."

She was stunned when the expected argument didn't transpire.

He reshuffled the crutches and turned to face her, resting both strong hands on her shoulders, tracing her collarbone with his thumbs.

She shivered at his touch.

"The problem," he said, "is your father isn't in there."

"What?" Had Pete learned something? For a moment her heart swelled with hope. Was her dad alive after all?

"What's in there is a cadaver. A dead body. Everything that made him your dad has been gone for a very long time."

She deflated. "I understand, but—"

Pete squeezed. Gently. "But nothing. Listen to me. I know you. I know what you want and where you're coming from. You need proof. Incontrovertible proof that your dad died twenty-seven years ago." Pete's voice grew softer. He lowered his face toward hers. "All you're going to see in there is a burnt shell of a man who's been long gone."

She couldn't hold Pete's gaze any longer and looked at the front of his wrinkled shirt. "But if that really is my father's body in there—"

Pete brought one hand up to cup her cheek. "Zoe, let me do this for you. Let me take your place in there. Let me make that ID for you."

She choked on tears that came out of nowhere. She tried to argue, but the words jammed in her throat.

"Zoe." Her name on Pete's lips sounded like a caress. "Do you trust me?"

She lifted her gaze to his clear blue eyes again and felt as though he'd connected to her thoughts, her soul. Her heart. Did she trust him? After all the bad choices she'd made in her life, did she trust this one man?

"Yes," she whispered.

"Then let me do this for you." He lowered his face a little more, until his forehead touched hers. "I promise I won't keep anything from you."

The air had been sucked out of the hallway. Except for Pete's warm breath on her face. Her lips. Thoughts swam, unfocused, across her brain. Her father's body. The closed casket. What lurked under that lid? The truth. But could she trust this truth to anyone else? Even Pete?

"Okay." Her voice sounded wet and strangled even to her own ears.

He skimmed his thumb across her lips. Pressed a lingering kiss to her cheek. And stepped back, breaking the link between them. Zoe struggled to regain her balance and her composure.

"I'll tell you everything I find out," Pete said. "Everything. You have my word."

She nodded, afraid to speak.

He reached out and touched her face again. This time, she leaned into his touch.

"I'll take good care of your dad." Pete's voice wavered. "You take care of mine."

"I want to go home." Harry sounded less like an eight-year-old and more like a stubborn old mule as Zoe guided him out of the elevator at the fourth floor and back toward the ICU.

"I know. I'm sorry. We have to wait for Pete to...get done with what he's doing." She touched the spot on her cheek Pete had kissed. The memory of his lips, the heat of his closeness, made her slightly woozy.

"How long is that going to take?" Harry demanded.

She switched from a mental picture of Pete's eyes to one of a closed casket. "A while I'm afraid."

Harry glowered. "I want to go home."

"I'll make you a deal. We'll check on Mrs. Kroll. See if I can get in to visit my landlord for a minute. Then you and I will go down to the snack bar and get a milkshake."

The frown vanished. "A milkshake? Chocolate?"

Zoe held her arms out from her sides. "Is there any other kind?"

"All righty then. Let's go."

She took Harry's arm, and they started toward the waiting room. At the end of the hall, the automatic doors to the ICU swung open, and a trio in scrubs carrying on an animated conversation breezed out. At the same moment, a painfully thin old man shuffled out of the waiting room and headed toward the elevator and Zoe and Harry. The old man lifted his head and his cold gaze seemed to settle on them.

Then he collapsed.

The trio in the scrubs leaped to his side. One of them managed to break the old man's fall, easing him to the floor. A second one knelt beside him. The third whipped her stethoscope from around her neck.

Zoe kicked into paramedic mode and pulled away from Harry. But he closed his fingers around her arm.

"No." Harry's voice was oddly low and deep. Authoritarian. Very much like Pete's.

Stunned, she turned to look at Harry. His expression was as stern and serious as his voice. "Harry, I'm a paramedic. I might be able to help."

He didn't release his grip. "No. Let someone else take care of him."

The way Harry said *him* sent a chill up Zoe's spine. She looked back at the group outside the waiting room. They were helping the old man to his feet. He brushed them off as if they were a swarm of gnats. "I'm fine," she heard him say. "I take these spells."

"Who is he?" she asked Harry.

"I don't remember. I just know he's not nice."

As they watched, the old man shook off the last of the medical team's attempts at assistance and continued toward Zoe and Harry with his head lowered. Watching his step. Or avoiding eye contact.

He passed them wide to their right without looking up. But Zoe never took her eyes off him. Something about him seemed familiar. Considering his age and frail condition, she'd probably transported him in the ambulance at some point.

Harry urged her forward. "Let's go."

She kept her gaze on the old man behind them as she allowed Harry to draw her toward the waiting room. The elevator doors pinged open, and the old man got on.

And Patsy Greene, loaded with a huge bouquet wrapped in green tissue, stepped off. She spotted Zoe and waved. "There you are," Patsy called and broke into a jog to catch up.

Zoe had to wrestle Harry to stop.

"Who's your date?" Patsy asked with a grin.

"Have you met Pete's dad?"

Patsy gave Harry a big smile and extended a hand. "Can't say I've had the pleasure. I can see where Pete gets his good looks."

Harry beamed as he took her hand.

"Harry, this is one of my very best friends, Patsy Greene. She boards her horse at my farm and helps me around the barn."

"Speaking of which," Patsy said to Zoe. "I quit."

Zoe choked. "What?"

"You should see the mess those cops are making."

She'd forgotten about that. The search for the missing gun. "Did they find something?"

"Nope. But they dumped all the manure out of the spreader inside the arena. Look, girlfriend, I don't mind cleaning stalls and loading that thing one time, but I'll be darned if I'm doing it a second time. I'm nice, but not that nice."

Zoe wasn't sure if she was more annoyed with the idea that she would be the one cleaning up that mess—or amused with the mental picture of Nate and the county guys sifting through all that horse crap.

Harry pointed at the bouquet. "Are those for me?" He grinned. "You shouldn't have."

Patsy laughed. "Sorry, Mr. Adams. They're for Mr. Kroll." Her smile faded as she glanced at Zoe. "How is he?"

Zoe slipped her arm through Harry's again and tugged him forward. "Pete spoke with him earlier. I guess he can't remember what happened on Saturday, so he wasn't able to tell who shot him."

Patsy swore under her breath. "That's too bad. I'll feel a whole lot better when they catch whoever did it."

Zoe thought of Tom back in Vance Township. Maybe they already had.

Patsy stepped in front of them and stopped. "Hey. What are you doing up here anyway? I thought your dad's autopsy was this evening."

"It is." Zoe's mind drifted down to the hospital's lowest floor and her heart sank equally far. "In fact, it's going on right now."

Pete had gratefully taken advantage of the stool Franklin Marshall offered. Perched there next to the door, Pete watched the coroner and Doc Abercrombie work on the body.

Pete had no regrets about sending Zoe away. The remains on the stainless steel table weren't something she should have to deal with even had they belonged to a total stranger. But odds were this charred corpse had been Zoe's dad.

Through the years, Pete'd had the misfortune of seeing things. Ugly things. Tragedies and horrors beyond the comprehension of anyone outside of law enforcement or emergency response personnel. He'd seen bodies pulled from burning wrecks.

Nothing compared to this.

Marshall and Abercrombie clearly felt the same way. During most autopsies Pete had observed in this morgue, the two men played music. Head pounding rock. This evening, as soon as they'd opened the body bag, the radio had been turned off.

The door next to Pete swung open and Wayne Baronick slipped in. "How's it going?"

Pete shrugged. "I don't know how much they can really do with a twenty-seven-year-old corpse, but they're working on it. How about you? Find anything at the Kroll farm?"

Baronick's wide-eyed gaze locked on Gary Chamber's body. "Not a damned thing. By the way, don't make me sift through a wagonload of horse shit ever again."

"I'm not your boss. I didn't make you do anything."

"Right." Baronick blinked and scanned the rest of the room. "Where's Zoe? I thought for sure she'd be here."

"I talked her out of it. She's with Harry."

The detective shot another glance at the remains. "Good."

A murmur passed between the two men at the table, and Marshall cleared his throat. "Chief? I believe we have something here."

Pete gathered his crutches and pushed off the stool. "What is it?"

Doc Abercrombie turned to face him, pinching a pair of forceps.

Pete didn't need to get any closer to see what they held.

"It's only preliminary until I finish here, but I feel pretty safe in saying cause of death was not smoke inhalation. Nor was manner of death accidental. We have a gunshot wound. And a homicide."

Pete wasn't surprised.

He watched as Doc dropped the slug into a specimen jar and packed the whole thing in a plastic bag. The pathologist scribbled on it and handed the package to Baronick, who also made a notation for the chain of evidence.

The detective held the bagged jar up so both he and Pete could see the contents. "I'll run this over the ballistics lab. I'll bet a week's pay it matches the others."

Pete blew out a breath. "No bet."

TWENTY-EIGHT

With Harry and Patsy in tow, Zoe found Mrs. Kroll in the waiting room. The older woman's eyes widened in delight when she spotted Patsy's bouquet.

"How lovely."

Patsy handed them over. "They're from all the boarders at the farm. We wanted Mr. Kroll to know we're thinking of him.

The green tissue crinkled as Mrs. Kroll buried her face in the flowers and inhaled. "That's sweet of you. But he's not allowed to have anything like this here in the ICU. Maybe once he gets into a regular room."

Patsy's shoulders sagged. "I wasn't thinking."

"Don't worry about it, dear. I'll take them home with me. We're leaving in a little bit anyway."

Harry patted Zoe's arm. "I want to go home, too."

"Pretty soon," she told him. "Mrs. Kroll, I was wondering if Mr. Kroll might be up for one more visitor." When her landlady appeared puzzled, Zoe pointed to herself.

"I'm sorry, Zoe. They just took him down for a CAT scan. He might be gone a while."

"Oh." Zoe glanced at Harry. Impatient-to-get-home Harry. He'd wandered over to the alcove by the door to watch a young volunteer pour more water into the coffeemaker. How long could she keep him distracted? How long would the autopsy on her father take? "Maybe I'll check back later. If not, I'll stop in tomorrow."

"That would be fine." Mrs. Kroll buried her nose in the flowers again. "These smell wonderful. I can't get over how kind everyone has been. Folks have been dropping off food at the house. Neighbors, farmers, have been coming by here to check on Marv and me. Even some I never would've thought would care. Or make the effort. Heavens, of all the people in this valley, the last person I'd expect to be so thoughtful is Wilford. Yet he's been here every single day."

The skin on Zoe's neck prickled as if a toxic wooly caterpillar had just crawled from her collar. "Wilford?"

Mrs. Kroll nodded.

"Wilford *Engle*?"

"Why, yes. He was just here a few minutes ago."

The man who had fallen. Who had avoided eye contact as he passed them on his way to the elevator. She hadn't seen him in years, which explained why she hadn't recognized him, yet he'd seemed familiar. She remembered Pete saying Harry had been with him when they'd gone to talk to James' brother. Harry's words, *he's not nice*, echoed in her mind.

Zoe spun on her heel toward the coffeemaker. The young volunteer was refilling the bins with packets of sugar.

But Harry was gone.

Pete didn't expect the autopsy to turn up anything else, so he followed Baronick out of the morgue. In the hall, he dug out his cell phone and called the station. Instead of Nancy, Seth answered.

"Is Tom Jackson still there?"

"Yeah, but not for much longer. His attorney is throwing a fit. Making all kinds of threats."

"Keep him there. I'm on my way back, and I have a few more questions for our houseguest."

"You got it, Chief."

Baronick, still holding the evidence bag containing the slug, looked around. "How're you getting back? Your driver is MIA."

Pete grunted and dialed Zoe's number. "Did you think she and my father were going to stand here in the hall all evening?"

Baronick shrugged. "To be honest, I figured she'd be leaning on the door with her nose pressed to the glass."

The thought had occurred to Pete, too. But Harry had been pretty rambunctious. More than likely Zoe had to resort to treating him at the snack bar to settle him down.

"Pete?" Zoe's voice sounded odd on the phone.

"I'm ready to go back to the station. Where are you?"

There was silence for a moment. "Um. I'm up in the ICU waiting room. I—um—don't know how to tell you this. I can't find Harry."

The tightness in Pete's shoulders from the crutches crept up into his skull. Not again. "How long has he been missing?"

"Just a couple of minutes. He was right here, and then I turned my back, and he was gone." Her voice tap-danced up the musical scale with each word.

"Don't panic." Pete had been guilty of that twice already and been made a fool of both times. "He probably wandered down the hall. Check the restrooms. Check the storage rooms. He hasn't gone far. I'll be there in a minute."

"Pete?"

"Yeah?"

"About the autopsy?" Her voice trailed off.

"We'll talk when I get there."

"Okay." Her voice sounded lost and vulnerable as she clicked off.

Pete closed his eyes for a moment. When he looked up, Baronick was studying him. "Harry's wandered off again?"

"So it would seem."

"You need some sort of GPS tracking device you can slip in the old man's shoe."

Pete snorted. "That's not a bad idea. He hasn't been gone long. Zoe probably will have tracked him down by the time I get there."

Baronick tucked the evidence bag into his jacket pocket and fell into step beside Pete. "We. By the time *we* get there."

Zoe peeked in yet another patient room. Both TVs on. Both patients in bed, sleeping. No visitors. No Harry.

This was all her fault. She was supposed to keep an eye on him. Everyone knew his tendency to wander off.

She moved to the next, her heart pounding harder than if she'd run a marathon instead of simply race-walking up and down the fourth floor hallways. One last room. No sign of Harry there either. She took off, sprinting around the corner, pausing for the automatic doors to swing open.

Zoe plunged through and pulled up short before colliding with Pete and Baronick.

The detective caught her by the shoulders. "Slow down there."

Pete nudged him aside. "I guess I don't have to ask if you've found Harry."

The weight of failing Pete crushed down on her. "Not yet. But I have Patsy Greene and Alexander Kroll checking the other wings on this floor. Mrs. Kroll is checking in ICU."

Baronick pulled out his cell phone. "I'll call security."

"I already did. They're on their way." She studied Pete. Stress showed through his poker face veneer. How could she ask about her own father when she'd just misplaced his?

"Harry does this all the time," Pete said, his voice soothing. "He'll turn up any minute now, wondering what all the fuss is about."

She hoped so. God, she hoped so.

Baronick cleared his throat. "I think I'll go call security *again*." He fingered his phone as he walked away.

Pete moved closer to her. "Zoe, the autopsy's been completed."

"I assumed as much." The questions she needed to ask were stuck. Pete had answers. But did she want to hear them? "And?"

"You know the standard line about ongoing cases and waiting for the lab to confirm results." Pete paused. "But dental records matched. The body in the casket is definitely your father."

The hospital hallway—the entire world—tilted. Zoe closed her eyes for a moment, but that only made it worse. Pete grabbed her by the arms. Kept her from spinning off into oblivion. He drew her against his chest. She leaned there trying to remember how to breathe.

Her father...her dad...was gone. For good. He hadn't run off. He hadn't entered the witness protection program. He hadn't disappeared in order to protect her. He was dead.

As she struggled to process reality, she realized Pete wasn't so much holding her in his arms as he was bracing her.

There was more.

Zoe eased back. "What else?"

He released her arms, taking her hands instead. "Abercrombie found a bullet. Baronick'll take it to the county lab."

Another bullet. Not only was her dad dead, he'd been murdered. "It's going to match, you know."

"That's what I figure."

The world around her that a moment ago had been whirling out of control became very still and focused. "You go with Baronick. Do what you need to do to track down who—whoever killed my father. Don't worry about Harry. I'll find him."

Pete tipped his head, eyeing her.

"You asked me to trust you. Now I'm asking you to trust me. I'll find Harry. I promise."

After Pete and Baronick left, Zoe headed back to her headquarters of search operations—the ICU waiting room.

Alexander Kroll shrugged and held up his hands. "I checked every men's room on this floor. He wasn't in any of them."

What if something had happened to Harry? She'd lost him. *She* had. And she knew what it was like to lose—really lose—a father. She wouldn't let Pete go through that. Not yet. Not like this. She'd given him her word.

Mrs. Kroll wrung her hands as if applying lotion. "I spoke with the nurses in ICU. No one has seen him."

A rapid *thud thud thud* of footfalls in the hall grew louder, and Patsy skidded around the bend into the room. "I looked in every room in the south wing." She paused, breathing hard. "All the storage and linen closets are locked with keypads, so he couldn't get in them. I checked both the men's and the women's restrooms. And none of the staff have seen him. I told them to keep an eye out."

Zoe turned a full circle, scanning the room, thinking—hoping Harry might suddenly reappear out of thin air. Where was security? She'd phoned them at least fifteen minutes ago.

As if on cue, a pair of uniformed guards ambled through the door. Zoe leaped to meet them. "Have you heard anything yet?"

"We need more information." The older guard, who carried himself like a retired cop or military officer, studied his notebook. "All I have is a missing elderly man with dementia wandered away. Can you give us a description?"

"He's about six feet tall," Zoe said, "white hair, blue eyes, athletic build. I'd guess late sixties, early seventies. His name is Harry Adams. He's Vance Township Police Chief Pete Adams' dad."

The older guard nodded and scribbled notes. The younger one waved a walkie-talkie. "I'll report it." He turned and strode away, speaking into the radio.

"How long has he been missing?"

Zoe looked at her watch. "About twenty minutes." Crap. Harry could have covered a lot of ground in twenty freaking minutes. And she couldn't quite shake that look Wilford Engle had given Harry when he'd spotted them. What was that all about anyway?

"Has he done this sort of thing before?"

She nodded. "But he doesn't usually go very far."

"I'm sure he hasn't this time either."

The younger guard returned. "I've put out an alert," he told them. Turning to Zoe, he asked, "You said he's alone, right?"

"Right. Why?"

"Because one of the volunteers at the front desk reported seeing two elderly men arguing in the lobby about ten minutes ago. One matches the description you gave us. Although that description could match any number of people."

Zoe's mind swam in a sea of muck. Two men arguing? "Did you get a description of the other man?"

"Approximately eighty years old. Tall, very thin. Very pale."

Wilford Engle. Zoe reached for her throat to claw away the invisible hand choking her. "You have to get someone down there to hold them."

"Sorry, ma'am," the young guard said. "The volunteer didn't know about your friend being missing. She said the two men in question left the building."

TWENTY-NINE

"Either charge my client or release him." Anthony Imperatore didn't bother with bluster or theatrics. He was all cool-headed, down-to-earth business.

Pete respected the man, grateful for his legal savvy and determination those times when someone Pete cared about—Sylvia last winter, for instance—was being unjustly accused. But right now, in the hallway of Pete's police station, the attorney reminded him of a pit bull guarding his territory. "I need five minutes with Jackson. That's all. Afterward, I'll cut him loose." Or formally arrest him. But no use mentioning the obvious to Imperatore.

The lawyer eyed Pete askance. "Five minutes. And I will be present during this interview."

"Wouldn't have it any other way."

With a miniscule nod, Imperatore agreed.

Minutes later, Pete once again faced Zoe's stepfather across a table. Jackson's demeanor hadn't improved. "I've just come from Gary Chamber's autopsy."

Jackson lowered his face. "I wish you hadn't done that."

"I'm sure."

Jackson's face came up again. "Not for the reason you seem to think."

"Oh?"

Imperatore tapped the table. "Mr. Jackson, be quiet."

He tipped his head toward his lawyer. "I have nothing to hide." His voice was a growl. "I didn't do anything." He met Pete's gaze and held it firm. "I gather you saw Gary's body."

"I did."

Jackson swallowed. Hard. "Did Zoe?"

"No."

Jackson seemed relieved. But his gaze darkened. "Why not?"

Pete considered reminding the man about who was asking the questions here. But maybe a little honey was in order to catch this fly. "I didn't think she should have to face that."

Jackson studied Pete in silence for a long moment before shifting in his chair. "I give you credit. You really do care for my daughter."

Pete knew where this was headed and let it ride.

"So do I," Jackson said. "And I cared for her—and her mother—when Zoe was eight. I knew how badly burned Gary's body was. I didn't want either of them to have to deal with that."

"How did you know?"

"What?"

"How did you know how badly burned Gary's body was? Unless you saw it."

"No. Froats told me."

"Warren Froats?"

"One and the same."

A knock at the door drew Pete's attention. The door swung open and Baronick entered without invitation.

The detective crossed to Pete's side, kept his back to Jackson and Imperatore, and leaned down to whisper in Pete's ear. "It's a match."

Not that Pete had doubted the result for a minute, but now the lab had confirmed. One gun had been used in every one of the shootings in this forty-five-year crime spree. "Do me a favor." Pete kept his voice low, but didn't care whether his suspect heard or not. "Get Warren Froats in here."

Baronick slipped out, shutting the door behind him.

Pete toyed with his pen. "I spoke with Marvin Kroll this afternoon."

Jackson gave a short laugh. "Then why am I still here if he told you I didn't shoot him?"

"Because he didn't. He has no memory of the incident."

"Son of a bitch." Jackson slammed both hands down on the table.

Imperatore cleared his throat. "Not another word." The lawyer pointed at Pete. "Time's up."

Pete held up his watch. "I still have two minutes."

Imperatore made a production of removing his Rolex and setting it on the table in front of him. "Two minutes. Not a second longer."

So be it. "Kroll received a letter from James Engle, same as you did. In it he stated that Bernice Kroll had nothing to do with the Miller brothers' deaths. Like you, Mr. Kroll went to talk to James. On Wednesday. The same day as you." Pete didn't mention Kroll had been there *after* Jackson. "Kroll believed James had killed the Millers and wanted him to admit it."

"Did he?" Jackson asked, his voice flat.

"Admit to it? No."

Jackson studied his hands, still palm-down on the table. Silent moments ticked away, cutting into Pete's remaining minute. But his gut told him to wait.

Tom Jackson took a long breath. "I was at James' house Wednesday."

"Mr. Jackson," Imperatore scolded.

"It's all right. The chief already knows I was there. And I didn't do anything."

"But—"

Jackson cut off his attorney with a look. Then he sat back in his chair. "I'd opened his letter to Kimberly. I know. I shouldn't have. But I did. And when I read it, I knew it would tear her apart. So I insisted we come north. I arranged things so I could come up a few days ahead of her and talk to Jim."

"Your two minutes are up," Imperatore snapped.

Jackson shook his head. "I acknowledge I have the right to remain silent. I'm waiving it."

Pete suppressed a smile. Under different circumstances, he might just like Zoe's stepfather.

"I wanted to find out what he knew about Gary's accident," Jackson said. "And—everything else, too. I don't know what happened with the Miller brothers. But before that whole incident, Jim had been a father figure. My own father never had much to do with me, so Jim filled a big void. But after all that happened, and his sister died—"

"Died?" Pete paused in his note taking. "Mae Engle is dead?"

"She died in childbirth. They kept it all very hush hush."

"Any idea what happened to the baby?"

"It was put up for adoption is all I know. Anyway, after all that, Jim started drinking. A lot. He began avoiding me. Wouldn't return my calls. If I stopped by, he was either blitzed or too busy to be bothered with me. One time I demanded to know what was going on. Told him I'd always wished he was my dad. He threw an empty whiskey bottle at me." Anguish deepened the creases in Jackson's forehead. "I'll never forget what he said to me that day. 'You're better off staying the hell away from me and my family. Nothing good ever came from being an Engle.'"

Jackson fell silent, his breath raspy. Pete waited for him to compose himself.

After clearing his throat, Jackson continued. "Did I think he killed Denver or Vernon? Or both? Yeah. I did. I still do."

Pete peered up from his notes. "During the autopsy this evening, the M.E. pulled a bullet out of Gary Chambers' body."

Jackson didn't blink.

"You knew."

He shook his head. "Not before I spoke with Jim last Wednesday. Up until then, I thought the same as Kimberly. That Gary had been killed by a drunk driver."

"Carl Loomis."

"Yeah. But after that letter from Jim, I demanded to know what he was talking about and he told me."

"That he'd shot Gary?"

"Not exactly."

If Pete's foot hadn't been throbbing like a diesel engine, he'd have jumped up and gone over the table at Jackson. Instead, he struck the table with his closed fist. "What *exactly* did he say?"

Jackson flinched, but recovered. "He said he felt responsible for Gary's death, but he hadn't been the one who killed him. He said he wasn't free to tell me who had, but he needed to clear his conscience while he still could."

"But James Engle didn't have cancer."

"I know that. Now. But he kept saying he didn't have long for this earth." Jackson rubbed his eyes, letting his fingers rest on the bridge of his nose. "That day, last Wednesday, he was as despondent a man as

I've ever seen. I honestly believed he was dying. I can't explain why he thought he had cancer. Or if he knew he didn't, why he told everyone else that he did. But I can tell you this. If I were a gambler, I'd bet every cent I have that Jim committed suicide."

"You think Wilford Engle *kidnapped* Harry?" Patsy's tone clearly indicated she thought Zoe was certifiable.

Maybe she was.

Zoe jogged through the hospital's parking lot with Patsy on her heels. One of the good things about having a big old pickup was being able to spot it towering over the newer, smaller cars and SUVs. "I'm not sure, but I think it's a possibility." No one had been able to locate Harry anywhere inside the building. "Harry recognized Wilford. Sort of. He couldn't place him, but told me he wasn't nice."

"But why would old Wilford Engle kidnap Harry?"

Reaching her truck, Zoe fumbled the key into the lock. "I guess he didn't know Harry couldn't remember who he was."

Patsy ducked around to the passenger door. Over the truck bed she raised her hands in exasperation. "So what?"

Zoe yanked open the door, hit the button to unlock Patsy's side, tossed her phone on the seat, and jumped in. "So Wilford thinks Harry has spotted him hanging around Mr. Kroll's room." She jammed the key in the ignition without telling Patsy she was figuring this story out as she went. "Wilford doesn't want Harry—or more precisely, Pete—to know he was lurking around the ICU."

Patsy climbed in and reached for the seatbelt. "What difference does it make if Wilford is showing concern for his neighbor?"

"Nothing. Unless it's not concern." The sickening reality settled hard in Zoe's gut. "Wilford was hanging around to find out if Mr. Kroll was going to pull through. And be able to identify him."

Patsy scowled. "Identify him?"

Zoe twisted the ignition. *Click.*

Nothing else. Just click.

Frantically, she glanced at the dashboard's gauges and buttons. To the left of the steering wheel, the toggle for the headlights was flipped.

"Crap!" She pounded the steering wheel. The bad thing about having a big old pickup truck was the warning bell alerting her she'd left the lights on had quit working six months ago. "My battery's dead."

"What were you saying about Mr. Kroll indentifying Wilford Engle?"

In the silence, the pieces clicked just like her crippled truck. "Wilford Engle shot Mr. Kroll."

Patsy gasped. "Why?"

"I'm not sure. But if Wilford thought he'd killed Mr. Kroll and then found out Mr. Kroll had survived, it makes sense he'd want to keep tabs on whether he pulled through or not. And if he regained consciousness, Wilford might have been waiting for an opportunity for a second chance."

Patsy fixed her with a skeptical glare. "You've been watching too many crime shows on TV."

Zoe ignored Patsy as her train of thought picked up speed. The bullet that had been used to shoot Mr. Kroll matched the one that had killed Denver Miller. And Carl Loomis.

And most likely Zoe's father as well. A chill skittered across her shoulders. Was Wilford the killer? Not Tom. But Wilford Engle. And now he had Harry.

Zoe turned to Patsy. "If it's true that Wilford is trying to get rid of Mr. Kroll because he can ID him, he might intend to get rid of Harry, too."

"I can't believe that." But Patsy's voice wavered.

"Why else would Wilford take Harry?"

Patsy frowned and twisted a strand of her hair.

Zoe didn't have time for Patsy to puzzle this out. "Harry's in danger. If I'm wrong, I'll owe Wilford Engle an apology. If I'm right..."

Patsy's hand dropped to her lap. "Come on. We'll take my truck."

They dove out of the Chevy. Zoe fell into step with Patsy as they pounded down the row toward Patsy's white Toyota Tundra. She chirped it open as Zoe circled to the passenger side. Patsy had the big truck fired up before Zoe clicked her seatbelt.

"Where to?" Patsy asked.

Zoe froze. Where to? Where would Wilford take Harry? His house? James' farm? Somewhere else entirely? There were too many possibilities. "Just start back to Vance Township. I need to call Pete." She'd hoped to have Harry safely back home without bothering Pete, but things had gone awry.

Patsy jammed the Tundra into reverse and screeched out of the space. Zoe reached in her pocket for her phone.

Nothing. Her mind raced back. She'd had the phone in her hand as they left the hospital. She'd tossed it on the seat of her truck as she climbed in. "Crap. I left my cell phone in my truck."

"Use mine. It's in the console."

Zoe flipped open the lid of the center cubby. She dug through a jumble of power cords and pulled out Patsy's phone. Except Patsy didn't have Pete's number on speed dial. Or in her address book. Zoe rubbed her forehead, trying to massage her memory into action. Was it...? Yes. She keyed in the number. Hoped it was right.

After one ring, her call went to voicemail. At least it was Pete's voice on the recording, so the number was right. "Pete, it's Zoe," she said after the beep. "I have a problem..."

Pete sat alone in the conference room, staring at the white board.

Tom and Kimberly Jackson were once again on their way to the airport. Pete wished they'd have stuck around and smoothed things over with Zoe—if that were possible.

Ignoring his throbbing foot, Pete pushed up from his chair and made his way across the room to the board with one crutch. He thumbed the cap from the dry-erase marker and drew lines through both Jacksons' names.

From his pocket, his phone chirped. He set down the marker and dug out the phone. The screen showed a number he didn't recognize.

Someone pounded on the door, and it swung open before Pete had a chance to say anything. Warren Froats stormed in with Baronick right behind. Pete pressed the key to silence his phone and slipped it back in his pocket.

"Dammit, Pete, you could've just called and invited me to come in," Froats said, hoisting a thumb at Baronick. "You didn't have to send the goddamn Boy Scouts."

"I wanted to make sure you got here," Pete said.

Baronick snorted. "Yeah. Old codgers like you might forget where the police station is."

Froats grumbled something and looked around. "First time I been in the station since you young punks moved it."

Pete braced the one crutch in front of him, resting his crossed arms on it. "What do you think?"

Froats grunted. "Too fancy schmancy. Lacks the charm of the old digs."

"At least the police department actually works cases now," Baronick said. "Unlike in your day when you just went through the motions and spent most of your time keeping the bars in business."

"Watch it, sonny. I'll take Pete's crutch there and break your leg to match his." Froats nodded at Pete's foot. "When are you gonna get that thing fixed up proper?"

"When I solve this case. I had a long chat with Tom Jackson."

Froats pulled out a chair, sat down, and propped one work-booted foot, then the other on the table, crossing his ankles. "Jackson didn't do it."

"Do what?"

"Anything you were accusing him of."

"And you know this how?"

"Because I'm an excellent judge of human nature."

Baronick barked a laugh. "Which is why your history of solving murders is so good."

"What murders?"

"Let's start with Gary Chambers," Pete said.

Froats waved a hand as if shooing a fly. "That was no murder. That was an accidental death. Drunk driver. You know that."

Pete shut up Baronick with a look. He wanted the pleasure of this revelation for himself. "Except it wasn't. We exhumed Chambers' body this afternoon and Franklin Marshall performed an autopsy. The autopsy that should have been done twenty-seven years ago. On your watch."

Froats' cocky attitude faded.

"Marshall dug a .38 caliber slug out of the body." Pete watched Froats as the words sank in. "It matches the one that killed Denver Miller forty-five years ago and Carl Loomis yesterday. Not to mention the one they dug out of Marvin Kroll."

Froats' summer-fishing-on-the-creek tan paled. "Well, I'll be damned."

Baronick huffed. "You said it. I didn't."

Pete recounted what they'd learned about Marvin and Bernice Kroll and Mae Engle. "Both Jackson and Kroll seem to think James Engle killed the Miller boys. And if Gary Chambers was asking a lot of questions about them before his death, it makes sense that James might have wanted to shut him up, too. That being the case, guilt combined with going off his depression meds could very well have driven James Engle to commit suicide." He paused and looked at Baronick, a six-foot sentry stationed by the door. Then back at Froats. "The problem with that otherwise perfectly reasonable scenario is there's no way James Engle shot Marvin Kroll or killed Carl Loomis."

Froats wheezed. "If we're going along with your theory, we could make a case that he had motive, though. He might've been afraid that Loomis was gonna talk after all these years."

Baronick shifted from standing soldier straight to leaning back against the wall. "But Loomis had no memory of that night."

"Engle could have been afraid Loomis might start remembering shit," Froats said.

Baronick smirked. "Except Engle was already dead. And I don't believe in ghosts."

Pete stuck the crutch under his right arm and leaned hard on it as he stared at the white board. There was one name on the board that was only there once—in the column under James Engle's homicide. Pete had become more and more convinced James' hanging had indeed been the suicide it first appeared to be, so he hadn't paid much attention to that list. He hobbled over to it, picked up the marker again and, using it as a pointer, pressed the cap to that one name. "What do we know about the brother? Wilford."

Behind Pete, Froats and Baronick fell silent. Pete looked over his shoulder, raising a questioning eyebrow at his "team."

Baronick shrugged. "From what I've seen of him, he's too frail to be much of a threat to anyone."

"It doesn't take much strength to pull a trigger," Pete said.

Froats rubbed the stubble on his chin. "As I recall, Wilford was always the quiet one. Had all the charm of a diamondback rattler. But he stayed out of trouble. And out of the spotlight."

"What kind of relationship did he have with James?"

"They were tight."

"Yet Wilford didn't know James' cancer was a ruse."

Baronick came away from the wall. "And why the ruse in the first place?"

Pete nodded to Froats.

"Why claim to have cancer when he didn't?" Froats appeared to contemplate the question. "How the hell should I know? But I will tell you this much. Now that I think about it, I always thought Wilford was the smart one and James was his puppet. Wilford stayed in the shadows. James did as he was told."

A sickening thought started to form in Pete's mind. "So James was afraid of his brother?"

"Maybe more than afraid." Froats grunted. "Something else that's odd, now that I'm thinking about it—"

"I sure wish you'd have thought about this stuff back at the time," Baronick snapped.

Froats shot him a look. "As I was saying, something else that's odd is the only time I remember Wilford being the one to step forward was the night of Gary Chambers' accident."

"Murder," Baronick corrected.

Froats' boots hit the floor with a thud and he came out of the chair, a finger pointed at the detective. "I've had enough of your insolence, you young punk. Just shut the hell up."

Pete shifted to one foot and lifted the crutch like a bat. "Both of you, cut it out. I don't need to be breaking up a fight in the middle of my station. Neither one of you are schoolboys. So stop acting like it." He aimed the crutch at Froats. "Now. What about Wilford the night of Chambers' crash?"

Froats glared at Pete for a moment, but finally answered. "The night of the crash, it was Wilford Engle who called it in to dispatch."

Son of a bitch. Pete turned to Baronick. "Drive me out to Wilford Engle's place."

Baronick checked his watch. "Now? It's kind of late, Pete."

"I don't give a damn if it's two o'clock in the morning. Let's go."

THIRTY

In spite of the long June days, by the time Zoe and Patsy pulled up in front of Wilford Engle's house, the valley had fallen into sultry shadows. Heavy evening air, thick as a dripping sponge, hit Zoe in the face the moment she opened the Tundra's passenger side door and stepped out.

"Is that his car?" Patsy tipped her head toward an old brown four-door sedan parked under a tree in the overgrown yard.

"Beats me."

The place was dark except for a faint glow at the front door. Perhaps a light from the back of the house. Zoe wished she had her truck there. More specifically, she wished she had the tire iron she kept under her seat.

She picked her way through the weeds to the sedan—an Oldsmobile—and rested a hand on the hood. "It's still warm. They're here."

Patsy shot an anxious glance toward her Tundra. "We should call the cops and wait out here."

But Zoe *had* called the cops. One of them at least. Why hadn't Pete called back? "You're right. You stay out here and call 9-1-1. I'm going to check the house." She started toward the front porch.

"I said *we* should wait," Patsy called after her.

Zoe heard Patsy curse followed by the soft thud of her boots as she jogged to catch up.

The first step screeched the moment Zoe stepped on it. So much for the element of surprise. As if they'd had any chance of that, rolling up in that glow-in-the-dark white Tundra.

"What are we gonna do?" Patsy whispered.

Zoe climbed the rest of the steps and crossed the rickety porch.

"I'm not sure." Knock? Expect to be welcomed into Wilford's home? Ask him flat out if he had Harry? Yeah, that would go over well.

"You're not sure?"

Zoe peered in the screen door. The front room was in total darkness. As best she could tell, it was a living room. If someone lurked there, he was hidden in the shadows. A doorway opened to another room in the rear of the house. What appeared to be a single low-wattage bulb glowed from back there. She made out a vintage chrome and Formica table with mismatched chairs around it.

She wrapped her fingers around the doorknob and turned. It clicked open. "I'm going in. You stay here."

"You can't go in there." Patsy sounded on the verge of a full-blown whispered panic attack.

"Look. Wilford's what? Eighty years old? I think I can take him."

"What if he's got a gun?"

"What if he's got Harry?"

Patsy let out a muted version of a frustrated scream. "If you go in there, I'm going with you."

"Fine."

Zoe gave the knob a tug. The wooden frame must have swollen and warped with age because it dragged. And scraped. Then opened with a screech. She shushed the door as if that might help. She stepped inside with Patsy right behind.

The air in the dark living room was stagnant and dank as a quagmire. How could anyone breathe in this place? It reeked of mold and rotted tobacco. She paused a moment, allowing her eyes to adjust to the dark. Scanning the room, she spotted what appeared to be a large ceramic ashtray on an end table. She picked it up and hefted it. Heavy enough to make a dent in someone's head, the ashtray also seemed to be the only good impromptu weapon within reach.

As she moved closer to the doorway at the back of the room, more of the kitchen came into view. The rest of the table. Another chair. And a pair of knees.

Someone was sitting at the table.

Zoe turned to Patsy with a finger to her lips. Wide-eyed, Patsy nodded. Zoe sidestepped so she could no longer see the man's knees. And he wouldn't see her if he happened to lean forward. She tiptoed closer. Prayed the floorboards of the old house wouldn't squeak with her next step. Another step. And one more.

She sidled against the wall next to the doorway. All she had to do was poke her head around and see who was attached to the knees. If only the room had more air circulation, maybe she could breathe. She swallowed. Took a deep rancid breath. And leaned into the opening.

The knees were still there. She leaned further, sticking her head into the room.

Harry.

His dazed eyes were fixed on the table in front of him. His hands folded in his lap.

Zoe took a final, quick look into the rest of the kitchen. Empty. She stepped through the door, bringing Patsy with her. "Harry? Are you all right?"

He looked up at her, no sign of recognition in his pale blue eyes. "I want to go home."

Zoe let out a breath and went to him. She knelt at his side, setting the ashtray on the floor. "I know you do. I'm going to take you there."

He smiled at her, but the same way she imagined he'd smile at a cab driver who'd made the same offer.

She took his hands and stood up. "Let's go."

A floorboard creaked. Without looking, she knew they had company. The voice behind her was raspy, but deadly. "Yes. Let's."

Zoe turned slowly. In the doorway she'd just crossed stood a man who looked as close to a walking cadaver as she ever hoped to see. His skin was so white, even in the low light she could see blue veins beneath it. But at the moment the most conspicuous part of Wilford Engle was the revolver in his hand.

The headlights of Baronick's black unmarked vehicle revealed an empty driveway and a darkened house as they parked in front of Wilford Engle's place. The flicker of distant heat lightning revealed Wilford's sedan parked under a tree. Pete noticed a hint of light at the front door.

"It's almost ten," Froats said from the backseat. "He's probably already in bed. Farmers are up with the chickens, you know."

Baronick cut the ignition and shot a pained look at Pete. "Tell me again why we had to bring him along."

Froats didn't wait for Pete to answer. "Because you knew danged well I'd have followed you in my own car if you didn't. If," Froats held up one finger, "and I'm only saying *if* this mess is my fault, I intend to be around to make it right."

Pete refrained from mentioning he also didn't quite trust his predecessor yet, and he'd rather have Froats close where he could keep an eye on him.

Baronick reached across Pete to the glove box, pulled out a walkie-talkie, and handed it to him. "Just in case."

Pete rammed it into his pocket.

Baronick and Froats climbed out of the car. Pete struggled with his crutches, but heaved himself up on the second try. Another flash of lightning gave them a momentary glimpse of the overgrown yard and dilapidated house. A muggy breeze hissed through the leaves of the massive silver maple.

Baronick led the way. Pete let him. The detective had two free hands for accessing his sidearm. Pete had insisted Froats leave his antique but effective Colt .45 locked up back at the station.

Wilford Engle would've had to be deaf to not hear Pete's cumbersome climb up the rickety steps. But no additional lights flicked on inside. Baronick pounded on the screen door's frame. "Mr. Engle? Police. We need to talk to you."

The only response was the wind whispering through the maple's leaves.

Something wasn't right. Tension gnawed at Pete's shoulders, and it was more than the crutches causing it. "Baronick, take the back."

The detective bounded down the steps. Stopped. Turned back. "What about him?" He heaved a thumb at Froats.

"He's with me."

Baronick snorted. "It's your funeral."

Pete and Froats leaned against the house, flanking the doorjamb. Pete shifted both crutches to his left side and unholstered his Glock.

"You should have let me bring my gun," Froats muttered.

"If old man Engle shoots me, you can use mine."

Froats grunted.

The walkie-talkie in Pete's pocket crackled to life. "I'm in position," Baronick said.

Gun in one hand, crutches in the other, Pete released a growling breath. He holstered his Glock, dug out the walkie-talkie, and tossed it to Froats. "Make yourself useful."

When Pete was set once again, he nodded to Froats.

"Go," the retired chief barked into the radio.

Wilford Engle sat in the passenger-side backseat of Patsy's Tundra with his gun aimed at Harry, who sat to his left. "Pull over here."

"Here?" Patsy squeaked. "There's nothing here."

Every time they'd passed a car going the other way, Zoe, who sat sideways next to Patsy, had a clear view of Engle, his gun, and Harry. Headlights provided snapshots of Harry's blank stare. Engle's dark, hard eyes. The evil glint of metal.

Zoe could also make out the strain in Patsy's face from the glow of the dashboard instruments. What Zoe didn't need to see was the spot along the game lands road where Engle had ordered Patsy to stop. Zoe knew it intimately. This was where her dad had gone over the hill to his death.

But that memory was a lie. Her dad had already been dead—gunned down by the same old revolver now aimed at Harry.

Engle leaned forward and pressed the muzzle of the gun into Patsy's neck. "Pull over *now*."

Patsy let out a small cry, over-steered, and nearly sent them down the hill. But she jammed the brakes, and the Tundra lurched to a stop.

"Turn it off," Engle ordered.

Trembling, Patsy obeyed.

Zoe's eyes burned, but she had no time for the luxury of tears.

Harry appeared oblivious, as if he'd been drugged. Had Engle given him something? Or was he simply immersed in his dementia fog?

"Let Harry go." Zoe held her voice steady. "He's got Alzheimer's. He doesn't remember who you are or where he saw you before."

As if his name had awakened him, Harry blinked and looked at Zoe.

Crap. This was not the time for a moment of clarity.

"Nadine? Is that you? Thank heavens. Will you please take me home?"

Zoe sighed in relief. "I'm working on it, Pop." To Engle she said, "See what I mean? He's harmless. Even if he did say anything, no one would believe him."

Engle leaned back against the seat, again taking aim at Harry. He appeared to consider it. "You people have been a pain in my ass."

Puzzled, Zoe asked, "What people?"

The gun stayed on Harry, but Engle's dark gaze flashed to her. "You're kin of them Millers, ain't you?"

"They were my great uncles."

Engle sniffed in disdain. "They weren't so great. That son of a bitch Vernie went and seduced my little sister. Got her knocked up. Then he flat out refused to make an honest woman of her. He even had the gall to offer her money to get an abortion. Now tell me. What's so great about that?"

"I didn't mean—"

"Poor sweet Mae." His voice wavered. "She's been gone from this earth forty-four years as of this coming Friday. Mae Flower, I used to call her. Figured she was destined to be an old maid. She was thirty and never had no man make a fuss over her before. But along came that Vernie Miller." Engle said the name as if it tasted rancid on his tongue. "He was a good ten years older than Mae, more wise to the ways of the world. She thought she loved that son of a bitch. And he broke her heart. Worse. He broke her spirit."

Zoe tried to imagine. It wasn't hard. She'd had a few heartbreaks of her own over the years.

"What was I to do? I was her brother. It was up to me to make him pay for what he'd done to her."

"You killed him?"

Engle sat straighter. "Wasn't my intention." As if that made it all right. "I just went to beat on him some. Make him hurt like he'd hurt my sister. But he was a smug bastard. Next thing I knew, my hands were around his throat and he wasn't moving no more."

Zoe risked glancing at Harry. He'd retreated into his mental fog again, his head lowered. In the dark, she couldn't see his eyes, but she guessed they were either closed or looking at his hands. In that moment she realized while searching for her dad, she'd come to love Pete's as if he were her own. She had to get him to safety. She and Patsy might stand a chance—somehow be able to jump old Wilford—disarm him—but she would not jeopardize Harry's life. "What about Denver?" she asked. Keep Engle talking.

"He walked in right about then. Must've heard the commotion. Saw I'd killed his brother. He had a gun." Engle held up the revolver. "This gun, as a matter of a fact. We fought over it. It went off and there he was. Dead." He brought the muzzle back down toward Harry. "You see? I didn't intend on killing neither of them boys. It was all an accident."

From the tone of his voice, Zoe figured he didn't believe that any more than she did.

"I called my brother Jim, and he came over and helped me string Vernie up to look like he'd hung himself. We set it up good. Spread the stories about them boys fighting over that other girl. And I kept this gun as a souvenir. Never know when someone's gonna need killin'."

Like her father. Zoe closed her eyes. Slowed her breathing. "Why would Jim go along with it? Why didn't he tell the truth?"

Engle fell silent for a moment then said, "He wanted to. But he's my brother. And moreover, Mae was his sister, too. Then when she died giving birth to her daughter, we both hated Vernie even more. It was his fault she died. He deserved what he got."

A daughter. Mae had a daughter. "What about the baby?"

Engle swung the gun toward Zoe. Even in the darkness, she could make out the gaping black maw aimed at her. But a flash of lightning emphasized the reality of being mere inches away from death.

"Enough with the questions." Engle waved the gun toward the door. "Get out." He turned the gun on Patsy. "You, too. And then you help this old buzzard-bait out."

Zoe released the latch. Eased her door open. This might be her chance. When Engle was climbing out behind her, she could ram his door closed on him. Maybe slam his arm—the one with the gun—in it.

But, no. As Patsy held the driver's side back door open for Harry, Engle kept the gun aimed at him and slid across the seat to get out on Patsy's side, too. Zoe stood alone on the passenger side, guardrails and the hill where her father had died behind her. She listened for the sound of an approaching car. Nothing. No one was coming to their aid. And no one knew where they were. She could make a break for it. Run like hell into the night. But that meant leaving Harry and Patsy to fend for themselves. No. Escape wasn't an option.

"Move." Engle herded Harry and Patsy toward Zoe. "I want this whole mess to be over. I don't know why folks can't leave well enough alone." He pointed the gun at Zoe again. "First your daddy starts asking questions. Gets everyone wondering about that night. He just wouldn't shut up. Until I made him."

The heat rising up Zoe's neck had nothing to do with the steamy night air. Her fingernails sliced into her palms. Gun or no gun, she wanted to pummel the life out of Wilford Engle.

"And then Kroll started poking around, trying to get Jim to talk," Engle muttered. "I had to shut him up, too. But the old fool didn't die. At least not yet. Then this old lamebrain went and spotted me at the hospital—" Engle brought the gun to Harry's ribs. "I could've handled him. He'd have been easy. Knock him over the head. Toss him in a ditch somewhere. Another old mental case wanders off, falls, hits his head, and dies. Happens all the time. Except you two have to show up at my house before I get it done. Now look at the mess I've got."

Harry, oblivious to the conversation going on about him, gazed into the night, his hands shoved into his pockets. The same man who'd killed Zoe's father now intended to take Pete's dad from him, too. She could not—would not—let that happen. "Don't hurt Harry. Let him go. Look at him. He's not a threat to you."

"Like hell. He may not remember now, but he might start remembering later. That's why I had to get rid of Carl. And it's why I'll have to finish what I started with Marvin Kroll."

"But it's different with Harry. His memory isn't going to get better. He's got Alzheimer's. His memory, what's left of it, is only going to get worse. Let him go."

For a moment, Engle seemed to consider it. But then he shook his head. "The only reason I've been able to live my life the way I want is because I made sure no one talked." He gave a raspy sigh. "I can see, though, that I'm going about this all wrong. I was going to take care of the old man first and then you two. Now that's not gonna fly. You're right. He's fairly harmless. But I don't think you two gals are gonna stand by while I club him like a baby seal."

Damn right.

Engle brought the revolver around, aiming it square at Zoe. Patsy cried out from behind her. For the second time in only a few minutes, Zoe faced the business end of Wilford Engle's gun.

"You know what they say." Engle chuckled. "Ladies first."

Like a statue come to life, Harry threw himself at Engle. The flash from the muzzle momentarily blinded Zoe at the same instant the blast exploded in her ears. Patsy screamed. Harry had Engle by the wrists. Wrestled him for the gun.

Zoe staggered forward, wanting to help. Harry was bigger. He should be able to take Engle down.

The gun fired a second shot. This time the flash and the blast were muffled. Harry groaned. His knees buckled. And he slid to the ground.

THIRTY-ONE

"This place sure is homey." Sarcasm oozed from Froats' voice.

He and Pete stood in the middle of Wilford Engle's stifling kitchen. Overhead, floorboards creaked as Baronick searched the rest of the house. "My pop said this place gave him the heeby-jeebies," Pete said.

The lack of any call from Zoe about Harry added to Pete's gut feeling that something was very wrong here. His father's voice and observation rising through the inner chaos didn't help. Pete pulled out his phone as Baronick's boots echoed *thud thud thud* down the stairs from the second floor.

"All clear," the detective called out.

Pete pressed Zoe's number into the phone. It rang and rang, finally going to voice mail. "Where are you? Call me."

Froats peered in the kitchen sink and shuddered. "Who're you trying to reach?"

"Zoe."

Baronick, wearing gloves and pinching a sheet of paper, appeared in the living room doorway. "She find your old man yet?"

Pete wished he knew. He pointed at the paper. "What's that?"

Baronick waved it in the air. "James Engle was a very prolific writer."

"Another letter?"

"Yep." The detective strode into the kitchen and smoothed the page on the table top. "And they keep getting better and better."

Pete dug out his reading glasses, rammed them on his face, and leaned over the table.

Dear Wilford,

By the time you read this I can only assume you will know I do not have cancer.

What I do have is a heavy burden of guilt for what you and I have done. I've often told you over the years that I wanted us to confess to our sins, but you, dear brother, would have none of it. I wanted you to believe I was a dying man with one dying wish: that you should admit it was you who killed the Miller brothers and Gary Chambers.

But you refuse to grant my "final request."

Years ago, I swore on our mother's grave that I would never betray you. But I cannot go on living with the knowledge that I took part in your madness. Without going back on my oath to you, I've tried to make some of it right with the survivors.

You should know by taking my own life in the same manner as we staged Vernon Miller's "suicide" and in the same spot, I hope to get the attention of someone who remembers and whose curiosity might drive them to look into the past and discover the truth.

I implore you to confess. Turn yourself in. Certainly, the legal system will go easy on an old man.

Please forgive me.

Your brother,
Jim

Froats, who had been reading over Pete's shoulder, let out a low whistle. "Where'd you find it?"

"In an envelope on his dresser." Baronick picked up the letter and slid it into a clear plastic evidence bag. "I recognized the handwriting from the other letters. By the way—it was postmarked last Wednesday."

"The same day he hung himself." The letter may have offered a solid answer to many of the questions that had plagued Pete over the past week, but it did nothing to quell the unease building in his gut. "Does Engle own another vehicle?"

"Nothing that's registered."

"So either he's here somewhere, or he caught a ride." Pete stared at the phone. Noticed the symbol indicating he had a message. The call he'd ignored earlier.

He pressed the button to retrieve it. While he waited for the automated prompts, he said, "Check outside. The garage. The barn. I think I remember a workshop out back."

Baronick handed the evidence to Pete and headed for the rear door. "On it."

The voice on the recording sent Pete reeling. He caught his balance on the tacky kitchen counter. "Pete? It's Zoe. I have a problem. I don't know how to tell you this, but I think Wilford Engle might have something to do with the shootings. At least Mr. Kroll's." There was a pause. When she continued, her voice trembled. "I'm afraid he might have snatched Harry. Patsy and I are on our way to Wilford's place now. I'll call you when we find him. I'm so sorry, Pete."

"What the hell's wrong with you?" Froats demanded.

Pete gripped the counter. He should have taken that call. How long had it been? Zoe must have already been here and gone. Engle had Harry. Where were they?

Pete pressed Zoe's number again. It rang. Rang again. So the phone wasn't turned off. Why wasn't she answering? Wait. He glanced at the phone. She'd called from a different number. He fumbled with the menu buttons. Pulled up the number from that last call and dialed. Like Zoe's, it rang until going to voicemail. At the tone, he shouted into the cell. "Damn it, Zoe. Call me. Now."

The last time he hadn't been able to reach her by phone—last winter—she'd been facing down a killer. He prayed history wasn't repeating itself.

But his gut told him otherwise.

Froats stepped in front of Pete, getting in his face. "What's going on?"

Pete stared into the old chief's eyes. "You worked those cases. You knew these people. If Wilford Engle were going to take someone somewhere—to kill them—where would he go?"

The question took a moment to sink in. Froats' eyes widened. "Holy hell. You think—"

Pete pushed away from the sink. Carrying his crutches he hobbled to the screened back door. "*Wayne*," he shouted into the night. "You find anything?"

"Nothing," Baronick called back. "It's clear."

"Then get in here and order a countywide BOLO." Pete hit speed dial for Seth's cell.

Froats appeared to have shrunk three inches. "You think Wilford Engle has your father."

"I don't think. I know." The line rang in Pete's ear. "Not just my father. The bastard has Zoe, too." When Seth picked up, Pete updated him on what they knew and what he suspected. "Be on the lookout for Zoe's truck. And use caution. Consider Engle to be armed and dangerous." Like an old wounded grizzly. A grizzly that had dragged off Zoe and his pop.

Baronick had come inside with his phone pressed to his ear. Froats paced the kitchen, rubbing his beard. Pete pivoted, looking around the filthy room, searching for some sign. Some tidbit. A breadcrumb to let him know Zoe and Harry were okay. Better yet, where to find them.

"An old codger like Wilford Engle doesn't like change," Froats said, his gravelly voice low. "His world's been rocked by the suicide of his brother. He's trying to bring it back to an even keel."

By getting rid of everyone Engle saw as a threat to his freedom. Not exactly a comforting thought.

Baronick turned around. From his expression, Pete knew it wasn't good news.

The detective lowered the phone. "We've located Zoe's truck."

Pete jumped toward him, forgetting about his foot. He winced, but ignored the razor-sharp pain. "Where?"

"In the Brunswick Hospital parking lot. Looks like she never left. But they said her cell phone's on the seat."

Pete yanked his phone back out of his pocket. Pulled up the voice message. Played it again. "She said she and *Patsy* were on their way here. This must be Patsy's number. Patsy Greene. Get a make, model, and plate number for her vehicle and put the BOLO out on it. Then we're going over to James Engle's place."

"Why there?" Froats asked.

"Because you said Wilford didn't like change. I'll bet he's a creature of habit. Criminals like to revisit the scene of the crime. Maybe he's going to use one he's used before." Besides, Pete couldn't think of anywhere else he'd go. He jammed the crutches under his arms and headed for the front of the house in long, swinging strides.

"Wait," Froats called from behind him.

"We don't have time to wait," Pete barked.

"I know that, damn it. Listen to me. Have one of your men check out James' place. They'll know where it is. You and me? We're gonna check someplace else. Someplace they're not gonna know. At least not the exact location."

Pete spun. Studied the gleam in the old police chief's eyes. "Wayne," Pete yelled. "Come on. Froats is navigating."

THIRTY-TWO

As Zoe dove for Harry, she wasn't sure if the scream came from her throat or Patsy's.

"Get away," Engle said, sputtering.

Zoe ignored him. Ignored everything but Harry sprawled on the ground. "I need light."

The hot metal of the recently fired gun muzzle pressed into her temple. "I said, get away from him."

She clenched her fists, too angry to be scared. Or maybe the adrenaline gave her courage. For a fleeting moment, she considered grabbing Engle's wrist and prying the gun from his hands. But she'd just seen Harry—a bigger stronger individual than she—lose that battle. She managed to turn her head enough so she could shift her eyes and fix Engle's dark silhouette with a hard stare. "You're planning to shoot me anyway. So either do it now or get that gun out of my face and give me some goddamn light."

Engle stepped back. For a moment, the gun barrel wavered then he clutched the grip with both hands, steadying his hold. "No use wasting your time, girlie."

In the darkness, Zoe could only imagine his finger tightening on the trigger. But instead of one final blast from the gun, the old man's knees buckled. He hit the ground hard, and the revolver clunked on the road's tar-and-chipped shoulder, disappearing into the black of night.

What just happened? Had Patsy clubbed Engle from behind? "Patsy?"

"I'm here." Patsy's soft voice was higher-pitched than normal, but wasn't near Engle. "Did he have a heart attack?"

"I don't know." Nor did Zoe know where the gun was. "I need light."

"I have a flashlight in my glove box."

"Get it." Triaging Engle's collapse to a lower priority at the moment, Zoe fingered Harry's neck for a carotid. She prayed for a pulse. Found one. And remarkably strong. Harry's mind might be failing, but he had a helluva big heart. "Harry? Can you hear me?"

He took a hoarse breath. "Yeah." He moaned. "Damn."

"Where's the pain?" She trailed her fingers down his shirt front, feeling for that unmistakable warm, sticky liquid that was no doubt draining from him in the dark.

The gravel crunched as Patsy jogged up. Suddenly Harry was bathed in light from Patsy's flashlight. Zoe almost wished they'd stayed in the dark.

A glistening deep crimson spot was spreading across Harry's polo shirt just above and left of his belt. With no ambulance and no supplies to work with, she pressed both her hands against the oozing hole in the center of the pool. "Patsy, do you have any towels in your truck?"

"I have a blanket."

"Great. Get it."

Patsy pivoted away, leaving Harry in darkness again.

"Wait. Leave me the flashlight."

As Patsy stepped toward her with the oversized black Maglite, Engle groaned. Patsy aimed the beam in his direction.

The old man was on his hands and knees, hunched over. "I take these spells," he mumbled.

Where was the gun? Zoe scanned the ground around Engle, searching. The old man slowly lifted his head. And his hand—with the .38 in it.

Fuck.

"Enough." With gun trained on Zoe, Engle lurched to his feet. "I've wasted enough of my time on the three of you."

Harry's fingers wrapped around her wrist. "Zoe?"

He knew who she was. Harry was bleeding to death on the side of a dark, deserted road, but he knew who she was. She choked. "Yeah, Harry, it's me."

"I'm sorry. I tried."

Tears blurred her vision. "I know you did."

The revolver's muzzle again jabbed into the side of her head.

Patsy swung the beam of light into Engle's face. "Wait," she cried.

Engle shielded his eyes with his free hand. "Turn that thing off."

"No. Wait. Listen to me."

What on earth was Patsy doing? But anything to delay Engle from pulling that trigger—and buy more time—was fine with Zoe.

"You said your sister Mae died in childbirth. Right?"

"Turn off that damned light."

Patsy seemed to ignore him. "You said she'd been gone from this earth forty-four years ago *as of Friday*, right?"

"What difference does that make now?"

Zoe's breath caught in her throat as the realization sunk in.

Friday. Barbecue and beer. Patsy's birthday.

Patsy's forty-fourth birthday.

"Is that right?" Patsy demanded.

Engle swung away from Zoe. The muzzle no longer pressed into her skin. She risked a glance.

He had the gun aimed squarely at Patsy. And she kept the flashlight on him. He squinted hard into the beam. "I'm going to shoot that damned light and you with it."

"Did your sister die in childbirth on June twentieth?"

Engle lowered the gun. A little. "That's what I said, ain't it? Why are you harpin' on it?"

Patsy's face was in darkness, but her voice trembled as she said, "It's my birthday. I was adopted. I've tried for years to find out about my birth parents, but all I've been able to come up with was they were from Monongahela County and were both dead." She paused. "I think your sister was my mother."

Zoe planted a hand against the sharp gravel to keep her balance. Wilford Engle was Patsy's uncle? She was his niece? As awful as it seemed for Patsy, this might be what could save their lives. Zoe had a quick mental picture of Wilford throwing down his gun and embracing his newfound family.

The night fell silent except for the sound of Wilford's wheezing breath. He didn't throw his gun down. Instead he tucked it into the waist of his trousers. He took an uneven step toward Patsy.

Then he let out a roar that sounded like a bear. He staggered toward Patsy, arms outstretched. He didn't hug her. He grabbed her by the throat. The flashlight clattered to the ground. "You're the bastard offspring of that son of a bitch Vernie Miller. You're the reason Mae's dead."

Patsy gave a garbled cry.

Zoe took Harry's hand that was on her wrist and placed it on his gunshot wound. "Press down, Harry. As hard as you can."

If he answered, she didn't hear. She launched toward the scuffle. Before she reached them, Wilford Engle shoved Patsy backwards. She stumbled. Zoe heard the dull thud of Patsy's legs against the guardrail. Caught a glimpse of Patsy's arms flailing. And then with a snarl, Engle heaved Patsy over.

She shrieked. Breaking twigs snapped and rustled as Patsy crashed down the rock face. The same rock face Zoe's father had been driven over.

A flash of lightning glinted off the gun in Engle's waistband. At the same moment, Zoe spotted Patsy's Maglite lying on the ground.

Engle must have sensed what Zoe planned. He wheeled toward her, the gun back in his hand. Zoe leaped. Snatched the flashlight. Engle raised the muzzle. And Zoe swung the heavy barrel of the Maglite with everything she had. It cracked against Engle's forearm. The gun sailed into the darkness. He swore and doubled over.

Zoe huffed a breath. Relaxed.

The old man lunged forward. He rammed the crown of his head into her, just below her ribs. Gasping, she slammed the ground with him on top. The flashlight flew from her grasp. Gravel bit into her elbows.

Engle struggled to his feet while Zoe fought for air. Even in the dark, she could make out his right arm hanging useless at his side. She clawed at the ground, fingers closing around pebbles and dirt. He tottered away from her, head lowered. Looking for his gun.

Air returned slowly. Zoe rolled to her side. Onto her knees. Engle bent down. Reached with his left hand.

The gun.

Zoe groped in the dark. Her hand fell upon something smooth and round. She dragged the flashlight to her. Held it close, shielded from view. A second chance. There would be no third.

Engle staggered toward her, the gun in his left hand. "You bitch," he hissed. He took another step toward her. And another.

Come closer, she thought. It's dark. You don't want to miss. Neither do I.

One more step. He stopped. Zoe, hunkered on the ground, hoping she looked to him as if she were hugging her ribs. She lifted her gaze to his hand. The gun trembled. He raised it. She tightened her grip on the flashlight.

And came up swinging. A big upward arc that caught Engle's left wrist from underneath. His arm and the gun snapped toward the sky. The blast nearly deafened her, but the bullet missed its target.

Before Engle had a chance to move, to fire another shot, to dodge out of the way, Zoe brought the flashlight down where she'd last seen his head. The heavy barrel connected with a sickening crunch.

Engle collapsed in a heap at her feet.

Swaying, breathless, and seeing spots from the muzzle blast, Zoe let the flashlight drop. Harry lay bleeding next to the road. Patsy had gone over the hillside. As Zoe struggled to decide who she should tend to first, she heard something in the distance. Wishful thinking? Or a car on this deserted back road? The sound grew louder.

The car squealed around the bend, the headlights blinding her. But not before she made out the red and blue emergency lights. Arms outstretched, she staggered toward Harry and flagged down the cavalry.

THIRTY-THREE

The reality of what Pete had almost lost and what he may lose yet, weighed heavier on him than if he'd tried to carry one of the horses at Zoe's barn on his shoulders. The world swirled around him in shades of blue and red. He leaned on his crutches behind one of the three Monongahela County ambulances that had responded to the dark country road. Inside, a trio of paramedics worked on Harry, who looked horribly pale under the bright interior lights of the medic unit. Pete wanted to be in there with his father, soothing him. But the medics had ordered him—nicely—to give them space. Besides, Harry was unconscious, the blood loss, immense.

Pete shifted the crutches and turned to look for Zoe in the crowd of fire fighters, emergency medics, and police swarming the scene. One of the medics with a different crew slammed the back door of a second ambulance and pounded on it with his fist. The rig lurched forward and pulled away, carrying Wilford Engle to the hospital. One of the county police vehicles, in which Froats was riding shotgun, fell in behind. Engle, also unconscious with a head injury, would be kept under close guard at the hospital.

Firefighters gathered at the guardrail. They'd set up a generator and lights to illuminate the wooded hillside and ropes to lower rescue workers over the side. Pete spotted Zoe standing near the search and rescue team, talking to Baronick, her fingers pressed to her mouth.

Pete thought of the drive here with Froats and Baronick. The heart-pounding terror of what they would find at the scene where Gary Chambers had died decades earlier. Froats had been right, the old cuss. They'd careened around that last bend on the dark road, their headlights falling on a white pickup at the berm, Zoe in the middle of the road waving, and a heap that turned out to be Harry lying on the yellow line.

Harry and Zoe. Pete had come so close to losing both of them. For the second time, he'd arrived too late to rescue Zoe from a crazed gunman. Both times he thanked God that Zoe had managed to defend herself. She was a hell of a woman. Pete heard Harry's words in his mind. *You should marry that girl.* At the very least, he should convince her that being "just friends" wasn't going to cut it.

A hand touched Pete's shoulder. Flinching, he turned to see one of the paramedics who'd been working on Harry. "Is Pop going to be all right?"

The young man's solemn face did little to offer optimism. "We've done all we can for him here. I wanted you to know we're transporting him to Phillipsburg. Life Flight is coming in and will land on that field behind the ambulance garage. From there, they'll take him to Allegheny General."

Pete took an unsteady hop toward the medic unit. "I'm going with you."

The paramedic blocked him. "You can't, Chief. There isn't room in the helicopter. You'll have to catch a ride from someone else."

How many times had Pete said the exact same words to a distraught family member? He growled deep in his throat, but nodded. "Tell him...tell Pop I love him and I'll see him soon."

The paramedic gave a quick nod and was gone. Within a minute, the back doors were closed and the vehicle pulled out, jouncing over the ruts.

A whoop went up from the woods. The firefighters and rescue crew cheered. "We got her! She's alive!"

Baronick put an arm around Zoe, and she collapsed against him.

Zoe in Wayne Baronick's arms? This was not good.

Clenching his jaw, Pete hobbled over to them.

Zoe must have seen his approach. She pushed free of the detective and turned. "How's Harry?"

"They're Life Flighting him to Allegheny General. He's lost a lot of blood."

She swiped a hand over her face. "I'm so sorry, Pete. I tried—" Her voice broke.

Baronick reached for her, but Pete threw down his crutches and pulled her into his arms. "You probably saved his life," he whispered into her hair. "I owe you."

She hiccupped. "I almost got him killed."

Pete held her tighter. "How do you figure that? Wilford Engle is the only one responsible for any of this."

"But if I'd kept a closer eye on Harry, maybe—"

Pete shushed her. Cupped her face in his hands and drew it back so he could look at her in the harsh emergency lighting. "You couldn't have stopped Engle from taking him. And you did find him." Pete would save scolding her about playing hero for another time.

Her face was a study in anguish. "Pete, you don't understand. *He* saved *me*. Wilford Engle was going to shoot *me*. Harry took the bullet that was meant for *me*."

"You're the one who doesn't understand. *That* was my pop. Superman. The man I grew up wanting to be like. The reason I became a cop. I'd thought I'd never see that man again."

She gazed up at him. The guilt and agony melted from her face.

"Even if—" Pete's voice caught. He swallowed and tried again. "If he doesn't make it, my pop will have died a hero. Because he adored you. In the shape he's been in the last few years, that's a helluva way to go."

Zoe managed a timid smile. "He's a hero either way. Like father, like son."

Another cry went up from the crew at the guardrail as Bruce Yancy barked orders to the man inside the truck, running the winch. "Bring her up. Slow."

Pete and Zoe turned to watch. He kept a protective arm around her shoulders, and she slipped her arm around his waist.

Pete shot a challenging glance at Baronick who gave him a nod and headed off to watch them haul Patsy Greene up.

"Patsy is Mae Engle's daughter," Zoe said.

"What?"

"She figured it out and told Wilford in the midst of everything. I think she hoped it would save us. Him knowing she was his niece. Instead, all he reacted to was that she was Vernon Miller's daughter. The reason Mae was dead. And he threw her over the hill."

Pete struggled to grasp this latest development. "Are you sure she's Mae and Vernon's daughter? Maybe she just said that to distract him."

Zoe shook her head. "Wilford mentioned that Mae had died in childbirth forty-four years ago Friday. That's Patsy's birthday. She's been planning a big barbecue at her place. When she told Wilford, he flipped out on her."

"Huh." Pete rolled it around in his brain. "That makes her your cousin."

"I was thinking that, too. Second cousins, I guess."

Two firefighters appeared at the edge of the precipice, guiding a rescue basket. Inside, Patsy lifted one arm as much as the straps would allow and waved. Another cheer went up from the rescue crew.

Pete felt Zoe pressed against his side, shaking. He thought she was crying again. But then he realized she was laughing. "What's so funny?"

Zoe shook her head. "I don't think Patsy's had a chance to think about her new family connections yet. Otherwise, she might have told them to leave her down there in the woods."

Confused, Pete gave Zoe a questioning look.

She grinned up at him. "I'm Patsy's second cousin. That means she's first cousins with…"

Pete finished the sentence for her. "Kimberly."

Zoe sat on the cool grass next to the fresh grave, mindlessly picking the thorns from the stem of one peach rose. Overhead, white billowing clouds drifted in a clear blue sky, finally void of humidity. She breathed in the scents around her. Damp earth. Delicate flower. A touch of cedar from the nearby tree.

Almost three weeks had passed since the awful night at the side of the road. That spot where one vindictive, evil man, so desperate to eliminate all witnesses to his chain of crimes had wreaked havoc yet again. At least now his secrets were out. Wilford Engle would never spend another day as a free man as long as he lived, which likely wouldn't be long. She'd heard he'd been diagnosed with lung cancer.

Behind her, tires crunched on the road that looped through the cemetery. The car stopped. The engine stilled. A door opened and closed.

She laid the rose on the mounded earth, which hadn't had time to settle yet. "I'm so sorry," she said to the ground and the heavens, hoping her regrets reached their intended recipient.

The grass rustled as uneven footsteps approached. She didn't look up. One brown leather shoe and one plastic and Velcro boot stopped next to her.

"I figured I might find you here," Pete said.

She looked up, squinting into the sun. "I needed to say goodbye. Just him and me." She shifted onto her knees and reached out to touch the granite plaque set into the ground at the grave's head. Traced the name. *Gary Chambers.* "I love you, Dad." Choking back all the emotion of knowing her father really did rest in peace, she climbed to her feet.

Pete caught her hand. "Have you talked to your mom?"

"No. I tried. I've called, but just get the machine. I leave messages." Zoe shrugged. "So far, no one's called back. Patsy's been in touch with them, though. She's planning to fly down there in a couple of weeks."

One corner of Pete's mouth tipped up. "That should be an interesting trip."

"Interesting? Yeah. And did you hear? James Engle left his farm—the Miller farm—to my mom."

"What's she going to do with a farm?"

Zoe shrugged. "Beats me."

They stood in silence, listening to the cicadas in the distant woods. After a few moments, Pete asked, "Are you all right?"

She forced a smile. "No. Yes. I will be." She studied him. Longer than she used to allow herself to maintain eye contact with him. There was something going on behind those ice blues, but she couldn't make out what. He seemed...sad. Haunted. "What about you? Are you all right?"

He huffed a laugh and looked down. "The hospital released Harry today."

"Oh?" Zoe thought he'd be happier about that.

"Nadine picked him up. Took him home."

"And by home, I gather you don't mean your house."

"Nope."

Zoe intertwined her fingers with his and bumped his shoulder with hers. "I thought you were looking forward to your sister taking him back."

"I thought I was, too. But I kind of got used to having him around."

"He's one tough old buzzard. Took that bullet and bounced back like a superhero."

"That's exactly what he is." Pete grinned. "He saved the girl. I came in after it was all over."

"You sound like you're jealous."

The grin faded. "I almost lost you both."

"But you didn't lose either of us. I'm still here." Zoe looked down at the grave. "You can visit your dad any time you want."

Pete pressed a warm kiss to her forehead. "And I will. Care to come with me? The orthopedist said I can drive."

She leaned against him. Inhaled his woodsy fragrance. "I don't know. What'll Harry think if we show up together?"

"What he already thinks. That you're my girl."

Zoe laughed. She stepped back, but Pete held onto her hand. "I shouldn't have let him keep thinking that," she said. "I should've convinced him we're just friends."

"You should consider yourself lucky he knows who you are at all." Pete turned to face her squarely. Hooked one finger under her chin. "And now that you mention it, I want to talk to you about this whole *just friends* thing."

Zoe stared at his mouth, aware of her heart doing the rumba inside her chest. "What about it?"

He leaned down and kissed her lips. She melted against him, closing her fingers around the fabric of his shirt, not trusting her legs to hold her.

When it ended, he said, "I think we need to renegotiate."

"That can be arranged."

"How about over dinner?"

"Okay." Zoe smiled and thought her dad—and Harry—would approve.

ANNETTE DASHOFY

Annette Dashofy, a Pennsylvania farm gal born and bred, grew up with horses, cattle, and, yes, chickens. After high school, she spent five years as an EMT for the local ambulance service. Since then, she's worked a variety of jobs, giving her plenty of fodder for her lifelong passion for writing. She, her husband, and their two spoiled cats live on property that was once part of her grandfather's dairy. Her short fiction, including a 2007 Derringer nominee, has appeared in *Spinetingler*, *Mysterical-e*, and *Fish Tales: the Guppy Anthology*. Her newest short story appears in the *Lucky Charms Anthology*.

In Case You Missed the 1st Book in the Series

CIRCLE OF INFLUENCE
Annette Dashofy

A Zoe Chambers Mystery (#1)

Zoe Chambers, paramedic and deputy coroner in rural Pennsylvania's tight-knit Vance Township, has been privy to a number of local secrets over the years, some of them her own. But secrets become explosive when a dead body is found in the Township Board President's abandoned car.

As a January blizzard rages, Zoe and Police Chief Pete Adams launch a desperate search for the killer, even if it means uncovering secrets that could not only destroy Zoe and Pete, but also those closest to them.

Available at booksellers nationwide and online

Visit www.henerypress.com for details

Don't Miss the 3rd Book in the Series

BRIDGES BURNED

Annette Dashofy

A Zoe Chambers Mystery (#3)

Paramedic Zoe Chambers is used to saving lives, but when she stops a man from running into a raging inferno in a futile attempt to rescue his wife, Zoe finds herself drawn to him, and even more so to his ten-year-old daughter. She invites them both to live at the farm while the grieving widower picks up the pieces of his life.

Vance Township Police Chief Pete Adams, of course, is not happy with this setup, especially when he finds evidence implicating Zoe's new houseguest in murder times two. When Zoe ignores Pete's dire warnings, she runs the very real chance of burning one too many bridges, losing everything—and everyone—she holds dear.

Available April 2015

Visit www.henerypress.com for details

Henery Press Mystery Books

And finally, before you go...
Here are a few other mysteries
you might enjoy:

ARTIFACT

Gigi Pandian

A Jaya Jones Treasure Hunt Mystery (#1)

Historian Jaya Jones discovers the secrets of a lost Indian treasure may be hidden in a Scottish legend from the days of the British Raj. But she's not the only one on the trail...

From San Francisco to London to the Highlands of Scotland, Jaya must evade a shadowy stalker as she follows hints from the hastily scrawled note of her dead lover to a remote archaeological dig. Helping her decipher the cryptic clues are her magician best friend, a devastatingly handsome art historian with something to hide, and a charming archaeologist running for his life.

Available at booksellers nationwide and online

Visit www.henerypress.com for details

THE AMBITIOUS CARD

John Gaspard

An Eli Marks Mystery (#1)

The life of a magician isn't all kiddie shows and card tricks. Sometimes it's murder. Especially when magician Eli Marks very publicly debunks a famed psychic, and said psychic ends up dead. The evidence, including a bloody King of Diamonds playing card (one from Eli's own Ambitious Card routine), directs the police right to Eli.

As more psychics are slain, and more King cards rise to the top, Eli can't escape suspicion. Things get really complicated when romance blooms with a beautiful psychic, and Eli discovers she's the next target for murder, and he's scheduled to die with her. Now Eli must use every trick he knows to keep them both alive and reveal the true killer.

Available at booksellers nationwide and online

Visit www.henerypress.com for details

LOWCOUNTRY BOIL

Susan M. Boyer

A Liz Talbot Mystery (#1)

Private Investigator Liz Talbot is a modern Southern belle: she blesses hearts and takes names. She carries her Sig 9 in her Kate Spade handbag, and her golden retriever, Rhett, rides shotgun in her hybrid Escape. When her grandmother is murdered, Liz hightails it back to her South Carolina island home to find the killer.

She's fit to be tied when her police-chief brother shuts her out of the investigation, so she opens her own. Then her long-dead best friend pops in and things really get complicated. When more folks start turning up dead in this small seaside town, Liz must use more than just her wits and charm to keep her family safe, chase down clues from the hereafter, and catch a psychopath before he catches her.

Available at booksellers nationwide and online

Visit www.henerypress.com for details

DEATH BY BLUE WATER

Kait Carson

A Hayden Kent Mystery (#1)

Paralegal Hayden Kent knows first-hand that life in the Florida Keys can change from perfect to perilous in a heartbeat. When she discovers a man's body at 120' beneath the sea, she thinks she is witness to a tragic accident. She becomes the prime suspect when the victim is revealed to be the brother of the man who recently jilted her, and she has no alibi. A migraine stole Hayden's memory of the night of the death.

As the evidence mounts, she joins forces with an Officer Janice Kirby. Together the two women follow the clues that uncover criminal activities at the highest levels and put Hayden's life in jeopardy while she fights to stay free.

Available at booksellers nationwide and online

Visit www.henerypress.com for details

FATAL BRUSHSTROKE

Sybil Johnson

An Aurora Anderson Mystery (#1)

A dead body in her garden and a homicide detective on her doorstep...

Computer programmer and tole-painting enthusiast Aurora (Rory) Anderson doesn't envision finding either when she steps outside to investigate the frenzied yipping coming from her own back yard. After all, she lives in Vista Beach, a quiet California beach community where violent crime is rare and murder even rarer.

Suspicion falls on Rory when the body buried in her flowerbed turns out to be someone she knows—her tole painting teacher, Hester Bouquet. Just two weekends before, Rory attended one of Hester's weekend painting seminars, an unpleasant experience she vowed never to repeat. As evidence piles up against Rory, she embarks on a quest to identify the killer and clear her name. Can Rory unearth the truth before she encounters her own brush with death?

Available at booksellers nationwide and online

Visit www.henerypress.com for details

SHADOW OF DOUBT

Nancy Cole Silverman

A Carol Childs Mystery (#1)

When a top Hollywood Agent is found poisoned in the bathtub of her home suspicion quickly turns to one of her two nieces. But Carol Childs, a reporter for a local talk radio station doesn't believe it. The suspect is her neighbor and friend, and also her primary source for insider industry news. When a media frenzy pits one niece against the other—and the body count starts to rise—Carol knows she must save her friend from being tried in courts of public opinion.

But even the most seasoned reporter can be surprised, and when a Hollywood psychic shows up in Carol's studio one night and warns her there will be more deaths, things take an unexpected turn. Suddenly nobody is above suspicion. Carol must challenge both her friendship and the facts, and the only thing she knows for certain is the killer is still out there and the closer she gets to the truth, the more danger she's in.

Available at booksellers nationwide and online

Visit www.henerypress.com for details